Sarton Selected

An Anthology of the Journals, Novels, and
Poems of May Sarton

BOOKS BY MAY SARTON

POETRY

Encounter in April
Inner Landscape
The Lion and the Rose
The Land of Silence
In Time Like Air
Cloud, Stone, Sun, Vine
A Private Mythology
As Does New Hampshire
A Grain of Mustard Seed
A Durable Fire
Collected Poems, 1930–1973
Selected Poems of May Sarton
(edited by Serena Sue Hilsinger and Lois Byrnes)
Halfway to Silence
Letters from Maine

NOVELS

The Single Hound
The Bridge of Years
Shadow of a Man
A Shower of Summer Days
Faithful Are the Wounds
The Birth of a Grandfather
The Fur Person
The Small Room

Sarton Selected

An Anthology of the Journals, Novels,

and Poems of May Sarton

Edited, with an Introduction and notes, by

Bradford Dudley Daziel

W.W. NORTON & COMPANY · NEW YORK · LONDON

Printed in the United States of America.

The text of this book is composed in Janson, with the display
set in Bernhard Modern Roman. Composition and manufacturing by the Maple Vail Book Manufacturing Group. Book design
by Guenet Abrahams.

First Edition.

Library of Congress Cataloging-in-Publication Data

Sarton, May, 1912–
[Selections, 1991]
Sarton selected / May Sarton ; edited, with an introduction and
notes, by Bradford Dudley Daziel.
p.   cm.
I. Daziel, Bradford Dudley.   II. Title.
PS3537.A832A6   1991
811'.52—dc20   90-46669

ISBN 0-393-02968-9

W.W. Norton & Company, Inc.,
500 Fifth Avenue, New York, N.Y. 10110

W.W. Norton & Company, Ltd.,
10 Coptic Street, London WC1A 1PU

1 2 3 4 5 6 7 8 9 0

ACKNOWLEDGMENTS

Grateful acknowledgment is made to the National Poetry Foundation for permission to reprint Constance Hunting's perceptive study " 'The Risk Is Very Great': The Poetry of May Sarton," from *May Sarton: Woman and Poet*, edited by Constance Hunting (Orono, Me.: National Poetry Foundation, 1982).

I wish to thank the *Puckerbrush Review*, vol. 7, no. 2, 1986 (Orono, Me.) for permission to reprint, in a revised version, the editor's article, "May Sarton and the Common Reader."

Especial gratitude must be expressed to Werner John Deiman, Professor of English at Bates College, for his assistance in selecting the poems; to the poet, John Tagliabue, who saw the need for this anthology; to Constance Hunting for her expert editorial guidance; to Nancy Hartley for her precise scholarship; to Michael Wayne Leonard for his critical acumen and proofreading ability; and for years of enthusiastic support from Westbrook College, where I teach, to its president, dean, faculty, and, most particularly, to Dorothy Healy, Curator of the Maine Women Writers Collection.

And for her invaluable guidance, generosity, and encouragement, May Sarton

Bradford Dudley Daziel
Portland, Maine
September 1990

CONTENTS

11

Contents

Contents

13

Contents

Contents

Introduction

MAY SARTON AND THE COMMON READER

BRADFORD DUDLEY DAZIEL

.... (ᵛᵢᵧ)

Virginia Woolf did not expect her contemporaries to appreciate fully her experiments in literary criticism or fiction so she appealed, over the heads of the newspapers and universities, to the general reading public. In the preface to her first volume of essays, she cites as her precedent the conviction of Dr. Johnson:

> "I rejoice to concur with the common reader; for by the common sense of readers, uncorrupted by literary preju-dices, after all the refinements of subtilty [sic] and the dog-matism of learning, must be finally decided all claim to poetical honours."
>   . . . The common reader, as Dr. Johnson implies, differs from the critic and the scholar. He is worse educated, and nature has not gifted him so generously. He reads for his own pleasure rather than to impart knowledge or correct the opinions of others.
>
> *(The Common Reader*, 1)

Clearly, later generations have validated Woolf's preference for the judgment of the common reader rather than that of the professional critic. Such too, I think, will be the fate of May Sarton. Contemporary critics have not fully appreciated Sarton because she employs (contrary to Woolf) traditional rather than experimental fictional forms and because she writes primarily about the world of women and celebrates traditionally female values (e.g. nurture) as opposed to someone like Joseph Conrad who writes primarily about the world of men and their values (ambition, competition, and aggression). Few critics have complained that Conrad's vision is too limited, but that has been often a criticism of Sarton's fiction. *The Birth of a Grandfather* (1957) offers "the feminine world of family and home. The delineation of the male characters is weak" (Elizabeth Janeway, *New York Times Book Review*, 8 September 1957). And writing in *The Times Literary Supplement* (I choose only two examples), Valentine Cunningham regards *A Reckoning* (1978) as flawed with "depressingly sophomoronic psycho-babble" primarily because the dying Laura's "dependence is on a world of women" instead of upon "other members of her own and the human family" (8 February 1980). Interestingly enough, it was a woman, again Woolf, who noticed the gender-restricted, yet not confined vision of Conrad:

> There are the ships, the beautiful ships. . . . They are more feminine than his women, who are either mountains of marble or the dreams of a charming boy over the photograph of an actress. But surely a great novel can be made out of man and a ship, a man and a storm, a man and death and dishonour.
>
> ("Mr. Conrad: A Conversation," *Collected Essays* I, 312)

Only the next generation of professional critics, apparently, will recognize that a valuable novel has been made by Sarton out of a woman and solitude, a woman and cancer, a woman and death and her honor.

The purpose of this anthology is to offer common readers a representative selection in one volume of Sarton's poems, journals, and novels. The introductory section begins with an essay on the sensitivity of common readers to the essence of Sarton's vision. The essay is followed by an appreciation of Sarton's craftsmanship as a poet by Constance Hunting, who has published Sarton's *Writings on Writing* (1980) and *Letters to May* (1986), as well as edited *May Sarton: Woman and Poet* (1982). The third part of the introduction includes excerpts, originally published together by Hunting in *Writings on Writing*, of Sarton's analysis of poetry, particularly her own method of composition and revision.

Following the introduction, the first third of the anthology consists of a selection of Sarton's poems. Given the extraordinary variety of form and subject which contributes to Sarton's excellence as a poet, the anthologist's attempt to make a representative selection is perhaps destined at the start to be imperfect. Nevertheless, the reader will find poems from the beginning of her career to the present, arranged in the order in which most appeared in *Collected Poems* (1974). Included are poems which are humorous. There are poems which capture landscape and celebrate the spiritual and aesthetic joy of gardening. Some offer the writer's appreciation of individuals; some, of animals as individual, feeling creatures worthy of the poet's empathy. There are love poems. There are also lyrics which give voice to the author's idealistic and profoundly intellectual responses to social injustice, as well as to the ultimate, existential questions at the heart of each human life. The selection also reveals Sarton's virtuosity, for her works explore the gamut of lyric forms, from free verse and blank verse to sonnets, sestinas, and villanelles. In each, the common reader may discern a master craftsman at work; in each may be heard one of the most significant voices of our age articulating the perennial problems of our race.

The middle portion of the anthology is a sampling of the eight journals Sarton published prior to 1990. An attempt has been made to include the broad range of experiences on which Sarton has brought her intellect to bear. The excerpts—fascinating, wise, and often deeply moving in themselves—comprise an autobiography, as it were, of the artist and the woman. Often in the journals Sarton alludes to her work, its composition and critical reception. The selections also provide a useful framework in which to read or reread her fiction and poetry because Sarton treats themes and describes individuals in the journals who appear in the novels and poems. Unifying these fragments from the journals is

Sarton's humanism—a passionate and critical appreciation of the ultimate mysteries of existence. A theme which pervades the journals, as well as her fiction and poetry, is the value of deep feeling when it is brought to the fore of consciousness. The fact that logic always accompanies honesty and passion prevents her work from ever verging on sentimentality. Consequently, as she explores the microcosm of her own experience, she defines the geography of the human heart in general and depicts the political, social, and moral landscape of contemporary American and European culture. In Sarton's vision of life, the present and the past are inseparable, the particular is inextricably linked to the universal, and logic and emotion are one. The journals testify amply to the truth of the philosopher Schleiermacher's conviction: "Feeling can never betray, for there being and consciousness are the same."

The final section of the anthology is devoted to fiction. Since *A Reckoning* is arguably her most profound and certainly most moving novel, the first chapter is included here, for, like an operatic overture, it stands on its own even as it announces the chief themes of the novel as a whole. *As We Are Now* is printed here in its entirety. A short novel, it is typical, as is the first chapter of *A Reckoning*, of Sarton's most compelling, realistic fiction, in which one character, catalyzed by trauma, achieves a heightened level of consciousness. Caro Spencer and Laura Spelman are ordinary individuals who free the hidden poet in themselves as they win from the chaos of their lives a moment of vision. Their hard-won spiritual growth and redemption is parallel to Sarton's own struggle and achievement as a poet, so richly revealed in each poem and journal entry included in this anthology.

If professional critics have failed to define adequately Sarton's gifts as a writer, the common reader has already conveyed his appreciation of Sarton's work to her. Thousands of letters written to her by her readers provide a sometimes unsophisticated but often wise literary criticism. Loaned to me by May Sarton, these letters provide a composite picture of her common reader and a useful key to the essence of Sarton's work. Moreover, they proved to the artist herself, especially when she did not receive appropriately significant or positive reviews, that she had an audience of intelligent, if not academic, readers. In a filmed interview she said that "the letters proved the word was getting out" (Martha Wheelock, *World of Light*, New York: Ishtar, 1980). And in a letter to me (7 June 1985), Sarton is quite frank about the role the letters have played in her professional development:

> You ask whether the letters have had any specific effect on my work . . . there is no doubt that especially in the Nelson years [1958–1973] they kept me from despair. After Faithful [the novel *Faithful Are the Wounds*, 1955] I never got a really good press. I used to be reviewed before that in both daily and Sunday Times and Herald Tribune (which existed then) and even the poems, now ignored for years, got good reviews. Then I suppose I became old fashioned, not interesting . . . and it is really Women's Studies . . . which have brought me back. Anyway you can see the letters persuaded me that I was not crazy to go on willy-nilly.

One should add, by the way, that *In Time Like Air* (1958), the volume of poems which came after *Faithful Are the Wounds*, also received a good press. Incidentally, both books were candidates for the National Book Award—a first for the same author with books in different genres in the same year.

· · Critic and Common Reader: The Appreciative Early · · Audience

During roughly the first third of Sarton's publishing career (1938–1958), the poet and novelist was able to depend upon positive reviews. Critics saw fit to praise rather than denigrate the beauty of her writing, its simplicity coupled with depth of vision, and her use of the poetic mode in her fiction. Writing in the *New York Times*, Jane Spence Southron concluded of Sarton's first novel, *The Single Hound* (1938): "Only a young poet could have written this beautiful and distinguished first novel" (20 March 1938). The individual whom Sarton has identified (interview, 30 July 1986) as the best critic of her poetry, Basil de Selincourt, praised her first novel in a letter to her (7 April 1939) as "definitely one of those novels that one thinks of as much as being a poem." In an equally positive notice in the Literary Supplement of *The Times*, the reviewer touched on another aspect of Sarton's work which was later to put her out of favor: "Her imagination leads the reader into a gracious and sunlit world, slightly unreal, perhaps. . . . The book, unusual in theme and atmosphere, will impress this writer's name on the discerning reader" (30 April 1938).

A cursory summary of the reviews accorded her poetry and fiction up to 1955 reveals similarly positive notices. Echoing de Selincourt's identification of her first novel as a poem, William Soskin praised *Bridge of Years* (1946) for its "lyrical" depiction of the confusions and crises which comprise a home and the "small perils and insecurities of a marriage" (*Herald Tribune* 27 April 1946). Elizabeth Bowen called *Shadow of a Man* (1950) "an unusual blend of scrupulous intelligence and poetry" (quoted by Sarton in a letter to Eric Swenson, 4 February 1961).

Similarly positive reviews of her next two novels appeared in the *New York Times*, whose authoritative voice failed to praise most of what Sarton produced in the last two-thirds of her publishing career. John Nerber wrote of *A Shower of Summer Days* (1952) that Sarton "ranks with our very best of novelists" (26 October 1952). Reviewing the same novel in Sunday's *Times*, Orville Prescott declared that Sarton "writes with affectionate perception about people who are much more good than bad"; further, he points to her "poetic skill in capturing the essence of a succession of fleeting moments" and the "niceties of human relationships so subtle that they lie outside the cosmos of most novelists" (5 November 1952). Finally, similar convictions inform William Goyen's review in the *Times* of *Faithful Are the Wounds* (1955): "It is a poet's work, all beauty, inwardness and intense personal feeling. Devoid of heroic exaggeration, unadorned and shining in a sunlit clarity [it] exists, finally, as a living segment of human life" (13 March 1955).

Critical notices of her poetry received equal approbation. Basil de

Selincourt, writing in *The Observer*, called the poet of *Inner Landscape* (1939) "deep-searching to the point of ruthlessness, and very delicate" (2 April 1939). It is Sarton's use of "the words of common speech" and her courageous "simplicity of statement" reminiscent of the pre-Elizabethan poets to which Martha Bacon points as she also extols *The Lion and the Rose* (1948) for its "subtle cadences and delicate, all-but-inaudible rhymes" (*Saturday Review of Literature*, 17 April 1948). *The Land of Silence* (1953) inspired Wallace Fowlie to write in *The New Republic*, "The admirable simplicity of May Sarton's poetry is something more than that. . . . She testifies to a deep experience of reality which far surpasses purely speculative philosophy" (14 December 1953). Of the same volume, Louise Bogan in *The New Yorker* notes "her mature power of recognizing the heart of the matter and of expressing it in memorable terms" (27 February 1954). More than one notice of *In Time Like Air* (1958) praised Sarton's simplicity; a good example is James Dickey's summation in *The Sewanee Review:* "In almost every poem she attains a delicate simplicity as quickeningly direct as it is deeply-given, and does so with the courteous serenity, the clear, caring, and intelligent human calm of the queen of a small well-ordered country" (Spring 1958).

Writing letters to Sarton after the publication of her second novel, *Bridge of Years* 1946, many readers echoed, as it were, the earlier professional criticism. Eleanor Blair, for example, implies that Sarton, her life-long friend, is like Emily Dickinson, except that Sarton's fiction allows her to communicate to a wider audience:

> [I am] thinking of your letter to the world and the wider circulation that it's bound to have now in this novel-reading age. There have been so many bitter books and frightened books and disillusioned books that this assertion of the sound value of honesty of mind, and of warmth of sympathy and of courage (especially the inner, unspectacular kind) . . . [represents] values that can stand through personal and national hurricanes.
>
> (3 May 1946)

Blair's assessment looks forward to the vision of life projected by Sarton in all of her works. Even in the disturbing *As We Are Now* (1973) and the tragic *A Reckoning* (1978), Sarton's *Weltanschauung* is positive, humanistic, and celebratory of the potential nobility in each life. Her portrayal in fiction of "honesty," "warmth of sympathy," and "inner, unspectacular . . . courage"—to use Blair's words—and her simplicity as a poet received from critics and those who wrote directly to Sarton equal approbation. The newspapers and the common reader provided Sarton with an intelligent and appreciative audience.

·· *The Common Reader as Patron: "Paymaster"* ·· *and "Inspirer"*

In her essay, "The Patron and the Crocus," Virginia Woolf examines how important it is for the writer to choose his audience:

> For a book is always written for somebody to read, and, since the patron is not merely the paymaster, but also in a very subtle and insidious way the instigator and inspirer of what is written, it is of the utmost importance that he should be a desirable man.
>
> . . . The Elizabethans, to speak roughly, chose the aristocracy to write for and the playhouse public. The eighteenth-century patron was a combination of coffeehouse wit and Grub Street bookseller. In the nineteenth century the great writers wrote for the half-crown magazines and the leisured classes. And looking back and applauding the splendid results of these different alliances, it all seems enviably simple, and plain as a pikestaff compared with our own predicament—for whom should we write?
>
> (*Collected Essays* II, 149)

This was by no means a simple question for Woolf herself. Clearly the author of *To the Lighthouse*, *The Waves*, and *Between the Acts* chose an alliance with a different sort of reader from that for whom *The Years* was aimed. In fact, Sarton told me that Woolf reported to her that shortly after the publication of *The Waves* a friend called her and said: "Virginia, you are getting too far away from us" (interview, 30 July 1986). Certainly, Woolf always wrote hoping for the approval of her most intimate friends and often in spite of the injunctions of critics such as F. R. Leavis, whose complaints seem today as foolishly prejudiced and beside the point as they were hurtful to Woolf in the 1930s.

Like Virginia Woolf, May Sarton chose the common reader as her patron. Never indifferent to the critics or their lack of praise for her work after 1957 and in the later two-thirds of her career, she nevertheless continued writing, as did Woolf, as if they did not exist. She wrote for the common reader, who became an extension of her friends and upon whom Sarton could depend to be sensitive to the excellence of craft in her fiction and poetry and to appreciate the vision of life so evident in all of her work. In a way, the increasing importance to Sarton of her nonacademic and nonprofessional readers was prefigured in a letter from her valued friend and critic, Basil de Selincourt, who agreed with Sarton's choice of an audience—in his words, her "ambition to write poetry that the normal mind responds to" (21 March 1948).

Perhaps the earliest supporter was Anne Thorp, whom Sarton has memorialized in *The Magnificent Spinster* (1985). The granddaughter of Henry Wadsworth Longfellow, Thorp was neither a professional nor an academic critic. She had been Sarton's teacher at the Shady Hill School and became a life-long friend of Sarton and her parents. Although Sarton has told me that Anne Thorp was not sensitive to the technical aspects of the poet's craft, Sarton also stressed that she has never written for other poets or for those who are experts in prosody, but rather for people "who are moved or changed" by her poems (interview, 30 July 1986). Herself a master of the poet's craft, Sarton has rarely sought to call attention to technique for its own sake. Subtlety of metrics and rhyme, as well as awareness of form as a whole, enable Sarton to "move" the common reader. And Thorp was such a one.

After May Sarton's mother died of cancer and Sarton composed "A Hard Death," Anne Thorp wrote her a long letter. I quote the first paragraph and put in italics words Thorp cites from the poem:

It is a joy to get your letter, yet I hardly want you to write me—or if so only the shortest word—for I know that hundreds of letters must be sifting into your letter box, to speak of your mother, and to speak of your poem. Yes, I think the poem has beauty and is full of a truth that all who have suffered can apprehend—You say that this grief has carried you into the centre of life. Perhaps because it is deep. Deep grief, like deep joy can make one aware that one's roots go down toward a Centre, that at that Level one intensely shares human experience; one is more clearly aware of being a part of mankind and of one's nearness to God. And that, I suppose, is to feel in the centre of life. Your mother's self has always awakened something of that feeling in me. . . . She has always heightened my perception of these things, and thinking of her continues to do so. Yes, *let us be gentle to each other this brief time*, as she was. That *we* must *die in exile* is a passing matter, and in the nature of things, but in living we can indeed choose to *stand before each presence with gentle heart and hand*—And bless you for putting it into words that help us perceive it afresh.

(13 January 1951)

Here was a reader who clearly mourns the loss of her friend—May Sarton's mother. But Sarton's poem has moved her afresh. Thorp is also brought by the poem to the universal experience of death and the loss of beauty. Yet Thorp also includes an oblique criticism of the poem she takes so seriously. She seems to argue against the poet's despair in the fifth and last stanza ("For we shall die in exile far from home") by jumping back to the third stanza ("stand before each presence") and by saying that dying "in exile" is "a passing matter, and in the nature of things." In her nonprofessional yet sensitive response to this poem, Anne Thorp is typical of the patron for whom Sarton chose to write.

Who exactly is Sarton's common reader? I have used a negative definition up to now: he who is neither a professional nor an academic critic, he who, Virginia Woolf says, "reads for his own pleasure rather than to impart knowledge or correct the opinions of others" (*The Common Reader*, 1).

Most letters Sarton received from celebrated writers reside now in the Berg Collection of the New York Public Library. Nevertheless, there remain in those loaned to me notes and letters from Leonard Woolf, Vita Sackville-West, Samuel Eliot Morrison, Howard Mumford Jones, Julian Huxley, Marianne Moore, Basil de Selincourt, Eva Le Gallienne, Archibald MacLeish, and William Rose Benet. To be sure, these letters meant much to Sarton in the beginning of her career, although she never asked these friends to give her publishers "blurbs" with which to sell her books (letter to Eric Swenson, 4 February 1961). Just as she was disinclined to burden her friends with such a reasonable request for commercial support, so also it may be argued that she saw these successful writers as sympathetic bystanders. She did not write to please them. She did not choose them to be her patrons.

The common reader rarely wrote to her as to a stranger, but usually as to an intimate friend. Many of the letters begin, as does one of the earliest from another writer, Patricia K. Page, "I have never written 'fan-mail' before." Page goes on to applaud Sarton's "achievement" in *The Single Hound* (1938): "I wish the average modern novelist could so infuse his works with people one feels one *could* know [as you have done]" (March 1939). The oddest letter is from a podiatrist, who in 1938 enclosed his photograph and offered to trade service to her feet for some of her books. Some of the letters—always poignant—are from men and women who are teachers, ministers, lawyers, and fellow writers. A larger proportion of the letters have been set by nuns, single women, and gay men and women. But approximately 80 percent of the letters (especially after 1957) come from women, most of them married with children.

I believe that Sarton chose as her patron the common reader—usually, the married woman sensitive to her potential as a nurturer—or males who are themselves more interested in healing or helping than in aggressively vying with one another for success. Typical of the letter bestowed by such a patron on May Sarton is this response to her first novel from a stranger: "I read the 'Single Hound' in two 'sittings' (which would have been *one*, but for myriad interruptions as the mother of a family). . . . [It is] a book which—in its apparent simplicity but actual depth—its anguish and its trueness seems to equal the best that has been done" (Mary T. Fremont-Smith, Spring 1938).

Occasionally men write, and in the last twenty years most of the letters are not about one book but about Sarton's total work. Typical of these recent letters is one, quoted in a letter from Sarton to me (26 August 1986) from a young man doing graduate work in Lubbock, Texas:

> Growth plays such an important role in your books: all the characters are struggling to grow, struggling to learn what it means to be human, in all their strengths in all their weaknesses. This seems to be the predominant message you send out: we must confront ourselves, because in this act lies the most workable solution to our troubles, whether they be our problems as individuals, or as a country. But this act requires a great amount of courage. I believe your books are courageous.

· · *The Common Reader's Sensitivity to Craft* · ·

Professional critics may at first have supported Sarton as a poet and as a poet writing novels. The tide of favorable critical opinion began to ebb in the late 1950s and seemed to fade beyond the horizon altogether by the time Lore Dickstein dismissed *A Reckoning* as a disguised lesbian novel (*The New York Times*, 12 November 1978). The sum total of the neglect of professional critics after *Faithful Are the Wounds* has been described by Sarton as a "public beating." Since that novel was highly praised in *The New York Times*, that newspaper "sneered at or attacked every book of mine. . . . You can rise above one or two public humiliations such as this, but finally after ten or more it gets to you. I felt finished. I felt that I would not again expose myself to such pain. I felt like a deer shot down by hunters" (*Recovering*, 21). The fact that she has published three novels, three volumes of poems, and two journals after that attack is a testament to her ultimate belief in herself and her trust in the common reader as an ultimately more important critic than the *Times*.

Since Dr. Johnson's common reader is "uncorrupted by literary prejudices," he is through "common sense" to decide all claim to "poetical honors." May Sarton's reader reveals such common sense first by admitting his lack of credentials and putting aside his prejudices. When *The Lion and the Rose* appeared in 1948, one of the first letters to the author came from the woman with whom she lived for many years, Judith Matlack (a professor of English at Simmons College, memorialized by Sarton in *Honey in the Hive*, 1988). With a common sense and generosity of spirit often lacking in professional critics, she denies being one of the "critics who are really competent judges" and, at the same time, puts aside her jealousy of those to whom the love poems were written:

Valentine's Day, 1948

Dearest one:

I have just read and read over again most of the poems. You see, for me, this is an experience I shall never have again, to see coming into the magic of print pure poetry, a little of which I was so close to that it was born almost next to my heart—and if not that exactly, next to my room.

It seems to me that *all* the emotional poems are especially lovely, and no matter who inspired them, I cannot feel anything but pride and joy in them. I like them better than the others, because I should be fooling no one but myself if I tried to imagine myself as intellectually sensitive or aware to the degree of other critics who are really competent judges.

God bless you, my sweet May,

Judy

If Sarton did not write poems and novels specifically to Anne Thorp or Judy Matlack, their "common sense," as Dr. Johnson speaks of the value of the best reader, identifies their sensibility as the sort which distinguishes Sarton's patron—the more general reader unknown to the author.

Sarton's common reader occasionally has tried to interpose himself between the harsh professional critic and the wounded author. When Louise Bogan gave *The Land of Silence* a very brief review in *The New Yorker* and characterized it as "conventionally literary" (27 February 1954), a housewife from Concord, New Hampshire, Mrs. Myleen Newton Morrison, wrote to Sarton:

> Please forgive the intrusion of a stranger, but I have long admired the work you have done, especially The Land of Silence. . . . [I feel] dismay at the condescension of its review in the New Yorker last week.
>
> I have been following you from afar for many years. . . . You seem in a sort of sense a legatee of Virginia Woolf. . . .
>
> My special gratitude to you for the sonnets of the Land of Silence and for the "self" poem ["Now I Become Myself"], which describes a rather specially feminine circumstance. Women, somewhat more than men, I think, have to wear other people's faces, because of the variety of demands which life makes of them, perhaps.
>
> (5 March 1954)

Infuriated by reading an apparently advance copy of Ciardi's review in *Nation* of the same book, a friend of Sarton wrote a long letter of defense. Ciardi objected to Sarton's use of words like "absolute," "anguished," "beautiful," and declared that her "aesthetic position [is one] to which I must register myself as absolutely, fiercely, implacably, violently opposed" (*Nation*, 20 February 1954). Sarton's friend, the poet Francis Minturn Howard, offered to loan her a copy of Virginia Woolf's *A Room of One's Own* even if Sarton had already read it (10 November

1953). Howard said that Woolf was right in asking why the critic felt the "desire to kill off the object of criticism."

When the common reader acts as a good critic, he appears as unpretentious, appreciative, and helpful. One of the earliest letters to Sarton came from a stranger in Atlanta, Georgia, who had just read her first novel, *The Single Hound*. After saying that it was "not a great novel, [but] it introduces a great novelist," Edgar A. Neely, Jr., offers some criticism: "(a) Please don't turn from the story to address the reader. (b) Avoid too obvious parallels. . . . (c) Continue to use the memory of a character as your principal time device (you did this expertly with Doro)" [24 January 1939].

Sarton's patron is often the homemaker, unknown to her, who has deep feelings about major events in the national macrocosm or in her own home-world; and Sarton has felt inspired to evoke those hidden passions, the recognition of which is often the first step toward growth for her reader. Of *Faithful Are the Wounds* a married woman, unknown to Sarton, wrote from Connecticut: "You have managed to say very well something that many of us felt, but have not been able to put into words—and in saying it, have caused us to think much more deeply about it" (7 February 1956). Another letter from a stranger is notable in that again a common reader recalls *Faithful Are the Wounds* a year after reading it and shows an attentiveness to poetic detail, as well as the analysis of deep feeling:

> When I think of it, what comes back first as a symbol of the whole is the scar on the tree on Brattle Street and the people now going by without remembrance.
>
> It had a further special meaning for me, because years ago my brother committed suicide. I have always resented bitterly the common feeling that suicide was a cowardly escape. . . . I feel strongly that the act in some cases is an attempt to say something that can be heard no other way. I am grateful to you for giving nobility to a sacrifice rarely understood.
>
> (Mrs. Robert A. Cushman, 10 March 1956)

Virtually all of the letters convey compliments to Sarton. Those responding to *The Fur Person* were effusive in their praise and often sent the author photographs of their own cats. A few letter writers, however, offered astute criticism. Writing from Surrey, for example, prolific author Beverley Nichols declared: "It has a wonderful tenderness, without a hint of sentimentality. And although, physically speaking, nothing very stupendous happens, it has a remarkable tension from start to finish."

How grateful must be the author whose reader remarks on a technical similarity among several books:

> You have a special gift for finding or inventing new frames for novels: the interview in *Mrs. Stevens Hears the Mermaids Singing*, the town history in *Kinds of Love* and now [*A Reckoning*]. It has a double interest, the facing one's own death, and the life-time relationships that emerge are examined and resolved.
>
> (Elizabeth Gray Vining, 1 December 1978)

Of course Vining, the former governess to the Crown Prince of Japan, is an uncommon person and perhaps not a "common reader." Nevertheless, she was not reviewing the book for a publication or writing about it in a scholarly setting. In reading for her own pleasure, as Woolf's common reader does, Vining observes a matter of form, the use of a framing device at the same time she attempts to sum up for herself the essence of *A Reckoning*.

·· *Sunlight from One Common Reader with* ·· *Declining Vision*

Emerging from the thousands of letters written to Sarton are many fascinating portraits of common readers. Of particular interest to me is Katharine Davis, dead now for many years. Although some of her letters and postcards are evidently missing, there exist ten typewritten letters averaging five pages in length, written from 1950 to 1961, in response to each of Sarton's major books. When I first read them, I ignored them because their often technical criticism seemed to touch on small points rather than larger issues in Sarton's work. Furthermore, the typing was so erratic and the letters so long-winded, I assumed that Sarton probably had not taken them seriously. I was wrong.

Living in Glens Falls, Davis was an elderly lady: at the beginning of their decade of correspondence Davis wrote, "I said good bye to sixty some years back" (13 June 1950). Her chief pleasure in life was the reading of poetry. Sarton has told me that Davis was "an expert on poetics," "a fine critic perhaps better than I," and had a fine ear for the "music of poetry." Sarton added, "I suppose I felt sorry for her" (interview, 30 July 1986). Davis was indeed pathetic: her eyesight was ever failing and she had to wait until a sunny day in order to see to read and to write the letters on her porch. She did not have enough money to buy Sarton's books.

At first, I was appalled at Katharine Davis. In the letters she reveals herself to be deeply prejudiced against, in particular, Polish and French Canadian immigrants to New England; Roman Catholics, in general; and Democrats, especially F. D. Roosevelt and Adlai Stevenson. Her rather domineering character and unfortunate snobbery come across in letters which complain about those with "steerage ancestors."

When she visited Sarton's home in Nelson and Sarton probably took her to visit one of Sarton's friends, Kay Martin, at the MacDowell Colony, Martin was not impressed:

> I'm not a "good critic" like that damned old bitch, K. Davis, who, in my estimation, represents a knife with no anaesthetics. But the day you brought her in the rain to the studio, I saw *you*, sitting there looking your most beautiful, radiant self in filmy green and white—shining through beside that awful old woman like moonbeams on a ramshackle, rickety, creaking old wooden structure falling apart not very gracefully.
>
> (2 November 1961)

Given the testimony of Martin, the occasionally narrow-minded comments on novels, and the unattractive world view of Davis, why then did May Sarton take seriously the letters from Katharine Davis?

Sarton's work has always revealed her great respect for the elderly and the wisdom they have accumulated from a lifetime of experience. From *The Single Hound* (1938) to *The Magnificent Spinster* (1985), major characters and sometimes heroines have been elderly women. If the old have been forced to see themselves as pariahs in American society, the opposite is true in Sarton's fictional world. Like authors as diverse, for example, as William Butler Yeats (e.g. "Sailing to Byzantium") and Sarah Orne Jewett (e.g. *Country of the Pointed Firs*), Sarton has always been attracted to the problems of the elderly and the potential spiritual liberation old age can bring. To my knowledge, few in the cavalcade of literature in the English language have written so frequently or so sensitively about the vicissitudes and potential "soul making" with which the aged find themselves cursed and blessed. Clearly, Caro speaks for her author in *As We Are Now* when she says: "The trouble is that old age is not interesting until one gets there, a foreign country with an unknown language to the young, and even to the middle-aged" (23). So Sarton has always been unusually sensitive to the old. (It is perhaps more than incidental to mention that she was on the founding board of directors of Elderhostel, Inc.—an organization which currently enables more than 100,000 elderly individuals to attend week-long courses at more than 1,000 educational institutions the world over.)

Was Sarton predisposed to take Davis seriously, then? In spite of her shortcomings, Davis's love of poetry seemed to render her capable of "reaching new wonders" as does one of Sarton's "Old Lovers at the Ballet" (*Halfway to Silence*). That poem is about an old woman whose envy of the younger dancers becomes metaphormosed into spiritual liberation. It is a poem, comparable to Yeats's "Sailing to Byzantium," about an old woman, rather than an old man. Not written for Katharine Davis, the poem's depiction of an elder, alienated from the natural world and attracted to the world of spirit, may describe, however, the respect Sarton had for Davis's potential nobility.

At first Davis wrote letters to a poet she did not know personally.

The bond which developed between Davis and Sarton represents another case of the fruitful alliance Virginia Woolf saw between the patron and the artist. Drawn to the early books of poems, Davis offered the ultimate accolade to Sarton—what Dr. Johnson called the "claim to poetical honors." Davis was an amateur reader. But she had common sense and good taste: for example, she loved equally the poems of William Wordsworth, T. S. Eliot (especially "Burnt Norton"), and W. H. Auden, though she could discriminate among their styles. Her greatest joy in life was reading a poem aloud: "Not only do I hear it, but in the poems which most appeal to me, I feel in my throat and tongue muscles, the sounds of the lines . . . and I have read over and over again poems in The Lion and the Rose" (24 February 1954).

And occasionally this common reader was also able to convey first-rate advice to Sarton. Objecting to her use of a quoted line in a poem, Davis urged Sarton to abjure the practice:

> The quotation-marks irritate the reader, like minute torpedoes. While I think Eliot often uses lines far too remote from even the devoted poetry reader who isn't a real hound, I do think his plan of putting the line right in without quote-marks is a good one. If the quote is apt and incremental, it is really part of the poem.
>
> (21 May 1950)

Davis offered comments on *Birth of a Grandfather:* "I loved your use of the Leech Gatherer in your novel" (7 October 1957). Sarton's allusion to Wordsworth's "Resolution and Independence" is seminal to her theme of the middle-aged Sprig's growth of a soul. And Davis recognizes "a large enveloping theme, the need to be oneself, so violently shown by Caleb . . . the change which can be made by a shift in the angle of vision; and finally the wider obligations of the marriage contract" (7 October 1957). Surely Davis's sensitivity helped to balance such mixed reviews as Whitney Balliett's comment in *The New Yorker:* "There are too many clichés in language; her prose lacks the sinew and tension that distinguish her best poetry" (5 October 1957).

Disqualifying herself as "not a good judge of the novel as a form" (21 May 1950) and as one who all her life has "tended to eschew books which might make me disturbed or depressed . . . with [my] ills and cares increasing" (7 October 1957), Davis nevertheless offers some acute appreciations of Sarton's novels. She calls *Shadow of a Man* a "philosophical romance" and calls its chief themes: "the need for Americans to learn to live more deliberately, more thoughtfully, more attentively in regard to ALL human relations; and also that . . . it should be incumbent on each person to stay himself or herself to grow along his or her own line."

Of the poem "Celebrations," the last in *The Lion and the Rose*, Davis had written: "This has that elan vital, the upsurge, the same kind of lift which makes William Wordsworth's ["Ode:] *Intimations* [of Immortality"] 'perhaps the greatest lyric poem in any language' (maybe I've not quoted Saintsbury quite right. . . . I recognize the difference in magnitude of theme . . . but it is the kind of lift you get from the *Intimations*" (21 May 1950). Of course I won't claim that Sarton included the allusion to Wordsworth's "Resolution and Independence" in *Birth of a Grandfather* because Davis had praised her earlier book of poems *The Lion and the Rose*. If the common reader in this case may not have been what Virginia Woolf called the "instigator" surely it is another example of the fruitful alliance of a writer and her appreciative patron. Thankful must be the poet that such a reader can help balance such a review of *The Lion and the Rose* as that which appeared in *Kirkus Review:* "Like so many women poets, her poems are not held together by any ordered continuity of thought" (1 January 1948).

One final aspect of this alliance points to the role of May Sarton as nurturer. Not only did she send the somewhat impoverished Davis several inscribed books, but she took seriously the questions raised by Davis: "How unselfish and kind of you to write me such a delightful letter . . . not merely thanking me (as though any thanks were needed!) but also really replying to remarks in my too-long epistle" (4 June 1950). It is moving to me that Katharine Davis, so domineering in her relations to others, so prejudiced and narrow-minded in some ways, was open to all that was new in literature. In many of her letters to Davis,

Sarton apparently urged Yeats upon her friend, answered questions about the Irish master and portions of his life relevant to his verse, such as his obsession with Maude Gonne. That Sarton would go to all this trouble, give Davis books and personal essays, rather than simply answering a loyal fan with postcards, testifies to her respect for the old. With all her shortcomings, Katharine Davis was typical of Sarton's common reader sensitive to craft. Along with countless others, Davis was, in Woolf's words, "in a very subtle and insidious way the instigator and inspirer of what is written."

· · *The Nature of Nurture* · ·

The common reader is attracted to May Sarton's work for many reasons. One might look again, for example, at the compliments cited earlier in this introduction from the reviews of her books up to 1957: the novels are good because they are "poetic"; they "assert the value of honesty of mind, and of warmth of sympathy and of [inner] courage"; they reveal an "affectionate perception about people who are much more good than bad." In fact, what the reviewer in *The New York Times* said of *Faithful Are the Wounds* is largely true of *all* her work: "It is a poet's work, all beauty, inwardness and intense personal feeling. Devoid of heroic exaggeration, unadorned and shining in a sunlit clarity [it] exists, finally, as a living segment of human life" (13 March 1955).

Sarton's work has not changed, though I think it has become even more "transparent" (a word she often uses); the critics' view of fiction and poetry and their jargon have changed. One cannot speak of "beauty" in this cycle of literary criticism. One cannot say a novel is good nowadays if it is "poetic." And here, in the state of Maine, for example, some feel that Carolyn Chute (whose artistry I admire greatly) has captured the "real" Maine, as opposed to someone like Sarton or Sarah Orne Jewett, whose characters may seem too good to be true. More uneducated, poverty-stricken, violent, and incestuous folk may walk the Maine byways than do gentle, dignified, noble souls like Sarah Orne Jewett's Mrs. Todd or Sarton's Jane Reid. But art is at least as real as life. Surely Shakespeare's Juliet is at least as *real* as a bride pictured in the *Maine Sunday Telegram*.

More out of fashion (with critics but not common readers) now than in the first third of her career, Sarton continues to convey in poems and novels an uplifting, inspiring, healing, and aesthetically beautiful vision of life. Ironically, it is perhaps more difficult to depict a happy, fruitful aspect of life so that the reader believes its reality than to do the opposite. Commenting on *A Shower of Summer Days*, Winifred Wilkinson, a British writer, recognizes this talent in Sarton:

> You have done something that is fiendishly hard to do and that is given an idea of a long-married couple's happiness . . . with the running surface-current of bickerings, stray affections, etc., which do not really disturb the reality any more than a leaf whirling about in a river disturbs its flow. It is a FEAT . . . like all happiness, it is much harder to capture than misery.

(1 December 1952)

Although thrice alienated from "normal society," for Sarton is a woman writer, a lesbian, and as much a European as an American, she is skilled at portraying long-standing, successful (heterosexual) marriages.

Unfashionably, again, Sarton puts her emphasis not on egocentric, passionate, violent, or erotic love but rather on what she repeatedly calls "deep feeling," "caring," and "growth." She does not write about ambition, competition, aggression, and disillusion. Nor, it should be emphasized, does she write escapist romances in which, to cite Dr. Johnson, the vicious are punished and the virtuous are rewarded. Her fictional worlds strike one as real as a crocus spattered with mud or the smile of Jane Reid, a retired teacher who has gone to Germany in the months after World War II to help orphans find homes. Sarton's fictional world does not invoke the reader's willing suspension of *belief*; it causes the common reader to believe in the "honesty" of the author. When Susan Warix was recovering from a long illness in Cleveland, for example, her husband "thoughtfully gave [her] *A Reckoning* for Christmas." She had already read *Journal of a Solitude* at college and *A House by the Sea:* "The wonderful thing you have given me is honesty—what it is really like to be a woman, to feel despondent—to question what life is really about. When sick everyone tried to cheer me up—the comfort I felt in your book was my saving! Thank you" (17 January 1979).

Sarton offers a valid, compelling mimesis. The values implicit in her vision are related to the idea of *nurture* in all its forms. It is not an accident that the most frequent images in her poetry and fiction are from gardening. One example is from "Now I Become Myself" much admired, as I specified earlier, by the common reader, Mrs. Morrison, who wrote to defend her against Louise Bogan's "condescending" review in *The New Yorker:*

> All fuses now, falls into place
> From wish to action, word to silence,
> My work, my love, my time, my face
> Gathered into one intense
> Gesture of growing like a plant.
> As slowly as the ripening fruit
> Fertile, detached, and always spent,
> Falls but does not exhaust the root,
> So all the poem is, can give,
> Grows in me to become the song,
> Made so and rooted so by love.

The work of the nurturer is "rooted" in love: its impetus (the life force issuing from the seed), its means (the nutrients), and the ultimate blossoming, dying, and casting forth a new seed. When May Sarton first began writing poems, her friend and valued critic Basil de Selincourt asked her: "What is it all about, anyway, unless there is communication of love—(love in the most inclusive sense). To read your own things to an audience and know at once that they had been cared for and understood must have been richly rewarding and a great inspiration too" (21 March 1948). When Sarton chose to celebrate her mother as a caring healer of her many friends, the poet found a metaphor in a poem linking two generations of gardeners, herself and her mother, as well as two kinds of art: the skill of raising plants and the craft of nourishing human beings:

AN OBSERVATION

True gardeners cannot bear a glove
Between the sure touch and the tender root,
Must let their hands grow knotted as they move
With a rough sensitivity about
Under the earth, between the rock and shoot,
Never to bruise or wound the hidden fruit.
And so I watched my mother's hands grow scarred,
She who could heal the wounded plant or friend
With the same vulnerable yet rigorous love;
I minded once to see her beauty gnarled,
But now her truth is given me to live,
As I learn for myself we must be hard
To move among the tender with an open hand,
And to stay sensitive up to the end
Pay with some toughness for a gentle world.

The heroes of her novels are such nurturers, "who could heal the wounded plant or friend / With the same vulnerable yet rigorous love." Her theme is always growth, rooted in love; and this is what the common reader finds so ennobling in her work. Most of her main characters are women. Few are career women, unless their careers involve nourishing the minds of others. Although Sarton is certainly not a didactic writer, many of her most memorable characters are teachers, authors, or editors. Some obvious examples include Doro in *The Single Hound*, Professor Cavan in *Faithful Are the Wounds*, Lucy in *The Small Room*, Joanna in *Joanna and Ulysses*, Mrs. Stevens in *Mrs. Stevens Hears the Mer-*

maids Singing, Caro in *As We Are Now*, Laura in *A Reckoning*, as well as both the narrator and her subject in *The Magnificent Spinster*. Other novels, such as *The Bridge of Years* or *A Shower of Summer Days*, have for the most part more traditional nurturers, mothers, or mother-figures, as their heroines. The common reader recognizes the teacher in his capacity as a nurturer. Responding to the second novel, *Shadow of a Man*, a teacher who never met the author wrote to thank her for the novel:

> So often we who teach lose sight of the broader significance of the work we are doing, the development of human relations, I agree with you completely where you say, through Francis, "We don't ask enough of each other. We're afraid," and again, through Fontanes, "We are wholly responsible to each other, in every exchange, even the least important."
>
> (Mary B. Austin, 21 September 1950)

What precisely is a nurturer? And how is his work "rooted in love"? The best definition occurs in *The Magnificent Spinster*, when the narrator thinks of how much planning her subject Jane Reid put into "daily life that seemed to saunter along unplanned! Somewhere Jung has noted: 'We must not forget that only a very few people are artists in life; that the art of life is the most distinguished and rarest of all the arts . . .' " (296).

Less than many of her contemporaries has Sarton written about the problems of the artist or the poet. Except for *Mrs. Stevens Hears the Mermaids Singing*, which has justly and often been called a Portrait of the Artist as a Woman, Sarton's books examine not the role of the artist in society but rather the way the ordinary person must become a kind of artist in order to control, shape, and ennoble his existence and the lives around him.

Sarton's major characters might be called artists-in-life or artists of their own lives. Among the many similarities between Virginia Woolf and May Sarton is the depiction of individuals who are sensitive to the needs of others, skillful at helping them fulfill them, and preoccupied with fostering growth rather than in imposing their will. Mrs. Dalloway, Mrs. Ramsay, and, in Woolf's masterwork *Between the Acts,* Isa Oliver and Mrs. Swithin are as much artists as the conscious artists, Lily Briscoe or Miss La Trobe. Sarton's reader is quick to notice a similar emphasis in her work. For example, in *Faithful Are the Wounds,* Mrs. Walter Kotschnig after mentioning the suicide of Cavan—the chief subject of the book—praised Sarton for her "portrayal of love beyond the erotic or the parental and [for] the guts to call it 'love' " (20 February 1956).

"Love beyond the erotic," or *caritas,* is the essence of the vision Sarton projects in her work. This is neither romantic nor unrealistic. It requires courage because it is out of fashion. And one might argue that the common reader understands the poet's vision of love. The necessity of growth, however painful, is the *ultimate* reality, more compelling than the subject matter of many a more celebrated novelist. When she conveyed her appreciation of *At Seventy* to Sarton, Constance Hunting might have been speaking of the Sarton oeuvre: "What strikes with such wonderful force is the full, rich, human love for this world and its friends; indeed, 'Love calls us' in this journal" (13 March 1984).

Perhaps the case may be made most convincingly by citing the least likely example. *A Reckoning* is Tolstoy's *Death of Ivan Ilyich* expanded to the length of a novel, stripped of its comforting mystic, religious ending, and without the satire of bourgeois values. It is a hard book to read without dissolving in tears, for it begins with Laura having just learned that her death from cancer is imminent and ends with her ending. Yet it is still in print; it is checked out with remarkable frequency in public libraries; it inspired hundreds of letters of gratitude from ministers, psychologists, teachers, mothers, daughters—common readers.

A Reckoning, about death from cancer, is really about nurture. A psychologist in New York City expresses his belief in the validity of Sarton's

> depth of insight about "the work" of dying; that the greatest affirmation of life is the continued search for personal identity, to one's last breath.

> In my own work with dying patients I learned more about
> life than about death. . . . The book is not about death but
> about the human spirit at its most magnificent and miracu-
> lous heights.
>
> (Lawrence LeShan, 21 October 1978)

Readers of *A Reckoning* feel uplifted because, as her doctor says to
Laura just before she dies, "It seems that you have been living your
death, living instead of dying it, I mean. It has been a meaningful journey, hasn't it?" (245). When Laura answers, "Yes," the common reader
recognizes that he or she is perhaps in an earlier stage of that same
journey. He recognizes that "we hurtle / toward the dark" ("Death and
the Turtle"), but also that he can be an artist of his own life. He can
try to reckon up what Laura calls "the real connections" (10). Sarton's
patron finds attractive in her work characters who nurture others and
who nourish growth within themselves.

Sarton's common reader often responds to her as if she were one of
her own heroines. Sometimes this response suggests that Sarton is, in
addition to being a novelist, something of a minister to human needs:

> I don't know what it is—you call to mind the things one
> forgets—or you remind us of all the things that help. And
> also, what you say hits some responsive chord in us, so we
> just think "yes—that's right." And so we feel at home and
> rested, as it were "in the head."
>
> (Phyllis Gleason, 25 June 1984)

It is significant that the Unitarian Women's Fellowship gave her their
Ministry to Women award in 1982.

In a letter to Sarton a Canadian woman, Deborah Sinclair, speaks
for many readers who find comfort in all of Sarton's work. Since this
letter is typical of so many, I quote the first third as it was written:

Dear Ms. Sarton,

It is with much thought and preparation that I send you these few words. For a long time I have often wanted to write you. I must add, that I have never been moved to write an author in my entire life and I am quite an avid reader!

Nonetheless, I feel so moved by your work that I felt I had to let you know what it has meant to me for a number of years now. I never go anywhere overnight without a copy of, at least, one of your books. Presently, your journal *At Seventy* is my bedtime companion. Your writing has been like a dear friend to me. I get great comfort and joy just knowing another person in the world thinks as I do. It's as if I've found a soul-mate and we've never and probably never will meet. . . . (29 June 1986).

At times the gratitude for the artist-as-healer arises from an assessment of Sarton's vision of life or its embodiment in her poetic novels as analogous to sacrament:

My "final thoughts" on *A Reckoning* are that you have worked a miracle. A heartbreaking subject has been handled with such sensitivity and a sharp eye devoid of either sentimentality or religiosity that one can consume it like a sacred (in the best sense) wafer of truth and be comforted thereby.

(Jean Burden, the poet, 10 October 1978)

To other readers *A Reckoning* seems a wholly secular document. For example, the Director of Nursing for the Cancer Control Agency of British Columbia expressed her gratitude succinctly: "The human and artistic integrity of *Reckoning* is a reprieve. I am afraid we were almost Kubler-Ross'ed to death" (Sue Rothwell, 27 February 1979). The praise of *A Reckoning* which Sarton most appreciated came from a retired professor of comparative literature at Columbia, Emery Neff, whose letter she quotes in *Recovering*. He believes the novel liberates the reader from "primal fears: fear of sexual deviation [and] fear of dying" (67).

Ultimately in her literary criticism, Virginia Woolf saw herself as typical of the common reader for whom she wrote; Woolf also wrote her best novels for those like herself and her friends. In that Sarton's common reader is not a professional critic, he is similar to Woolf's. But Sarton has tried to reach a wider audience than Woolf. She began to publish novels to bring her vision to a popular audience as opposed to the select few in America and Britain who read new poets. And when she began publishing her journals, she sought an even wider public.

In Wheelock's filmed interview, Sarton mentions her acquaintance, Virginia Woolf, and praises her ability to project on every page of her books her unique vision of life. Sarton adds with off-the-cuff humility: "I think this is true to a not such a geniusy [sic] extent of my work" (Wheelock). It is not a question of genius; it is surely in part a matter of Sarton having chosen a slightly different common reader for whom to write.

Woolf's common reader resembled to some extent her father, the celebrated critic Sir Leslie Stephen, and the world of letters over which he had helped preside in the previous generation. Sarton's father was similarly intellectual and founded an academic discipline, the history of science; and Sarton's mother resembled Woolf's mother, whose interest in improving the art of nursing led her to publish a pamphlet *Notes from Sick Rooms*. May Sarton chose as her patron and common reader not her academic father but rather her mother, "who would heal the wounded plant or friend / With the same vulnerable yet rigorous love."

In Sarton's *The Magnificent Spinster* the narrator has chosen to write her first work of fiction at the age of seventy in order to celebrate a friend of fifty years. Jane Reid had been her teacher, as Anne Longfellow Thorp had been May Sarton's mentor at the Shady Hill School in Cambridge. Of course, Sarton is memorializing Thorp, but one might argue that the narrator's purpose ("to celebrate an extraordinary woman," 13) suggests that Sarton has made her common reader and her patron the hero of the book. Sarton's composite vision of virtue in a woman resides in Jane Reid. That some of Reid's superficial facets are ignored (e.g. did she have a love life?) may have bothered the novel's reviewers who missed the point. This novel, again, is about a woman more good than bad. Jane is a political liberal with the financial means to help society's victims either in Cambridge's black neighborhood or in war-ravaged Germany. Her essence is the artist's sensibility residing in an ordinary person: "the source or spring, something that cannot be polluted, that can withstand whatever happens to throw one off balance, that is there, a foundation that sometimes seems to me below the personal. It is what the artist, the poet, draws on" (279).

Like her model in Sarton's own life, Reid invites friends to an island off the coast of Maine in the summer. *The Magnificent Spinster* begins with Jane as a child on Wilder Island and ends with Jane as an old woman helping children discover buried treasure—psychological and real—at her ancestral summer home. As a nurturer, she is herself like her home: "after all, this was what the island was for, to give a hard-pressed friend a respite, to shelter and make well" (310). Her common reader has found such an island in Sarton's work. And the healer has been sustained by those to whom she has offered respite.

In an amusing essay, "Middlebrow," Woolf says she is, like Shakespeare, Dickens, Byron, Shelley, Keats, a "highbrow . . . who rides his mind at a gallop across country in pursuit of an idea." She goes on to say that she "honours so wholeheartedly and depends so completely upon lowbrows. By a lowbrow is meant of course a man or a woman of thoroughbred vitality who rides his body in pursuit of a living at a gallop across life." The "middlebrow," according to Woolf, is something of a nonentity in between. Like Yeats, Woolf was suspicious of the middle class. Her essay is an indictment particularly of the middlebrow's intellectual point of view and concludes: "If any human being, man, woman, dog, cat, or half-crushed worm dares call me 'middlebrow' I will take my pen and stab him, dead" (*Collected Essays* II, 196–203).

If Woolf's middlebrow must ride, at a gallop, his body in pursuit of a living *and* must ride his mind, perhaps at a canter, in pursuit of an idea, he or she is not such a bad person. In fact, most of us—I include myself—must balance our lives between the needs of the intellect and those of the purse. Woolf's loathing for the middlebrow arises from her refusal to compromise her intensely personal, poetic vision. Like Shelley's "Epispsychidion," *The Waves* and much great literature was written for the intellectual elite.

A highbrow herself, Sarton's success as a writer and a poet lies in the fact that she is neither addressing the highbrow, as does Woolf, nor offering a mimesis of the lowbrow, as does Carolyn Chute. She has chosen for her patron the middlebrow, often the housewife. She tries to reform the middlebrow's stereotypical disdain for the elderly or the homosexual—a disdain rooted, of course, in fear. She wishes her common reader no longer to accept the second-class status of women. Above all, she wishes the common reader to be cognizant of the artist's sensibility which resides in the ordinary person. Sarton chose as her patron her mother and all those with the potential to be similar nurturers themselves: not the Lord Jims but the Jane Reids.

Sarton as visionary-healer is neither sentimental nor always comforting. The most poignant letters come from readers who speak of many of her works and of her vision as a whole. They recognize her for the social critic she is, at least in part. "On the surface my work has not looked radical, but perhaps it will be seen eventually that in a 'nice, quiet, noisy way' I have been trying to say radical things gently so that they may penetrate without shock" (*Journal of a Solitude*, 90). Apart from the journals where she expresses herself forthrightly, in her novels she reverses social stereotypes: homosexuals are not depraved but ordinary. The elderly and physically ill are not, like T. S. Eliot's Prufrock, pathetic, secondary characters "to swell a progress, start a scene or two" but, like homosexuals, capable of being heroic or at least noble in their own right. And Sarton's "nice, quiet, noisy way" has allowed her to say "radical things gently" about the women's movement, too. The common reader appreciates Sarton's conviction, for example, that "women are at last becoming persons first and wives second, and that is as it should be" (*Journal of a Solitude*, 57).

> I especially appreciated [*The Small Room*, and then *Kinds of Love*] . . . *Mrs. Stevens Hears the Mermaids Singing* and *As We*

Are Now . . . and *A Reckoning . . .* your people are real and
try to be honest. You say and do more for women than all
the militant feminists put together.

(Sister Stefanie Weisgram, February 1979)

More than anything else, the common reader of Sarton senses in
her fiction the importance of recognizing and nourishing the inner life.
Her readers understand that this journey of discovering, nurturing,
and accepting the real self is often a painful discovery and also depends,
in part, on an honest assessment of the world beyond the self. This
journey has been the daily business of Sarton the poet, as the journal
entries in this anthology testify. Common readers feel nourished by *all*
of Sarton's work because her fiction and poetry are as honest as the
journals in facing the most difficult of life's problems. Sarton has not
evaded troubling political questions. Equally in poems, novels, and
journals, she has written of the horror of the Holocaust, as well as the
other major social and political crises of her time. Although her fiction
is obviously different from that of Virginia Woolf, it must be acknowl-
edged that just as both are poets working in prose, so also do both look
unflinchingly at the terrors (as well as the joys) of human experience.
Woolf focuses on the existential tensions which form the fabric of each
discrete moment of consciousness; similarly, in *As We Are Now* and *A
Reckoning*, to choose as examples those novels represented in this
anthology, Sarton offers, in a series of related moments, a convincing,
honest representation of the physical and spiritual agonies of old age
and death by cancer.

The journey toward the discovery of one's real self is also, in Sarton's
work, that road on which highbrows and middlebrows may gallop
alongside a highbrow and attain the poet's heightened state of consciousness. Sarton's common reader is her inspired and inspiring patron.

50

"THE RISK IS VERY GREAT": THE POETRY OF MAY SARTON

CONSTANCE HUNTING

In his preface to *A History of Science*, George Sarton, the preeminent scholar in his field, writes:

> Nature is full of wonderful things—shells, flowers, birds, stars—that one never tires of observing, but the most wonderful things of all to my mind are the words of men, not the vain multiplicity of words that flow out of a garrulous mouth, but the skilful and loving choice of them that falls from wise and sensitive lips. . . . The words and phrases used by men and women throughout the ages are the loveliest flowers of humanity. (vii)

This passage is remarkable not only for its tone of animated reverence but for its unself-conscious sentiments and simplicity of language. These qualities, easy and amazing as sunlight, shine throughout the work—volume after volume on shelf after shelf in private and public libraries in most of the world—of George Sarton's daughter, May Sarton. They have caused her work to be labeled sentimental, genteel, privileged, simplistic: all those pejoratives of an age in which reason is less than venerated and in which violence is confused with emotion. Let us see. Let us begin by looking at Sarton's essay, "The Writing of a Poem," in which she calls poetry "a holy game":

In what does the "holiness" of the game of poetry consist?
Is it not in the quality of the experience that precedes the
writing? For the writing of poetry is first of all a way of life,
and only secondarily a means of expression. It is a life discipline one might almost say, a discipline maintained in order
to perfect the instrument of experiencing—the poet himself—so that he may learn to keep himself perfectly open
and transparent, so that he may meet everything that comes
his way with an innocent eye?

(*Writings on Writing*, 40)

First, then, the poet's life and his response to it. Next, the height-
ening of consciousness, akin to that of the mystic: "The mystic induces
a state of extreme awareness, the visionary state, by his own disciplines" (40).

We move, if we are worthy of our task, toward a purer
innocence and a purer wisdom until at the very end we may
attain what Coleridge has defined as the function of poetry,
that state when the familiar is wonderful and the wonderful
is familiar, and when the simplest object has seeds of revelation in it.
    Simone Weil puts it, "Absolute attention is prayer." The
eye of the poet must give to the object this kind of attention.
He is to see what he sees as if it had been just created, and
he is to communicate it to us as if we had never seen it
before. But if you look at almost anything, a rock, a tree, a
lizard in this way, you learn something. The prayer is in
the looking; the answer to the prayer is the poem which
describes the object and also does something more, is something more than the object itself. (42)

She continues, "Poetry one might say is the perpetual reincarnation
of the spirit through a concrete image" (43). But do these adjurations

seem, to late twentieth-century ears, too pietistic, with their religious vocabulary—"holiness," "disciplines," "prayer," "reincarnation"? Are they, in George Sarton's words, too "severe and uncompromising" (*A History of Science*, vii)? What about that alternative old-shoe attractiveness of Robert Frost's mischievous "Poetry is the kind of thing poets write" (cited in X. J. Kennedy, *Literature*, 453); is May Sarton not only too sober but too serious?

Here is "Prayer Before Work," which opens, in her *Collected Poems* (1974), the selection from *Inner Landscape*, first published in 1939, when Sarton was twenty-seven:

> Great one, austere,
> By whose intent the distant star
> Holds its course clear,
> Now make this spirit soar—
> Give it that ease.
> Out of the absolute
>
> Abstracted grief, comfortless, mute
> Sound the clear note,
> Pure, piercing as the flute:
> Give it precision.
>
> Austere, great one,
> By whose grace the inalterable song
> May still be wrested from
> The corrupt lung:
> Give it strict form. (31)

Three stanzas, three attributes invoked. To take the last first, "form." The stanzas run a,a,a,a,b; c,c,c,c,d; e,e,e,e,f. The patterning seems rigid in its consistency, but in fact Sarton has allowed herself great scope in the play of sound, using both exact and slant rhymes, internal and external assonance and alliteration, and the semi-cesurae which surround the many spondees and make the sound-sense of the latter stand out, as in "course clear," "clear note," "strict form." Next, "precision." Each word in "Prayer Before Work" has been *chosen*, not one is unnecessary. Most are linked by the process of interweaving vowels and consonants: "*aus*tere" to "*whose*" to "*dis*tant," "au*stere*" to "*star*," "course" to "soar" to "ease," to cite examples from only the first stanza. And the effect of the nonrhyming last line of each stanza is to open it upward, in a gesture eloquent as lifting arms to the sun. Thirdly, "ease." This kind of ease has nothing to do with facility, which Sarton in her essay "The School of Babylon" terms "the enemy of poetry" (*Writings on Writing*, 19). Rather it evokes the image of the eagle resting on the wind, or of Shelley's skylark which "singing still doth soar, and soaring ever singest." Such ease does not come without effort. This early poem is not only the answer to its own prayer but a presage of hundreds of poems to come. It is manifestly the poem of a calling. A further comment: one test of a successful poem is that it have an element of technical surprise which is so subtle that most readers or listeners will notice it only subliminally. Yet it will be this paradoxically hidden element which ensures the poem's power. In "Prayer Before Work," it is not the stunning image of the "corrupt lung"; not the skillful change rung of "Great one, austere" to "Austere, great one"; not the ingenious contradiction of "mute / Sound." Seen or heard, it is the wrenching of "from" in the line "May still be wrested from" to "form" in the line "Give it strict form." Preposition to noun, becoming to being—Sarton has "wrested" as well as been given the poem's "form." Upon this action, the poem stays.

Not all of Sarton's poetry is so compressed. In fact, her structures are Protean in their variety. Tercets, sestinas, couplets, quatrains, free verse, blank verse, imagistic verse, lyrics, letter poems, sonnets, the entire range of poetic territory is explored in her eleven separate volumes. Her themes too are large: nature, love, art, death, *ephémeros*, permanence, inner and outer landscape. Her technical, intellectual, and temperamental scope is such as to launch her into the environs of greatness. Yet she also touches on smaller, homelier subjects: gardening, teaching, housekeeping, friends. If, then, her poetry is so inexhaustibly varied, in what consists its individuality? What have the lines "Downstairs the plumber / Is emptying the big tank, / Water-logged" to do with these which face them on the opposite page, "All lovers sow and reap their harvests from / This flesh ever to be renewed and reconceived / As the bright ploughs break open the dark loam?" (*Halfway to Silence*, 56–57).

What keeps the poems hers is the mind and spirit behind them, a mind at once complicated and straightforward, a spirit both sensitive and resilient. The mind of an educator and a learner, the spirit of a lover and a child. But these are not separate; and they are both private and public. Hence the political poems like "The Invocation to Kali" and "A Ballad of the Sixties," charming animal poems like "A Parrot" and "Eine Kleine Snailmusik," the "brushstroke" poems like "Japanese Prints" and "A Country House," and the splendid sonnet sequences like "These Images Remain" and "A Divorce of Lovers" are not only possible but achieved. But *how* are they achieved? What are their salient *like*nesses?

Colors, for one thing. Random lines show "The fresh watercolor / Green of rice" ("Notes from India"); "we come to Chartres, riding the green plain" ("Return to Chartres"); "Country of still canals, green willows, golden fields" ("Homage to Flanders"); "In leaf-rich golden winds" ("The First Autumn"); "In Kashmir the sheer sapphire of that flight" ("Ballads of the Traveler"); "At dawn we wake to rose and amber meadows, / At noon plunge on across the waves of white" ("The House in Winter"). Not colors for their own sake, but colors melded with image. Image! Concerning which Sarton writes in her essay, "The Writing of a Poem":

> I believe that if one were to isolate one quality and one only as essential to the poetic nature, it would be the poet's instinctive tendency to translate the abstract into the concrete, *to think in images*. For the business of poetry is to bring thought alive, to make a thought into an experience, and we experience through the senses. The means of doing this is the image.
>
> (*Writings on Writing*, 45).

Poets usually gather in their works a cluster, a constellation of images whose connotative meanings are expressive of certain aspects of existence which are important, even necessary to them and which they use as indices of concepts and emotions. George Sarton, who began by wanting to be a poet, uses "shells, flowers, birds, stars" to show that "nature is full of wonderful things." This is a very simple, though by no means simple-minded, method of bringing "thought alive," by examples. His daughter uses a similar cluster as title for her volume *Cloud, Stone, Sun, Vine* (1961). Other recurrent images in her poems are swans (serenity, pure grace), silence (the still point of passion), fields (rich existence), the seacoast (battling existence), air (ecstasy of spirit), light (benison). Not always are these connotated thus, but often enough to suggest such meanings consistently. They are not obtrusive but they are intrinsic. They seem simple—poets have used them for centuries— but the more Sarton's poems are read and pondered, the more depth they reveal. Hers is, in a way, deceptive art: the clarity of the images obscures their tenacious roots. They bloom, they do not explode.

The breath of their blooming is Sarton's supple line, which by no means lacks gentle shock. Again and again she bends it, provides it with an unexpected rhythm or rhyme which at first reading seems not true, seems even somewhat awkward:

> All fuses now, falls into place
> From wish to action, word to silence,
> My work, my love, my time, my face
> Gathered into one intense
> Gesture of growing like a plant.

> (from "Now I Become Myself")

"Silence," "intense" surely appear ill-yoked, and the line "Gathered into one intense" scans inconveniently compared to the effortless accents and flow of the other tetrameters. To "fit it in" is to distort it: "Gathered into one intense." Very well, do not attempt exactitude but read it as ordinary speech: "Gathered into one inténse / Gésture . . ." and discover how the line break acts to heighten the intensity of forcing exhalation, then inhalation, then exhalation on "gésture," which now becomes a substantial experience toward the image "growing like a plant." Sarton has here brought "thought alive," brought "thought into experience," and not the other way around as with didactic poets (and she has been called didactic).

Beyond breath there is sound, and commingled with sound, sense. Two poems in *A Private Mythology* (1966) treat the same scene but different subjects. They are thus instructive to examine for techniques toward effect and to measure the extent of Sarton's daring:

In Kashmir

Lovers of water and light
Rest on a silvery fleece,
Lost among willows and sheep.

The lake, a quiet eye,
Reflects on interchanges
Between clouds and the ranges.

And on this shallow mirror
The narrow long boats glide,
Turning white peaks aside.

While on his watching-pole,
A kingfisher, intent,
His long bill water-bent,

Makes a black, slanting line.
He focuses the scene,
The silver and the green.

Long pause, complete suspense—
And then the piercing dive
Shakes all the reeds alive.

The flash of sapphire blue
And mirror-breaking lance
Makes even mountains dance.

Back on his watching-pole
The king who got his wish
Swallows a little fish.

FROM "BALLADS OF THE TRAVELER"

O tell us, friend, what wonders there are
In far Kashmir, in ancient Srinagar?
In Srinagar, a world of snow and sky
Wher the *shikaras*, shallow long boats, ply,
I saw a kingfisher, watching a fish,
Sit his long pole with concentrated wish—
Wait, wait, wait—then take the dive
And swallow his bright wriggling catch alive.
In Kashmir the sheer sapphire of that flight
Hit like a shot the bull's-eye of delight.

"In Kashmir" is written in tercets, a trimeter. The first line of each stanza is unrhymed. This much is clear at a glance. Now the subtleties begin. The metrical foot of the first stanza is dactylic, the beat of Virgil's *Aeneid*, and the lines are in trimeter, exactly half the length of Virgil's hexameter. The poem, therefore, is to be an epic in miniature. The fact that the second, sixth, and seventh stanzas are iambic does not vitiate the announcement of the first, nor does the fact that the third, fourth, fifth, and eighth are mixed dactylic and iambic. There variations point up the playfulness of Sarton's approach, its technical sense of humor. (She is serious; not sober, here.) It is the last line of the third stanza, the first of the fourth and fifth stanzas which are dactylic, and the first and last of the eighth, all either announcing or reminding of the main scheme. The focus of the scene, as Sarton states, is the kingfisher. The sounds depicting the setting are, like it, calm, meditative: alliterative, too, those l's, for example, so innocently scattered through the first four stanzas, until they come together in the single line "Makes a b*l*ack, s*l*anting *l*ine" and make that mark actually visible. The dash after "Long pause, complete suspense—" is the mark of that suspense and the presentiment of the "piercing dive" after which the sounds become plosive: "shakes," "flash," "breaking." The final stanza has the quality of an ironic fable. This "king" gets a little "wish," the august personage is in contrast to the smallness of his desire. Is this the lesson? That humans, too, these beings little less than angels, set their desires too low? Yet the kingfisher's wish is also proper to him, for even kings must eat. Here is the thought of the experience; and "little" in the phrase "little fish" echoes ripples on the surface of the poem as it does on the lake.

The seven stanzas of "Ballads of the Traveler" are fuller and longer than those of "In Kashmir." The second, "kingfisher" stanza is typical, being written in couplets and in ten lines. Although the first stanza is wholly pentameter, the second varies the beat to tetrameter in the first and fifth lines. (The lines of the other stanzas are, with one exception, also in pentameter.) After the regular iambic pentameter of the initial stanza, "O tell us, friend, what wonders there are" comes like a fold in a hitherto smooth garment. It is startling; it seems slightly clumsy compared to the poem's opening couplet, *"O traveler, tell, what marvels did you see / In old Japan over the shining sea?"* It requires effort; and rightly so, for its effect is that of the questioner's interest truly aroused—it is as though the questioner is now leaning forward in anticipation of a response as unusual as that of the first stanza, which speaks of "a thinking garden" made "of rocks arranged in sand." Nor is the listener disappointed, for the response is once more mysteriously simple: "I saw a kingfisher, watching a fish." This line too is in tetrameter, thus responding in kind to the opening phrase of the interrogator. Further, its foot is dactylic, endowing it with a hint of mythical grandeur in contrast to the more ordinary predominantly iambic foot of the stanza. Although the scene is the same as that of "In Kashmir," in "Ballads of the Traveler" the emphasis is on the kingfisher's dive rather than on his getting his wish. The dive is redescribed in the closing couplet, and in high poetic language. Very different from the plain "take the dive" is

"In Kashmir the sheer sapphire of that flight / Hit like a shot the bull's-eye of delight," and different again from "The flash of sapphire blue / and mirror-breaking lance" of "In Kashmir." In the first place, the line in "Ballads of the Traveler" is longer; so, therefore, is the "flight." Also there are two dashes here, used for the same purpose as the single dash in "In Kashmir," but presaging as well the redescription of the dive. And how relatively unextraordinary is "The flash of sapphire blue"; compared to "In Kashmir the sheer sapphire of that flight"! With its multiple s's and sh-ph sounds, its extended vowels, the downturn of the sound of "flight" echoing the visual action to "Hit like a shot," the lines themselves are the pure experience that poetic image gives. The lesson is in the experience rather than in thought, and the "delight" can be endless. That is the lesson of the art and of the artist.

Sarton is, after all, her mother's daughter also. Anyone who has seen the exquisitely embroidered dresses and accessories that Mabel Elwes Sarton made for the child May is affected by wonder at the inventiveness of the curving designs of flowers and vines, at the soft, brilliant colors—pomegranate, emerald, flame. Done in a mixture of silk and wool threads, much like crewelwork but more delicate in execution, often on voile, that sturdy, fragile-looking fabric, the designs are images of poignancy and joy. The wool deepens; the silk gleams. Each stitch enhances the whole composition.

In the Preface to *A History of Science*, George Sarton writes:

> Nothing is more moving than the contemplation of the means found by men to express their thoughts and feelings, and the comparison of the divers means used by them from time to time and from place to place. . . . There is so much virtue in each word; indeed, the whole past from the time when the word was coined is crystallized in it; it represents not only clear ideas, but endless ambiguities; each word is a treasure house of realities and illusions, of truths and enigmas. (vii)

If May Sarton inherits her attitudes toward work and words from her father and his graceful, generous stance, like him she does not "write for philologists" but "for educated people in general" (*A History of Science*, vii). She does not write for academics, although she loves learning and teaching, but for the educable of heart and spirit as well as of mind. That is why her poetry is deceptively clear. Light falls poorly on stagnant pools. Her aim is to clarify the water so that the light of art shines at its best. The prayer for "ease," "precision," and "form" forms the ground of all of her work. Then comes the "delight," the spell of sound and sense, music and image. But craft must also enter in, and Sarton's skills are at once bold and fine, daring in the defiance of banality, intricate in the minute patterning of the large design. May Sarton's poetry is indeed a splendid achievement. "The risk is very great" (*Writings on Writing*, 46). It is, after all, a life.

FROM "THE WRITING OF A POEM"

MAY SARTON

$(\sqrt{|\mathbf{Y}|})$

Sometimes an idea for a poem must tease the mind for years before it is ripe. And there are themes that must go on being explored as long as one lives. One of these is surely time. May I share with you one more set of my own worksheets, one of my struggles with this immense theme?

The poem is called "On Being Given Time." The occasion was my being given a Guggenheim Fellowship and for the first time in some years able to foresee an open space; I might at last hope to induce the state of peculiar awareness from which poems spring. I had finished a long and difficult novel; I was feeling tired and empty; and with this great news of imminent freedom in my pocket, I went for a walk. It happened that I came to one of the small ponds along The Fenway in Boston and stood for some moments watching the ducks swim about, watched, and suddenly experienced one of those "moments of vision" of which I spoke earlier. It is hard to define just what this moment contained; the worksheets we shall look at will gradually define it. At any rate I was seized by some intimation about time and what it is, and some weeks later the idea teased me into sitting down to try to capture it.

The first sheet is very much crossed-out, as well as written over along the margins. But I see I have circled a title: "Time as Creation." This evidently was the theme. I did not begin to write the poem until some weeks after watching the ducks, and in the interval I had evidently forgotten the original key to the experience. The early worksheets are really hunting expeditions in pursuit of an image. There are three separate tries; each of them shows the signs of battle:

The first reads:

> Time is the joker in every pack
> A mechanical toy that life winds up
> The magician who makes time disappear
> The necromancer
> The gangster, the shady thief—

One can see clearly in the lines that poets work by association just as the analysand does within a psychoanalytic analysis. The second try goes off on a different track. There are two or three versions of this one:

> I stalked it all day among the pigeons
> The automobiles, the jet-planes, faster, faster,
> Laid in wait for it at street corners
> Spreading my nets of silence over the noisy regions
> As if to catch a cloud and make time fall like rain
> But at the end the joke was on me
>
> As, yes, the target of the day hunted the hunter
>
> Hit by my own target at the end

But although this evidently had possibilities, since I gave it three tries, I was still not in the groove. So there is a third:

> Children know better than to take it
> Playing the long game of morning large and free
>
> Animals rest within it and never let it—

(I might interpolate here that these lines were finally the focussing ones for the poem, but I did not recognize this yet. I went off on another tangent):

> Only do *we* make this mechanical toy
> Count it like money as if so large and free
> It could be hoarded and amassed.
> It cannot ever be spent.
>
> We can be part of its flowing and so spend ourselves
> But spend time? Take time? Give it away?

This last seemed for awhile to be *it*, and after playing around with three or four versions based on the suggestion of the last line above, I came out with what looked like a poem, and titled it,

JOURNEY TOWARD TIME

> They say "it takes time"
> Or "take your time," they say.
> Mine? My time? My lifetime?
> And how do you "take it" anyway?
>
> Once I clenched my fist
> And snuffed time like a moth;
> I learned there's more of a twist
> To catching it than truth
>
> They say, "Time's money," too,
> But could you count it piece by piece
> Hoard or keep the river's flow?
> Invested, would it still increase?
>
> "Tell me the time." Who can?
> Watches are time's worst enemy;
> The little tick is fatal.
> It's not mechanical at all.

> Oh it's no friend to men
> The winged chariot or jet-plane
> That screams him round and round the sun
> Until his heart bursts and he's done.
>
> Yet I've come close to seeing
> The angel out of the corner of an eye—

There I left it. Why? Because I sensed just about here that what I was doing was writing *about* the subject; I was playing with words, instead of translating the experience. The tone of voice also was not quite my own. It seemed a little slick, too light. What I really wanted to do was to make the reader actually feel time opening out while he read, not to tell him what had happened to me or how I felt about it, but to communicate the experience itself. I remember I gave up at the end of that day. And waited for several days, with the poem knocking around in the back of my mind, while I did other things.

Then I picked up the crossed over, re-written, mess of worksheets and studied them. I found that the first one seemed the most alive; I re-read it in its various versions and found a note I had overlooked:

> The ripple behind the duck as it swims
> The release after music

This was clearly the kind of image I was looking for, the image that made the thing happen instead of just talking about it. There then began the search for the stanza form:

> We may be sick of time, but time's the healer,
> Angry with time, but time's the peace-giver
> Afraid of time, but time—
> Destroyed by time, but time is also saviour

But this was obviously playing with words again, allowing the rhyme to distort the idea. However, I was getting warm, and a few pages further on I find this:

There might be some device worth discussing
The riple behind the duck as it swims
Opening the way to time without fussing
Or that other ripple after music that breaks down walls.
I have taken a walk round the block in the evening
After the crowded day, renewed acquaintance
With time as the most natural thing.
I have seen it floating through a dance.

Here is the first appearance of what turned out to be crucial in the final poem, the idea that form releases the sense of time. I hope that under all these words that cannot come close to the complex of feelings, thoughts, analysis that go into the hours of working at a poem—I hope that under the words you have sensed that I was all the time clarifying my idea. The search for the image was part of that clarification. I only knew, you see, what the experience had really contained when I had discovered the true image for it. When this happened I had the form, a rather slow-moving rhythm, a five-line stanza. For as Emerson puts it so beautifully: "It is not metre but a metre-making argument that makes a poem, a thought so passionate and alive that like the spirit of a plant or animal, it has an architecture of its own." Just as the poem makes the poet, so the idea also creates its own form.

I was now well on my way. At the end of another five or six hours I had the poem. Here it is in the version I sent out to my friends at Christmas in 1953.

ON BEING GIVEN TIME

Sometimes it seems to be the inmost land
All children still inhabit when alone.
They play the game of morning without end,
And only lunch can bring them, startled, home
Bearing in triumph a small speckled stone.

Animals, too, live in that open world.
We may tease up the sleeping furry ball,

But starfish paws will gently be unfurled
And furled again, and the cat all recurled
So roundly, the interruption quite unreal.

Scholars and lovers make the midnight blaze,
Spring an hour open to hold three centuries.
They are the joyful jugglers of the days,
Replacing clocks, those rigid enemies,
With thought and passion conjured as they please.

We have been long aware that time's no toy
To be manipulated like a clever engine
With little hands that tick away all joy.
Sweet flowing time the children still enjoy
Has natural and nonchalant dimension.

Yet even for them, too much dispersal scatters;
What complex form the simplest game may hold!
And all we know of time that really matters
We've learned from moving clouds and waters
Where we see form and motion lightly meld.

Not the fixed rigid object, clock or mind,
But the long ripple that opens out beyond
The duck as he swims down the tranquil pond,
Or when a wandering falling leaf may find
And follow the formal downpath of the wind.

It is, perhaps, our most complex creation,
A lovely skill we spend a lifetime learning,
Something between the world of pure sensation
And the world of pure thought, a new relation,
As if we held in balance the globe turning.

Even a year's not long, yet moments are.
This moment, yours and mine, and always given,
When the leaf falls, the ripple opens far,

And we go where all animals and children are,
The world is open. Love can breathe again.

Yes, there does come the moment, the wonderful moment when the poem is finished, when you have rolled a page into the typewriter for the last time and are ready to send it out to friends. There is nothing more you can do. It is on its own. This, of course, is the moment when it is quite necessary to try it out on someone, preferably at once, for already in a few hours the "first fine careless rapture" of achievement will be attacked by doubts, and the revulsion that may have something to do with fatigue will begin to creep in. W. B. Yeats in a letter to a friend comments:

> One goes on year after year gradually getting the disorder
> of one's mind in order, and this is the real impulse to create.
> Till one has expressed a thing it is like an untidy, unswept,
> undusted corner of a room. When it is expressed one feels
> cleaner, and more elegant, as it were, but less profound, so
> I suppose something is lost in the expression.

> (*The Letters of W. B. Yeats*, New York: Macmillan, 1955).

Is that the end? Not quite. Much later on I had a letter from Archibald MacLeish suggesting that the poem would benefit by some cutting. He suggested cutting everything except stanza four and the last three. Well, I have been thinking about this now for three years and playing around with various cuts, and I have finally put the poem in my new book, *In Time Like Air*, with five stanzas, cutting two, three, and four of the version I read to you.

I cannot imagine whether in all I have said there has been some small part of the "usable truth" for you. Perhaps, if nothing else has emerged, at least the idea that inspiration is facile, or that poems spring like Athene fully-armed from the poet's brow has been exploded! But surely whatever I have failed to communicate, I trust that I have not failed to communicate my faith that poetry is a way of life as well as a complex and fascinating intellectual game, that poets must serve it as a good servant serves his master, must revere and woo it as the mystic reveres and woos God through self-discipline toward joy. And I hope that you may feel under all these words the inexhaustible enthusiasm that drives us on, that willingness to break down in order to refashion closer to the heart's desire that makes the creative process among the most fruitful and awe-inspiring disciplines of the mind.

REVISION AS CREATION

MAY SARTON

.... (ᐱᵢᐱ)

My thesis is that revision *is* creation and that it is a far more exciting and revelatory process than the mere manipulating of word and
idea, though at its lowest level it is, of course, also that. My thesis is
that we *earn* form as we earn understanding; my thesis is that metaphor
("to see the world in a grain of salt") is the great teacher of the poet as
he wrestles to discover what he really means, just as it is the point for
the reader where intellect and emotion fuse and he meets the poem as
he might meet a person with whom he is to fall in love at first sight.
But this impact, the impact of a true poem, must have been preceded
by a long adventure on the part of its creator: for him what is the value
of the finished work compared to what he has found out on the journey
of its making?

   I understand very well why Valéry simply could not bear to "finish"
a poem; what interested him was revising it—indefinitely—because he
was discovering so much on the way; because he felt that a moment of
inspiration could be, in fact, mined forever. It was the same attitude
that Yeats expressed in four lines:

> The friends that have it I do wrong
> Whenever I remake a song

> Should know what issue is at stake:
> It is myself that I remake.

For me a true poem is on the way when I begin to be haunted, when it seems as if I were being asked an inescapable question by an angel with whom I must wrestle to get at the answer. We all experience at times the pressure of the unresolved crude matter that we need to set outside ourselves and to examine; the poet's way of doing it is to begin to make some notes, to ease the tension by writing something down on a pad and looking at it. At this point it is often not at all clear what the poem is really about. At this point what goes down on the page may be quite incoherent, *because* whatever has been set in motion is complex . . . and because it has probably come out of a strong emotion, but one that is, for one reason or another, troubling. One thing is sure: somewhere among the jottings there will be an image, because it is the nature of poetry to turn the abstract into the concrete. Very possibly there are several images and I begin to know what the poem is telling me as I probe them, turn them over like pebbles picked up on a beach, hold them in my hands, feel their substance and weight, dream them alive in my mind. "Here we are at a place," says Gaston Bachelard* who has taught us so much about the psychology of image-making, "where ideas dream and where images meditate."

The image must be complex enough to carry the weight of complex feeling; it must be absolutely exact. This is where the beginner often bogs down; he is too easily satisfied with the flotsam and jetsam the wave of what might be called inspiration has brought him. He is unwilling to analyze, to probe, to push the limits on what seems to him marvelous, unexpected, and a gift from the gods. Beginners are narcissistic and conservative; it takes time to learn to be daring and radical enough to break down again and again, and by doing so to explore the most

---

*See especially *L'air et les songes* (Paris: Corti, 1943) and *L'eau et les rêves* (Paris: Corti, 1942).

elusive realities of experience in the most concrete and exact possible terms.

It has happened to me at least once that the image preceded the poem by years. I tucked it away for the moment when it would meet the experience worthy of it for intensity and complexity. Such an image was suggested to me by that same Bachelard: "Salt dissolves and crystallizes; it is a Janus material. To dream salt intimately is to penetrate into the most secret habitation of one's own substance." When I first came upon that image I knew I was not ready to use it but that someday I would be. The poem, a love poem, which finally got built on that image is itself an example of how one tests a metaphor. If you like, the whole poem analyzes the image to prove something about the nature of love in relation to time.

IN TIME LIKE AIR

Consider the mysterious salt:
In water it must disappear.
It has no self. It knows no fault.
Not even sight may apprehend it.
No one may gather it or spend it.
It is dissolved and everywhere.

But, out of water into air
It must resolve into a presence,
Precise and tangible and here.
Faultlessly pure, faultlessly white,
It crystallizes in our sight
And has defined itself to essence.

What element dissolves the soul
So it may be found and lost,
In what suspended as a whole?
What is the element so blest
That there identity can rest
As salt in the clear water cast?

Love, in its early transformation,
And only love, may so design it
That the self flows in pure sensation,
Is all dissolved, and found at last
Without a future or a past,
And a whole life suspended in it.

The faultless crystal of detachment
Comes after, cannot be created
Without the first intense attachment.
Even the saints achieve this slowly;
For us, more human and less holy,
In time like air is essence stated.

(*Cloud, Stone, Sun, Vine*, New York:
Norton, 1961)

Perhaps you can imagine what a long struggle it was to get inside this metaphor and through it to discover what I was trying to say about love! "What do you go into a poem for?" asks Robert Frost. "To see if you can get out!"

It is hard to talk about revision because it is a complex matter. One of the ways one is helped to "get out" what is "in" the poem, is form. The poem I have just read is exceedingly compressed; the form itself creates intensity. You can't wallow—you have to *control*. I have said that form is earned. What I mean by that is that the music of a poem does not show itself unless one's whole being is at a high pitch of concentration. The experience back of the poem must have been revelatory. The trouble with free verse is that very rarely (D. H. Lawrence comes to mind as an exception) does the intensity seem great enough; the danger is the diffuse, self-indulgent, not closely enough examined content. There is a wonderful poem by Laurence Lerner which says this better than I can say it in prose.

TO SCHOOL

I sent my Muse to School:
   They taught her to walk straight,
To bear her body well,
   Scan, and alliterate.
So perfect was her poise
Men turned to watch her pass.

Skin deep, some said: those airs
   But fascinate the sight;
No true delight is hers.
   I thought, they must be right.
She plays a flawless part:
True verse is from the heart.

But when my heart was hurt,
   Too dumb to find relief,
She took voice till her art
   Sang the true shape of grief.
And the unschooled who heard
Loathed their own broken words.

(The Directions of Memory, London:
Chatto and Windus, 1963)

If the pressure back of the poem is great enough, then I find almost always that among those rough chaotic notes I jot down in the moment of inspiration, there is one line that suggests meter, and sometimes I can sense the whole first stanza. It is here in the music of the poem that the greatest mystery lies. I suppose that a practising poet has inside him the rumor of many sounds, the patterns of poems by others which he has totally absorbed. He doesn't say—ever—that he is going to write a sonnet; he has a sonnet idea; a sonnet hums inside this idea, and the form is inevitable if it is to be valid. We do not impose form on the poem; form is organic. But just as with the image, the poet in a state of inspiration may go wrong unless he is extremely self-critical. The enemies of creation are and have always been facility, cleverness, self-indulgence, and above all a misunderstanding about what inspiration is. I know that I am inspired when I become a fury of self-criticism to dig out what I really mean from a lot of irrelevancies that have poured down on the page in the first excitement of the start.

Revising a poem means being possessed by a driving need to clarify a powerful and complex experience by means of image and form. When one is well into it and maybe ten or twelve pages of the struggle are already strewn about, it is clear that the feeling which drove one to make the struggle for expression is no longer the point. Something else has taken its place, which I must call the act of *creation*, and the act of creation implies a conscious exploration and manipulation of what the subconscious brings. The poet has become a critic. He must be capable from now on in of unremitting ruthless analysis.

Sometimes one has to wait a long time before one can sense the form. "It is not meter," says Emerson, "but a meter-making argument that makes a poem, a thought so passionate and alive that like the spirit of a plant or animal, it has an architecture of its own." Some poems are inward gestations; they haunt; they bother; they work their way through a long inward process of refinement. During the time when the Nazi camps were being uncovered I needed to speak about it (we all felt the crushing weight of horror and had to come to terms with it somehow). I had the image—it was that of a gentle cousin of mine in Belgium, the weakling of the family who had never made much of himself, but who, when the supreme test came of withstanding torture and not telling, found it in him to die rather than to speak. Now here was an example of an emotion at first too strong to do anything with; I just had to live with it for a long time, to come through it into some usable truth. It had to be completely *faced* first with a cold honest look. Revision is creation because we are making ourselves through the making of the poem. There are no notes. A poem is not a scream and good poems are never hysterical, so the scream must have been inwardly suppressed before the poem, that which will communicate, and in this instance make the unbearable bearable, can find its way out. One of the ways in which poetry does what Rilke asks of it ("you must change your life") is because of its *music*. But I could not find the music for a long time, because I had not resolved the emotion. Perhaps you can imagine the relief when I was able to write what turned out to be a ballad, a rather simple song. I hope it does not run away from the reality, but transforms it into usable truth.

THE TORTURED

Cried Innocence, "Mother, my thumbs, my thumbs!
The pain will make me wild."
And Wisdom answered, "Your brother-man
Is suffering, my child."

Screamed Innocence, "Mother, my eyes, my eyes!
Someone is blinding me."
And Wisdom answered, "Those are your brother's eyes,
The blinded one is he."

Cried Innocence, "Mother, my heart, my heart!
It bursts with agony."
And Wisdom answered, "That is your brother's heart
Breaking upon a tree."

Screamed Innocence, "Mother, I want to die.
I cannot bear the pain."
And wisdom answered, "They will not let him die.
They bring him back again."

Cried Innocence, "Mother, I cannot bear
It now. My flesh is wild!"
And Wisdom answered, "His agony is endless
For your sake, my child."

Then whispered Innocence, "Mother, forgive,
Forgive my sin, forgive—"
And Wisdom wept. "Now do you understand, Love,
How you must live?"

(Cloud, Stone, Sun, Vine)

There was no problem with the image here, of course. It was given and it was archetypal. The problem was the music, was the *form*.

If we earn metaphor by being extremely open to experience of all kinds, and able to examine it with a cold clear eye, and if we earn form only as we are able to experience at a high level of intensity, then might one not say that the revising of a poem is a constant revising, disciplining, and refining of the poet himself? Each true poem has been an act of *growth*, and growth is not something that can be pasted on or arrived at by putting on a new dress or cutting one's hair in a new cut. Let me suggest, then, that the art of poetry as a lifetime adventure will demand the capacity to break down over and over again what has already been created, and to break down barriers within the poet's self so that he may keep on growing within the whole form and shape of his life. Creation is revision within the whole person as he moves on from youth to middle age and from middle age to old age. Yeats is, of course, the great exemplar, for he molded his whole art when he was an old man. It is exhilarating to contemplate on this spring day when renewal is in the air.

ON GROWTH AND CHANGE

MAY SARTON

(งฺ๊โฃ)

AT LINDOS

"What are ruins to us,
The broken stones?"
They made for the sea,
These elementals
Possessed by Poseidon.
"And what is Athene?"
The sun flamed around them.
The waters were clear green.

What compelled us
To face the harsh rock?
Why did we choose
The arduous stairways?
There lay the crescent
Of white sand below us,
And the lucky swimmers.

But at last we came out,
Stood high in the white light,
And we knew you, Athene,
Goddess of light and air,
In your roofless temple,
In your white and gold.
We were pierced with knowledge.
Lucidity burned us.
What was Poseidon now,

Or the lazy swimmers?
We looked on a flat sea
As blue as lapis.
We stood among pillars
In a soaring elation.

We ran down in triumph,
Down the jagged stairways
To brag to the bathers,
But they rose up to meet us
Mysterious strangers
With salt on their eyelids,
All stupid and shining.

So it is at Lindos
A place of many gods.

(*A Private Mythology*, New
York: Norton, 1966)

    I have believed from the start that it would be possible to go on growing indefinitely as a poet, believed it against some of the evidence: Rimbaud, who ceased to write; Wordsworth who doddered on too long—though each had powerful genius. But there are stars we can hitch our wagons to, Yeats for one, who broke and re-made his style when he was in his forties and wrote some of his great poems in his seventies.

    The poet in middle age must take risks at an age when this is harder than it was in youth, must learn how to remain open, "transparent" is my word for it, at a time in life when his friends in less demanding professions are consolidating gains and deepening the groove of hard-won personal style. Poetry is a dangerous profession between conflict and resolution, between feeling and thought, between becoming and being, between the ultra-personal and the universal—and these balances are shifting all the time. We move softly because we tread on swords; we move quietly to remain aware of the slightest stir in the grass, as well as of the plane breaking the sound barrier overhead; we move about without defense, totally open to experience whatever it may bring. The instinct to protect oneself is very strong; the poet cannot afford to allow this instinct to preserve him from growth. His mastery, I sometimes think, is chiefly the mastery of anguish and doubt.

I have chosen "At Lindos" as the thread on which to hang these observations for more than one reason. We need to rejoice in the fertility of poetry in the United States today. We too are nourished and renewed by many gods; we have poets of genius who range all the way from a traditionalist like Richard Wilbur to those new voices who are breaking the sound barrier in *their* way, the beatniks. It is this wide spectrum that makes poetry so rich and exciting; it is being read in a way that perhaps the novel has ceased to be—perhaps because it is alive in a way that the novel is no longer.

I have chosen "At Lindos" also for personal reasons. It was the breakthrough from formally structured verse into free verse, which I have not found appropriate to my uses for many years. Is this return to a more fluid, and elusive, style one of the demands of middle age, a time when the need is felt for a less strained breathing, for a larger dimension? I have believed that intensity commands form. The poem I was writing seemed explosive and vital in proportion to the tension it could support, and that tension presupposed formal structuring. When I was in a state of intense perception, lines ran through my head and would have their way, and taught me, as I put an average lyric through thirty to sixty drafts, where the poem meant to go and how it would get there.

Formal structure satisfied the need for the absolute. After those thirty drafts had been worked through, I could sometimes feel, "There, it's finished. All is held solid and clear and contained; there is nothing ragged or spilled over. I can hold it in my hand like a rock."

Yet my book *A Private Mythology* is about half in free verse. We have seen the same phenomenon in our great poet Robert Lowell, for he has moved from the explosive intensity and formal structure of his early poems to a much freer style in these last years.

It took me three years of abortive attempts at putting the essence of a first visit to Japan, India, and Greece into formal verse, before I could admit that I was on the wrong path. The poems felt over-manipulated, and died. I had embarked on that great adventure to celebrate my fiftieth birthday, and I sensed that this was to be a time of painful transition.

Finally, after three years, I took a deep breath and plunged into a new element . . . ; it was all risk and tremor at first. I had to break down a grooved response to meter; iambic pentameter had become my natural way to write poems. This fluid element of free verse was frightening. I found that its value for the reader of apparent spontaneity, casualness, was just as hard to come by as the sustained dancing quality of formal structure. In the first place, in free verse the alternatives are almost without limit, and so the temptation to revise indefinitely is always there. I found it hard to bring the poem out to the sense of finality I had grown accustomed to, the joy of achievement. These poems felt not like rocks in my hand, but like water flowing over it. Free verse is far closer to normal breathing. I missed the tension between the speaking voice and the strict form of which Robert Frost has spoken so eloquently.

But little by little I learned to breathe with the line; I enjoyed the sensation of being floated on an image, on a sentence to its very end. The free verse poem, I discovered, runs on unbroken. It achieves momentum, and rounds itself out chiefly by means of metaphor. Where the poem in meter dances, the free form saunters, stopping here and there, as a walker does. The silences within it are, perhaps, even more important than those within metrical form, but they are achieved by more subtle means. In "At Lindos" every break between the lines should create a space in the mind, should simulate the passage of time, a pause.

Because free verse approaches the conversational, every device which can make it immediate is to the point. In "At Lindos" one of the problems I had to solve was to explain the setting, and to set up a dialogue, and I hope that the opening question does just this. But of course the conversation in a poem is as stylized as it is in any work of art, as stylized as the dialogue in a Hemingway short story.

The greatest peril in free verse seems to be that of over-charging, or of rambling along, so that cutting to the bone becomes mandatory. It must feel shaped, though in a far less obvious way than in a sonnet, for instance. And I fear, even now, after being subjected by the adventure, that no free verse poem is as *memorable* as a poem in form may be. It exists more like a light-bird on the ceiling than like a rock. It is always in flight. It does not, perhaps, give rest. But what it can give the reader as well as the writer is a sensation of things opening out, a horizon, not a boundary. It has its own way of disturbing.

For poetry exists to break through to below the level of reason where the angels and monsters that the amenities keep in the cellar may come out to dance, to rove and roar, growling and singing, to bring life back to the enclosed rooms where too often we are only "living and partly living."

Poems

.... (ソ|ソ)

FROM *ENCOUNTER IN APRIL* (1930–1937)

FIRST SNOW

This is the first soft snow
That tiptoes up to your door
As you sit by the fire and sew,
That sifts through a crack in the floor
And covers your hair with hoar.

This is the stiffening wound
Burning the heart of a deer
Chased by a moon-white hound,
This is the hunt, and the queer
Sick beating of feet that fear.

This is the crisp despair
Lying close to the marrow,
Fallen out of the air
Like frost on the narrow
Bone of a shot sparrow.

This is the love that will seize
Savagely onto your mind
And do whatever he please,
This the despair, and a moon-blind
Hound you will never bind.

Editor's Note: Following the practice observed in *Collected Poems*, I have cited the title of the volume in which the poems first appeared. Unless there is a note to the contrary, the text of the poems which follow is taken, however, from that of *Collected Poems*. I have, however, corrected typographical errors which appeared in *Collected Poems*. Of course, *Halfway to Silence* (1980), *Letters from Maine* (1984), and *The Silence Now* (1988) appeared following the publication of *Collected Poems* (1974).

"SHE SHALL BE CALLED WOMAN"

Genesis II, 23

1

She did not cry out
nor move.
She lay quite still
and leaned
against the great curve
of the earth,
and her breast
was like a fruit
bursten of its own sweetness.

She did not move
nor cry out—
she only looked down
at the hand
against her breast.
She looked down
at the naked hand
and wept.

She could not yet endure
this delicate savage
to lie upon her.
She could not yet endure
the blood to beat so there.
She could not cope
with the first ache
of fullness.

She lay quite still
and looked down

at the hand
where blood was locked
and longed to loose the blood
and let it flow
over her breast
like rain.

2

Not on the earth
but surely somewhere
between the elements
of air and sea
she lay that night,
no rim of bone to mark
where body clove to body
and no separate flesh,
strangely impenetrable—
O somewhere surely
did she come
to that clear place
where sky and water meet
and lay transparent there,
knowing the wave.

3

She bore the wound of desire
and it did not close,
though she had tried
to burn her hand
and turn one pain
into a simpler pain—
yet it did not close.
She had not known

how strong
the body's will,
how intricate
the stirring of its litheness
that lay now
unstrung,
like a bow—
she saw herself
disrupted at the center
and torn.
And she went into the sea
because her core ached
and there was no healing.

4

Not in denial, her peace.
For there in the sea
where she had wished
to leave her body
like a little garment,
she saw now
that not by severing this
would finity be ended
and the atom die,
not so the pure abstract
exist alone.
From those vast places
she must come back
into her particle.
She must put on again
the little garment
of hunger.
Not in denial
her appeasement,
not yet.

5

For a long time
it would be pain
and weakness,
and she who worshiped
all straight things
and the narrow breast
would lie relaxed
like an animal asleep,
without strength.

For a long time
a consciousness possessed her
that felt into all grief
as if it were a wound
within herself—
a mouse with its tiny shriek
would leave her
drained and spent.

The unanswerable body
seemed
held in an icy pity
for all livingness—
that was itself
initiate.

6

And then one day
all feeling
slipped out from her skin
until no finger's consciousness remained,
no pain—
and she all turned
to earth

like abstract gravity.
She did not know
how she had come
to close her separate lids
nor where she learned
the gesture of her sleeping,
yet something in her slept
most deeply
and something in her
lay like stone
under a folded dress—
she could not tell how long.

7

Her body was a city
where the soul
had lain asleep,
and now she woke.
She was aware
down to extremity
of how herself was charged,
fiber electric,
a hand under her breast
could hear the dynamo.
A hand upon her wrist
could feel the pulse beat.
She felt the atoms stir,
the myriad expand
and stir

She looked at her hand—
the mesh
with its multitude of lines,
the exquisite small hairs,
the veins

finding their way
down to the nails,
the nails themselves
set in so firmly
with half-moons
at their base,
the fine-set bone,
knuckle and sinew,
and she examined
the mysterious legend
upon the palm—
this was her hand,
a present someone had given her.

And she looked at her breasts
that were firm and full,
standing straightly
out from her chest,
and were each a city
mysteriously part
of other cities.
The earth itself
was not more intricate,
more lovely
than these two
cupped in her hands,
heavy in her hands.
Nothing ever was
as wonderful as this.

8

She let her hands
go softly down her skin,
the curving rib,
soft belly

and slim thigh.
She let her hands
slip down
as if they held a shift
and she were trying it
for the first time,
a shining supple garment
she would not want to lose:
So did she clothe herself.

9

She would not ever be naked
again—
she would not know
that nakedness
that stretches to the brim
and finds no shelter
from the pure terrific
light of space.
The finite self
had gathered
and was born
out of the infinite,
was hers
and whole.
For the first time
she knew what it meant
to be made so
and molded into this shape
of a pear,
this heaviness of curving fruit.

10

There were seeds
within her
that burst at intervals
and for a little while
she would come back
to heaviness,
and then before a surging miracle
of blood,
relax,
and reidentify herself,
each time more closely
with the heart of life.
"I am the beginning,
the never-ending,
the perfect tree."
And she would lean
again as once
on the great curve of the earth,
part of its turning,
as distinctly part
of the universe as a star—
as unresistant,
as completely rhythmical.

STRANGERS

There have been two strangers
Who met within a wood
And looked once at each other
Where they stood.

And there have been two strangers
Who met among the heather
And did not look at all
But lay down together.

And there have been two strangers
Who met one April day
And looked long at each other,
And went their way.

FROM *INNER LANDSCAPE* (1936–1938)

PRAYER BEFORE WORK

Great one, austere,
By whose intent the distant star
Holds its course clear,
Now make this spirit soar—
Give it that ease.

Out of the absolute
Abstracted grief, comfortless, mute,
Sound the clear note,
Pure, piercing as the flute:
Give it precision.

Austere, great one,
By whose grace the inalterable song
May still be wrested from
The corrupt lung:
Give it strict form.

SUMMARY

In the end it is the dark for which all lovers pine.
They cannot bear the light on their transparent faces,
The light on nerves exposed like a design.
They have a great need of sleep in foreign places,
Of another country than the heart and another speech.
In the end it is escape of which all lovers dream
As men in prison dream of a stretch of beach.
When they toss wide-eyed in their beds they may seem
To think of the cruel mouth and the hard breast
But it is simply murder that their hearts conceive,
Grown savage with the need of dark and rest.
They are ever innocent. They are found to believe
That love endures and their pain is infinite
Who have not learned that each single touch they give,
Every kiss, every word they speak holds death in it:
They are committing murder who merely live.

ADDRESS TO THE HEART

You cannot go back now to that innocence—
the pure pain that enters like a sword
making the bright blood flow
and the slow perfect healing, leaving you whole.
This is a deeper illness,
a poison that has entered every tissue:
Cut off your hand, you will not find it there.
This must be met and conquered in each separate atom,
must be lived out like a slow fever.
No part is mortally afflicted.
Each part will have its convalescence surely,
and yet you will arise from this infection
changed,
as one returns from death.

CANTICLE

We sat smoking at a table by the river
And then suddenly in the silence someone said,
"Look at the sunlight on the apple tree there shiver:
I shall remember that long after I am dead."
Together we all turned to see how the tree shook,
How it sparkled and seemed spun out of green and gold,
And we thought that hour, that light and our long mutual look
Might warm us each someday when we were cold.

And I thought of your face that sweeps over me like light,
Like the sun on the apple making a lovely show,
So one seeing it marveled the other night,
Turned to me saying, "What is it in your heart? You glow."—
Not guessing that on my face he saw the singular
Reflection of your grace like fire on snow—
And loved you there.

A LETTER TO JAMES STEPHENS

James, it is snowing here. It is November.
Think of the good day when we talked together,
For it is time to think of it, remember
What the warm wine, warm friendship, summer weather
Raised in our minds now that it is so cold,
Now that we sit alone and half the world apart,
This bitter season when the young grow old
And sit indoors to weigh the fiery heart:
What of it now? What of this personal all,
The little world these hands have tried to fashion
Using a single theme for their material,
Always a human heart, a human passion?
You said "Seek for a sterner stuff than this,
Look out of your closed spaces to the infinite,
Look beyond hunger and the longed-for kiss
To what there is beyond your love and in it,
To the whole heavy earth and all it bears;
Support the sky. Know the path of the planet,
Until you stand alone, a man who stares
His loneliness out of its depth to span it,
Till you can chisel substance out of space.
Forget your love, your little war, your ache;
Forget that haunting so mysterious face
And write for an abstracted beauty's sake.
Contain a large world in a small strict plan,
Your job is to draw out the essence and provide
The word that will endure, comfort, sustain a man.
This is your honor. This should be your pride."
Dear James, pure poet, I see you with that shell
Held to your sensitive abstracted ear,
Hunting the ocean's rumor till you hear it well,

Until you can set down the sound you hear:—
Fixed to a shell like that you made immortal,
This heart listens, this fragile auricle
Holds rumor like your ocean's, is a portal
That sometimes opens to contain the miracle.
If there are miracles we can record
They happen in the places that you curse.
Blessèd the pure in heart and the enduring word
Sings of that love that spins the universe.
My honor (and I cherish it for it is hardly won)
Is to be pure in this: is to believe
That to write down these perishable songs for one,
For one along, and out of love, is not to grieve
But to build on the quicksand of despair
A house where every man may take his ease,
May come to shelter from the outer air,
A little house where he may find his peace.
Dear James, if this fire seems only the strange
Quick-burning fire of youth unfounded on the earth
Then may it be transformed but never change.
Let Him in whose hands lie death and birth
Preserve its essence like that bush of flame
That stood up in a path, and, fiery-plumed,
Contained the angel who could speak God's name—
The bush that burned and still was not consumed.

FROM *THE LION AND THE ROSE* (1938–1948)

MONTICELLO

This legendary house, this dear enchanted tomb,
Once so supremely lived in, and for life designed,
Will none of moldy death nor give it room,
Charged with the presence of a living mind.

Enter, and touch the temper of a lively man.
See, it is spacious, intimate and full of light.
The eye, pleased by detail, is nourished by the plan;
Nothing is here for show, much for delight.

All the joys of invention and of craft and wit,
Are freely granted here, all given rein,
But taut within the classic form and ruled by it,
Elegant, various, magnificent—and plain,

Europe become implacably American!
Yet Mozart could have been as happy here,
As Monroe riding from his farm again,
As well as any silversmith or carpenter—

As well as we, for whom this elegance,
This freedom in a form, this peaceful grace,
Is not our heritage, although it happened once:
We read the future, not the past, upon his face.

The time must come when, from the people's heart,
Government grows to meet the stature of a man,
And freedom finds its form, that great unruly art,
And the state is a house designed by Jefferson.*

---

*The last stanza appeared in the version of the poem printed in *The Lion and the Rose* but was omitted in *Collected Poems*.

MEDITATION IN SUNLIGHT

In space in time I sit
Thousands of feet above
The sea and meditate
On solitude on love

Near all is brown and poor
Houses are made of earth
Sun opens every door
The city is a hearth

Far all is blue and strange
The sky looks down on snow
And meets the mountain range
Where time is light not shadow

Time in the heart held still
Space as the household god
And joy instead of will
Knows love as solitude

Knows solitude as love
Knows time as light not shadow
Thousands of feet above
The sea where I am now

Who wear an envelope
Of crystal air and learn
That space is also hope
Where sky and snow both burn

Where spring is love not weather
And I happy alone
The place the time together
The sun upon the stone.*

---

*The last two stanzas appeared in the version of the poem printed in *The Lion and the Rose* but were omitted in *Collected Poems*.

SANTOS: NEW MEXICO

Return to the most human, nothing less
Will nourish the torn spirit, the bewildered heart,
The angry mind: and from the ultimate duress,
Pierced with the breath of anguish, speak for love.

Return, return to the deep sources, nothing less
Will teach the stiff hands a new way to serve,
To carve into our lives the forms of tenderness
And still that ancient necessary pain preserve.

O we have moved too far from these, all we who look
Upon the wooden painted figure, stiff and quaint,
Reading it curiously like a legend in a book—
But it is Man upon the cross. It is the living saint.

To those who breathed their faith into the wood
It was no image, but the very living source,
The saviour of their own humanity by blood
That flows terribly like a river in its course.

They did not fear the strangeness, nor while gazing
Keep from this death their very precious life.
They looked until their hands and hearts were blazing
And the reality of pain pierced like a knife.

We must go down into the dungeons of the heart,
To the dark places where modern mind imprisons
All that is not defined and thought apart.
We must let out the terrible creative visions.

Return to the most human, nothing less
Will teach the angry spirit, the bewildered heart,
The torn mind, to accept the whole of its duress,
And pierced with anguish, at last act for love.

[FROM] POET IN RESIDENCE

Carbondale, Illinois

• • •

Before Teaching

These nights when the frog grates shrilly by the pond
And fireflies' points of flame flicker the gloom,
Where birds are stilled in the dense thicket-heat,
And I have seen through haze a bloody moon
Rise through the trees to make the sober town
A legendary place, a place of fearful glory,
These nights when, knowing I shall have to teach
When morning comes again, are close to fear,
I ask myself, fumbling and full of doubt, angry with time,
How stamp for you as if a gold coin in relief
The single signature of passion and belief?

What through the years endures, the only joy,
The one delight age does increase, the discipline
That fosters growth within it and is ever fertile,
And the great freedom too that comes with this—
And if I cannot do it, why be a poet then,
Or talk of art, or weep for its defeat?
These nights the frog grates and the firefly
Pricks the dense thickets of the gloomy heat
Have known the heart's will and its savage cry,
And too the delicate cool wind, the blessing on the air.

. . .
Place of Learning

Heavy, heavy the summer and its gloom,
The place, a place of learning, the difficult strange place,
And for what reason and from how far did you come,
To find the desolation and the thin soil,
To find the great heat and the sudden rain,
To listen for the long cry of the through train?

The time, a time of teaching, a curious time.

The birds alone made welcome in the morning sun
And all else strange. But this familiar, this well known,
This, in a sense, always the world where one moves
Opening the doors, opening the doors to push through alone,
And it is a way of many isolated deepening loves.
This we have known. It has been like this before.
The place of learning. The fear and trembling. The final opening of a
    door.

But here in the place of learning, in the time of teaching,
To find also, and surely not by accident,
Among the gifts of trees, of birds, the various gifts:
Coolness after long heat, a lightening sky after
Much heaviness, also to find—
The open heart, detached and open,
So feeling it has become impersonal as sunlight,
To find this curious one, creative and aloof:
From how far and for what reason did you come,
Stranger with a fire in your head, to this deep kind of welcome?

So what you gave was given and what you taught was learned,
Striking rock for water and the water falling from air,
Opening a door to find somone in the room, already there.

THE WORK OF HAPPINESS

I thought of happiness, how it is woven
Out of the silence in the empty house each day
And how it is not sudden and it is not given
But is creation itself like the growth of a tree.
No one has seen it happen, but inside the bark
Another circle is growing in the expanding ring.
No one has heard the root go deeper in the dark,
But the tree is lifted by this inward work
And its plumes shine, and its leaves are glittering.

So happiness is woven out of the peace of hours
And strikes its roots deep in the house alone:
The old chest in the corner, cool waxed floors,
White curtains softly and continually blown
As the free air moves quietly about the room;
A shelf of books, a table, and the white-washed wall—
These are the dear familiar gods of home,
And here the work of faith can best be done,
The growing tree is green and musical.

For what is happiness but growth in peace,
The timeless sense of time when furniture
Has stood a life's span in a single place,
And as the air moves, so the old dreams stir
The shining leaves of present happiness?
No one has heard thought or listened to a mind,
But where people have lived in inwardness
The air is charged with blessing and does bless;
Windows look out on mountains and the walls are kind.

THE CLAVICHORD

She keeps her clavichord
As others keep delight, too light
To breathe, the secret word
No lover ever heard
Where the pure spirit lives
And garlands weaves.

To make the pure notes sigh
(Not of a human grief, too brief)
A sigh of such fragility
Her fingers' sweet agility
Must hold the horizontal line
In the stern power of design.

The secret breathed within
And never spoken, woken
By music; the garlands in
Her hands no one has seen.
She wreathes the air with green
And weaves the stillness in.

MY SISTERS, O MY SISTERS

Nous qui voulions poser, image ineffaceable
Comme un delta divin notre main sur le sable.

Anna de Noailles

1

Dorothy Wordsworth, dying, did not want to read,
"I am too busy with my own feelings," she said.

And all women who have wanted to break out
Of the prison of consciousness to sing or shout

Are strange monsters who renounce the treasure
Of their silence for a curious devouring pleasure.

Dickinson, Rossetti, Sappho—they all know it,
Something is lost, strained, unforgiven in the poet.

She abdicates from life or like George Sand
Suffers from the mortality in an immortal hand,

Loves too much, spends a whole life to discover
She was born a good grandmother, not a good lover.

Too powerful for men: Madame de Stael. Too sensitive:
Madame de Sévigné, who burdened where she meant to give.

Delicate as that burden was and so supremely lovely,
It was too heavy for her daughter, much too heavy.

Only when she built inward in a fearful isolation
Did any one succeed or learn to fuse emotion

With thought. Only when she renounced did Emily
Begin in the fierce lonely light to learn to be.

Only in the extremity of spirit and the flesh
And in renouncing passion did Sappho come to bless.

Only in the farewells or in old age does sanity
Shine through the crimson stains of their mortality.

And now we who are writing women and strange monsters
Still search our hearts to find the difficult answers,

Still hope that we may learn to lay our hands
More gently and more subtly on the burning sands.

To be through what we make more simply human,
To come to the deep place where poet becomes woman,

Where nothing has to be renounced or given over
In the pure light that shines out from the lover,

In the pure light that brings forth, fruit and flower
And that great sanity, that sun, the feminine power.

2

Let us rejoice in
The full curve of breast,
The supple thigh
And all riches in
A woman's keeping
For man's comfort and rest
(Crimson and ivory)
For children's nourishment
(Magic fruits and flowers).
But when they are sleeping,
The children, the men,
Fed by these powers,
We know what is meant
By the wise serpent,
By the gentle dove,

And remember then
How we wish to love,

Let us rejoice now
In these great powers
Which are ours alone.
And trust what we know:
First the green hand
That can open flowers
In the deathly bone,
And the magic breast
That can feed the child,
And is under a hand
A rose of fire in snow
So tender, so wild
All fires come to rest,
All lives can be blest—
So sighs the gentle dove,
Wily the serpent so,
Matched in a woman's love.

3

Eve and Mary the mother are our stem;
All our centuries go back to them.
And delicate the balance lies
Between the passionate and wise:
Of man's rib, one, and cleaves to him;
And one bears man and then frees him.
This double river has created us,
Always the rediscovered, always the cherished.
(But many fail in this. Many have perished.)

Hell is the loss of balance when woman is destroyer.
Each of us has been there.
Each of us knows what the floods can do.

How many women mother their husbands
Out of all strength and secret *Virtu;*
How many women love an only son
As a lover loves, binding the free hands.
How many yield up their true power
Out of weakness, the moment of passion
Betrayed by years of confused living—
For it is surely a lifetime work,
This learning to be a woman.
Until at the end what is clear
Is the marvelous skill to make
Life grow in all its forms.

Is knowing where to ask, where to yield,
Where to sow, where to plough the field,
Where to kill the heart or let it live;
To be Eve, the giver of knowledge, the lover;
To be Mary, the shield, the healer and the mother.

The balance is eternal whatever we may wish;
The law can be broken but we cannot change
What is supremely beautiful and strange.
Where find the root? Where re-join the source?
The fertile feminine goddess, double river?

4

We think of all the women hunting for themselves,
Turning and turning to each other with a driving
Need to learn to understand, to live in charity,
And above all to be used fully, to be giving
From wholeness, wholeness back to love's deep clarity.
O, all the burning hearts of women unappeased
Shine like great stars, like flowers of fire,
As the sun goes and darkness opens all desire—
And we are with a fierce compassion seized.

How lost, how far from home, how parted from
The earth, my sisters, O my sisters, we have come!

For so long asked so little of ourselves and men,
and let the Furies have their way—our treasure,
The single antidote to all our world's confusion,
A few gifts to the poor small god of pleasure.
The god of passion has gone back into the mountain,
Is sleeping in the dark, deep in the earth.

We have betrayed a million times the holy fountain,
The potent spirit who brings his life to birth,
The masculine and violent joy of pure creation—
And yielded up the sacred fires to sensation.
But we shall never come home to the earth
Until we bring the great god and his mirth
Back from the mountain, until we let this stranger
Plough deep into our hearts his joy and anger,
For we shall never find ourselves again
Until we ask men's greatness back from men,
And we shall never find ourselves again
Until we match men's greatness with our own.

THE LADY AND THE UNICORN

The Cluny Tapestries

I am the unicorn and bow my head
You are the lady woven into history
And here forever we are bound in mystery
Our wine, Imagination, and our bread,
And I the unicorn who bows his head.

You are all interwoven in my history
And you and I have been most strangely wed
I am the unicorn and bow my head
And lay my wildness down upon your knee
You are the lady woven into history.

And here forever we are sweetly wed
With flowers and rabbits in the tapestry
You are the lady woven into history
Imagination is our bridal bed:
We lie ghostly upon it, no word said.

Among the flowers of the tapestry;
I am the unicorn and by your bed
Come gently, gently to bow down my head,
Lay at your side this love, this mystery,
And call you lady of my tapestry.

I am the unicorn and bow my head
To one so sweetly lost, so strangely wed:

You sit forever under a small formal tree
Where I forever search your eyes to be

Rewarded with this shining tragedy
And know your beauty was not cast for me,

113

Know we are woven all in mystery,
The wound imagined where no one has bled,

My wild love chastened to this history
Where I before your eyes, bow down my head.

PERSPECTIVE

Now I am coming toward you silently,
Do not say anything. Stay as you are—
Suspense between my love and your despair.
Like a stone figure on a fountain, be
The center of an arc of paths and trees.
Now I am coming toward you, freeze!
Be nothing but yourself, not even mine,
You as you are when all alone and free,
Suspended outside love and outside time—
Look at me as I am, as if I were a tree.
Now I am coming toward you, say nothing,
Shine in your own light, purer than my joy,
And I shall, coming toward you, make no cry,
But try to sense the nearness and the space
Between my windswept leaves and your still face,
Between the tree and the stone figure drawn
Together, if at all, by shadow or some simple dawn.

WHO WAKES

Detroit, June 1943

Who wakes now who lay blind with sleep?
Who starts bright-eyed with anger from his bed?
I do. I, the plain citizen. I cannot sleep.
I hold the torturing fire in my head.

I, an American, call the dead Negro's name,
And in the hot dark of the city night
I walk the streets alone and sweat with shame.
Too late to rise, to raise the dead too late.

This is the harvest. The seeds sown long ago—
The careless word, sly thought, excusing glance.
I reap now everything I let pass, let go.
This is the harvest of my own indifference.

I, the plain citizen, have grown disorder
In my own world. It is not what I meant.
But dreams and images are potent and can murder.
I stand accused of them. I am not innocent.

Can I now plant imagination, honesty,
And love, where violence and terror were unbound—
The images of hope, the dream's responsibility?

Those who died here were murdered in my mind.

THE BIRTHDAY

What shall we give The Child this day,
On this shining day
In a starving world,
What gifts, what toys, for this, Love's dearest birthday?

For gold, give the heart's hunger,
The heart's want give for myrrh,
For hunger and want are stronger
And purer and deeper than anything
We have, than any joy we sing.

These and one more, the third,
These and one saving grace,
The balsam-scented word,
Green in the desolate place;
Give to His Innocence
Our hope for frankincense.

Now lay down thirst and hunger
There in the lonely manger,
And in the desolate place
Lay the green saving grace,
The bough without a thorn,
For God in man is born;
Out of all grief and pain,
Love, be renewed again!

FROM *THE LEAVES OF THE TREE* (1948–1950)
·· (ᵛᵢᵧ)

MYTH

The temple stood, holy and perfect,
Each pillar bearing its limit of strain serenely,
Balance and order shining in the dark.

And then a rush of swans' wings in the air,
A shower of stars. Thunder. All cracked apart.
Disorder of marble. Pockets of violet shadow.
Strange black gashes filled with the thrust of flowers.
The single arch which had enclosed the heart
Split open to the huge arches of the dark.

There was a rush of swans' wings through the air.

And those who had built the temple with such care
Came to a splendor of ruins,
Saw the perspectives altered
And all the pillars thrown to the ground,
And silent in their astonishment,
Learned what the gods can do.

KOT'S HOUSE

If the house is clean and pure,
Fiercely incorruptible,
God is ever at the door,
The Father and the Prodigal.

Should He never be aware
Of the order of each plate,
Still they will be shining there
And the floor immaculate.

Though at times the things revolt,
Fickle water or damp wall,
The chipped cup or stiffened bolt
(Love, where is your Prodigal?)

Still the house waits and is glad;
Every tea cup is a welcome,
Every cup aspires to God
Even if He never come.

And whether He exists at all,
The Father and the Prodigal,
He is expected by these things
And each plate Hosannah sings!

EVENING MUSIC

We enter this evening as we enter a quartet
Listening again for its particular note
The interval where all seems possible,
Order within time when action is suspended
And we are pure in heart, perfect in will.
We enter the evening whole and well-defended
But at the quick of self, intense detachment
That is a point of burning far from passion—
And this, we know, is what we always meant
And even love must learn it in some fashion,
To move like formal music through the heart,
To be achieved like some high difficult art.
We enter the evening as we enter a quartet
Listening again for its particular note
Which is your note, perhaps, your special gift,
A detached joy that flowers and makes bloom
The longest silence in the silent room—
And there would be no music if you left.

ISLANDS AND WELLS

In the private hour of night,
There are islands of light:
There is one, there is one
Ill in a great bed alone
Who without moving, moves
Like a delicate wind of caring
Over the earth, showering her loves
As a tree the leaves it has shed,
As a ship, world-faring,
Though anchored fast in her island-bed.

In the dry hour of the heart,
There are still wells in the desert:
There is one, there is one
To whom I once came down
From terrible Los Alamos of the bomb.
She opened wide the door.
She made me loving welcome,
And as we watched the setting sun, she spoke
Of suffering Europe, Asia. The world was near.
O human eyes! O deep imploring look!

In the dark night of the sense
When God is only felt as absence,
Prevenient grace is there
To tell us to endure
Since islands of pure light,
Since desert wells exist.
However dark our private night,
However far from Him, and how unsure,
There still is human love, moments of trust
That make us suddenly rich, however poor.

POETS AND THE RAIN

I will lie here alone and live your griefs.
Outside it rains and here the empty walls
And my own shoes empty beside the bed—
Strange tides pour through the river in my head.
I will lie here and answer outside calls:
I listen to the books and the beliefs.

I will receive you, passive and devout,
But soon must stand up in my shoes and shout.

Here the old man, hawk-cries and hawk-crest,
Looks out and taunts the world, sick of mankind,
Watching us tread like monkeys in the dance,
Riddled with doubt, hysteria and ignorance—
Old man, I hear your bird-scream on the wind.
I hear your voice shriller than all the rest.

Soon I must stand up in my shoes and dream
A hunting song to make the old hawk scream.

Here is the woman, frustrate and most pure,
Who builds a nest of blessings and there sits
Singing the lighted tree and the dark stone
(Many times to this woman I have come),
Who bids us meditate and use our wits
And we shall, with the help of love, endure—

Soon I must stand up in my shoes and weave
A simple song the birds would all believe.

Here the great girl, the violent and strong,
Who walks accompanied by dreams and visions,
Speaks with the blurred voice of a giant sleeping
And wakes to hear the foreign children weeping
And sees the crystal crack, the fierce divisions,
Asking deep questions in her difficult song.

Many times have I started up to answer them
And, standing, lost myself within her dream.

But winding through the labyrinth of mind
My song comes through and soon must speak aloud
I hear it in my ears, the roar of seas,
A swarming as of thousands of uprushing bees,
A sudden sweep of raindrops from the cloud,
I stand, rapt with delight, though deaf and blind,

And speak my poem now, leaves of a tree
Whose roots are hidden deep in mystery.

SUMMER MUSIC

Summer is all a green air—
From the brilliant lawn, sopranos
Through murmuring hedges
Accompanied by some poplars;
In fields of wheat, surprises;
Through faraway pastures, flows
To the horizon's blues
In slow decrescendos.

Summer is all a green sound—
Rippling in the foreground
To that soft applause,
The foam of Queen Anne's lace.
Green, green in the ear
Is all we care to hear—
Until a field suddenly flashes
The singing with so sharp
A yellow that it crashes
Loud cymbals in the ear.
Minor has turned to major
As summer, lulling and so mild,
Goes golden-buttercup-wild.

AS DOES NEW HAMPSHIRE

Could poetry or love by the same lucky chance
Make summer air vibrate with such a brilliance?
A landscape which says little—
Grave green hills diminishing to blue
Against the foreground of a long blond meadow,
While from the near pine elegantly falls
The nuthatch's neat syllable—
A landscape which says little,
But says this simple phrase so well
That it takes on forever the dimension
(Space, sound, silence, light and shade)
Of which a summer's happiness is made.
Only most daring love would care to mention
So much, so simply, and so charge each word
As does New Hampshire, "mountain," "meadow," "bird."*

---

*The quotation marks in the last line appear in the first published version of the poem in the volume entitled *As Does New Hampshire*.

TAKE ANGUISH FOR COMPANION

If the one certainty is suffering,
And if the only absolute is doubt,
From these alone belief must be wrung
Or else the bitter poverty found out:
Take anguish for companion and set out.

It leads us back to man himself, to sit
Down by his side whom we have killed and starved;—
Brother and sister, criminal and half-wit,
For each of us there is a place reserved,
To sit beside the one we have not served.

Wake as he dreams, dream as he wakes, to see
Man always at our side, starving and weeping,
Curved like a mother over his misery,
Huge and abandoned like a giant sleeping,
And we ourselves this creature we are keeping.

But if we dare to keep anguish companion,
We feel spring in our throats a living song,
See man leap from the rocks toward the sun,
Refuse to be imprisoned for too long,
His anger storming at the walls of wrong.

He is suddenly willing joy instead of power;
Shaken to the marrow by joy as by a flame,
Bending with mad delight toward a flower,
Secret and tender, violent, he came
Up from the darkness toward his haunting name.

He is the one who always sings and cries,
Believes, in spite of every proof, he will
Out of the darkness see with clearer eyes,
Conquer himself and learn to be an angel,
Who finds his only peace within the struggle.

For to be desperate is to discover strength.
We die of comfort and by conflict live
Who grow in this knowledge till at length
We find it good, find it belief enough
To be anguish alive, creating love.

INNUMERABLE FRIEND

Ainsi du temple où seul l'ami entre, mais innombrable.

St. Exupéry

Let us forget these principalities,
Nations, governments, these mythical powers,
These real walls, these beleaguered cities;
We are theirs perhaps, but they are not ours
We move, and must move always, one by one
Across the perilous frontiers alone,
And what we build be builded severally.
But who are "we" and is there still a "we"
Not lost under the weight of history?
The poet, scientist and teacher know
How fast the seeds of hate and fear can grow,
What passions can take over peaceful nations,
What anguish lurk in the safe reservations.
Can we not start at the small roots again,
Build this "we" slowly, gently, one by one,
From each small center toward communion?
Reach over the frontier, stranger to stranger,
To find the only sure relief from danger?
Take the immense dangerous leap to understand,
Build an invisible bridge from mind to mind?
Swung out from letters or the briefest meeting
(Lives have been changed by a simple greeting)
Build an invisible bridge toward one person.
So the slow delicate process is begun,
The root of all relationship, and then
Learn that this stranger has become all men,
Flows through the open heart as a great host
Of all the human, solitary, lost.

His longing streams through the conventions
Of diplomats and their meager intentions,
Hunting for home like a great hungry wind.
He is the one, this our innumerable friend!

Let us forget these principalities, these powers:
We are theirs perhaps, but they are not ours.
Turn toward each other quietly and know
There are still bridges nations cannot overthrow.
And if we fight—if we must at the end—
These are the bridges we fight to defend.

THE LAND OF SILENCE

1

Time beats like a heart; we do not hear it
But we are nourished as by sleep after pain.
Death is so close to life that we can bear it.
The smallest veins drink time and breathe again.

2

Now I am here in the land of silence,
Of the near dove and the distant hills,
I know that the surface is the essence,
No stripping down to what is already bare,
No probing what is absolutely here.
This is the land of bones and violent dreaming
Where Heaven is woven in and out of Hell
And each not essence but actual and near.

More than for love we search for faith
Who in this high air must gasp for breath.

LETTER TO AN INDIAN FRIEND

Was it a long journey for you to begin
To grow peaceful green things,
To harvest well, to watch the sun
Go down, to find the ancient springs?
What human pain, what wild desire
Did you burn in the fire,
Long ago, Tilano?

What is the first step, Tilano,
Toward the wisdom of your feet,
Treading the dust or the snow
So quiet, so tender, so fleet?
I have come from far
To the warm sun and the shelter,
A long journey to reach here,
And now it is clear
That I do not know
The first step.

What is the first act, Tilano,
Toward the wisdom of your hands?
They plant the corn;
They bring in the lamp in the evening,
Wood for the fire, and each thing done
With rigorous love, with devotion.
It was a long journey to you and the sun,
And now it seems I clasp in your hand
A land of work and silence, a whole land.

What is the first prayer, Tilano?
To go into the forest
And be content to sit
For many days alone,
Not asking God to come,
Since He is present in the sun,
Simple and quiet in the tree and stone.
How many times have you watched the sun rise
That when I look into your eyes,
So old, so old and gay, I see there
That I have never learned the first prayer?

OF PRAYER

Straining the dark
For some answer,
Calling the strange dancer
With our formal prayers,
Hope for a private sign,
A secret world of grace,
We never meet your face,
Prince of the Imagination:
Not to our prayers have you been merciful.
Always the human faces
Open their eyes behind our lids
And all our questions become human questions,
So when we seek we do not find you
And you offer no suggestions.

But in that hour least expected
When we are most ourselves and not deflected
Even by remembrance of your name,
We stream down the paths of grace—
Hour of the poem or that hour
When two people war to the bone
And meet each other's skeleton.

Here desire is a tremendous flower;
Petals have steel in their growing,
Balance in power as the pillar
That supports arched leaves of stone.

It is a mistake, perhaps, to believe
That religion concerns you at all;
That is our own invention,
Longing for formal acceptance
To a formal invitation.
But yours to be the anarchist,
The thrust of growth,
And to be present only in the
Prayer that is creation,
In the life that is lived,
Love planted deeper than emotion,
Pure Idea that cannot break apart,
Creator of children or the work of art.

BECAUSE WHAT I WANT MOST IS PERMANENCE

Because what I want most is permanence,
The long unwinding and continuous flow
Of subterranean rivers out of sense,
That nourish arid landscapes with their blue—
Poetry, prayer, or call it what you choose
That frees the complicated act of will
And makes the whole world both intense and still—
I set my mind to artful work and craft,
I set my heart on friendship, hard and fast
Against the wild inflaming wink of chance
And all sensations opened in a glance.
Oh blue Atlantis where the sailors dream
Their girls under the waves and in the foam—
I move another course. I'll not look down.

Because what I most want is permanence,
What I do best is bury fire now,
To bank the blaze within, and out of sense,
Where hidden fires and rivers burn and flow,
Create a world that is still and intense,
I come to you with only the straight gaze.
These are not hours of fire but years of praise,
The glass full to the brim, completely full,
But held in balance so no drop can spill.

SONG

This is the love I bring,
Absolute and nothing:
A tree but with no root,
A cloud heavy with fruit,
A wide stone stair
That leads nowhere
But to empty sky,
Ambiguous majesty.

This is the love I bear:
It is light as air,
Yet weighs like the earth;
It is water flowing,
Yet adamant as fire.
It is coming from going.
It is dying and growing.

A love so rare and hard
It cuts a diamond word
Upon the windowpane,
"Never, never again,
Never upon my breast,"
Having no time to bring,
Having no place to rest,
Absolute and nothing.

PROTHALAMION

How pure the hearts of lovers as they walk
Through the rich quiet fields
Where the stiff wheat grows heavy on the stalk,
And over barley and its paler golds
The air is bright—

Would touch it all, embrace, learn it by hand,
Plunging their faces into the thick grain,
To stroke as well as see the cow's soft flank,
To feel the beech trunk harsh under the palm,
And oh, to drink the light!

They do not even walk yet hand in hand,
But every sense is pricked alive so sharp
That life breathes through them from the burning land,
And they could use the wind itself for harp,
And pluck the vibrant green.

At first the whole world opens into sense:
They learn their love by looking at the wheat,
And there let fall all that was shy and tense
To walk the season slowly on propitious feet
And be all they have seen.

While all around them earth moves toward an end,
The gold turning to bronze, the barley tasseled,
Where the great sheaves will be stored up and bend
Their heads together in that rich wedding bed
All are about to enter.

The hearts of lovers as they walk, how pure;
How cool the wind upon the open palm
As they move on toward harvest, and so sure
Even this ripening has a marvelous calm
And a still center.

WITHOUT THE VIOLENCE

Without the violence, the major shift,
The shudder of the earth's foundations torn,
Without the great upheaval which could lift
That fiery core, it would not have been born,
And yet when chaos cooled, this land was here,
Absolute and austere—
Then, not before,
It snowed.
Later, by centuries and centuries,
The saving water flowed,
The grass arrived, dark little trees.
After a terrible and rending war,
This land took on its fearful peace,
After, and not before.

LETTER FROM CHICAGO

For Virginia Woolf

Four years ago I met your death here,
Heard it where I had never been before
In a city of departures, streets of wind,
Soft plumes of smoke dissolving—
City of departures beside an aloof lake.
Here where you never were, they said,
"Virginia Woolf is dead."

The city died. I died in the city,
Witness of unreal tears, my own,
For experience involves time
And time was gone,
The world arrested at the instant of death.
I wept wildly like a child
Who cannot give his present after all:
I met your death and did not recognize you.

Now you are dead four years
And there are no more private tears.
The city of departure is the city of arrival,
City of triumphant wind lifting people,
City of spring: yesterday I found you.
Wherever I looked was love.
Wherever I went I had presents in my hands.
Wherever I went I recognized you.

You are not, never to be again,
Never, never to be dead,
Never to be dead again in this city,
Never to be mourned again,
But to come back yearly,
Hourly, with the spring, with the wind,
Fresh as agony or resurrection;
A plume of smoke dissolving,
Remaking itself, never still,
Never static, never lost:
The place where time flows again.

I speak to you and meet my own life.
Is it to be poised as the lake beside the city,
Aloof, but given still to air and wind,
Detached from time, but given to the moment—
Is it to be a celebration always?

I send you love forward into the past.

NOW I BECOME MYSELF

Now I become myself. It's taken
Time, many years and places;
I have been dissolved and shaken,
Worn other people's faces,
Run madly, as if Time were there,
Terribly old, crying a warning,
"Hurry, you will be dead before—"
(What? Before you reach the morning?
Or the end of the poem is clear?
Or love safe in the walled city?)
Now to stand still, to be here,
Feel my own weight and density!
The black shadow on the paper
Is my hand; the shadow of a word
As thought shapes the shaper
Falls heavy on the page, is heard.
All fuses now, falls into place
From wish to action, word to silence,
My work, my love, my time, my face
Gathered into one intense
Gesture of growing like a plant.
As slowly as the ripening fruit
Fertile, detached, and always spent,
Falls but does not exhaust the root,
So all the poem is, can give,
Grows in me to become the song,
Made so and rooted so by love.
Now there is time and Time is young.
O, in this single hour I live
All of myself and do not move.
I, the pursued, who madly ran,
Stand still, stand still, and stop the sun!

A CELEBRATION FOR GEORGE SARTON

I never saw my father old;
I never saw my father cold.
His stride, staccato, vital,
His talk struck from pure metal
Simple as gold, and all his learning
Only to light a passion's burning.
So, beaming like a lesser god,
He bounced upon the earth he trod,
And people marveled on the street
At this stout man's impetuous feet.

Loved donkeys, children, awkward ducks,
Loved to retell old simple jokes;
Lived in a world of innocence
Where loneliness could be intense;
Wrote letters until very late,
Found comfort in an orange cat—
Rufus and George exchanged no word,
But while George worked his Rufus purred
And neighbors looked up at his light,
Warmed by the scholar working late.

I never saw my father passive;
He was electrically massive.
He never hurried, so he said,
And yet a fire burned in his head;
He worked as poets work, for love,
And gathered in a world alive,
While black and white above his door
Spoke Mystery, the avatar—
An Arabic inscription flowed
Like singing: "In the name of God."

And when he died, he died so swift
His death was like a final gift.
He went out when the tide was full,
Still undiminished, bountiful;
The scholar and the gentle soul,
The passion and the life were whole.
And now death's wake is only praise,
As when a neighbor writes and says:
"I did not know your father, but
His light was there. I miss the light."

THE FURIES

One is large and lazy;
One is old and crazy;
One is young and witty;
One is a great beauty,
But all feed you the wind,
And each of them is blind.

How then to recognize
The hard unseeing eyes,
Or woman tell from ghost?
Human each is, almost—
That wild and glittering light—
Almost, and yet not quite.

Never look straight at one,
For then your self is gone.
The empty eyes give back
Your own most bitter lack,
And what they have to tell
Is your most secret Hell:

The old, the sad pursuit
Of the corrupting fruit,
The slightly tainted dish
Of the subconscious wish,
Fame, love, or merely pride
Exacerbate, provide.

Wrap you in glamour cold,
Warm you with fairy gold,
Till you grow fond and lazy,
Witty, perverse, and crazy,
And drink their health in wind,
And call the Furies kind.

THE ACTION OF THE BEAUTIFUL

I move through my world like a stranger
Where multiple images collide and fall,
Fragments of lakes, eyes—or a mirror.
How to include, make peace with them all?

Only your face (is this too illusion?)
So poised between silence and speech
Suggests that at the center of confusion
An inward music is just within reach.

Can so much be spoken by an eyelid,
Or the bent forehead so much light distill?
Here all is secret and yet nothing hid,
That tenderness, those deep reserves of will.

There is no future, past, only pure presence.
The moment of a glance is brimmed so full
It fuses consciousness to a new balance—
This is the action of the beautiful.

Lakes, mirrors, every broken radiance
Shine whole again in your reflective face,
And I, the stranger, centered in your presence,
Come home and walk into the heart of peace.

LAMENT FOR TOBY, A FRENCH POODLE

The great Toby is dead,
Courteous and discreet,
He of the noble head,
Remote and tragic air,
He of the trim black feet—
He's gone. He is nowhere.

Yet famous in New Hampshire
As one who fought and killed—
Dog-bane and dog-despair—
That prey that all resign,
The terrible and quilled,
Heraldic porcupine.

He will become a legend,
Black coat and royal nature,
So wounded he was blind,
As on a painted shield
Some lost heroic creature
Who fought and would not yield.

If we were brave as he,
Who'd ask to be wise?
We shall remember Toby:
When human courage fails,
Be dogged in just cause
As he before the quills.

THE OLIVE GROVE

Here in the olive grove,
Under the cobalt dome,
The ancient spirits move
And light comes home,

And nests in silvery leaves.
It makes each branch a cloud,
And comes and goes, and weaves
Aerial song aloud.

Here every branch is gifted
With spiritual fruit
And every leaf is lifted
To brightness from the root.

Where the terrestrial plane
Meets vision and desire,
The silver and the green
Are strung on a great lyre,

And leafy seraphim
The sun and shade among
Turn each grove to a hymn;
Whole hillsides are in song.

Silvery, shadowy now
The fruit over our head,
Who lie and hardly know
which is light, which is bread.

AT MUZOT

In this land, Rilke's country if you will,
Nothing is closed or intact.
The mountains open out an airy world and spill
Height as an ethos. We live in the vertical.
Angels, often invoked, become a fact.

And they have names, Cloud, Stone, Sun, Vine,
But the names are interchangeable.
All meld together in making the same flowing design;
We drink conjunction in the mingled wine.
The journey is infinite and it is immobile.

This is what he found after all the busy wanderings,
This childhood dream of a lonely tower
Set in a mountain-meadow world where the air sings
And the names are interchangeable of cloud and flower.
This is what he found: the grass full of springs.

A sacramental earth; reality both stalked
and made the vision clear.
And here the living waters sprang up where he walked.
It was the clouds and not himself who talked.
Was he the ghost who felt himself so near?

At Muzot he stood at last at the intersection
Of God and self (nothing is closed).
The voice he heard came from dissolving stone.
Even the mountains ascended and were gone,
And he himself stood naked and disclosed.

AFTER FOUR YEARS

How to lay down her death,
Bring her back living
Into the open heart, the overgrieving,
Bury once and for all the starving breath
And lay down her death?

Not on love's breast
Lay down this heavy prize
And close at last the open, the gray eyes
Of her who in my woe can find no rest—
Not on love's breast.

And not in solitude
Lay the long burden down,
For she is there awake when I'm alone,
Who cannot sleep, yet sorely, sorely would—
Oh, not in solitude!

Now everywhere I'm blind;
On the far journeys
Toward the magical old trees and cities
It's the same rooted sorrow that I find,
And everywhere I'm blind.

Is there a human prayer
That might unknot prolonged
Unnatural grief, grief that has surely wronged
Her very radiant presence in the air,
Is there a human prayer?

It is poor love, I know,
Mother and marvelous friend,
Over that final poverty to bend
And not remember all the rich life too:
It is poor love, I know.

"Rich love, come in,
Come home, my treasure.
All that you were and that no word can measure
Melt itself through me like a healing balm,
Rich love, come home."

And here lay down at last
Her long hard death,
And let her be in joy, be ash, not breath.
And let her gently go into the past,
Dear world, to rest at last.

SOMERSAULT

Not to rebel against what pulls us down,
The private burdens each of us could name
That weigh heavily in the blood and bone
So that we stumble, clumsy half the time
Unable to love well or love at all!
Who knows the full weight that another bears,
What obscure densities sustains alone,
To burst fearfully through what self-locked doors?
So heavy is our walk with what we feel,
And cannot tell, and cannot ever tell.

Oh, to have the lightness, the savoir faire
Of a tightrope walker, his quicksilver tread
As he runs softly over the taut steel thread;
Sharp as a knife blade cutting walls of air,
He's pitted against weights we cannot see,
All tension balanced, though we see him only
A rapture of grace and skill, focused and lonely.

Is it a question of discipline or grace?
The steel trap of the will or some slight shift
Within an opened consciousness?
The tightrope walker juggles weights, to lift
Himself up on the stress, and, airy master
Of his own loss, he springs from heaviness.
But we, stumbling our way, how learn such poise,
The perfect balance of all griefs and joys?
Burdened by love, how learn the light release
That, out of stress, can somersault to peace?

THE FROG, THAT NAKED CREATURE

The frog, that naked creature,
Arouses immediate pity;
He does not burst except in fables, but
He looks as if he might,
So violent his anxiety,
So exposed his nature.
His brilliant eyes look wildly out
As if the pulse were leaping from his throat.

We feel his being more, now
We have grown so vulnerable,
Have become so wholly exposed with the years
To primeval powers;
These storms are often terrible,
Followed by sudden snow.
It is alarming to feel the soul
Leap to the surface and find no sheltering wall.

Is this growth, we wonder?
But it makes us tremble,
Because we are not able to conceal
The rage, the fear we feel,
Nor able to dissemble
Those claps of thunder
When we are seized and shaken beyond our will
By the secret demon or the secret angel.

To show the very pulse
Of thought alive,
Transparent as the frog whose every mood
Glows through his cold red blood—
For whom we grieve
Because he has no walls—
Giving up pride, to endure shame and pity,
Is this a valid choice, choice of maturity?

THE PHOENIX

It is time the big bird with the angry neck,
We have cajoled and cursed,
Went home to die, or whatever he must do
When his heart would burst.

For his wild desire pulses over our heads
And opens the secret night,
Passage of wings that madden without release,
When the phoenix is in flight.

Let him go, stretching his long legs, clumsy
On this harsh ground. Let him flee
To the soft black marshes he remembers
Or the gentle mother tree.

Let him go. He has shaken the house at night;
His wings have clouded our dream,
And there is no peace for his lost cry at daybreak
And at night his terrible scream.

He flames through the morning yet he never sings;
He only makes that strange lost cry.
He is angry all the time. Let him find his tree
And make his nest and die.

Though he is God's own angel in disguise,
We cannot bear another angry word,
Nor look into those cold and jeweled eyes,
O pitiless strange bird!

Will he come back, will he come back all shining
From his dark death, to bring
The true message, the gentle, that all his torment
Was desperate to sing?

Or—what if it were not he at all, not he
Who must consume himself to be reborn,
But we ourselves, who drove an angel from us
Because our hearts were torn?

IN TIME LIKE AIR

Consider the mysterious salt:
In water it must disappear.
It has no self. It knows no fault.
Not even sight may apprehend it.
No one may gather it or spend it.
It is dissolved and everywhere.

But, out of water into air,
It must resolve into a presence,
Precise and tangible and here.
Faultlessly pure, faultlessly white,
It crystallizes in our sight
And has defined itself to essence.

What element dissolves the soul
So it may be both found and lost,
In what suspended as a whole?
What is the element so blest
That there identity can rest
As salt in the clear water cast?

Love, in its early transformation,
And only love, may so design it
That the self flows in pure sensation,
Is all dissolved, and found at last
Without a future or a past,
And a whole life suspended in it.

The faultless crystal of detachment
Comes after, cannot be created
Without the first intense attachment.
Even the saints achieve this slowly;
For us, more human and less holy,
In time like air is essence stated.

NATIVITY

Piero della Francesca

O cruel cloudless space,
And pale bare ground where the poor infant lies!
Why do we feel restored
As in a sacramental place?
Here Mystery is artifice
And here a vision of such peace is stored,
Healing flows from it through our eyes.

Comfort and joy are near,
Not as we know them in the usual ways,
Personal and expected,
But utterly distilled and spare
Like a cool breath upon the air.
Emotion, it would seem, has been rejected
For a clear geometric praise.

Even the angels' stance
Is architectural in form:
They tell no story.
We see on each grave countenance,
Withheld as in a formal dance,
The awful joy, the serene glory:
It is the inscape keeps us warm.

Poised as a monument,
Thought rests, and in these balanced spaces
Images meditate;
Whatever Piero meant,
The strange impersonal does not relent:
Here is love, naked, lying in great state
On the bare ground, as in all human faces.

BINDING THE DRAGON

"The dragon's Proteus. He must be fought,
And fighting dragons is my holy joy,"
The poet says, although he may look caught
And blood is spurting from one eye.

"Sublimate," says the cautious analyst.
The poet answers, "Let him do it first.
Look, I have got this dragon in my fist.
I'll hold him here until he dies of thirst."

But suddenly the dragon flows away.
The dragon is a river: you can't do it,
Hold up a river in your hands all day.
"And what is sublimation?" asks the poet.

"Is it to translate water into fire?
Is it to follow birds along the air?
Is it to be the master of desire,
Or ride a cycle with no handlebar?

Gentle a dragon to lie quiet there,
Beautiful in his power but asleep,
Image of dragon resting on the air?"
The poet asked, and then began to weep.

He did not want the dragon to be caught.
He wanted it alive and in his fist.
For who would kill the god with whom he fought?
And so he wept and cursed the analyst.

MY FATHER'S DEATH

After the laboring birth, the clean stripped hull
Glides down the ways and is gently set free,
The landlocked, launched; the cramped made bountiful—
Oh, grave great moment when ships take the sea!
Alone now in my life, no longer child,
This hour and its flood of mystery,
Where death and love are wholly reconciled,
Launches the ship of all my history.
Accomplished now is the last struggling birth,
I have slipped out from the embracing shore
Nor look for comfort to maternal earth.
I shall not be a daughter any more,
But through this final parting, all stripped down,
Launched on the tide of love, go out full grown.

FROM *CLOUD, STONE, SUN, VINE* (1958–1961)

.... (ViVi)

[FROM] A DIVORCE OF LOVERS

5

What price serenity these cruel days?
Your silence and ungiving, my small cries,
Followed by hours when I can lift some praise
and make the wound sing as in Paradise.
What price the poise you ask for, the unharried?
Four rooted years torn up without a qualm,
A past not dead perhaps, but quickly buried:
On one side anguish, on the other calm,
Both terrible because deprived of hope
Like living eyes still open in a grave.
And we shall lunch, you say, that is our scope.
Between what we have lost and still might save
Lies, very quiet, what was once too human,
And lovely, and beloved, a living woman.

. . .

10

So drive back hating Love and loving Hate
To where, until we met, they had been thrown
Since infancy: forever lock that gate
And let them lacerate themselves alone,
Wild animals we never learned to tame,
But faced in growing anguish through the mist,
Elusive beasts we did not dare to name,
And whom we could not dominate or trust.
Now bury childish hunger, childish greed
In play-pen, zoo-pen, whatever pen will hold
The wild frustration and the starving need:
This is your method, so I have been told.
And mine? Stand fast, and face the animal
With the full force and pardon of the soul.

． ． ．

16

The cat sleeps on my desk in the pale sun;
Long bands of light lie warm across the floor.
I have come back into my world of no one,
This house where the long silences restore
The essence and to time its real dimension;
All I have lost or squandered I examine
Free of the wars and the long searing tension;
And I am nourished here after the famine.
Though this was time that we had planned to spend
Together, circled on the calendars,
To walk my woods for one weekend,
Last night I looked alone at the bright stars.
Nor time, nor absence breaks this world in two.
You hold me in your heart, as I hold you.

． ． ．

20

Now silence, silence, silence, and within it
The leap of spirit upward and beyond;
We take the heart's world in our hands and spin it
Out to the distant stars above this ground,
And let it go at last, and let it go
With those illusions that we held too long;
Against our will now we are forced to grow
And push out from all safety into song.
This is one half of it, the saving grace;
The other, the dark struggle, as, like worms,
We riddle darkness, tunnel some small space
Where we can lie with patience through the storms.
And of these two, who knows where wisdom lies,
Deep in the earth, or wandering the skies?

DER ABSCHIED

Now frost has broken summer like a glass,
This house and I resume our conversations;
The floors whisper a message as I pass,
I wander up and down these empty rooms
That have become my intimate relations,
Brimmed with your presence where your absence blooms—
And did you come at last, come home, to tell
How all fulfillment tastes of a farewell?

Here is the room where you lay down full length
That whole first day, to read, and hardly stirred,
As if arrival had taken all your strength;
Here is the table where you bent to write
The morning through, and silence spoke its word;
And here beside the fire we talked, as night
Came slowly from the wood across the meadow
To frame half of our brilliant world in shadow.

The rich fulfillment came; we held it all;
Four years of struggle brought us to this season,
Then in one week our summer turned to fall;
The air chilled and we sensed the chill in us,
The passionate journey ending in sweet reason.
The autumn light was there, frost on the grass.
And did you come at last, come home, to tell
How all fulfillment tastes of a farewell?

Departure is the constant at this stage;
And all we know is that we cannot stop,
However much the childish heart may rage.
We are still outward-bound to obligations
And, radiant centers, life must drink us up,
Devour our strength in multiple relations.
Yet I still question in these empty rooms
Brimmed with your presence where your absence
blooms,

What stays that can outlast these deprivations?
Now, peopled by the dead, and ourselves dying,
The house and I resume old conversations:
What stays? Perhaps some autumn tenderness,
A different strength that forbids youthful sighing.
Though frost has broken summer like a glass,
Know, as we hear the thudding apples fall,
Not ripeness but the suffering change is all.

THE BEAUTIFUL PAUSES

Angels, beautiful pauses in the whirlwind,
Be with us through the seasons of unease;
Within the clamorous traffic of the mind,
Through all these clouded and tumultuous days,
Remind us of your great unclouded ways.
It is the wink of time, crude repetition,
That whirls us round and blurs our anxious vision,
But centered in its beam, your own *nunc stans*
Still pivots and sets free the sacred dance.

And suddenly we are there: the light turns red,
The cars are stopped in Heaven, motors idle,
While all around green amplitude is spread—
Those grassy slopes of dream—and whirling will
Rests on a deeper pulse, and we are still.
Only a golf course, but the sudden change
From light to light opens a further range;
Surprised by angels, we are free for once
To move and rest within the sacred dance.

Or suddenly we are there: a hotel room,
The rumor of a city-hive below,
And the world falls away before this bloom,
This pause, high up, affecting us like snow.
Time's tick is gone; softly we come and go,
Barefoot on carpets, all joyfully suspended,
And there, before the open morning's ended,
The beautiful pause, the sudden lucky chance
Opens the way into the sacred dance.

I write this in October on a windless morning.
The leaves float down on air as clear as flame,
Their course a spiral, turning and returning;
They dance the slow pavane that gives its name
To a whole season, never quite the same.
Angels, who can surprise us with a lucky chance,
Be with us in this year; give us to dance
Time's tick away, and in our whirling flight
Poetry center the long fall through light.

BIRTHDAY ON THE ACROPOLIS

1

In the fifth grade
We became Greeks,
Made our own chitons,
Drank homemade mead,
And carved a small Parthenon
Out of Ivory soap.
It never seemed real,
The substance too soft,
An awkward miniature.
But over these labors
Athene towered,
Life-size.
She was real enough.

She was mine, this one,
From the beginning,
Not she of the olive,
But she of the owl-eyes,
A spear in her hand.

Any day now the air would open,
Any day . . .

2

Forty years later
I was hurled to the bright rock,
Still merged with the dark,
Edgeless and melting,
The Indian ethos—
Stepped out from the plane

To stand in the Greek light
In the knife-clean air.

Too sudden, too brilliant.
Who can bear this shining?
The pitiless clarity?
Each bone felt the shock.
I was broken in two
By sheer definition:

Rock, light, air.

3

I came from the past,
From the ancient kingdoms
To this youth of my own world,
To this primary place.

I stood at the great gate
On my fiftieth birthday,
Had rounded the globe
Toward this Acropolis,
Had come round the world
Toward this one day:

O Pallas Athene,
You of the shining shield,
Give me to stand clear,
Solid as this, your rock,
Knowing no tremor.

Today, you, Pandrosos,
Who cherish the olive,
Bring from my battered trunk
The small silver leaves,
Fresh and unshielded.

Make the olives rich
In essential oil;
May the fruit fall lightly
As small drops of rain
On the parched fields.
Protect the small trees.

Today, you, Aglauros,
Pure prow of Athens,
Poise me in balance
So that all clarity
May meet all mystery
As on the spear's point.

4

When proportion triumphs,
When measure is conscious,
Who is to protect us from arrogance?

The presence of the gods. They are here:
Fate's ambiguities and jealous Athene.

No, it is not a place for youth,
This bastion where man's reason grew strong.
These pillars speak of mature power.

Imagined as white, they are rough gold,
The spaces between them open as justice
To frame mountains
And the distant, blue, world-opening sea.

5

On my fiftieth birthday I met the archaic smile.
It was the right year
To confront
The smile beyond suffering,
As intricate and suffused
As a wave's curve
Just before it breaks.

Evanescence held still;
Change stated in eternal terms.
Aloof. Absolute:
The criterion is before us.

On my fiftieth birthday
I suffered from the archaic smile.

AT DELPHI

The site echoes
Its own huge silences

Wherever one stands,
Whatever one sees—

Narrow terror of the pass
Or its amazing throat,
Pouring an avalanche of olives
Into the blue bay.

Crags so fierce
They nearly swallow
A city of broken pillars.
Or Athene's temple,
Exquisite circle,
Gentled on all sides
By silvery leaves.

Eagles floating
On high streamers of wind,
Or that raw cleft,
Deep in the rock,
Matrix
Where the oracle
Uttered her two-edged words.

Wherever one stands,
Every path leads to Fate itself:
"Speak! Speak!"

But there is no answer.

Choose the river of olives.
Choose the eagles.
Or choose to balance
All these forces,
The violent, the gentle;
Summon them like winds
Against a lifted finger.
Choose to be human.

Everyone stands here
And listens. Listens.
Everyone stands here alone.

I tell you the gods are still alive
And they are not consoling.

I have not spoken of this
For three years,
But my ears still boom.

A FUGUE OF WINGS

Each branching maple stands in a numb trance,
A skeleton fine-drawn on solid air,
No sound or motion . . . summer's rippling dance
Has been abstracted to this frozen stare
Of black, and blue, and white.

Until the wings—the wings alive!—excite
The marbled snows; and perpendiculars
Of tree and shadow thrown across the light
Are shivered by minute particulars.
The opening phrase is there.

A fugue of wings darts down through the still air,
A dancing passage of staccato notes,
Now up, now down, and glancing everywhere,
Glissandos of black caps and neat white throats.
Here come the chickadees!

Parabolas fly through the static trees;
They dart their pattern in like an assault
On all defined and frozen boundaries.
Their beat is off-beat. Chickadees exalt
Erratic line, rebound,

Hang upside down, play with the thread of sound,
But cede to those blue bandits, the big jays,
Who plummet down like daggers to the ground;
The rhythm changes with their boisterous ways;
They scream as they feed.

Now finches flock down to the scattered seed,
Disperse on the forsythia's light cage
In rosy clusters, sumptuous indeed—
With them, we come into a gentler passage.
They form a quiet cloud

Thick on the ground, and there in concert crowd.
A nuthatch follows, he of modest mien
And dangerous beak; the music grows too loud.
The fugue is cluttered up. What we have seen,
What we did hear is done.

Until woodpeckers take it up, and drum
The theme; finches fly up with jays;
A whirling passage spirals the fugue home.
Afterward silence, silence thronged with praise
Echoes and rounds the phrase.

AN OBSERVATION

True gardeners cannot bear a glove
Between the sure touch and the tender root,
Must let their hands grow knotted as they move
With a rough sensitivity about
Under the earth, between the rock and shoot,
Never to bruise or wound the hidden fruit.
And so I watched my mother's hands grow scarred,
She who could heal the wounded plant or friend
With the same vulnerable yet rigorous love;
I minded once to see her beauty gnarled,
But now her truth is given me to live,
As I learn for myself we must be hard
To move among the tender with an open hand,
And to stay sensitive up to the end
Pay with some toughness for a gentle world.

A VILLAGE TALE

Why did the woman want to kill one dog?
Perhaps he was too lively, made her nervous,
A vivid terrier, restless, always barking,
And so unlike the gentle German shepherd.
She did not know herself what demon seized her,
How in the livid afternoon she was possessed,
What strength she found to tie a heavy stone
Around his neck and drown him in the horse-trough,
Murder her dog. God knows what drove her to it,
What strength she found to dig a shallow grave
And bury him—her own dog!—in the garden.

And all this while the gentle shepherd watched,
Said nothing, anxious nose laid on his paws,
Tail wagging dismal questions, watched her go
Into the livid afternoon outside to tire
The demon in her blood with wine and gossip.
The gate clanged shut, and the good shepherd ran,
Ran like a hunter to the quarry, hackles raised,
Sniffed the loose earth on the haphazard grave,
Pressing his eager nose into the dust,
Sensed tremor there and (frantic now) dug fast,
Dug in, dug in, all shivering and whining,
Unearthed his buried friend, licked the dry nose
Until a saving sneeze raised up the dead.

Well, she had to come back sometime to face
Whatever lay there waiting, worse than horror:
Two wagging tails, four bright eyes shifting—
Moment of truth, and there was no escape.
She could face murder. Could she face redeeming?

Was she relieved? Could she perhaps pretend
It had not really happened after all?
All that the village sees is that the dog
Sits apart now, untouchable and sacred,
Lazarus among dogs, whose loving eyes
Follow her back and forth until she dies.
She gives him tidbits. She can always try
To make them both forget the murderous truth.

But he knows and she knows that they are bound
Together in guilt and mercy, world without end.

DEATH AND THE TURTLE

I watched the turtle dwindle day by day,
Get more remote, lie limp upon my hand;
When offered food he turned his head away;
The emerald shell grew soft. Quite near the end
Those withdrawn paws stretched out to grasp
His long head in a poignant dying gesture.
It was so strangely like a human clasp,
My heart cracked for the brother creature.

I buried him, wrapped in a lettuce leaf,
The vivid eye sunk inward, a dull stone.
So this was it, the universal grief;
Each bears his own end knit up in the bone.
Where are the dead? we ask, as we hurtle
Toward the dark, part of this strange creation,
One with each limpet, leaf, and smallest turtle—
Cry out for life, cry out in desperation!

Who will remember you when I have gone,
My darling ones, or who remember me?
Only in our wild hearts the dead live on.
Yet these frail engines bound to mystery
Break the harsh turn of all creation's wheel,
For we remember China, Greece, and Rome,
Our mothers and our fathers, and we steal
From death itself rich store, and bring it home.

DEATH OF A PSYCHIATRIST

For Volta Hall

1

Now the long lucid listening is done,
Where shame and anguish were subtly opposed:
His patients mourn this father as their own.

Each was accepted whole and wholly known,
Down to the deepest naked need exposed.
Now the long lucid listening is done.

For the raw babe, he was a healing zone.
The cry was heard; the rage was not refused.
Each has a father to mourn as his own.

When someone sees at last, the shame is gone;
When someone hears, anguish may be composed,
And the long lucid listening is done.

The ghostly child goes forth once more alone,
And scars remain, but the deep wound is closed.
Each has a father to mourn as his own.

A guiltless loss, this shines like a sun,
And love remains, but the deep wound is closed.
Each has a father to mourn as his own,
Now the long lucid listening is done.

2

It was not listening alone, but hearing,
For he remembered every crucial word
And gave one back oneself because he heard.

Who listens so, does more than listen well.
He goes down with his patient into Hell.

It was not listening alone, but healing.
We knew a total, yet detached response,
Harsh laugh, sane and ironical at once.

Who listens so, does more than merely pity,
Restores the soul to its lost dignity.

It was not listening alone, but sharing.
And I remember how he bowed his head
Before a poem. "Read it again," he said.

Then, in the richest silence he could give,
I saw the poem born, knew it would live.

It was not listening alone, but being.
We saw a face so deeply lined and taut
It wore the passion of dispassionate thought.

Because he cared, he heard; because he heard,
He lifted, shared, and healed without a word.

THE WALLED GARDEN AT CLONDALKIN

1

For a long time they merely left it there;
They were too full of pity and distress
To breathe again that choked and choking air.
The rusty gate closed on a wilderness.
The walled garden, an old dying princess
From a lost country, had grown very strange.

A snow of petals fell on the rich loam:
Gloire des Mousseux, Star of Holland, Night,
Ladies in waiting in a spacious room,
Those roses dressed in small clouds of light.
All, all, destroyed, invaded, overgrown,
The formal beauty gone, formal delight,
And none to reclaim now, to heal, save
Order and beauty buried here alive.

"Where are the roses gone?" they whispered, shaken,
On those rare sad occasions when they stood,
Remembering the safer land of childhood,
And saw this feverish ruin, overtaken
By squitch and groundsel and the woody nightshade.
"Where are the goldfish, where the pond?" And fled,
As children do, this world grown out of range.
"The times have changed. We cannot help the change."

2

Think of her, remember
The brilliant queen of phlox,
Of roses without number,
Disciplined in box—
Of delphinium, the duchess;
A hierarchy of herbs
Sweetened in order—
Rosemary, mignonette—
Each trim border.
She wore mock orange
In her green hair,
Marvelously strange;
The birds in the air,
The goldfish came
To her summer voice
And knew her by name.
Her peaches were choice.
Camellias, carnations
In warm glass prisons
Were subject nations.
Her winter princes
Were hothouse quinces.
Walled, glassed in vain
The royal domain:
Quick grows the grass
In flowery places,
And the wilderness,
And the crude green faces.

3

And there it was they found him, standing splendid
Among his thirty thousand leeks and lettuces,
The empty pots filled and the glass all mended;
He looked indulgently on the sweet peas,
Lord of the greenhouses, and so pure his joy
That as he picked a peach, he seemed a boy.

The garden was scarcely breathing when he came,
A gentle foreigner with mud on his shoes,
Not even a relative, poor, and of no fame,
A water-carrier, trundler of wheelbarrows.
Quiet and slow, his pockets full of seeds,
He cleared the wild disordered past of weeds.

"All gone, all sold, the princess dead, my dears!"
The peacock on the wall screamed and was still.
The watchers felt perplexed by shifting years.
They suffered all the past and future till
The tangled skein was smoothed out and resolved,
As if some hopeless muddle had been solved.

No new world ever could have moved them as
This dying one revived by gentleness.
Their thoughts were tender for the dying princess,
But not for her sake did the warm tears rise:
They gave this homage to patient human ways,
The hired man's common and heroic days.

A RECOGNITION

For Perley Cole

I wouldn't know how rare they come these days,
But I know Perley's rare. I know enough
To stop fooling around with words, and praise
This man who swings a scythe in subtle ways,
And brings green order, carved out of the rough.
I wouldn't know how rare, but I discover
They used to tell an awkward learning boy,
"Keep the heel down, son, careful of the swing!"
I guess at perils and peril makes me sing.
So let the world go, but hold fast to joy,
And praise the craftsman till Hell freezes over!

I watched him that first morning when the dew
Still slightly bent tall, toughened grasses,
Sat up in bed to watch him coming through
Holding the scythe so lightly and so true
In slow sweeps and in lovely passes,
The swing far out, far out—but not too far,
The pause to wipe and whet the shining blade.
I felt affinities: farmer and poet
Share a good deal, although they may not know it.
It looked as easy as when the world was made,
And God could pull a bird out or a star.

For there was Perley in his own sweet way
Pulling some order out of ragged land,
Cutting the tough, chaotic growth away,
So peace could saunter down a summer day,
For here comes Cole with genius in his hand!
I saw in him a likeness to that flame,
Brancusi, in his Paris studio,
Who pruned down, lifted from chaotic night
Those naked, shining images of flight—
The old man's gentle malice and bravado,
Boasting hard times: "It was my game!"

"C'était mon jeu!"—to wrest joy out of pain,
The endless skillful struggle to uncloud
The clouded vision, to reduce and prune,
And bring back from the furnace, fired again,
A world of magic, joy alone allowed.
Now Perley says, "God damn it!"—and much worse.
Hearing him, I get back some reverence.
Could you, they ask, call such a man your friend?
Yes (damn it!), and yes world without end!
Brancusi's game and his make the same sense,
And not unlike a prayer is Perley's curse.

So let the rest go, and heel down, my boy,
And praise the artist till Hell freezes over,
For he is rare, he with his scythe (no toy),
He with his perils, with his skill and joy,
Who comes to prune, to make clear, to uncover,
The old man, full of wisdom, in his prime.
There in the field, watching him as he passes,
I recognize that violent, gentle blood,
Impatient patience. I would, if I could,
Call him my kin, there scything down the grasses,
Call him my good luck in a dirty time.

FROM *A GRAIN OF MUSTARD SEED* (1967–1971)

·· (√|Ϋ)

THE INVOCATION TO KALI

> . . . *The Black Goddess Kali, the terrible one of many names, "difficult of approach," whose stomach is a void and so can never be filled, and whose womb is giving birth forever to all things.* . . .

Joseph Campbell

1

There are times when
I think only of killing
The voracious animal
Who is my perpetual shame,

The violent one
Whose raging demands
Break down peace and shelter
Like a peacock's scream.

There are times when
I think only of how to do away
With this brute power
That cannot be tamed.

I am the cage where poetry
Paces and roars. The beast
Is the god. How murder the god?
How live with the terrible god?

2

The Kingdom of Kali

Anguish is always there, lurking at night,
Wakes us like a scourge, the creeping sweat
As rage is remembered, self-inflicted blight.
What is it in us we have not mastered yet?

What Hell have we made of the subtle weaving
Of nerve with brain, that all centers tear?
We live in a dark complex of rage and grieving.
The machine grates, grates, whatever we are.

The kingdom of Kali is within us deep.
The built-in destroyer, the savage goddess,
Wakes in the dark and takes away our sleep.
She moves through the blood to poison gentleness.

She keeps us from being what we long to be;
Tenderness withers under her iron laws.
We may hold her like a lunatic, but it is she
Held down, who bloodies with her claws.

How then to set her free or come to terms
With the volcano itself, the fierce power
Erupting injuries, shrieking alarms?
Kali among her skulls must have her hour.

It is time for the invocation, to atone
For what we fear most and have not dared to face:
Kali, the destroyer, cannot be overthrown;
We must stay, open-eyed, in the terrible place.

Every creation is born out of the dark.
Every birth is bloody. Something gets torn.
Kali is there to do her sovereign work
Or else the living child will be stillborn.

She cannot be cast out (she is here for good)
Nor battled to the end. Who wins that war?
She cannot be forgotten, jailed, or killed.
Heaven must still be balanced against her.

Out of destruction she comes to wrest
The juice from the cactus, its harsh spine,
And until she, the destroyer, has been blest,
There will be no child, no flower, and no wine.

3

The Concentration Camps

Have we managed to fade them out like God?
Simply eclipse the unpurged images?
Eclipse the children with a mountain of shoes?
Let the bones fester like animal bones,
False teeth, bits of hair, spilled liquid eyes,
Disgusting, not to be looked at, like a blight?

Ages ago we closed our hearts to blight.
Who believes now? Who cries, "merciful God"?
We gassed God in the ovens, great piteous eyes,
Burned God in a trash heap of images,
Refused to make a compact with dead bones,
And threw away the children with their shoes—

Millions of sandals, sneakers, small worn shoes—
Thrust them aside as a disgusting blight.
Not ours, this death, to take into our bones,
Not ours a dying multilated God.
We freed our minds from gruesome images,
Pretended we had closed their open eyes

That never could be closed, dark puzzled eyes,
The ghosts of children who went without shoes
Naked toward the ovens' bestial images,

Strangling for breath, clawing the blight,
Piled up like pigs beyond the help of God. . . .
With food in our stomachs, flesh on our bones,

We turned away from the stench of bones,
Slept with the living, drank in sexy eyes,
Hurried for shelter from a murdered God.
New factories turned out millions of shoes.
We hardly noticed the faint smell of blight,
Stuffed with new cars, ice cream, rich images.

But no grass grew on the raw images.
Corruption mushroomed from decaying bones.
Joy disappeared. The creature of the blight
Rose in the cities, dark smothered eyes.
Our children danced with rage in their shoes,
Grew up to question who had murdered God,

While we evaded their too attentive eyes,
Walked the pavane of death in our new shoes,
Sweated with anguish and remembered God.

4

The Time of Burning

For a long time, we shall have only to listen,
Not argue or defend, but listen to each other.
Let curses fall without intercession,
Let those fires burn we have tried to smother.

What we have pushed aside and tried to bury
Lives with a staggering thrust we cannot parry.

We have to reckon with Kali for better or worse,
The angry tongue that lashes us with flame
As long-held hope turns bitter and men curse,
"Burn, baby, burn" in the goddess' name.

189

We are asked to bear it, to take in the whole,
The long indifferent beating down of soul.

It is the time of burning, hate exposed.
We shall have to live with only Kali near.
She comes in her fury, early or late, disposed
To tantrums we have earned and must endure.

We have to listen to the harsh undertow
To reach the place where Kali can bestow.

But she must have her dreadful empire first
Until the prisons of the mind are broken free
And every suffering center at its worst
Can be appealed to her dark mystery.

She comes to purge the altars in her way,
And at her altar we shall have to pray.

It is a place of skulls, a deathly place
Where we confront our violence and feel,
Before that broken and self-ravaged face,
The murderers we are, brought here to kneel.

5

It is time for the invocation:

Kali, be with us.
Violence, destruction, receive our homage.
Help us to bring darkness into the light,
To lift out the pain, the anger,
Where it can be seen for what it is—
The balance-wheel for our vulnerable, aching love.
Put the wild hunger where it belongs,
Within the act of creation,
Crude power that forges a balance
Between hate and love.

Help us to be the always hopeful
Gardeners of the spirit
Who know that without darkness
Nothing comes to birth
As without light
Nothing flowers.

Bear the roots in mind,
You, the dark one, Kali,
Awesome power.

"WE'LL TO THE WOODS NO MORE, THE LAURELS ARE CUT DOWN"

At Kent State

The war games are over,
The laurels all cut down.
We'll to the woods no more
With live ammunition
To murder our own children
Because they hated war.

The war games are over.
How many times in pain
We were given a choice—
"Sick of the violence"
(Oh passionate human voice!)—
But buried it again.

The war games are over.
Virile, each stood alone—
John, Robert, Martin Luther.
Still we invoke the gun,
Still make a choice for murder,
Bury the dead again.

The war games are over,
And all the laurel's gone.
Dead warrior, dead lover,
Was the war lost or won?
What say you, blasted head?
No answer from the dead.

GIRL WITH 'CELLO

There had been no such music here until
A girl came in from falling dark and snow
To bring into this house her glowing 'cello
As if some silent, magic animal.

She sat, head bent, her long hair all aspill
Over the breathing wood, and drew the bow.
There had been no such music here until
A girl came in from falling dark and snow.

And she drew out that sound so like a wail,
A rich dark suffering joy, as if to show
All that a wrist holds and that fingers know
When they caress a magic animal.
There had been no such music here until
A girl came in from falling dark and snow.

BEARS AND WATERFALLS

Kind kinderpark
For bear buffoons
And fluid graces—
Who dreamed this lark
Of spouts, lagoons,
And huge fur faces?

For bears designed
Small nooks, great crags,
And Gothic mountains?
For bears refined
Delightful snags,
Waterfalls, fountains?

Who had the wit to root
A forked tree where a sack
Of honey plumps on end,
A rich-bottomed fruit
To rouse a hearty whack
From passing friend?

Who ever did imagine
A waterspout as stool,
Or was black bear the wiser
Who sat down on this engine
To keep a vast rump cool.
Then, cooled, set free a geyser?

Who dreamed a great brown queen
Sleeked down in her rough silk
Flirting with her huge lord,
Breast-high in her tureen?—
"Splash me, delightful hulk!"
So happy and absurd.

Bear upside-down, white splendor,
All creamy, foaming fur,
And childhood's rug come true,
All nonchalance and candor,
Black pads your signature—
Who, above all, dreamed you?

When natural and formal
Are seen to mate so well,
Where bears and fountains play,
Who would return to normal?
Go back to human Hell?
Not I. I mean to stay,

To hold this happy chance
Forever in the mind,
To be where waters fall
And archetypes still dance,
As they were once designed
In Eden for us all.

EINE KLEINE SNAILMUSIK

The snail watchers are interested in snails from all angles. . . . At the moment they are investigating the snail's reaction to music. "We have played to them on the harp in the garden and in the country on the pipe," said Mr. Heaton, "and we have taken them into the house and played to them on the piano."

The London Star

What soothes the angry snail?
What's music to his horn?
For the "Sonata Appassionata,"
He shows scorn,
And Handel
Makes the frail snail
Quail,
While Prokofieff
Gets no laugh,
And Tchaikovsky, I fear,
No tear.
Piano, pipe, and harp,
Dulcet or shrill,
Flat or sharp,
Indoors or in the garden,
Are willy-nilly
Silly
To the reserved, slow,
Sensitive
Snail,
Who prefers to live
Glissandissimo,
Pianissimo.

A HARD DEATH

We have seen how dignity can be torn
From the naked dying or the newly born
By a loud voice or an ungentle presence,
Harshness of haste or lack of reverence;
How the hospital nurse may casually unbind
The suffering body from the lucid mind.
The spirit enclosed in that fragile shell
Cannot defend itself, must endure all.
And not only the dying, helpless in a bed,
Ask for a little pillow for the head,
A sip of water, a cool hand to bless:
The living have their lonely agonies.
"Is there compassion?" a friend asked me.
"Does it exist in another country?"

The busy living have no time to see
The flowers, so silent and so alive,
That paling to lavender of the anemone,
That purpling of the rose no one can save,
Dying, but at each second so complete
A photograph would show no slightest change.
Only the human eye, imperfect but aware,
Knows that the flower arrested on the air
Is flying through space, doing a dance
Toward the swift fall of petals, all at once.

God's Grace, given freely, we do not deserve,
But we can choose at least to see its ghost
On every face. Oh, we can wish to serve
Each other gently as we live, though lost.
We cannot save, be saved, but we can stand
Before each presence with gentle heart and hand;
Here in this place, in this time without belief,
Keep the channels open to each other's grief;
Never accept a death or life as strange
To its essence, but at each second be aware
How God is moving always through each flower
From birth to death in a multiple gesture
Of abnegation; and when the petals fall
Say it is beautiful and good, say it is well.

I saw my mother die and now I know
The spirit cannot be defended. It must go
Naked even of love at the very end.
"Take the flowers away" (Oh, she had been their friend!),
And we who ached could do nothing more—
She was detached and distant as a star.

Let us be gentle to each other this brief time
For we shall die in exile far from home,
Where even the flowers can no longer save.
Only the living can be healed by love.

THE WAVES

Even in the middle of the silent firs,
The secret world of mushroom and of moss,
Where all is delicate and nothing stirs,
We get the rumor of those distant wars
And the harsh sound of loss.

This is an island open to the churning,
The boom, the constant cannonade,
The turning back of tides and their returning,
And ocean broken like some restless mourning
That cannot find a bed.

Oh love, let us be true then to this will—
Not to each other, human and defeated,
But to great power, our Heaven and our Hell,
That thunders out its triumph unabated,
And is never still.

For we are married to this rocky coast,
To the charge of huge waves upon it,
The ceaseless war, the tide gained and then lost,
And ledges worn down smooth but not downcast—
Wild rose and granite.

Here in the darkness of the stillest wood,
Absence, the ocean, tires us with its roar;
We bear love's thundering rumor in the blood
Beyond our understanding, ill or good—
Listen, once more!

FROM *A DURABLE FIRE* (1969–1972)

.... (ᛩᛁᛩ)

GESTALT AT SIXTY

For ten years I have been rooted in these hills,
The changing light on landlocked lakes,
For ten years have called a mountain, friend,
Have been nourished by plants, still waters,
Trees in their seasons,
Have fought in this quiet place
For my *self*.

I can tell you that first winter
I heard the trees groan.
I heard the fierce lament
As if they were on the rack under the wind.
I too have groaned here,
Wept the wild winter tears.
I can tell you that solitude
Is not all exaltation, inner space
Where the soul breathes and work can be done.
Solitude exposes the nerve,
Raises up ghosts.
The past, never at rest, flows through it.

Who wakes in a house alone
Wakes to moments of panic.
(Will the roof fall in?
Shall I die today?)
Who wakes in a house alone
Wakes to inertia sometimes,

To fits of weeping for no reason.
Solitude swells the inner space
Like a balloon.
We are wafted hither and thither
On the air currents.
How to land it?

I worked out anguish in a garden.
Without the flowers,
The shadow of trees on snow, their punctuation,
I might not have survived.

I came here to create a world
As strong, renewable, fertile,
As the world of nature all around me—
Learned to clear myself as I have cleared the pasture,
Learned to wait,
Learned that change is always in the making
(Inner and outer) if one can be patient,
Learned to trust myself.

2

The house is receptacle of a hundred currents.
Letters pour in,
Rumor of the human ocean, never at rest,
Never still. . . .
Sometimes it deafens and numbs me.

I did not come here for society
In these years
When every meeting is collision,
The impact huge,
The reverberations slow to die down.
Yet what I have done here
I have not done alone,
Inhabited by a rich past of lives,

Inhabited also by the great dead,
By music, poetry—
Yeats, Valéry stalk through this house.
No day passes without a visitation—
Rilke, Mozart.
I am always a lover here,
Seized and shaken by love.

Lovers and friends,
I come to you starved
For all you have to give,
Nourished by the food of solitude,
A good instrument for all you have to tell
me,
For all I have to tell you.
We talk of first and last things,
Listen to music together,
Climb the long hill to the cemetery
In autumn,
Take another road in spring
Toward newborn lambs.

No one comes to this house
Who is not changed.
I meet no one here who does not change me.

3

How rich and long the hours become,
How brief the years,
In this house of gathering,
This life about to enter its seventh decade.

I live like a baby
Who bursts into laughter
At a sunbeam on the wall,

Or like a very old woman
Entranced by the prick of stars
Through the leaves.

And now, as the fruit gathers
All the riches of summer
Into its compact world,
I feel richer than ever before,
And breathe a larger air.

I am not ready to die,
But I am learning to trust death
As I have trusted life.
I am moving
Toward a new freedom
Born of detachment,
And a sweeter grace—
Learning to let go.

I am not ready to die,
But as I approach sixty
I turn my face toward the sea.
I shall go where tides replace time,
Where my world will open to a far horizon
Over the floating, never-still flux and change.
I shall go with the changes,
I shall look far out over golden grasses
And blue waters. . . .

There are no farewells.

Praise God for His mercies,
For His austere demands,
For His light
And for His darkness.

MOZART AGAIN

Now it is Mozart who comes back again
All garlanded in green.
Flute, harp, and trumpet, the sweet violin—
Each sound is seen.

Spring is a phrase, repeated green refrain,
Sound of new leaves springing.
I see the wind flowing like slanted rain,
Wind winging.

I learn this loving fresh, in ancient style
(Lightly time flows),
And mine a green world for pure joy awhile.
Listen, a rose!

Leaves are glissando. A long haunting phrase
Ripples the air—
This harpsichord of light that the wind plays.
Mozart is there.

BURIAL

The old man who had dug the small pit
Opened the two boxes with a penknife
And let the ashes fall down into it,
The ashes of this husband and his wife,
My father and my mother gently laid
Into the earth and mingled there for good.

We watched the wind breathe up an ashen breath
And blow thin smoke along the grass—
And that was all: the bitterness of death
Lifted to air, laid in the earth. All was
Terribly silent where four people stood
Tall in the air, believing what they could.

OF GRIEF

You thought it heartless
When my father fell down
Dead in his splendid prime,
Strong as a green oak thrown,
That all I did was praise
Death for this kindness,
Sang with a voice unbroken
Of the dear scholar's days,
His passion of a lifetime—
And my loss never spoken.

Judge of another's grief?
Weigh out that grief in tears?
I did not weep my father,
The rich, the fulfilled years.
What slow death have you known?
When no hope or belief
Can help, no loving care?
We watch and weep alone.
My heart broke for my mother.
I buried grief with her.

It is the incomplete,
That unfulfilled, the torn
That haunts our nights and days
And keeps us hunger-born.
Grief spills from our eyes,
Unwelcome, indiscreet,
As if sprung from a fault
As rivers seam a rock
And break through under shock.
We are shaken by guilt.

There are some griefs so loud
They could bring down the sky,
And there are griefs so still
None knows how deep they lie,
Endured, never expended.
There are old griefs so proud
They never speak a word;
They never can be mended.
And these nourish the will
And keep it iron-hard.

PRISONER AT A DESK

It is not so much trying to keep alive
As trying to keep from blowing apart
From inner explosions every day.
I sit here, open to psychic changes,
Living myself as if I were a land,
Or mountain weather, the quick cycles
Where we are tossed from the ice age
To bursts of spring, to sudden torrents
Of rain like tears breaking through iron.
It is all I can do to keep tethered down.

No prisoner at a desk, but an ocean
Or forest where waves and gentle leaves
And strange wild beasts under the groves
And whales in all their beauty under the blue
Can gently rove together, still untamed,
Where all opens and breathes and can grow.

Whatever I have learned of good behavior
Withers before these primal powers.
Here at the center governess or censor
No longer has command. The soul is here,
Inviolable splendor that exists alone.

Prisoner at a desk? No, universe of feeling
Where everything is seen, and nothing mine
To plead with or possess, only partake of,
As if at times I could put out a hand
And touch the lion head, the unicorn.
Here there is nothing, no one, not a sound
Except the distant rumor, the huge cloud
Of archetypal images that feed me . . .

Look, there are finches at the feeder.
My parrot screams with fear at a cloud.
Hyacinths are budding. Light is longer.

OLD TREES

Old trees—
How exquisite the white blossom
On the gnarled branch!
Thickened trunk, erratic shape
Battered by winter winds,
Bent in the long cold.

Young ones may please
The aesthete,
But old trees—
The miracle of their flowering
Against such odds—
Bring healing.

Let us praise them,
And sing hosannahs
As the small buds grow red
Just before they open.

THE COUNTRY OF PAIN

In the country of pain we are each alone.
Only joy brings communion, the light game
When passion tosses the ball high in air
And we forget Medusa who turns love to stone,
And Circe who knows every pig by name,
And manic-depressive Eros in despair.

In the country of pain there is no defence.
Tears scandalize. If we try to get through
To some rock of truth we are chastised
Like children whose anguish may be immense,
And told not to make scenes when all we know
Is terrible loss and true love ill-used.

In the country of pain we are animals
Who cannot understand a sudden blow
Or trust in a redeemer. There is none.
For pain is the country of lost souls
Which the gods flee because they know
They cannot re-humanize the pig or stone.

What redeemer now could return lost joys
Imprisoned by an ethos, beaten down,
The things made cheap within a damaged psyche,
The mysterious, magical, fantastic toys
Love showers on us with beautiful abandon
When manic-depressive Eros has a high?

For always what looked like an easy game
Becomes too frightening for innocence to play.
The country of Eros becomes the country of pain.
And the beglamoured pigs who gladly came
To Circe's call die in some horrible way
As Medusa begins her cold cruel reign.

OF MOLLUSCS

As the tide rises, the closed mollusc
Opens a fraction to the ocean's food,
Bathed in its riches. Do not ask
What force would do, or if force could.

A knife is of no use against a fortress.
You might break it to pieces as gulls do.
No, only the rising tide and its slow progress
Opens the shell. Lovers, I tell you true.

You who have held yourselves closed hard
Against warm sun and wind, shelled up in fears
And hostile to a touch or tender word—
The ocean rises, salt as unshed tears.

Now you are floated on this gentle flood
That cannot force or be forced, welcome food
Salt as your tears, the rich ocean's blood,
Eat, rest, be nourished on the tide of love.

OLD LOVERS AT THE BALLET

In the dark theatre lovers sit
Watching the supple dancers weave
A fugue, motion and music melded.
There on the stage below, brilliantly lit
No dancer stumbles or may grieve;
Their very smiles are disciplined and moulded.

And in the dark old lovers feel dismay
Watching the ardent bodies leap and freeze,
Thinking how age has changed them and has mocked.
Once they were light and bold in lissome play,
Limber as willows that could bend with ease—
But as they watch a vision is unlocked.

Imagination springs the trap of youth.
And in the dark motionless, as they stare,
Old lovers reach new wonders and new answers
As in the mind they leap to catch the truth,
For young the soul was awkward, unaware,
That claps its hands now with the supple dancers.

And in the flesh those dancers cannot spare
What the old lovers have had time to learn,
That the soul is a lithe and serene athlete
That deepens touch upon the darkening air.
It is not energy but light they burn,
The radiant powers of the Paraclete.

FROM *LETTERS FROM MAINE* (1984)

SHELL

Outside,
The sea's susurration,
Inside,
A terrible silence
As though everything had died,
One of those shells
Abandoned by the creature
Who lived there once
And opened to the tide.

Lift it to an ear
And you will hear
A long reverberation
In its tiny cave,
The rumor of a wave
Long ago broken
And drawn back
Into the ocean—
And so, with love.

INTIMATION

There is nowhere, no corner of a room, no garden,
No time of all times that is isolated, ours.
Between the tension of these actual walls,
We live, and the specific gravity of hours.

But there are instants. Suddenly you are.
I see arrested, sculptured, you set forth
Upon the landscape like a pillar casting
A long shadow to my feet on whirling earth.

Afterwards I remember the sight clearly,
As something unexplained, still strange.
But definite as dream when, upon waking,
The dreamed event becomes incapable of change.

THE CONSUMMATION

There on your bed lay poetry alive
With all that it can ever hope to give,
And there at last for one transcendent hour
You gave yourself into its gentle power.
Now the long tension slowly falls away
And we may be together in the simple day,
Not lovers, but by loving truly blest,
So take the light, my soul, and let us rest.

There on your bed you held me in your eyes,
Held me alive in your clear quiet gaze,
And even as your voice made strange lament
The light poured out, unfaltering, and sent
Beyond your power to hold it back from me
The shining of your inmost clarity.
Not lovers we, but strangely joined and blest,
So take the soul, my light, and let us rest.

There on your bed lay poetry alone
With all its hungers nourished at the bone,
And all its prayers and its long fierce desire
Held in the cool of your dark, magic fire,
As your cold hand, forgetful as a leaf,
Lay in my hand as if some human grief
Or some long praise could find a home at last,
So take this flesh, my soul, and let us rest.

There on your bed lay poetry beside
Neither a living bridegroom or a bride,
As if we two lay there already dead,
Hands, eyelids, heavier than lead,
And in this consummation, all withheld,
Except the soul upon a shining field,
And all received and given, and all lost—
So take the soul, my flesh, and let us rest.

FROM *THE SILENCE NOW* (1988)

THE COSSET LAMB

I met the cosset lamb
Carried in human arms
Because, dog-mauled,
Her mother would not nurse her
And baas in desolation
Along the fence.

I met the lamb and was
Stunned by this innocence.
What is there whiter?
Not milk of even bloodroot.
What is there softer?
Not even a fresh snow.
What is there sweeter
Than horizontal ears
And strange blank eyes?
There came a poignant calm,
Then that faint baa
That lingers on . . .
I knew I was
In Paradise.

For all that is so dear
And may be mauled,
For terror and despair
And for help near,
I weep, I am undone.
For all that can be healed,
The cosset lamb you hold,
And what cannot be healed,
The mother in the field,
I pray now I'm alone.

THE PHOENIX AGAIN

On the ashes of this nest
Love wove with deathly fire
The phoenix takes its rest
Forgetting all desire.

After the flame, a pause,
After the pain, rebirth.
Obeying nature's laws
The phoenix goes to earth.

You cannot call it old
You cannot call it young.
No phoenix can be told,
This is the end of song.

It struggles now alone
Against death and self-doubt,
But underneath the bone
The wings are pushing out.

And one cold starry night
Whatever your belief
The phoenix will take flight
Over the seas of grief

To sing her thrilling song
To stars and waves and sky
For neither old nor young
The phoenix does not die.

Autobiographical
Writings

(ץוץ)

FROM *A WORLD OF LIGHT: PORTRAITS AND CELEBRATIONS*

.... (ऒ।ऒ)

During the first two years of my life in the small heaven of our house in Wondelgem, Belgium, I was snatched away from my mother for weeks at a time because of her illnesses, sent to stay with friends, or, for one period of more than a month, given into the care of a dear friend who came to Wondelgem to look after me. When I was two we were driven out by the war, and again I was sent to cousins in England while my mother and father tried to find a means of livelihood in London. What all these uprootings did, I think, was to make the baby and small child learn to put out roots very quickly for survival. I became passionately attached to whomever took care of me, and perhaps this explains what someone called "emotional facility" when I was grown up. We were not able to settle anywhere for the first six years of my life. Then at last we reached Cambridge, Massachusetts, where my parents stayed for good, which became home; even so, we moved every seven years when my father had a sabbatical and we all went to Europe, the furniture being put in storage and a new apartment found on our return. It is not surprising, then, that I have always felt nostalgia for families rooted in one place, for the rites and routines of "family life."

My parents were remarkable, since I was an only child, in always leaving me free to do what I wanted and to be myself. My mother's theory of education was to be quite severe when I was an infant and until I was about ten years old, and then to give me almost absolute freedom of choice. As a child I left the house for the Shady Hill School at about seven every morning on my bicycle and came home often after dark. No one ever said, "Don't climb that tree; you might fall." When I wanted to go to camp, my mother made it possible for me to do so; I spent summers or parts of summers with the families of school friends—the Hockings in Vermont, the Runkles in Duxbury, Massachusetts, the Copley Greenes at Rowley, Massachusetts, the Boutons at Kearsage, New Hampshire. After I graduated from high school I had only one dream—to enter Eva Le Gallienne's Civic Repertory Theatre in New York. It was not easy, especially for my father, to accept the idea of a perilous life in the theatre in lieu of four years at Vassar. He battled it out with me for months before he consented, and then agreed to one hundred dollars a month allowance. My mother went to New York and found a club where I could stay near the theatre, where I would have some protection. How marvelous it was of them both to back me as they did with both moral and financial support when the whole precarious plan must have created great anxiety! There are few holidays in the theatre and sometimes I did not get home for months. So I had really left the nest for good at the remarkably early age of seventeen.

My father had never been a father in the the usual sense. He could not, absorbed as he was almost totally in his work, really pay attention, and when I was small I learned to be very silent, for he worked at home and the slightest noise interrupted his concentration. So at an early age I witnessed the fact that work was of the first importance, and that it justified rather inhuman behavior. I don't know when I began to be aware of the rifts in the marriage, but certainly before I was ten. My father, for instance, hated Christmas. (It was not in the Belgian tradition, where presents are given on St. Nicholas on the 6th of December.) We always had a small tree and my mother stayed up late making marvelous clothes for my dolls. One Christmas Eve I heard from my bed my father's rage at what he said was "spoiling May" and my mother's sobs. I woke the next day, Christmas day, with a high fever. That was a dramatic instance of his lack of sensitivity (also perhaps unconscious jealousy, for he had lost his own mother when he had been a baby and nobody "spoiled" him); but every Christmas was a time of strain because of his feelings about it. So, in the usual sense of the word, we did not have a family life. I had to grow up before I could understand that he himself was a child who never grew up in the emotional areas of his being. He usually gave me for my birthday a book that he wanted—for instance, when I was eleven and could have had no possible interest in it, an expensive French-English, English-French two volume dictionary, which then of course disappeared into his own library! I found it there after his death, and it came in very handy when I was translating Valéry with Louise Bogan.

Because of his need to concentrate absolutely on his work George Sarton had developed extreme resistance to anything that might prove disturbing, such as my mother's health or lack of it, or any need I might have that would require painful discussion. It is amazing, since both my mother and I suffered because of this, that I never resented that work, any more than she did. We honored him for it, and never doubted that, whatever the cost, .we were contributing to something of real importance. It was George Sarton's example as a scholar not as a human being that molded me. I did not come to love him as a human being until after my mother's death, when I myself was middle-aged.

But what my father represented was in extreme contrast to what my mother expected of herself and of me in human terms. I thought of her always as my dearest friend, an equal, *the* person with whom I could discuss anything and everything—my passions, my admirations, my griefs, my discoveries, my torments. She backed me to the limit, but she was also my best critic, with an unerring eye for self-dramatization or any false attitude. She was simply inside my life, as my father was simply outside it. And for her, especially in the later years, I was also the best friend, the one who could understand and share.

She had married an extraordinary man who loved her deeply, as she loved him. Never did either of them look at any other person with such love as they gave each other. But she had also married an emotional cripple, unable ever to discuss money (of which there was always too little) and fleeing any emergency that might require real self-giving on his part.

My mother never made scenes. She buried her anger, because, however angry she was—and with reason—she still felt that George Sarton must be protected, never upset by any demands of hers, for the sake of his work. The cost was high, high in ill health, migraine, and I have sometimes wondered whether the cancer of which she died might not have been caused by buried rage. And the cost was high for me because I suffered for and with her, yet could do nothing. But of course I learned from all this, and slowly learned to love my father (as she had done) for what he was, and to forget what he could not be.

On less emotional levels we were a trio who enjoyed each other immensely and who were quite independent of each other, for we all had consuming interests of our own. I began to write poetry when I was ten or eleven; my mother had her own inventive ways of teaching and her own work. When we met at meals there was always passionate discussion of books and art. And I have wonderful memories of summers we spent together in Ogunquit, and one memorable journey for a summer in the Pyrenees after my mother and I had spent a hard winter in Belgium. That journey has kept its dreamlike happiness for nearly fifty years. Our slow progress from one mountain village to another, where we took long walks, and I collected wild flowers to press . . . the vivid rural scenes—once we came upon a sheepshearing, and I watched with amazement the thick golden fleece gradually being clipped by hand and rolled over in a great rich furl . . . the awesome Cirque de Gavarnie . . . and especially my curiosity about the Basque people, which drove me to read all I could about them. But most of all what keeps its glow was the fact that we were happy that summer, all three.

Being the child of George and Mabel Sarton was an intense experience and an immensely rich one as I look back on it now. It was a rich experience to grow up between two such powerful personalities and to absorb their values, little by little.

Through my father I witnessed that if the vision were there, a man could work eighteen hours a day, with joy, and never seem to tire. I understood that a talent is something given, that it opens like a flower, but without exceptional energy, discipline, and persistence will never bear fruit.

Through my mother I witnessed extreme awareness of all forms of beauty, and extreme sensitivity to human beings and human relationships. Mother, wife, friend as well as artist—she had to balance a thousand things into a complex whole, and often felt torn among them. I see her as giving a little more than she could afford in every direction; the demands she made on herself were enormous.

And quite early on I began to experience the conflict implied in an effort to be as human as my mother and as dedicated as my father, for these two qualities are often in opposition. Though not always. My father, like me, answered every letter—that was his way of being human. I always knew that I had a responsibility toward life itself to do something in my own right, to contribute, to create. That was simply taken for granted in the ethos in which I grew up.

But an historian can believe that his work is bound to be of value if he goes to primary sources and is diligent and perceptive. No writer can have that assurance, filled as he is with the same anxiety and doubt during the creation of each new work. The work of an historian is cumulative; for the artist each new work is the rival of all that has gone before. And beyond even self-doubt no writer can justify ruthlessness for the sake of his work, because being human to the fullest possible extent is what his work demands of him. The conflict between life and art is bound to be acute and the finding of a balance an excruciating daily struggle, the more so for me because I had before me such extreme examples of each mode in my remarkable parents.

Both had died before I was forty-five. The imprint was deep, and I realized its depth party because I felt great relief. When my mother died I felt relief for her (it had been a long hard death from cancer), and relief for myself because I knew that the worst thing that could ever happen to me had happened. Never again would I wake up in tears from the nightmare that she had died. Only my own death would ever take from me as much. My father bore his loss with great dignity and courage, and in the six years before he himself died suddenly of a heart attack, I came to know and to love him in a new way. But when they were both gone, I felt freed of a great burden, the burden of being a child. I felt free to be wholly myself, especially as a writer. I could not, I think, have come out as I did in *Mrs. Stevens Hears the Mermaids Singing* while they were alive. I also felt a new responsibility, since a person without any family can afford to be honest in a way that perhaps no one with any close ties can be.

But I miss my parents, the more lately as the world around us darkens and there seems so little foundation of belief on which to stand. I long to run over to Channing Place for tea, to find my mother lying on the chaise longue in the garden, a cat on her lap, my father smoking a cigar in a chair beside her—the two people in the world with whom I could feel in total communion about politics, art, religion, all that really matters, to be reassured by their unfailing and concerned idealism, and to laugh again as we three often laughed together at this "preposterous pig of a world." Without them I sometimes feel the wind at my back— they had such vitality and strength.

When I was thirty I once said to my mother, "If I died now, I would feel that I had lived an extraordinary life. . . ." I meant as a human being, not as an artist. I was acknowledging that I had already then been given the friendship and love of many different people, people as rare and precious as stars, people whom I had watched and learned from and admired with the intensity of an astronomer discovering a new brilliant in the heavens. In ten years I had experienced a great flowering inside myself, a flowering, not a harvest, for it had had that poignance of a long-delayed spring, almost too much happening too quickly, and not to be held fast, only adored for a moment, and let go. Fulfillment would come much later, and in solitude. (pp. 16–23)

This excerpt from May Sarton's preface to *A World of Light* constitutes a succinct first chapter, as it were, of her unwritten autobiography. Lacking in some details which would be of interest to her readers, this sketch nevertheless offers a portrait of the emerging artist as a daughter. Like the heroine of *A Reckoning*, the author explores the "real connections" in her early life. Although *A World of Light* was published in 1976 and belongs, perhaps, two-thirds of the way through these excerpts of her journals, arranged chronologically by date of publication, this appreciation of her parents provides a useful touchstone for the reader who will encounter Sarton's parents throughout this book in one literary form or another.

FROM *I KNEW A PHOENIX: SKETCHES FOR AN AUTOBIOGRAPHY* (1912–1937)

.... (ฝฝฝ)

In my father's house—," my father used to begin, wreathed in an enormous smile. As he grew older, after my mother's death, his memories of this rather somber house opposite the church of St. Michel in Ghent, took on a rich patina. Sitting opposite him in his house in Cambridge, Massachusetts, for our ritualistic Sunday dinner, I savored the short pause while some shadowy glory took on substance in his mind. I could hear the sound of herbs being chopped for the soup in that faraway kitchen, for in my grandfather's house this was the sure sign that dinner was about to be served. I could see the long table set for a dinner of twelve, the hard rolls wrapped in damask turbans at each place, the rows of wineglasses, including *flûtes* for champagne at dessert. (Of this glittering army, one survived the '14–'18 war, a green glass on a crystal stem.) My father and I poured ourselves another glass of American Pinot, but our palates were far away, soothed by the glowing sequence of Chablis, Burgundies, Sauternes and Champagnes poured by my grandfather with proper solemnity, and honored, no doubt, with a long and flowery toast by Oncle Adolphe, the literary member of the family, who taught French literature in a Lycée in Brussels, and was convinced that anything written since Chateaubriand had better be passed over in silence. "In my father's house," my father used to remind me, "at formal dinners we allowed two bottles per male guest and one per female guest." (pp. 11–12)

[George Sarton's mother died one year after his birth, at age twenty-four]

. . . And all around her hangs the perfume of sadness, the silence her husband never broke to tell little George something of that vanished young mother who so soon became younger than her son. Her charm, her little ways, her smile, the tenderness for which the boy starved, were locked up with the piano, and never opened again.

Instead George was pampered and neglected by the maids. If he was ill, they kindly took his medicine for him, especially if it had a nasty taste, but, ignorant and irresponsible, they were about as far from an English Nanny as can be imagined. Loneliness haunted his memories of babyhood, but it was an active imaginative loneliness, not without a streak of Flemish humor. When he was still eating in a high chair, George was allowed to be present at dinner, but if he so much as babbled a single word, his father, without raising his head from his newspaper, reached forward to touch the bell (a round brass bell on a stand, tapped with one finger) and when the maid appeared, said simply, *"Enlevez-le."* When George was alone at a meal, formally served him in the dining room in his high chair, and he did not like something he was given to eat, he repeated the lordly gesture and the lordly phrase and was delighted to see that, like "Open Sesame" in reverse, he could thus have the unhappy cabbage, or whatever it was, removed form sight. (pp. 14–15)

[He gained] the reputation of being an eccentric by the time he was twenty. The most shocking of these [decisions], worse even than his vegetarianism, or his socialism, must have been the auction of his father's famous wine cellar after Alfred Sarton's death—and the most important was surely his determination to write a history of science. But the first made it possible for my parents to buy the lovely house in the country near Ghent, where I was born, and the second changed in forty years from a preposterous dream to the monumental *Introduction to the History of Science*, which is such a fertile reality to scholars today. (p. 23)

There were the cafés where a habitué kept his clay pipe with his name written on it. During one year of great fatigue, George had pipes all over the city, like a clubman with many clubs. Here he wandered, smoking and composing the early romantic books he wrote under the pseudonym of Dominique de Bray, when he thought he would be a poet, and with no idea yet that he would soon be getting a doctorate in celestial mechanics. . . . (p. 24)

[Gervase Elwes, the father of May Sarton's mother, was a civil engineer whose family was of Suffolk, England. He spent long periods of time away from home laying out railways, roads, and bridges in India, Spain, and Canada. When his daughter Mabel was, at the age of seven, sent for two years to live on a farm in Wales, her nine-year-old brother was sent to boarding school.]

I know what a radiance of remembered happiness crossed my mother's face when she spoke of Wales, as of some lost Paradise, and what this long period of solitary communion with nature did for one who was always a discerning and passionate observer of flowers, trees and animals—one who would later have to remake her home many times among strangers, and twice even change her nationality. (p. 26)

Her relationship with her father had been an especially close one; Gervase Elwes was a Fabian, an agnostic, a highly intelligent but unworldly man, with a delightful sense of humor and adventurous courage. At twenty-four, before his marriage, he was building bridges for one of the first railroads in the Himalayas, and the same spirit of adventure led him later in his life to make risky investments in mines. By the time his daughter Mabel had been educated (she was sent to a finishing school in Ghent), his affairs were in a bad way. It was clear that Mabel would have to earn her own living as soon as possible, and to that end she was sent to the Black Heath Art School, where she learned to do miniature portraits. By the year of 1906, when she first met George Sarton, she was a professional portrait painter, and was also doing some interior decorating for the firm of Dangotte. (p. 50)

[The father of May Sarton's mother died suddenly, leaving his family penniless.]

But fortunately Mabel's heart had already been transplanted to Belgium. There Madame Dangotte and her daughter Céline offered her a home, the most tender, loving care and understanding, during the time, after this shock, when she was seriously ill. Most important of all, Madame Dangotte had faith in Mabel's talent, gave her work to do, and that supportive belief more precious than money. (p. 51)

[May Sarton's mother and father] began as friends, the kind of friends who demand a great deal of each other, who confide in each other, and who learn from each other because they are each passionate in conviction, and able to express themselves. (p. 54)

And on the first day of spring, the day Mabel appeared in the little studio . . . where George had a study, they became fiancés and celebrated the event by hiring a boat, rowing down the Lys, and eating an engagement luncheon of asparagus and hard-boiled eggs, in true Flemish style. The long rich wanderings and digressions of youth were over. (p. 63)

. . . shortly before [George Sarton's] marriage, he had come to a firm decision, even at the risk of having no permanent job, and no visible means of support: "I have decided now, as soon as I have the doctorate, to devote myself to my own work without further preoccupations about getting a stable position. That exclusive need for security did in fact seem to me suddenly a cowardice:—to work, let the chips fall where they may! Mabel thinks as I do about this; and it's not she, God knows! who would turn me from my ideal." (p. 64)

Two houses stand behind me—one, my grandfather's somber house in the city of Ghent, where my father grew up; the other, all light and sunshine, the country house three miles outside, in Wondelgem, where I was born. "Wondelgem," the name itself sounded like magic to me as a child. It was part of that faraway paradise "before The War." It was quite literally in another world, since I did not remember it myself (I was two and a half when we left Belgium), a little girl who, in Cambridge, Massachusetts, heard the peculiar tenderness the word evoked in my mother's voice, as if the walls of the tiny apartment where we lived opened out at its sound into a secret garden, into a still airy house with roses climbing all over it, and inside, the walls covered with books.

It had been bought by the sale of my grandfather's wine cellar after his death; connoisseurs, many of whom had sat at his table, were at the same time scandalized that such a sale should take place at all, and delighted to be "in" on it: they paid high prices, and the result was a small fortune. Instead of water being turned into wine, in this instance wine had been turned into strawberry beds, into a small orchard, into great oaks at the bottom of a long green lawn, into the dear house itself, and its gradual furnishing with cupboards, tables, beds designed by my mother and made under her supervision. Never mind if she and her young husband slept on mattresses on the floor for three months while cabinetmakers lovingly polished the bird's-eye maple and walnut, fitting together the patterns in the wood so each piece seemed in the end to show the opened heart of the tree. It was all alive, this house and garden in the process of creation. (pp. 65–66)

[George Sarton's uncle wrote letters to the newspaper asking why the Germans were building large railway stations near the Belgian border, but most Belgians did not anticipate the beginning of the First World War.]

People planned their lives for peace. Deep in the country, under the shade of the oaks, my tall slim mother was sewing at the printed linen curtains, so strong and delicate they would last a lifetime. The blue flax from which they had been made waved in the fields along the Lys. And my father wrote letters to scholars all over the world announcing that he was founding a review to be devoted to the history of science and civilization. *Isis*, as it was named, was born in the spring of 1912, and Eléanore Marie, as I was named, shortly after. My father always referred to us together and dedicated one of his books to "Eleanor Mabel, mother of those strange twins, May and Isis." By now my name had shortened itself. (p. 69)

Meanwhile in Wondelgem in the spring and summer of 1914, we were beautifully happy and independent, all three. My mother was busy designing the furnishings of a room for the firm in Brussels for whom she worked, a room to be shown at the international exhibition of Arts and Crafts due to open in August. She had made a trip to Austria to work with the craftsman responsible for the inlay of wreaths of flowers in brilliant colors, for this was not done in Belgium. Belgian craftsmen, on the other hand, were polishing the birds's-eye maple a smoky blue, and bringing the insides of drawers to a satin finish. She had designed the rugs, the curtains, the pillows, as well as the furniture, which was amazingly modern for the period, and would seem modern now but for its rich decoration. (p. 74)

[After the conclusion of World War I, the Sartons returned to Wondelgem.]

She had lifted out of a pile of rubbish [in the war-ravaged house] a single Venetian glass on a long delicate stem, so dirty it had become opaque, but miraculously intact. How had this single fragile object survived to give us courage? It went back with us to Cambridge and it was always there, wherever we lived. And now it is here, in my own house, a visible proof that it is sometimes the most fragile things that have the power to endure, and become sources of strength, like my mother. . . . It seems that two German officers lived in the house during the first two years of the war. . . .

I was beginning to feel frightened, as if we were ghosts, entirely unreal, and only the rubbish and desolation was real, when we heard someone tearing through the flowers. One of our peasant neighbors stood shyly at the door. She held out to my mother a pile of beautiful old plates. . . .

All these years she had stored them up, one by one, as the officers paid for eggs and butter with some object from the house. Never knowing whether we would be back, she had saved them; she had hoped; she had foreseen the possible happiness she might one day have in her hands to give back. Only then, with the dear old plates in her own hands, so clean, so brilliant, so untouched, so wrapped in human kindness, did my mother weep. (pp. 81–82)

[When the German armies invaded Belgium, the Sartons resettled in America. George Sarton was able to continue his research and writing, eventually, at Harvard University; May Sarton's mother continued her career, as opportunities arose.]

My mother was the designer and her friend, Margaret Gillespie, the businesswoman of [Belgart], which created embroidered dresses and coats, using designs based on peasant embroideries, executed in bright wools and silks. . . . It was, for a time, during the 'twenties and' thirties a considerable business, filling orders from Neiman Marcus, Marshall Field and Lord & Taylor as well as many individuals, among them Nazimova. And, although in the end, it did not withstand the depression, it helped put me through school, sent me to camp, and did indeed "help make ends meet" at a time when a considerable per cent of my father's income had to go to the support of my twin, *Isis*. But above all it satisfied my mother's need to "create" something of her own, to use her talents, and to find her own place in the new world. (pp. 95–96)

[At the age of twelve, May Sarton attended, for one winter, the Institut Belge de Culture Française in a suburb of Brussels.]

. . . Its founder and presiding genius, Marie Closset, a friend of Gide and Francis Jammes, was well known in the world of Belgian and French letters as the poet Jean Dominique: my father had carried a volume of hers in his pocket in 1904, believing perhaps that the author was a young man. . . . (p. 120)

[Marie Closset] was herself a tiny figure, rather stooped and diminished by constant ill health; this frail aspect served perhaps to exaggerate her enormous luminous gray eyes behind dark glasses, which she put on and took off with a rhythmical gesture as she read or spoke. It was not a beautiful face in any ordinary sense, but it was a face so filled by the spirit and the intellect, so transparent to its own inwardness, that it was memorable. She had small hands with the lightness and grace of wings, and a grave, quietly expressive voice made for the reading of poetry. No wonder she hid those amazing eyes; they were too revealing. Genius in its purest form—love—looked out of them.

She taught literature almost entirely by reading from great works and commenting upon them, and these ranged from Plato and Aristotle to Tolstoy and the moderns of all nations. She also gave a course in Japanese Art, a course in Renaissance Art, a course in Greek Art, and many more; in fact, she chose to teach what moved her deeply, and nothing else. Later on, when I was grown up, I attended some of these classes as a listener, and I never heard her say a disparaging word about a work of art. What she wished to instill in her students was enlightened homage—homage enriched by intellectual analysis but rooted in passion. (p. 129)

FROM *PLANT DREAMING DEEP* (1958–1967)

.... (ᶹᵢᵞᵢ)

For forty-five years or so, I lived very happily without owning property, and in fact would have considered the owning of property a definite hazard. I felt then no responsibility except to a talent. I wandered, borrowing other people's lives, other people's families, with the nostagia of the only child; and for many years could not decide whether I was a European or an American at heart. As for roots, they were there in my parents' house in Cambridge, on Channing Place, where the Flemish chests, my mother's desk, and the big *bahut* with its pillars of glowing walnut seemed to have found a permanent home. There my mother's garden grew and flowered. . . .

Those years between my twenty-sixth (when my first book of poems came out) and my forty-sixth (when I came to Nelson) *were* adventurous because, luckily for me, I had to earn my living. I am sure it is a good thing for a writer in the formative years to be forced out into the world from his self-enclosed preoccupations and anxieties. It happened that I was good at lecturing, partly because I had been schooled in the theater to project to an audience, to use my voice well, and not to be afraid of public appearances.

When I made the first of many lecture trips, in 1939–1940, I was unknown, the former director of an off-Broadway theater that had failed during the Depression, the author of a slim volume of poems and one novel. The lecture circuit for poets had not yet become the big business it is now. I simply wrote to fifty colleges and offered to read for twenty-five dollars if they would put me up for a few days, and before I knew it I was beginning to plan and pin-point twenty or more such visits scattered all the way from Sterling, Kansas, to New Orleans, and from Charleston, South Carolina, to Santa Fe, New Mexico. My father came forward with a new Mercury convertible and the promise of fifty dollars a month to help me along, and I set out alone on an autumn, winter, and spring of unhurried exploration.

There were considerable gaps between engagements when my funds ran low, but then I holed in somewhere and wrote poems—ten unforgettable days in Eureka Springs, Arkansas; three weeks in New Orleans, where I managed to find a boardinghouse for eleven dollars a week, meals included. The whole trip was not at all what a lecture trip usually is, a hurried kaleidoscope of places and people, but rather a leisurely odyssey, the discovery of my America. I was always looking for the humanizing and illuminating perception of writers and poets about these landscapes I was seeing for the first time, and was amazed at how much has not yet been celebrated. Where is the poet of the secret wild Arkansas valleys? Of the great golden empty Texas plains? Of the Delta?

For me, the place of the greatest intensity turned out to be New Mexico, around Santa Fe, where I spent two months. The austere landscape, the great sunlit plateau dominated by the Sangre de Cristo Mountains, the "leopard land" dotted with piñon, affected me deeply. I had found one of the places on earth where any sensitive being feels exposed to powerful invisible forces and himself suddenly naked and attacked on every side by air, light, space—all that brings the soul close to the surface. There the poems flowed out.

Later on I was alone for days in Charleston, where I felt sharply, and for the first time, how in these United States a whole way of life may come and go in the space of fifty years—as in Charleston where rice built those exquisite plantation houses, then left them abandoned; as here in New Hampshire where Australian wool knocked out the sheep, and the painfully cleared fields went back to second growth. But in Santa Fe time is not that shallow. There one can go deep into a continuity as the pueblos and the culture they represent take one back at least eight hundred years through a single Indian dance. For a European that continuity is life-giving.

I came home from that trip not only enriched in every way as an American but with the good will of a nucleus of college presidents who have since asked me to return over and over again. That initial adventure has brought me many more. Through it I became the inhabitant of a continent and not just a refugee form Europe in a tiny corner of it.

But entering deeply into the life of a college for a few days and then moving on, or spending a week in a boardinghouse in a strange city is not the same as *living* somewhere, and what I meant by "life" was still rooted in Europe. During those years I went back whenever I could to the strong ties in England, France, Belgium, and Switzerland. I had not yet cut the umbilical cord.

> I too have known the inward disturbance of exile,
> The great peril of being at home nowhere,
> The dispersed center, the dividing love;
> Not here, nor there, leaping across ocean,
> Turning, returning to each strong allegiance;
> American, but with this difference—parting.

That stanza of a poem called "From All Our Journeys" was written in the 1940's. But then, while my parents were still living, I could come back "from all the journeys" to Channing Place.

. . .

[After Sarton's parents died and she felt that she needed to make a home of her own.]

. . . I behaved like a starving man who knows there is food somewhere if he can only find it. I did not reason anything out. I did not reason that part of the food I needed was to become a member of a community richer and more various, humanly speaking, than the academic world of Cambridge could provide: the hunger of the novelist. I did not reason that part of the nourishment I craved was all the natural world can give—a garden, woods, fields, brooks, birds: the hunger of the poet. I did not reason that the time had come when I needed a house of my own, a nest of my own making: the hunger of the woman. I only knew that the old Belgian furniture must be rescued from that cellar [at Channing Place].

If "home" can be anywhere, how is one to look for it, where is one to find it? For me, there was no ancestral "connection" that might have drawn me here or there, no magnet that might have narrowed down the possible choices. I could settle anywhere within a wide perimeter of Cambridge, for I intended to keep what I would not part with, my life with Judy, my place in her house, and the friends of many years. (pp. 19–23)

[In June 1958 Sarton bought an eighteenth-century farmhouse (with five fireplaces and thirty acres of land, bounded by a brook) in Nelson, New Hampshire, and moved to it from Cambridge those belongings associated with her family's European heritage.]

Well, once an old lady in her late eighties walked into the big kitchen-living-room [in the Nelson house] where "the ancestor" now hangs, looked about her, and asked in a rasping old-American voice, "Why do you have all this *Belgian* furniture in an old *American* house?"

I was too dismayed to answer. But I think this book is the answer, although she, brave soul, is dead; and will never read it. The answer is, "Katherine Davis, I have brought all that I am and all that I came from here, and it is the marriage of all this with an old American house which gives the life here its quality for me. It is a strange marriage and its like does not exist anywhere else on earth . . . and just that has been the adventure. (p. 25)

I was troubled by what to hang in the space above the mantelpiece in my study—a wide empty space between wall-to-ceiling bookshelves. . . . I had brought up a silk panel, turquoise damask, embroidered by my mother with a geometric design in blue and gold. That panel had never found a place on the walls at Channing Place, but both the shape and the color fitted perfectly in my study. It was, I saw when I had hung it experimentally, surely meant as a background for flowers, and so it became a kind of stage where the whole glorious sequence could be played out, from daffodils and tulips in May, to iris, and then to the great white peonies, the vivid blue delphinium, the long sequence of lillies, to end with chrysanthemums and asters in the fall. It is the *tokonoma* of the house, the sacred place where beauty is kept alive in memory of the dead.

Sunlight pours into my study from four windows. Year by year the turquoise silk has faded to a gentle watery blue, the brilliant embroidery has softened, and it is lovelier than ever. "We love the things we love for what they are," Robert Frost reminds us. And he means, I think, that we love them as they change—he is speaking in the poem of a brook gone dry—as well as for what they once were. My mother's face changed from that of an English beauty to that of a wrinkled old woman and never lost its sweetness. But the eyes did not change, those grave gray eyes that could suddenly twinkle with merriment, but through which fierce grief and tenderness flowed out toward a mouse rescued form the cat's jaws, toward the fallen bird with a broken wing, toward all living things including flowers and her husband and child. In exactly the way her creations have done—the inlaid desk, the embroidered panel—she grew old only to grow more beautiful, though changed.

I suddenly realized that what I had brought with me into the house, and the house itself, were making it possible for the first time since the death of my parents to evoke their joys. For the first time the joy that surrounds them in my mind could be rooted again, and had a place to root in. The long grief rose and melted away as I have so often seen mist do over my fields in the early morning. (pp. 47–48)

The dark came suddenly, flowed into the house, and filled me sometimes with a second of dread. It was time then to light the fire and put on the lights in the big room, like round moons in their Japanese paper lanterns, time to come back to a human world, where a Japanese print or a blue-and-white jug bring a long train of thought with them into the warm room.

If I got snowed in, I could shovel myself out. The trees, which groaned in a heart-rending way in storms, did not fall. Though it did often feel like the edge of nowhere, I found that I was very much alive on the edge of nowhere.

. . . I have wept bitter tears in this house. At any moment solitude may put on the face of loneliness. Life here has been, from the start, a challenge. And that is the point—not, perhaps, happiness, but life lived at its most aware and intense. Would not "Aunt Cora" [the previous owner of the house] have said as much when the first old-fashioned rose by the granite step, that rose so tightly folded into its hairy bud, opened each spring? Not happiness, perhaps, but something like New England itself—struggle, occasional triumph over adversity, above all the power to endure and to be renewed. For here the roses grown beside the granite. (p. 94)

Then one June day, the ancient bell on my front door tinkled rather more imperatively than usual, and there he [Perley Cole] was. He launched at once into a long speech which managed to seem laconic because of the manner in which it was delivered. It went something like this: "I know I'm an old man, an old fool some might say, but I've done some farming here and there in my time, and it might happen that you could need some help . . . Mind you, I ain't goin' to starve, one way or t'other, and I have plenty to do on my own place, but . . ."

I let him know that there were about a million things that needed doing, and pointed out a few of them.

"I'll be around one of these days," he said, and vanished.

It was my first experience of his abrupt departures. Every now and then Perley comes to a boil, and utters. When he has uttered, he vanishes into thin air. It can be disconcerting until you get used to it. He is shy and touchy, and I have come to believe that he vanishes because he is suddenly afraid that the answer he has elicited may not be the one he wants to hear.

I watched him walk away that day, his back slightly stooped, his stride the long slow stride of the farmer who can keep going from daylight to dark without tiring. And I thought over the face I had just seen for the second time, an American Gothic face, lean, sharply lined, with a high forehead and a long stubborn chin, a sharply defined nose, shy, piercing eyes. Why had he settled here among us? "I'm an old man," he said, but there was a certain fierceness in the tone that clearly meant "an untamed old man." (p. 108)

Then early one morning, I was woken by a soft sound I could not place, a kind of whispering out in the field between house and barn. From my bed, I pulled the shade up and looked out on a clear bright summer morning, the dew shining on the grass, and there was Perley Cole scything down the jungle. It was the first time I had seen a man scything (even around here we are motorized these days). I watched the long steady sweeps, and how often he stopped and stood the scythe up to whet it—watched and hugely enjoyed the whole operation, repeated over and over, as if in slow motion, the continuous rhythm of it, and the man himself, as tall and angular as his tool. I saw how he handled it with a wary, loving touch. And I saw, too, that this was no rough-and-ready job but a matter of skill and grace. When I went out, later on, he was on his knees trimming with a sickle, although the scythe itself had been used so delicately that only a perfectionist would have seen the need for additional work around the edges. The old barn stood up now as trim as could be.

"See that?" Perley said, lifting the scythe to show me. "Made in England. I wouldn't take a hundred dollars for it!"

The collar of his dark-gray shirt was turned in, and I could see a dew of sweat on his throat; his eyes looked dark blue in the morning light, and his cheeks were pink. There, triumphant, he was surely in the prime of life, and I would never have guessed that he was then over seventy. But he has learned to handle himself as skillfully as a fine tool.

We didn't talk much that day, nor for many days to come. But gradually he shaped and pruned and cleared the place for me. (pp. 109–110)

Little by little we began to tame each other, finding our way slowly into friendship, sealed with many a glass of sherry when Perley knocked off at noon. The sherry is downed in one gulp. Down it goes, and then, after a moment, up comes a story.

"Court's in session. Now you listen to me!"

I sit on the kitchen stool, drink my sherry slowly, and listen.

So it is that I have come to know a good deal about him, about him and his "bird," as he sometimes calls Angie, and about Parker, their son, who came back from World War II with a permanent cloak of silence around him, as shy as a deer. Parker and his mother are made of the same delicate stuff, but Perley arrived in this world weighing eleven pounds and screaming. He was the youngest of four brothers, and he was not the favorite; he ran away at twelve to work for a neighboring farmer. (p. 110)

I have never heard him say anything that did not come from deep inside his own experience, and when he tells me to be patient and not to be in such a hurry, I take it because I know that he has learned his own patience and his own rhythm through a long life. In the years I have known him, he has taught me a great deal. I have soaked him up like some healthy primal source, and he has nourished the poet as well as the gardener. He uses language like a poet himself, and savors his own pithy turns of phrase, so they come back like recurring themes in a fugue. One of my favorites is "He knows as much about farming as a goose knows about Jesus." (pp. 111–112)

He might have been an apparition from another age, an age when a workman still had the time and the patience and the wish to do a patient, perfect job, not for the money, not even for the praise he might get at the end of the day, but out of self-respect and out of the love of the work for its own sake. In this Perley is very much like a poet, and he stands before me as an exemplar. Thinking of the way he kneels down to clip a border after he has cut the grass, I sometimes have revised a page for the fifth time instead of letting it go after the fourth. (p. 113)

But little by little, together, Perley and I have lifted the place out of its neglect and chaos into something like beauty and order. (p. 114)

There is nothing that pleases Perley more than to survey a tangled jungle of rotten trees and brush and to carve it into shape. Contemplating what would look to most of us like an impossible task, he begins to hum with anticipation; his face, often harsh in repose, lights up with the joy of battle, with the artist's joy. Hours later he emerges, his straw hat pulled down over his eyes, his shirt collar tucked in, and swallows a glass of sherry as if it were water. Behind him beauty and order have been restored.

When he and I are working side by side here, as we do, for a few hours anyway we are neither old nor young. We are outside time. (p. 117)

Making a garden is not a gentle hobby for the elderly, to be picked up and laid down like a game of solitaire. It is a grand passion. It seizes a person whole, and once it has done so he will have to accept that his life is going to be radically changed. There are seasons when he will hesitate to travel, and if he does travel, his mind will be distracted by the thousand and one children he has left behind, children who are always in peril of one sort or another. However sober he may have been before, he will soon become an inveterate gambler who cuts his losses and begins again; he may think he intends to pare down on spending energy and money, but that is an illusion, and he soon learns that a garden is an ever-expanding venture. Whatever he had considered to be his profession has become an avocation. His vocation is his garden. (pp. 119–120)

. . . Arranging flowers is like writing in that it is an art of choice. Not everything can be used of the rich material that rushes forward demanding utterance. And just as one tries one word after another, puts a phrase together only to tear it apart, so one arranges flowers. It is engrossing work, and needs a fresh eye and a steady hand. When you think the thing is finished, it may suddenly topple over, or look too crowded after all, or a little meager. It needs one more note of bright pink, or it needs white. White in a bunch of flowers does a little of what black does in a painting, I have found. It acts as a catalyst for all the colors. After that first house I have used up my "seeing energy" for a while, just as, after three hours at my desk, the edge begins to go, the critical edge.

Flowers and plants are silent presences; they nourish every sense except the ear. . . . (p. 124)

For the joys a garden brings are already going as they come. They are poignant. When the first apple falls with that tremendous thud, one of the big seasonal changes startles the heart. . . . the flowers ring their changes through a long cycle, a cycle that will be renewed. That is what the gardener often forgets. To the flowers we never have to say good-by forever. *We* grow older every year, but not the garden; it is reborn every spring.

Like any grand passion, my garden has been nourished by memory as well as by desire, and is a meeting place, an intersection where remembered joys can be re-created. I first say shirley poppies—and if I had to choose only one flower, I might choose them—in Basil de Selincourt's garden near Oxford, in the Cotswolds. Basil sowed shirley poppies on a long bank a little above a more formal perennial border; and when they flowered, a diaphanous host, shaken by the light and wind, playing their endless variations on the themes of pink, white, and red, they were a wonder to behold. Everything about this flower is magic—its curious hairy stem; the tightly folded petals, a little damp, that open out of nothing like Fortuny dresses, to show the shaggy crown of gold or black stamens; and finally the intricate turret of the seed pod. So when my shirley poppies flower, it is Basil who comes back with them. (p. 125)

There are late joys just as there are early joys. Young, who has time to look at the light shine through a shirley poppy? The outer world is only an immense resonance for one's own feelings. But in middle age, afternoon light marbling a white wall may take on the quality of revelation. (p. 180)

FROM *JOURNAL OF A SOLITUDE* (1970–1971)

.... (ง่เง่เ)

On the way back [from a poetry reading in at a new Unitarian church in Brattleboro], I stopped to see Perley Cole, my dear old friend, who is dying, separated from his wife, and has just been moved from a Dickensian nursing home into what seems like a far better one. He grows more transparent every day, a skeleton or nearly. Clasping his hand, I fear to break a bone. Yet the only real communication between us now (he is very deaf) is a handclasp. I want to lift him in my arms and hold him like a baby. He is dying a terribly lonely death. Each time I see him he says, "It is rough" or "I did not think it would end like this."

I like to think that this last effort of Perley's had a certain ease about it, a game compared to the hard work of his farming years, and a game where his expert knowledge and skill could be well used. How he enjoyed teasing me about my ignorance!

Everywhere I look about this place [Sarton's home in Nelson] I see his handiwork: the three small trees by a granite boulder that he pruned and trimmed so they pivot the whole meadow; the new shady border he dug out for me one of the last days he worked here; the pruned-out stone wall. . . . What is done here has to be done over and over and needs the dogged strength of a man like Perley. I could have never managed it alone. We cherished this piece of land together, and fought together to bring it to some semblance of order and beauty.

While he scythed and trimmed, I struggled in somewhat the same way at my desk here, and we were each aware of the companionship. We each looked forward to noon, when I could stop for the day and he sat on a high stool in the kitchen, drank a glass or two of sherry with me, said, "Court's in session!" and then told me some tall tale he had been cogitating all morning.

It was a strange relationship, for he knew next to nothing about my life, really; yet below all the talk we recognized each other as the same kind. He enjoyed my anger as much as I enjoyed his. Perhaps that was part of it. Deep down there was understanding, not of the facts of our lives so much as of our essential natures. Even now in his hard, lonely end he has immense dignity. But I wish there were some way to make it easier. I leave him with bitter resentment against the circumstances of this death. "I know. But I do not approve. And I am not resigned" [Edna St. Vincent Millay's, "Dirge Without Music" (1928)]. (pp. 13–15)

September 21st
  Yesterday, Sunday, was Perley Cole's birthday. I went to see him in the afternoon and took him some pajamas. This time we were able to have a little talk. He is suffering from the change to a new place, although to an outsider this seems such an improvement on the horrible old one, that dirty old farmhouse sinking into the ground, and the atmosphere of lies there and of neglect, a place where more than one child has simply abandoned a senile parent, buried him alive. But Perley had put out roots there, had to, to keep his sense of himself. And now those roots have been torn away. (p. 21)

Eliot's statement comes back to me these days:

> Teach us to care and not to care
> Teach us to sit still.

It is there in Mahler's *Der Abschied*, which I play again every autumn (Bruno Walter with Kathleen Ferrier). But in Mahler it is a cry of loss, a long lyrical cry just *before* letting go, at least until those last long phrases that suggest peace, renunciation. But I think of it as the golden leaves and the brilliant small red maple that shone transparent against the shimmer of the lake yesterday when I went over to have a picnic with Helen Milbank. (p. 34)

Why is it that poetry always seems to me so much more a true work of the soul than prose? I never feel elated after writing a page of prose, though I have written good things on concentrated will, and at least in a novel the imagination is fully engaged. Perhaps it is that prose is earned and poetry given. Both can be revised almost indefinitely. I do not mean to say that I do not work at poetry. When I am really inspired I can put a poem through a hundred drafts and keep my excitement. But this sustained battle is possible only when I am in a state of grace, when the deep channels are open, and when they are, when I am both profoundly stirred and balanced, then poetry comes as a gift from powers beyond my will.

I have often imagined that if I were in solitary confinement for an indefinite time and knew that no one would ever read what I wrote, I would still write poetry, but I would not write novels. Why? Perhaps because the poem is primarily a dialogue with the self and the novel a dialogue with others. They come from entirely different modes of being. I suppose I have written novels to find out what I *thought* about something and poems to find out what I *felt* about something. (pp. 40–41)

The delights of the poet as I jotted them down turned out to be light, solitude, the natural world, love, time, creation itself. Suddenly after the months of depression I am fully alive in all these areas, and awake. (p. 48)

My father was theoretically a feminist, but when it came down to the nitty gritty of life he expected everything to be done for him, of course, by his wife. It was taken for granted that "his work" must come before anything else. He was both a European bourgeois in upbringing and a man of the nineteenth century, so my mother didn't have a prayer. My father didn't like her to work and never gave her credit for it, even in some years when she was designing embroidered dresses for Belgart in Washington, D.C., and made more money than he did. Her conflict— and it was acute—came from her deep belief in what he wanted to do and at the same time resentment of his attitude toward her and his total lack of understanding of what he asked of her. . . . Women are at last becoming persons first and wives second, and that is as it should be. (pp. 56–57)

Thinking of writers I cherish—Traherne, George Herbert, Simone Weil, and the novelists Turgenev, Trollope, Henry James, Virginia Woolf, E. M. Forster, all of them modest, private, "self-actualizers"—I see that they are all outside the main stream of what is expected *now*. The moderate human voice, what might be called "the human milieu"—this is supremely unfashionable and appears even to be irrelevant. But there always have been and always will be people who can breathe only there and who are starved for nourishment. I am one of those readers and I am also one who can occasionally provide this food. That is all that really matters to me this morning. (p. 68)

My own belief is that on regards oneself, if one is a serious writer, as an instrument for experiencing. Life—all of it—flows through this instrument and is distilled through it into works of art. How one lives as a private person is intimately bound into the work. And at some point I believe one has to stop holding back for fear of alienating some imaginary reader or real relative or friend, and come out with personal truth. If we are to understand the human condition, and if we are to accept ourselves in all the complexity, self-doubt, extravagance of feeling, guilt, joy, the slow freeing of the self to its full capacity for action and creation, both as human being and as artist, we have to know all we can about each other, and we have to be willing to go naked. (p. 77)

How unnatural the imposed view, imposed by a puritanical ethos, that passionate love belongs only to the young, that people are dead from the neck down by the time they are forty, and that any deep feeling, any passion after that age, is either ludicrous or revolting! The

French have always known that our capacity for loving mellows and ripens, and love if it is any good at all gets better with age. Perhaps it is not the puritan in us who has spread this myth. Perhaps it is just the opposite; the revolt against puritanism has opened up a new ethos where sex is the god, and thus the sexual athlete is the true hero. Here the middle-aged or old are at a disadvantage. Where we have the advantage is in loving itself—we know so much more; we are so much better able to handle anxiety, frustration, or even our own romanticism; and deep down we have such a store of tenderness. These should be the Mozartian years.

On the surface my work has not looked radical, but perhaps it will be seen eventually that in a "nice, quiet, noisy way" I have been trying to say radical things gently so that they may penetrate without shock. The fear of homosexuality is so great that it took courage to write *Mrs. Stevens [Hears the Mermaids Singing]*, to write a novel about a woman homosexual who is not a sex maniac, a drunkard, a drug-taker, or in any way repulsive. . . . (pp. 90–91)

[In *Psychological Reflections*, Carl] Jung says, "The serious problems in life are never fully solved. If ever they should appear to be so it is a sure sign that something has been lost. The meaning and purpose of a problem seem to lie not in its solution but in our working at it incessantly. This alone preserves us from stultification and petrifaction." And so, no doubt, with the problems of a solitary life.

After I had looked for a while at that daffodil before I got up, I asked myself the question, "What do you want of your life?" and I realized with a start of recognition and terror, "Exactly what I have—but to be commensurate, to handle it all better."

Yet it is not those fits of weeping that are destructive. They clear the air, as Herbert says so beautifully:

> Poets have wronged poor storms: such days are best;
> They purge the air without, within the breast.

What is destructive is impatience, haste, expecting too much too fast. (p. 101)

We have had to accept civilized man as the most cruel of all animals, to recognize that, given absolute power, we all become sadists (the German camps, Lieutenant Calley, et cetera), that wickedness is not a religious concept useful to terrify people into submission but an absolute reality, that each of us battles within the self. (p. 176)

August 3rd
[Sarton describes her father as a "typical bourgeois Belgian." To his wife he doled out a monthly allowance that was never quite enough, and would not discuss money matters with her.] Money, from the start, had been the wound in this marriage, a poisoned and poisonous wound. I suppose it is because I suffered so much from it myself, from knowing too much about my mother's sleepless nights of anxiety about bills, that I myself am quite irresponsible (at least by my father's standards) about money. I believe it must flow through me as food does, be spent as it is earned, be given away, be turned into flowers and books and beautiful things, be given to people who are creators or in need, never be counted except as what it is—a counter against more life of one kind or another. It must remain convertible, not allowed to lie fallow. Probably I talk too much about it like someone who has been brought up repressed about sex and tells risqué jokes as a sign of freedom. (p. 185)

There is only one real deprivation, I decided this morning, and that is not to be able to give one's gifts to those one loves most. In the months when X seemed withdrawn what was hardest to handle was the feeling I had that it no longer meant very much [for her] to hear me read a poem. The gift turned inward, unable to be given, becomes a heavy burden, even sometimes a kind of poison. It is as though the flow of life were backed up. (p. 191)

And what would I do without the evening news on TV? It is not only that I am passionately concerned about what is going on, but equally that the coming into the house of human faces seems like a necessity when I have been alone here all day.

There is no doubt that solitude is a challenge and to maintain balance within it a precarious business. But I must not forget that, for me, being with people or even with one beloved person for any length of time without solitude is even worse. I lose my center. I feel dispersed, scattered, in pieces. I must have time alone in which to mull over any encounter, and to extract its juice, its essence, to understand what has really happened to me as a consequence of it. (pp. 195–96)

Because of various encounters recently I am haunted by Basil de Selincourt's remark to me years ago, "You Americans give too much." How unconscious we are, often, that giving may actually be asking, asking at the very least for attention. I am sure I err in this way myself. This kind of giving for selfish reasons often ends in frustration and even in recrimination: "I have given you so much. Why don't you answer or respond?" which is to say, "When I love you so much, why can't you love me?" There are times lately when I dream only of disappearing, taking another name, settling in to some place where no one would recognize me or care. I suffer because I know too much about the people who project their needs onto me (often people I have never seen who regard me as an intimate friend and who pour out their lives, taking it for granted that I must care). I have been there myself, and so I too give too much. I create the illusion of caring out of compassion and out of guilt—and that only makes matters worse. For then the reckoning comes—the hurt question, "Why did you answer at all if you didn't mean to take me into your life?"

Many years ago I had a vivid dream after Virginia Woolf's suicide. I dreamt that I saw her walking in the streets of a provincial town, unrecognized, unknown, and somehow guessed that she had not committed suicide at all, but had decided that she had to disappear, go under as her famous self, and start again.

Last night I skimmed through the new edition of *The Bridge of Years* just to see how it tasted now after twenty-five years. Not too bad, although I would not write like that now. I have pared my style down. It is less obviously "poetic" these days. I was struck by this statement made by Paul: "It takes a long time, all one's life, to learn to love one person well—with enough distance, with enough humility, he thought."

Yesterday Judy and I talked about this very thing in relation to Z, who has been such a trial these last days. Perhaps the greatest gift we can give to another human being is detachment. Attachment, even that which imagines it is selfless, *always* lays some burden on the other person. How to learn to love in such a light, airy way that there is no burden? (pp. 200–201)

I begin to have intimations, now, of a return to some deep self that has been too absorbed and too battered to function for a long time. That self tells me that I was meant to live alone, meant to write the poems for others—poems that seldom in my life have reached the one person for whom they were intended. (p. 207)

FROM *HOUSE BY THE SEA: A JOURNAL* (1974–1975)

.... (ง|ง)

[In 1973 Sarton moved from Nelson to York, Maine, where she now resides.]

People who say they do not want to pick flowers and have them indoors (the idea being, I suppose, that they are more "natural" in the garden than in the house) don't realize that indoors one can really look at a single flower, undistracted, and that this meditation brings great rewards. The flowers on my desk have been lit up one by one as by a spotlight as the sun slowly moves. And once more I am in a kind of ecstasy at the beauty of light through petals. . . .

I come back to my happiness here. I have never been so happy in my life, never for such a sustained period, for I have now been in this house by the sea for a year and a half. I have not said enough about what it is to wake each day to the sunrise and to that great tranquil open space as I lie in my bed, having breakfast, often quietly thinking for a half hour. That morning amplitude, silence, the sea, all make for a radical change in tempo. Or is it, too, that I am growing older, and have become a little less compulsive about "what has to be done"? I am taking everything with greater ease. When I was younger there was far more conflict, conflict about my work, the desperate need to "get through," and the conflict created by passionate involvement with people. There are compensations for not being in love—solitude grows richer for me every year. It is not a matter of being a recluse . . . I shall never be that; I enjoy and need my friends too much. But it is a matter of detachment, of not being quite so easily pulled out of my own orbit by violent attraction, of being able to enjoy without needing to possess. (p. 61)

Sunday, August 3rd
(on Greenings Island)
My mother's birthday. Even two years ago it would have been celebrated here, but now dear Anne [Thorp] is beyond that kind of focus and when I mentioned it there was little or no response. Anne is one of the very few people I ever see now who knew and loved my mother and it felt like a second death at breakfast this morning—one so loved no longer alive in the consciousness of Anne. . . .

I think of my mother, late in her life having to take on the housework and cooking, the immense daily effort, and the determination not to be "downed." Yet she was in the last years like a wild bird caught in a net, struggling, struggling, and at times only a kind of fury kept her going. . . . Growing old is, of all things we experience, that which takes the most courage, and at a time when we have the least resources, especially with which to meet frustration. (pp. 126–128)

Yesterday I had a letter from a young woman who is living alone, a film maker of some reputation. She wants to do a film on people who live alone, and will come next week to talk about her plans. I gather she has some doubts about the solitary life. I told her that I feel it is not for the young (she is only thirty-three). I did not begin to live alone till I was forty-five, and had "lived" in the sense of passionate friendships and love affairs very richly for twenty-five years. I had a huge amount of life to think about and to digest, and, above all, I was a *person* by then and knew what I wanted of my life. The people we love are built into us. Every day I am suddenly aware of something someone taught me long ago—or just yesterday—of some certainty and self-awareness that grew out of conflict with someone I loved enough to try to encompass, however painful that effort may have been. (p. 135)

Yesterday Ed and Susan Kenney came for lunch. I had looked forward so much to their visit, and it was a beautiful hot, clear day, comfortable because of the low humidity, and a bright blue sea to welcome them. We plunged at once into talk about Elizabeth Bowen. Ed has written an excellent monograph on her work. (I discovered him through his review of her posthumous book *Pictures and Conversations* in *The New Republic* and had written to thank him for it.) Ed and Susan saw Elizabeth in Hythe and described the tiny house where she lived. The second time they went, she was ill and received them in bed, but her great gift for instant intimacy was at work as she lay with their year-old Jamie beside her. I keep that image of the dying old woman with little Jamie. And I was comforted by Ed saying she had written him to warn that she longed to hear but that she simply did not write letters. It may partly explain her long silence as far as I am concerned. (pp. 139–140)

Charles Barber arrived. . . . With so much grief and hard luck around, it is lovely to be with someone on the brink of a great adventure, bursting with joy . . . and it does seem a miracle that he found a way of getting to college in England, after all.

I looked at his lovely, but unformed, face, the face of a very young man (he is nineteen) and wondered what life would do to tauten and shape it. He is so open and full of sweetness now, but thought has not yet written anything on his smooth face, nor pain tightened his mouth. (pp. 145–46)

When the news of the seven-year persecution of Martin Luther King by the FBI came out yesterday and the day before, I felt rather *sick*. We live in such a dirty world, and as individuals seem more and more helpless to change it. When I am tired, it all becomes overwhelming like a dismal fog that never lifts. Of course, Franco's death the other day had reminded me of the idealism, the lifting up of so much courage thirty-six years ago in the rallying of youth from all over the world to help the Republic—long, long ago. Then there was still hope and now there is not. Then, before the Nazi camps, we could still believe in the goodness of man. Now man looks more and more like the murderer of all life, animals too—he is the killer of whales and of his own species— the death bringer. Under everything I do here is this sense that there is no foundation anymore. In what do we believe? can we believe? On what to stand firm? There has to be something greater than each individual—greater, yet something that gives him the sense that his life is vital to the whole, that what he does affects the whole, has meaning. (pp. 167–168)

I feel now very much at peace, even happy, as I start a new year with poetry. It is the first time in three years that I have dared look down into the depths or play records while I am working. Until now music has been too painful . . . if I opened that door I began to weep and couldn't stop. I had been traumatized by the final year at Nelson.

My experience with senility has been gentle with Judy, but it was traumatic with Dr. Farnham. For mental torture the paranoia of one's psychiatrist directed against oneself is pretty bad. I was accused of trying to murder her. Lawyers were involved. But at least some of the anguish was transformed into *As We Are Now*, so it was not all waste. What deep experience, however terrible, is? And I think I came out stronger and more sure of my own powers than I have ever been.

The sea has erased the pain. I have never been so happy as I am here, and I welcome the new year with great expectations. Since they are expectations that I can myself fulfill and have to do with inner life and with the beauty of the world around me, I dare to say this. (p. 176)

After writing the poem I spent an hour cutting and reading aloud from *As We Are Now* for the evening at Notre Dame University when, at their suggestion, I shall take half the hour for that and half for poems. It's an experiment . . . I have never before read prose for an audience in such a sustained way. But the book is, as one critic pointed out, a *récit*, so it should work. I was a little dismayed to see at what a pitch of intensity it lives, that book. Now three years later that kind of intensity, which came from anguish, is so remote that I can hardly imagine how it felt. I am far happier now, but in some ways less alive, and I miss that acute aliveness. (p. 197)

I wonder why it is that "inspirational" writing such as appears in *The Reader's Digest* and in religious magazines so often, far from consoling or "uplifting," makes me feel angry and upset. Most of the platitudes uttered are true, after all. But the fact is that this kind of superficial piety covers the real thing with a sugary icing meant to make it more palatable. It makes me feel sick. And the sickness is because I feel cheated. It debases God (by making him a kind of universal pal), and sentimentalizes Jesus, *and*—what is more dangerous and unchristian—it makes its communicants feel superior, part of an élite club where the saved can gather, shutting everyone else out. Into all this Tillich enters like a cleansing, ruthless wind. The thing that moved me so deeply when I read *The Shaking of the Foundations* came as an answer to my long anguish over the absence of God. The chapter called "Waiting" begins

> Both the Old and New Testaments describe our existence in relation to God as one of waiting. . . . The condition of man's relation to God is first of all one of *not* having, *not* seeing, *not* knowing, and *not* grasping. A religion in which this is forgotten, no matter how ecstatic or active or reasonable, replaces God by its own creation of an image of God. . . . I am convinced that much of the rebellion against Christianity is due to the overt or veiled claim of the Christians to possess God, and therefore, also, to the loss of this element of waiting, so decisive for the prophets and the apostles. . . . They did not possess God, they waited for Him. For how can God be possessed? Is God a thing that can be grasped and known among other things? Is God less than a human person? We always have to wait for a human being. (pp. 207–208)

I had to go to Cambridge and take away everything of mine from 14 Wright Street, where Judy and I spent ten happy years before I moved to Nelson. I had left paintings, hundreds of books, and some furniture because I didn't want to spoil that house as long as Judy lived there. . . .

As I talked [to Judy's nephew], it all came back—our life together in that house and two others in Cambridge before it, for over twenty years, and I was happy to remind myself of the remarkable person she was, her dark eyes that sometimes reflected somber moods and always suggested a strong inner life, as was indeed true, for Judy was a birthright Quaker and, in a most unassuming way, a good example of what being a Quaker means. She carried a heavy teaching load as professor of English literature at Simmons College, corrected papers till late at night, and was off to school by seven in the morning. Nevertheless, she spent many summers of volunteer work for the Quakers, once working with the Japanese Americans we treated so badly during World War II, and, after we met, teaching English with recently emigrated Latvians. Her Quakerhood showed itself in little ways too in her moderation in daily living . . . she never had more than one drink, for example, one drink for sociability, and that was enough. But, above all, she was a real Quaker in her tolerance of and quiet grace before my extravagance of temperament, and that is partly why our relationship endured.

Judy was born rich in the safe gentle world of West Newton, but by the time she was nineteen, a freshman at Smith College, that world had cracked under her feet in terrible ways—her mother's complete breakdown—she lived out the rest of her life in a sanatorium—and her father's bankruptcy. Charles Matlack was a charming cultivated man who had inherited a fortune with not the slightest trace of business acumen with which to invest it, and the results were tragic. His eldest daughter had married very young, fortunately, but Judy and her younger sister were faced with not only the loss of their mother, but the necessity to earn a living at once. Judy managed to work her way through Smith with the help of scholarships and then embarked on a career of teaching, after a winter at Oxford University, thanks to the generosity of a friend.

Judy always had a genius for friendship, and I think it came partly from her marvelous capacity for really listening to other people. She shared *with* her friends in a rare way, and it was just this that had drawn me to her when we first met as fellow lodgers in Santa Fe.

We had a beautiful life together. In the winter she was away all day while I worked at writing and waited happily for her to come home for tea and a little walk before she went upstairs to read papers and prepare her classes. But in the summer more than once we took off for Europe

. . . one memorable trip after World War II, when we drove down through the Dordogne to the South with two English friends, starved for sunlight and good food and France itself after the long hard years of war in London. And after I moved to Nelson we still spent all holidays together and Judy came to me for a month in the summer. So what is unknitting now, as she grows more and more absent, had been knitted together for many years, and is still the warp and woof, the deepest relationship I have known. (pp. 208–211)

The island is a dying world, at least as we knew it, under Anne's command for the past twenty years. Now she is senile too, worse off than Judy. To be the witness of this decline in two women who have been rocks in my life, to feel the quicksand under my feet, was not easy. (p. 282)

FROM *RECOVERING: A JOURNAL* (1978–1979)

.... (ꞌꞀꞌꞀꞀ)

   . . . For families are often not in perfect communion, and Judy and I for over thirty years have been able to rest on a foundation of wordless understanding. There is no one now with whom I can feel perfectly "at home" in just the way I did with Judy. She knew me, warts and all, and had long ago accepted me, warts and all, as I had her, for this was a true love. (p. 11)

To close the door on pain is to miss the chance for growth, isn't it? Nothing that happens to us, even the most terrible shock, is unusable, and everything has somehow to be built into the fabric of the personality, just as food has to be built in. (p. 13)

Tenderness is the grace of the heart, as style is the grace of the mind, I decided when I couldn't sleep last night. Both have something to do with quality, the quality of feeling, the quality of reasoning. (p. 16)

The *Times* has sneered at or attacked every book of mine since *Faithful Are the Wounds*—that got a rave and I am everlastingly grateful to Brendan Gill who wrote it—except *Crucial Conversations* which Doris Grumbach reviewed thoughtfully. So the effect of this last public beating [the *Times* review of *A Reckoning*] was as bad as it was, I think, because it was cumulative. You can rise above one or two public humiliations such as this, but finally after ten or more it gets to you. I felt finished. I felt that I would not again expose myself to such pain. I felt like a deer shot down by hunters. (pp. 20–21)

One of the first letters that came in on *[A Reckoning]* was from Eda LeShan and it meant a great deal to me because this was word from the horse's mouth. She says in part:

> I have been reading *A Reckoning* for about three days during which time I had a great many appointments and assignments, but the reality of my days had nothing to do with any of it—my only absorption was following a dying woman's quest for identity.
>
> I am convinced that your book is the most important statement about the experience of dying since Tolstoy's *Death of Ivan Illych*. It is a subject about which my husband and I know a good deal—he especially, since he worked on a research project for about twenty years in which he worked with the dying, constantly.
>
> . . . In his work with terminal cancer patients (psychotherapy) the search was always to help the person find his or her own authenticity, sense of personal identity—and this was important and necessary, no matter what the outcome. What you have done so magnificently as an artist, he struggled to do through scientific research—but we always knew the artist's vision was clearer, more necessary and ultimately all that counted. (pp. 21–22)

I have been in Paradise all month reading Virginia Woolf's fourth volume of letters and the biography of E. M. Forster, grazing with immense pleasure in those rich pastures. . . .

My heaven is Bloomsbury, as Virginia Woolf so perfectly described it in a letter to her nephew, "We are merely wild, odd, innocent, artless, eccentric and industrious beyond words." The richness and variety of what they produced is simply astounding, from Woolf's and

Forster's novels to Keynes' economic theories and Leonard's, to the paintings of Vanessa Bell and Duncan Grant, to Roger Fry's art criticism, to Strachey's style as a historian. They were incredibly productive, but the main charm is not that, but is, I think, the honesty, courage, and taste with which they honored and explored personal relationships. . . .

They had such a vivid sense of life that I have been haunted for forty years or more by that laughter of Virginia Woolf's, as I heard it when I went to Tavistock Square for tea, like some saving grace never to be found again. Why was the conversation so good? Partly because everything including private life could be openly discussed (Virginia Woolf loved to pin one down to what was really happening in one's life), and partly because the frame of reference was so wide. I got a little taste of it long ago, and it has set a standard that I have never met since. The sheer energy required to work as hard as they did and still be as social as they were is rare. I could never myself sustain the pace that V. Woolf did. Astonishing fertility. (pp. 47–48)

. . . I went down to Phillips Academy at Andover for two nights to talk to faculty and students and read poems as the Stearns Memorial lecturer. I set out in a happy frame of mind, looking forward to delicious meals at the Inn: a kind of holiday. This time the poems I had chosen to read were built around the theme, "The Joys and Hazards of Being a Poet," how to keep oneself open and vulnerable and still keep one's balance. That is it in a nutshell. It is not easy. Six of the good poets of roughly my generation have been suicides. If I have survived it may be because I can write novels, journals, and so on in the dry spells. I have the tools for climbing out of depression as I am doing now.

It all began well with cocktails with the English faculty and dinner at the Inn, followed by an informal talk about teaching poetry around Kelly Wise's fireplace. But after midnight I woke in a cold sweat and felt so ill and so strange that I thought for an hour that it must be a heart attack and for about fifteen minutes I believed I was dying. My hair was plastered to my head, my pajamas soaked. My teeth were chattering though the room had been uncomfortably hot. Finally I threw up repeatedly for an hour and got some relief. At three that morning it seemed impossible to read poems at ten to the students and give a big speech at eight that night. But by morning I was able to swallow some tea and slept till nine again and finally dressed and went downstairs. I found that I could manage, read animal poems to a kind and attentive group of students, and realized that I was going to make it. I slept for the rest of the day, and the speech went well that evening. Oh the relief of that! Of having a voice and finding the energy to project to a full house, after all, the guardian angel not far off. For how could I have done it without her help?

Next day I signed books at the Andover Bookstore, under perfect circumstances, for I sat at a round table by an open fire with chairs placed around it so people could sit down while they waited. A fine crowd showed up including a small child, a girl about eight who solemnly handed me a poem she had spoken and her mother written down for her. It was a good poem about the sun. A grandmother came with her little granddaughter bearing two red and white tulips for me. . . . What is difficult these occasions is to get the names one is to inscribe rightly spelled and at the same time pay attention to the *person*. Each has something he or she wants to tell me about himself or herself, about what some book or poem of mine has meant, so one has, in about sixty seconds, to recognize, to acknowledge, to respond on several levels at once. I was tired at the end of an hour and a half, but it was well worth the effort.

How happy I was to get home, unpack, read the mail, and then lie down with Tamas and Bramble and be very still for an hour, slowly "coming back" into myself. (pp. 49–50)

The day was happy, too, because after four months, the *New York Times* printed a long splendid letter from the LeShans to defend *A Reckoning* against Dickstein's mean review. I had given up hope that any one of the twenty or more letters I know were sent in, would be published. Dickstein in her answer to this sticks to her guns that it is a concealed homosexual novel.

As I think over all the letters I have had on this book the one that pleased me the most, I think, was from Emery Neff who taught comparative literature at Columbia (he and his wife among my dear Nelson friends.) He says:

> *A Reckoning* liberates from primal fears: fear of sexual deviation, fear of dying. Laura frees herself from resentment against her mother (conventional sex repression) and from the hospital, a mechanism for unnatural prolongation of life. All in a small space, vividly detailed. *De Nobis Fabula.* You assure us, in our eighties, that we can to a large extent control the circumstances of our dying and forgive wounds received in the course of living.

Dickstein failed to see the wood for the trees. And because of her misuse of a poem ["My Sisters, O My Sisters"] to prove her point I cannot but believe that she had made an *a priori* judgment.

Last night reading Virginia Woolf's journal written at the time *Jacob's Room* came out, I noted, "The only review I am anxious about is the one in the *Times Literary Supplement:* not that it will be the most intelligent, but it will be the most read and I can't bear people to see me downed in public." *Exactly.* (pp. 66–67)

So many people write me that the journals and memoirs and the poems are the better part of my work. And I always remember Virginia Woolf teasing me (when I first met her I had published only one book—of poems) about how much easier poetry is than the writing of novels. I suspect the journal as a form because it is too easy, too quick perhaps. But I still believe that a few of my novels will prove to have value in the end, *Mrs. Stevens, Faithful Are the Wounds, As We Are Now,* and possibly *A Reckoning,* when it comes to be read in depth, and what I actually *said* becomes clear.

The two sins I am accused of in the novels are 1) careless style and 2) over-idealism. "Marriages are not like that." "People do not talk as your characters do," etc. Sometimes letters come as saviors. In the midst of this low feeling about the novels a letter came from my Episcopal minister friend in Chapel Hill saying "You have been a superb writer for a long time, haven't you? I suppose I am first of all conscious of your style—because I am sensitive to this trait, perhaps too much so. But there it is, and I am filled with joy when a writer's style is excellent."

I have worked toward a transparent style, as simple and plain as possible, a tool with which to communicate complex relationship. When I began to write I was praised for a "poetic style," but it is just that I have tried to get rid of as too self-conscious. I have come to believe that too elaborate a style gets in the way, dazzles, but makes a wall between writer and reader. I try for a flowing line that suits breath and the voice, that does not stumble, and people discover this when they read a prose work aloud. (Carol Heilbrun says she did so when she read part of *I Knew a Phoenix* aloud to a class one day.)

The other question is more complex—or maybe simpler, who knows?—and has to do with a vision of life. But I might add that all dialogue in fiction has to be stylized to some extent to give an illusion of reality. No one has ever talked like a Hemingway character though after he had created the pared-down speech he uses, life sometimes imitated art. Real people talking are apt to be verbose and repetitive. Virginia Woolf uses to great effect sentences that float off into silence, half-finished. But actually living people rarely do this either. . . . in all cases of real art, the writer does have a recognizable voice. I believe that I do.

As for idealism, who is not flawed and human and complex? There are certainly no saints. If the vision of life communicated were unreal why does it speak to so many people of all ages, both sexes and all backgrounds? This is why the letters, whatever burden they present, are really what keep me from despair. Here is one sentence—what a marvelous letter it is that makes its point in a single sentence!—this from a director of Nursing in a Vancouver hospital: "The human and artistic integrity of *A Reckoning* is a reprieve. I am afraid we were almost Kubler-Ross'd to death. Thank you." (pp. 77–79)

I have hoped to provide the bridge between women of all ages and kinds, between mothers and daughters, between sisters, between women as friends; (the friendship between Ellen and Christina in *Kinds of Love* as an example), between the old and the young (Mar and Mrs. Stevens) and I have wished to be thought of in human terms. The vision of life in my work is not limited to one segment of humanity or another and it has little to do with sexual proclivity. It does have to do with love, and love has many forms and is not easy or facile in any of them. (p. 81)

In my one free day in San Francisco Sheila Moon, a poet and Jungian therapist, gave me a whole day, and my heart's desire which was to go to Muir Woods, the redwood forest in Marin County. I was hungry for the silence of the huge trees, unlike any other, awesome silence because the trees are alive and have been alive for so long, so it is not like a cathedral built of stones, but has the same effect. People talk in hushed voices, and one hears nothing but the sound of the water, the brook that runs through the valley. We walked slowly and talked or were silent, and again I felt the power of presence of someone who has thought and felt deeply and in a wide range. Sheila is a little older than I. We talked about old age. She feels that the pain is not less, but the joys perhaps are greater. I believe that to be true. The pure joys, the joy of a wild flower or a bird, or simply the silence of trees is there in old age because we are less distracted by personal emotion. Is that it? (pp 86–87)

My sixty-seventh birthday. A perfect, still day, sunshine for a change, and an unutterably blue, pale Fra Angelico sea. The daffodils are out in great garlands lighting up the dark brown field, and inside the fence there is a border of hyacinths, scillas, a few daffodils, and a trout plant just coming out, brilliant as the border in a tapestry. Against the wall on the terrace I did get the pansies in and now the blue windflowers are coming out.

I woke before six thinking of my mother who on this day sixty-seven years ago was determined to get strawberry plants in and went right on, lying down with labor pains then getting up to finish. I was born at ten-thirty in the evening after a hard labor, hard partly because the chauvinist brute of a doctor sat in an armchair with his feet up, smoking a cigar (!) and saying periodically "Poussez, Madame, poussez!" They brought her a bunch of lilies of the valley from the garden . . . today they are not yet in sight, but this is a late spring. (p. 98)

The day before yesterday as I read the *Times* I came upon Marynia Farnham's obituary. It is a blessing to know that she has been allowed to go at last, after these last years when she did not recognize anyone, talked only to herself in a strange singing monotone, the words incomprehensible. Now the long decline can be forgotten and the rich snowy days can come back when I used to drive over to Winchester to drink champagne in her great room filled with works of art, listen to music, and talk. The real Marynia can come back into memory, her flashing dark eyes, her laughter, and her salty wisdom.

I had been very lonely in Nelson when I first met her, and I shall never forget walking into that big room the first time . . . I felt I had come home at last. This was after I had been her patient and we had begun to be friends. She seemed, with her whippets around her, like some lady in a tapestry. Unbelievable in the midst of the cultural poverty with which I was surrounded to be in the presence again of such a civilized life and ethos! Not since Edith Kennedy, who had been dead thirty years or more then, had I found a person with whom I could talk about everything in depth, and who could bring to our exchanges such a wide frame of reference. In that room I learned a great deal. For her I wrote many poems, a whole book that has never been published. Let me place [one] of them here, in memoriam.

THE PLACE BEYOND ACTION

In these airy balances
Between music and poetry
Between kinds of love
And kinds of deprivation,
How softly we must tread!
Of course you, secret person,

Learned long ago to walk the tightrope
Between attachment and detachment,
Learned never to stumble
On its perilous tension . . .

Nevertheless,
Attentive to a whisper,
I know your passion
And feel your violence.

Sometimes I love the somber person
Who rises up from a glass of wine
To curse the "cultural desert"
Where we both live,
God knows why.

Sometimes I hate the somber person
Who makes me feel like a desert
Where nothing can bloom,
For I am the prisoner
Of what I see
And can do nothing to change.

You are alone and should not be,
Rich Ceres, great giver,
That is the truth,
And it is hardly to be borne.
I bear it with an ill grace,
Trying to remember
Your valor, resilience,
The fertile mind,
The changing moods
Like clouds over a landscape
Of hills and lakes, light-shot,
Never at rest, expecting surprises.

In the airy balance
Where we sometimes achieve communion
It will always be possible
To move outside the deprivations,
Yours and mine,
Into a curious detached region
Natural to you, achieved by me,
That is music, that is poetry.
It is the place beyond action
And even sometimes beyond thought—
At worst unnatural
So much must be denied,
At best, nourishing,
So much has been accepted.

It all ended badly, because of senility, but what does that matter now? Now I can come back to the essence, and the essence was life-giving, and remains so. (pp. 105–106, 108–109)

Martha and Marita [Martha Wheelock and Marita Simpson] and their crew, six men and women in all, have been here since Friday filming and recording. By great good luck the first three days gave us ideal filming weather, dry and cool with lovely light splashing through leaves on the walk through the woods, and one section of interview outside on the terrace where the wisteria is at perfection. Otherwise it's an in-between season here, the greens still fresh and brilliant, but no flowers until the azaleas and rhododendron come out, then iris and peonies.

It has been a joyous experience for me to be present and watch how the group works together and with what delicacy and consideration they have treated me. Of course we have been working on tiny segments, half an hour to get cameras up for a minute's walk with Tamas, so it's not possible yet to imagine what it will all look like in the end. I feel sure that the surroundings will come through like a poem, but am less certain about my part in it. One difficulty is that there is such a large body of work involved, how to choose what is most important, also which poems to read. Martha and Marita have managed, in spite of their necessary preoccupation with technical matters and the minutiae of setting the scene, to create an atmosphere so appreciative that I have not felt self-conscious but able to transcend physical weight and old age, and to feel transparent and alive. I am grateful. . . .

One thing I have not managed to talk about in the film is why strict form in poetry still has value and always will. We forget, perhaps, that poetry began eons ago and was associated with dance. Meter is how the body still gets involved on the subconscious level. We no longer dance to poetry or as we listen to it, but way below the conscious level, the beat opens doors. Why when the beat is so much a part of popular music, does it seem "old-fashioned" to use it as a tool in poetry? (pp. 111–112)

Because passionate love breaks down walls and at first does it in such a sovereign way, we are rarely willing to admit how little that initial barrier-breaking is going to count when it comes to the slow, difficult, accepting of each other, when it comes to the irritations and abrasions, and the collisions, too, between two isolated human beings who want to be. joined in a lasting relationship. So the walls go up again. The moment's vision is clouded, and mostly, I believe, by the fear of pain, our own and that of the other's, by the fear of rejection. To be honest is to expose wounds, and also to wound. There is no preventing that. Union on a deep level is so costly that it very rarely takes place. But withdrawal, censorship, the wish to keep the surfaces smooth because any eruption spells danger and must therefore be prevented, is costly also. Censorship simply drives conflict deeper inside. What is never discussed does not for that reason cease to exist. On the contrary, it may fester and finally become a killing poison. (p. 115)

For most of us Eros is an earthquake. There is fear and trembling and, above all, radical change involved . . . it is quite foolish to deny that our sexuality is deeply disturbing at any age. And most of us have a built-in censor to deal with this—too bad. On the other hand to pretend that Eros is not a primordial being of the same order as Earth and Chaos is to trivialize or screen off what has to be faced and experienced if we are to come into our humanity as whole beings, and if we are to reach Agape. Perhaps every serious love affair is the reexperiencing of history—psychic history. (p. 117)

. . . I had imagined that the loss of a breast would create catharsis, that I would emerge like a phoenix from the fire, reborn, with all things made new, especially the pain in my heart. I had imagined that real pain, physical pain, and physical loss would take the place of mental anguish and the loss of love. Not so. It is all to be begun again, the long excruciating journey through pain and rejection, through anger and not understanding, toward some regained sense of my self. I have in the past six months been devalued, as a woman, as a lover, and as a writer. How to build back to a sense of value, of valuing myself again? (p. 119)

So I did ask, and the only hard thing about these days was having to ask for help from the young. I should have remembered what Jean Dominique taught me long ago, that accepting dependence with grace was one of the last lessons we all have to learn. With the help of such tact and understanding, it has turned out to be revelatory. Perhaps it is teaching me to bury the one-pointed heart, that fierce infant demand that there must be one person, my person, on whom I could and must depend. Perhaps it is teaching me to rest lightly on the palms of the many hands that have been lifting me so gently all these days, an ever present sense of thought flowing toward me. I felt when I went into the hospital that I was carrying with me an invisible bunch of flowers, each flower a dear friend. (pp. 120–121)

Not the easiest of times, but I think I am doing well as a physical being at least. It is half past nine, and all night we had a much-needed rain so my anxiety about the parched garden can rest and that is a relief. Since seven I have got my breakfast and washed it up, washed the sheets and put fresh ones on my bed, fresh towels in the bathroom, a fresh dressing on my wound, went down cellar to put the lights on over seedlings down there, and now I am dressed and up here on the third floor for some hours of writing. The hardest thing is letters for the moment, as my head is worse off than my body these days. There appears to be very little psychic juice available—but then it is only thirteen days since the operation.

I have been thinking a lot about the body and what a miracle it is, the extraordinary summoning of aids and defenders and healers so hard at work now mending the big gash where my left breast was. The body is a universe in itself and must be held as sacred as anything in creation, as every miraculous bird and beetle and moth and tiger. It is dangerous to forget the body as sacramental . . . because the minute one does then mutilation, the mutilation of a wound, or simply the mutilation of old age can kill the spirit. An old body when it is loved becomes a sacred treasure; and sex itself must always, it seems to me, come to us as a sacrament and be so used or it is meaningless. The flesh is suffused by the spirit, and it is forgetting this in the act of love-making that creates cynicism and despair.

What I am fighting now is depression, but it is not, I think, wholly and perhaps at all, the result of the shock of a major operation on the body. The body can handle shock with amazing resilience. Shock calls out hidden powers.

It is that I feel devalued and abandoned at the center of my being. I sometimes feel that everyone else manages to grow up and harden in the right way to survive, whereas I have remained a terribly vulnerable infant. When poetry is alive in me I can handle it, use it, feel worthy of being part of the universe. When I can't, as now, when the source is all silted up by pain, I think I should have been done away with at birth. Absurd overreacting to the loss of love. (pp. 121–122)

I have been thinking about that baby in me who has tantrums and cries, trying to accept that it and the wise old woman who I am at times, are part of a single whole. And I have been thinking also that twice in my life people who discovered me through the work, who came to me as admirers and became intimate friends ended by being unable to accept the whole person, the flawed human being because they had somehow falled in love with an image besides which the reality of a living, suffering being who is not perfect, who is temperamental, who "has no surface" as someone has said of me, became disillusioning. (p. 123)

I am thinking of making a list of thing *not* to say to someone recovering from surgery and in a weak state. One of them is surely "count your blessings"—as though one didn't, and as though to discount tragedy. Another is to emphasize that millions of women have had the same problem like saying to a child who has fallen and torn a knee open, "hundreds of children do this every day." You can't lump people together in a large inchoate mass, for that is to diminish each one's selfhood. No two loves are alike, no two deaths, and no two losses: these are paths we travel alone.

What the mastectomy does to each individual woman is, at least temporarily, to attack her womanhood at its most vulnerable, to devalue her in her own eyes as a woman. And each woman has to meet this and make herself whole again in her own way. (It is much harder, I feel sure, for a young woman for obvious reasons.) (p. 131)

We did get some rain two or three days ago, but now I must begin hauling the hoses around again. It does not involve stooping, which is still difficult, and I enjoy it. Is there a greater pleasure than giving drink to the thirsty? It satisfies some atavistic need to take care and the very thought of thirsty roots drinking is reviving to the spirits.

Other recent joys have been a darling letter from a ninety-two-year-old woman who has been reading *The House by the Sea*, is full of life and able to cope in spite of the loss of her dear friend of sixty years. I wonder why it is that letters from the very old and from the very young give me the most pleasure. In the first instance perhaps because it is good to be younger than someone whom one can please, and in the second because it is good to be much older and still able to connect. . . . It has been ground into me by the bitter experiences of last year that I am old, that I must be denied some things, that the door has closed forever on passionate communion with another human being. The mutilated body appears then to be the physical evidence of that fact. But the phoenix rising again from the flames tells me otherwise. The more our bodies fail us, the more naked and more demanding is the spirit, the more open and loving we can become if we are not afraid of what we are and of what we feel. I am not a phoenix yet, but here among the ashes, it may be that the pain is chiefly that of new wings trying to push through. (p. 138)

I would like to believe when I die that I have given myself away like a tree that sows seed every spring and never counts the loss, because it is not loss, it is adding to future life. It is the tree's way of being. Strongly rooted perhaps, but spilling out its treasure on the wind. (p. 140)

My mother's birthday. And for the first time since her death twenty-nine years ago (is that possible?) I have opened the folders of letters and read some of her letters to me. I have dreaded doing this for years but instead of grief, they have brought me deep joy, a reaffirmation of our relationship, which was so rare in its freedom, as though we were intimate friends rather than mother and daughter. For my birthday when I was thirty-one she wrote me a little note,

> Dear heart, I thought of you last night—remembering the hour you were born and the lovely day I had spent in the garden sowing seeds and hiding my pains (which were not bad until much later). I was beautifully alone in the kitchen garden and could curl up on the mossy path in the warm sun till the pain passed and then go right ahead! And I so wondered if you would be a boy or a girl and what you would be like: would you be very intelligent like Daddy and perhaps have little use for me when you grew up? And so on, endlessly, but not painfully. (I wasn't *really* afraid of you) it was a dreamy wondering and with a warm secret conviction that you would be very close to me whatever and whoever you proved to be . . . and I was right, wasn't I? and I haven't held you too tight, dear Pigeon, have I? because

I do count freedom as among the most precious things in the world . . . and so have always wanted it for you. (p. 146)

One thing happened yesterday that seems a miracle, a release at last from a long bondage, for I have been perhaps too aware for too long that, in spite of all I was able to do for Mother in the last months, I failed in one way that I cannot forget, that has haunted me all these years. One day she asked me to sit with her for a while, and I said "I can't" and rushed out of the room in tears. Much of what I tried to suggest in *A Reckoning* about just that need for someone to be there in silence, and perhaps to speak out of the silence, came from this hard haunting memory of what I myself failed to do.

Yesterday I found the letters about my mother, a little bundle of them, written at the time of her death. Among them a letter from Anne Thorp, blessed Anne, who wrote, "In the dear letter your mother wrote she spoke with joy of the imaginative and wonderful sharing of living and dying that you and she had had together."

It is good that I know that now. But I believe that things happen when the time is ripe and perhaps it is right that I was given yesterday that balm, and not before. Failure cannot be erased. It is built in to a life and helps us grow. Failure cannot be erased, but it can be understood. I think today that Mother *understood*, and that has made all the difference. (pp. 150–151)

To see a person for himself or herself, not for one's feelings about them, requires wisdom, and I must assume that it is part of the ascension of true love beyond the initial passion and need. On the way there are frightful resentments and irritations caused by intrinsic differences of temperament and many a marriage or love affair bogs down as a result. How does one achieve perfect detachment? Partly perhaps by accepting the essence of a being for what it is, not wishing to change it, accepting. (p. 163)

I have been thinking about the image of a journey as the image for a love affair and its ending as the coming home to one's self again. The value of loving someone passionately, often a person very unlike one-self, is that one is taken literally out of one's self on a journey into unknown territory. As in a journey to a foreign country there is culture shock; one often feels lonely, even attacked by the differences. One is also all the time in a state of strange excitement, there are glorious moments, unforgettable scenes that make one tremble with joy and surprise, and there are days of great fatigue when all one longs for is home, to be with the familiar that does not ask for stretching to under-stand it, which can be taken for granted. Where one can rest. And above all where one is accepted as one is, not stammering in an unfa-miliar language, not trying desperately to communicate from one ethos to another.

For a week or more I have been in a state of extreme excitement, as though on the brink of revelation. It began at once as soon as I had decided to bring myself to the point of decision and to break off, not to cling out of need and desperation to something that perhaps was never there. The central person focuses the world and when there is no one to be that, one is at first terrified. But once the decision is made that had to be made, one is free at last to go home to the self, that self which has been censored, without even being aware of it, by the effort to please and to become acceptable to the one one loves. Now I believe we can be friends in a clearer air, she and I.

One of the censors that has been at work has been the notion that to be in love at our age is ludicrous and somehow not proper, that pas-sionate love can be banished after sixty shall we say? That is one of the myths that has been around a long time, but it was never true. Love at any age has its preposterous side—that is why it comes as a kind of miracle at any age. It is never commonplace, never to be experienced without a tremor. But to stop arbitrarily the flow of life because of a preconceived idea, any preconceived idea, is to damage the truth of the inner person . . . that is dangerous. Are we not on earth to love each other? And to grow? And how does one grow except through love, except through opening ourselves to other human beings to be fertilized and made new? (pp. 204–205)

Pain is the great teacher. I woke before dawn with this thought. Joy, happiness, and what we take and do not question. They are beyond question, maybe. A matter of being. But pain forces us to think, and to make connections, to sort out what is what, to discover what has been happening to cause it. And, curiously enough, pain draws us to other human beings in a significant way, whereas joy or happiness to some extent, isolates. (p. 208)

I began this journal ten months ago as a way of getting back to my self, of pulling out of last year's depression, and now I am truly on a rising curve. What has changed in a miraculous way is the landscape of the heart, so somber and tormented for over a year that I was not myself. Did letting go last month do it? What has happened, that quite suddenly some weeks ago the landscape became luminous and peaceful, no anger, no irritation, as though the screen that had separated us for so long had simply lifted away as fog sometimes does in these parts? Whatever the cause it feels like a miracle. Perhaps Agape has entered the scene and driven manic-depressive, neurotically dependent Eros away. I feel blest in my love, and able to give blessing as a result.

So it is time for a pause in these reflections and to welcome joy and praise back, so long absent. (p. 224)

FROM *AT SEVENTY: A JOURNAL* (1982–1983)

Such a peaceful, windless morning here for my seventieth birthday—the sea is pale blue, and although the field is still brown, it is dotted with daffodils at last.

. . .

What is it like to be seventy? If someone else had lived so long and could remember things sixty years ago with great clarity, she would seem very old to me. But I do not feel old at all, not as much a survivor as a person still on her way. I suppose real old age begins when one looks backward rather than forward, but I look forward with joy to the years ahead and especially to the surprises that any day may bring.

In the middle of the night things well up from the past that are not always cause for rejoicing—the unsolved, the painful encounters, the mistakes, the reasons for shame or woe. But all, good or bad, painful or delightful, weave themselves into a rich tapestry, and all give me food for thought, food to grow on.

. . . In the course of [a poetry reading at Hartford College] I said, "This is the best time of my life. I love being old." At that point a voice from the audience asked loudly, "Why is it good to be old?" I answered spontaneously and a little on the defensive, for I sensed incredulity in the questioner, "Because I am more myself than I have ever been. There is less conflict. I am happier, more balanced, and" (I heard myself say rather aggressively) "more powerful." I felt it was rather an odd word, "powerful," but I think it is true. It might have been more accurate to say "I am better able to use my powers." I am surer of what my life is all about, have less self-doubt. . . . (pp. 9–10)

. . . We are never done with thinking about our parents, I suppose, and come to know them better long after they are dead than we ever did when they were alive. (p. 30)

I realize that seventy must seem extremely old to my young friends, but I actually feel much younger than I did when I wrote *The House by the Sea* six years ago. And younger than I did in Nelson when I wrote the poem "Gestalt at Sixty." Those previews of old age were not entirely accurate, I am discovering. And that, as far as I can see, is because I live more completely in the moment of these days, am not as anxious about the future, and am far more detached from the areas of pain, the loss of love, the struggle to get the work completed, the fear of death. I have less guilt because there is less anger. Perhaps before I die I shall make peace with my father and be able to heal the wound. . . . (p. 37)

Why is it that people who cannot show feeling presume that that is a strength and not a weakness? Why is it common in our ethos to admire reserve, the withholding of the self, rather than openness and a willingness to give? To show vulnerability remains suspect. Marcie [Hershman, a friend interviewing Sarton for *Ms.*] and I are in agreement about this. We have each suffered from people who cannot give because that is too dangerous, people for whom self-protection becomes a way of life at the expense of growth. It is rather a relief now to be able to speak of these things, not out of pain but from detachment. (p. 38)

What I want most to convey [in a speech to the Unitarian Universalist Assembly] is that, in spite of the baffling state of the world around us . . . it is still possible for one human being, with imagination and will, to move mountains. The danger is that we become so overwhelmed by the negative that we cannot act. I am going to talk about H.O.M.E. (Homeworkers Organized for More Employment), Sister Lucy's community in Orland, near Bangor. I hear about it very directly from Karen Saum, and it has been for me a point of light for the past year.

Sister Lucy, like Mother Teresa, left a contemplative order because she saw so much need outside the convent wall. Ten years ago she began to build and to attract others to help her build a center for helping the very poor in that poverty-stricken part of Maine where lumbering is just about the only employment.

She began by creating a center where women could learn a craft, or if they had one, teach it to others, and sell the products. At present, ten years later, five hundred people have been able to make a little money in this way. But in ten years the project has expanded to include most of life. The people at H.O.M.E. cut wood and see that the old have enough for the winter; they take the sick to the hospital or to a doctor; they help alcoholics to join AA and get them to the meetings; they teach night classes so people can get high school diplomas; they teach reading and writing to illiterates; they are finding ways to improve livestock and plan to breed workhorses themselves. But the most amazing achievement is that they have built five houses, solar-heated, for five families who needed shelter, and built them with mostly volunteer labor. How all this has been achieved on next to no money only God knows.

The community is doing more than helping the poor, for at the same time it is giving hope to the young volunteers who troop up in summer from schools and colleges, helping them to understand what life is all about, helping them out of the apathy or depression of wondering what is the matter with the United States these days, creating in microcosm a true democracy of the spirit, which is also a practical democracy. Things get done at H.O.M.E. Impossible things get done.

Karen gets up at five in winter, builds a fire in the stove and writes me letters, so I feel close to the joys and problems. There is no running water in the main house. They drag it up from the lake, bucketful by bucketful. There is no electricity, so Karen writes by lamplight. At half-past six the resident priest offers Mass, and at seven they have breakfast. After breakfast Sister Lucy plans the day and may announce,

"Well, I think I'll chop down three or four trees this morning," and goes out and does so.

That is only the start of the tasks they handle and the crises they meet every day. A family is found living in an automobile (temperature 30° below!) and the family scheduled to move into the next new house gives it up so the automobile family can be housed. A prisoner is released from prison with nowhere to go and is taken in. It is a little like being God in the middle of Creation, although I'm afraid the people of H.O.M.E. do not rest on the seventh day!

I look forward very much to sharing this with the Unitarians. They will understand what H.O.M.E. is all about. I shall end up with the last lines of my poem "To the Living."

> Speak to the children now of revolution
> Not as a violence, a terror, and a dissolution,
> But as the long-held hope and the long dream of man,
> The river in his heart and his most pure tradition.

That was written in 1944, thirty-eight years ago. Poems do last. (pp. 62–64)

How touched I was in the afternoon (when I also read a few poems) to be given the UUWF's [Unitarian Universalists] Ministry to Women award. I have not thought of myself as ministering to women, but I am happy that they feel I do. It is good to be seventy and honored in such a nonacademic way for more than literary achievement, as a human being. (p. 81)

I woke this morning thinking about the strange chances that rule lives. Had it not been for the German invasion of Belgium in 1914, I should have turned out to be a Belgian writer with French as my language! I am so happy to be an American. For me, as for my father, it was a lucky disaster that forced us to leave Belgium; for my mother (twice transplanted) less so. I do feel that English is the best language for poetry, with its weaving together of Anglo-Saxon and Latin words, so it is both earthy and lucid. Even the difficulty of rhyming in English makes for a certain tension and toughness; in French it is a little too easy. (pp. 84–85)

Harold Bloom in *The Breaking of the Vessels* brings to light an amazing passage from a review T. S. Eliot wrote a few weeks before the famous "Tradition and Individual Talent" appeared. Eliot writes: "We do not imitate, we are changed; and our work is the work of a changed man; we have not borrowed, we have been wakened, and we become bearers of a tradition."

In my own life I recognize this as having happened twice, perhaps more. But two such passions altered my ideas about transforming life into art. The first was W. B. Yeats. His severity toward his own early poems, his ability to change his style from sensuous and diffuse to clear and rocklike forced me to clean up my own poems. To condense, to be willing and able to revise almost indefinitely. He also taught me, whatever Louise Bogan said to me to the contrary, that a poem has to be responsible and that political poems could be more than empty rhetoric. Mauriac had a profound influence on the novels. I saw, through reading and studying him, that what I must do was cast aside the "poetic" style (for which I had been praised) and to embed the poetry into the substance, that poetry in the novel is something that lives between the lines. I worked then toward a style that would not be noticed, precise and clear.

When I was in high school I became enamored of Edna St. Vincent Millay, as so many of my contemporaries did, and this brings me back to those who have found a muse in me and in my work. The danger, when the passion aroused is for a living writer, is that one confuses life and art. At the height of her fame Millay resembled a movie star. A movie star can hardly be a role model; instead, she magnetizes her audience into a fantasy world, and that, as far as creating literature goes, is dangerous and unproductive. I was saved perhaps from trying to *be* Millay by a wise friend, Giorgio de Santillana, who said, "Don't imitate Millay, go back to what influenced her," and so I read Donne and Marvell. (pp. 120–122)

My mother and father are buried in Mt. Auburn [Cemetery in Cambridge], their ashes mixed. Judy was with me that day, and Aunt Mary Bouton, dear old friend, and I always remember how moving it was that some of the ash was blown upward on a light breeze, such a delicate kind of burial—no heavy coffin to be lowered—that death itself seemed ephemeral. (p. 146)

But then I had to go shortly after lunch to drive to Concord to see Judy for the first time in months, since before Christmas. There she was, there she will be until she slips away, in her wheelchair, singing to herself. I know now that she will not recognize me, but I held her cold little hand and talked about old times. . . . Her face is still so distinguished, the dark eyes, the cap of white hair, that it seems incredible that she herself is far away and what is left is a baby, for whom food is the only real pleasure. The truth is I go to see her for me, not for her. After a time I feel a strong compulsion to touch base, as it were. True love does not die. (p. 147)

After all, at seventy not only do I have many readers who want to tell me their stories (always interesting) but, at seventy, I have accumulated many friends. So the bulk of what is on my desk is not "fan mail" but letters from real friends. I suppose my address book has a thousand names in it, and I write to every one at least once a year and often many times more. So what is the solution? There is none. And that is what makes me feel overcrowded and uneasy at the end of this much interrupted summer.

Yet always, in each mail, there is something that makes me rejoice to be alive and grateful that the books are reaching people and are proving useful. What does come through always is what burdens people carry, how hard any life is at best—any life where there is caring and sensitivity—and the need to reach out. I have been given a great deal by strangers; their letters have enlarged my heart. (pp. 157–159)

. . . After our lobster rolls, we sallied out to walk the Marginal Way [in Ogunquit] and sit down frequently on a bench to watch a race of catamarans. Those sails banded in brilliant colors, red, green-blue, orange, against the dark-blue ocean looked like a Monet painting, and we might have been on the French coast. . . . And it is always breath-taking when one emerges around a bend and there across the way is the immense stretch of white beach, five miles of it, that goes from Ogun-quit to Wells. The rugosa roses are gone now. I associate that walk with waves of their scent and also bayberry leaves squeezed to spice the air. But the fascination of the waves, curling in foam around the rocks, advancing and retreating in an endless dance, which always reminds me of Frost's "I Could Give All to Time"—that is always there. It was a just-about-perfect outing. (pp. 166–167)

As I came over the mountain from Milford [New Hampshire], I saw Mount Monadnock standing there, lavender against the pale-blue sky; such a solid comfort it was I had a wave of nostalgia for New Hamp-shire and my fifteen years of communion with the grand old mountain. Nothing will ever replace Nelson in my life, even the spacious world where I now watch sunrise over the ocean. Deep down inside me Nel-son is home, and I am glad I shall be buried in the cemetery there under the maples, and next to Quig [a painter, celebrated in *A World of Light*]. (p. 178)

I am happy because there is someone to focus the world for me again and to hold time still. Everything falls into place; I have even managed to write a lot of letters since I got back nine days ago, as though floated, instead of struggling against intolerable pressures. How mysterious it is! And what is it that suddenly opens the door into poetry? A face, a voice, two hours of rich communion and the world has changed. I am back in my real life again.

So it all seems good. I can do what has to be done. I am alive. And seventy feels very young—but that is not new. What is new perhaps is to accept that this time it will not be a love affair. Circumstances preclude that consummation, and I sense that there the guardian angel has been wise. For I really do not feel up to either the excitement or the inevitable rousing of the daimon that, in my case at least, a sexual encounter brings out of its lair. So there are some changes at seventy that mean old age. I don't mind. All I ask is to write poems, and that I am doing these days, trying a new form, a series of prose poems, called "Letters from Maine." (pp. 192–193)

[T. S.] Eliot's is a negative view, because (I dare to think) he was not a believer. Never is the joy of religion expressed, never is there transcendence. I remember seeing *Murder in the Cathedral* when it was first produced in London in a tiny theater. I left in a kind of black rage, because I had been put through a wringer but there had been no catharsis. The choruses especially left nothing but sand in my mouth. But that is partly why Eliot had such an influence in the twenties when people did not want to hear good news, at least not good religious news. The Zeitgeist was violently against such a view as George Herbert's, but now we go back to him who never denied the desert in himself but pierces us still with the humanness of his faith and his intimate relation with his God, often complaining but never arid for long. He was a believer, and that is a huge difference. (p. 199)

. . . Judy was the precious only love with whom I lived for years, the only one. There have been other great loves in my life, but only Judy gave me a home and made me know what home can be. She was the dear companion for fifteen years, years when I was struggling as a writer. We were poor then, for a time had no car even. But strangely enough I look back on those days as the happiest ones. And that is because there was a "we."

We met in Santa Fe and it is to that austere flaming landscape, sunset on the Sangre de Cristos, that my heart goes now and to a poem I wrote for Judy that ends:

For after love comes birth:
All we have felt and said
Is now of air, of earth,
And love is harvested.*

. . . The mother of someone I stayed with is dying in her own house, beautifully cared for by round-the-clock nurses, unable now to speak (she has Parkinson's). On her bed table is *A Reckoning*, and from it the nurses read aloud to her. It is what she wants most to hear. (p. 298)

As I think over this year I wish I had a long empty time in which to think it over instead of a few minutes before I take Tamas out into the wet green world! In spite of the pressures of what is ahead—to clear my desk, sow the annuals, plant perennials, get back to the novel—I feel happy and at peace. My life at the moment is a little like a game of solitaire that is coming out. Things fall into place. The long hard work is bearing fruit, and even though I make resolves to see fewer people this summer than last, I know I shall be inundated as usual, be unable to say "no," but it does not matter, for I am coming into a period of inner calm. There will be months of seeing people and months of public appearances, but as surely as the dawn, there will be months of solitude and time to work. Who could ask for more? As Robert Frost says:

I could give all to Time except—except
What I myself have held. But why declare
The things forbidden that while the Customs slept
I have crossed to Safety with? For I am There,
And what I would not part with I have kept.
(p. 334)

Editor's note: This is the last stanza of "The Harvest" from *The Lion and the Rose* (p. 213).

FROM *AFTER THE STROKE: A JOURNAL* (1986–1987)

.... (ง̌ı̌ง̌)

It may prove impossible because my head feels so queer and the smallest effort, mental or physical, exhausts, but I feel so deprived of my *self* being unable to write, cut off since early January from all that I mean about my life, that I think I must try to write a few lines every day.

It is a way of being self-supporting. I long for advice from someone like Larry LeShan who is himself recovering from a severe heart attack with many days in intensive care, yet has had the kindness to phone three times, the blessed man. He says I have no surface energy because reserve energy has to be built back first and that makes sense.

Meanwhile I lie around most of the afternoon, am in bed by eight, and there in my bed alone the past rises like a tide, over and over, to swamp me with memories I cannot handle. I am as fragile and naked as a newborn babe.

[I am too vulnerable to all the losses and often the pain connected with personal relationships. I have had too many lives, have attached myself to so many people over the fifty years since I was twenty-five and began my real life after my theater company failed in 1934. It is hard to imagine being able to say "fifty years ago," but during those fifty years I have lived hard and to the limits of my capacity as a human being and as a writer. So it is a huge bundle of feelings and thoughts that ride on those tides when I lie awake at night. My mother dies again, and again

I have to face that I did not have the courage to sit with her, which is what she needed. Perhaps I wrote *A Reckoning* partly to help readers do what I could not do . . . and people write me that it did help.

Then I come back often to Santa Fe where I met Judy on my second visit there when we were paying guests in the same house . . . what a piece of luck that proved to be! Our joining together, our living together in Cambridge was the good end of a long struggle and doubt on her part as to whether she wanted to accept me as a lover and friend. Judy had kept her personal life entirely apart from her professional life as a distinguished professor of English at Simmons College; she hesitated to be pinned down perhaps in the minds of her associates. She was not entirely prepared for the intensity of feeling on her side as well as mine. She was then forty-five and had had no intimate relationship before. And she had suffered from serious depression which she shared with no one until I came along, and even then in all the years we lived together I did not always know when she was in the valley of the shadow. Judy was as inverted and secretive as I am open and indiscreet. What drew us together was mysterious, as true love always is.

Basil de Selincourt was often in my thoughts, the first major critic to recognize my poems, and later a true friend. He looked like a hawk and could be quite brutal. But he read my poems with complete attention all through the years, and wrote his queries to me, and those letters with mine to him are now at the Berg collection with so much else, my correspondence with S. S. Koteliansky for one. It has made me aware that it is men not women who have held my work in high regard, with the one great exception of Carol Heilbrun who came into my life after I was forty-five.

. . .

But the disturbing, the unresolved memories that flood me have to do, of course, with love affairs. The fascinating but sometimes deadly Muses who seem to have brought me poetry and rage and grief in almost equal measure. Is it perhaps that I have been a bad lover, but a good friend? Or simply that passionate love at its most romantic and demanding has already the seeds of death in it, the fresh leaves will inevitably fall in time? At best it changes and grows into friendship as I am now in a kind of epiphany with Juliette Huxley through letters.

. . .

All of this and so much more—as they say on television—is contained in one person, dreaming it all like a dream and pursued by it sometimes like an inescapable nightmare. No life as rich can ever be perfectly resolved . . . it can be done only in a poem or two, only through a work of art. It is too complex, too terrible, too astonishing and so the wave of memory dashes itself against rocks.]*

I have been rather smug perhaps about solitude versus loneliness— "loneliness is the poverty of self, solitude the richness of self." Now I am frightfully lonely because I am *not* my self. I can't see a friend for over a half hour without feeling as though my mind were draining away like air rushing from a balloon. So having someone here would not work. (pp. 15–18)

If I have learned something in these months of not being well it may be to live moment by moment—listening to the tree frogs all night for I couldn't sleep, waking late to the insistent coos of the wood pigeons— and at this moment the hush-hushing of the ocean. Being alive as far as I am able to the *instant*.

But I think it is necessary before coming back to the present to adumbrate briefly where I am coming *from*.

First an autumn of poetry readings from September through early December—I was riding a wave. And even if it was a bit too much for me, I have no regrets. Would I have missed the great audience at the Smithsonian in Washington, D.C., (sold out months in advance) or across the continent the theater full in San Francisco? Or seeing Moscow, Idaho, in November, when the land lay below a small plane in

---

*The brackets in this excerpt are Sarton's. They indicate material added by her after the journal was first completed, but before it was published.

huge fertile folds, rich black earth—like the body of a mythical goddess—so feminine and restorative an earth, I had tears in my eyes?
Would I have missed all that?

[Sarton describes poignantly a series of setbacks which preceded her
stroke—the loss of her beloved cat, Bramble; her Christmas tree catch-
ing fire; and a diagnosis of her congestive heart failure and a fibrillating
heart.]
    Then on February twentieth I woke in the middle of the night ter-
rified as I felt as though a numb, perhaps dead, arm were strangling
me. It was actually my own left arm. I could not extricate myself.
Finally I did manage to and got up—with great difficulty, and staggered about. I knew something was wrong, but went back to bed. At
six I called Nancy [Hartley] and asked her to come, went down to let
Tamas out as usual, forced myself to make breakfast, carried the tray
up to bed, but couldn't eat it. Then I called Janice, my dear friend who
is an R.N., and said, "I think I have had a small stroke," She was very
firm. "Call your doctor. Get the ambulance—I'll be right over."
    It was a great relief when I knew help was on the way. I even man-
aged to pack a small suitcase to be ready, but I could not dress. My left
side felt very queer and dead.

                              .   .   .
    Then followed six days of tests and confabulations. The CAT scan
showed a small hemorrhage of the brain—perhaps a clot thrown out by
the irregular heartbeat. Then I came home, lucky indeed to be able to
speak and take care of myself—the telephone my lifeline. . . .
    It was a *mild* stroke, thank heavens. But what neither I nor my sup-
portive friends could quite realize is how strange one feels—and how
depressed—after even a slight stroke—that is what I have been learning
slowly for seven weeks. (pp. 19–24)

    When I came home from the hospital after the stroke the daily chores
seemed insuperable. Making my bed left me so exhausted that I lay
down on it at once for an hour. I realized that I had always hurried
through the chores in order to get up here to my desk as fast as pos-

sible—it felt strange not to be pressured for the first time since I moved here fourteen years ago—and I tried to learn from it, to learn to take the chores as an exercise, deliberately slowing down, savoring the smoothing of a sheet, the making of order as delightful in itself—not just something to get out of the way.

Often when I lay in bed after my breakfast which I take up on a tray, the light shone through the stained glass phoenix Karen Saum had had made for my seventieth birthday. It always felt like a good augury to watch it glow, blue and red.

Perhaps the phoenix can only begin to rise from its embers when it has reached the very end, death itself. With Bramble's death I felt the wilderness die in me, some secret place where poetry lived. She was so wild—passionate and distant at the same time. . . .

The hardest thing for me to give up after the stroke was writing to Juliette Huxley. Forty years ago we were intimate friends, but time and change intervened, misunderstanding broke the bond, and only now in these last months has she opened the door—and we are communicating again at last. She is eighty-nine. Time is running out—and the frustration of being unable to keep the slight thread intact between us is very hard to bear.

So I made up a dream of flying over to England in June and taking her to a country inn for a few days where we could talk instead of writing. That was the final thing I realized I had to give up. I'm not well enough, and she has had several bouts with flu and herself hesitated to come.

I spent a sleepless night trying to accept that I shall probably never see her again—that was the death of the spirit, the end of dreaming impossible dreams. Strangely enough, the next day I began this journal, and knew that my real self was coming back. (pp. 29–30)

Youth, it occurs to me, has to do with not being aware of one's body, whereas old age is often a matter of consciously *overcoming* some misery or other inside the body. One is acutely aware of it.

I simply never thought about this until the stroke—even when all my teeth had to be removed last year! So I have been lucky. But I see now that the stroke has made me take a leap into old age instead of approaching it gradually.

The kitten is so perfectly at ease inside his body that it is a joy to contemplate him, sometimes lying on his back with back legs stretched straight out and front legs stretched straight over his head. Such ease! (p. 35)

Yesterday, off Lanoxin and expecting to feel better, I felt so ill I could do nothing but lie around and *wait* for things to change inside my body. So it was especially moving to find a letter about *As We Are Now* in the mail that spoke to me with force.

The writer, Kathleen Daly, S.N.D., wrote in bed with the flu where she suddenly remembered an experience she had had as a nurse's aide in a nursing home in 1982–1984—and what the novel had meant. She says:

> The relationship you describe between the main character and Mrs. Close had so much likeness to a relationship I experienced that I always find comfort in reading those tender passages. . . . The woman I cared for was eighty-three years old and had had a severe cerebral hemorrhage that left her paralysed on one side and speechless and angry. Her family did not know how to relate to her in this state and were frightened and depressed by her uncontrollable anger and bitterness.
>
> I, having never known her in any other way, fell in love with her. Perhaps I sensed in her anger a spirit that had not yet given up or in her inability to speak (even though her eyes spoke volumes) a voice that needed to be heard and needed help to be heard. (I was experiencing similar things in other ways.) Whatever, I had the gift of caring for her until she died, and at her coffin and at her grave the only words that came to me were "thank you" and many tears.
>
> She helped me experience myself as tender and compassionate *and* limited. I had to learn how to forgive myself for

the many mistakes I made in trying to care for her in the ways that were best for her.
(pp. 35–36)

[Sarton's convalescence was difficult but by summer her vitality returned in full measure.]

Yesterday was perfect, clear and cool, and again today everything shines and sparkles with just a hint of autumn in the air. I went out to the garden and worked for a happy hour, cutting back the autumn-flowering clematis which had taken over half the fence, smothering the larger and more beautiful clematis that flower in June. Of course I am discovering all the things Karen did not have time to do. The lilies are doing very well; they had to be staked with longer stakes. It does seem very odd that the picking garden is finally, in late August, giving me flowers. . . .

It is impossible to write letters morning *and* afternoon, so I have decided to get back to my old routine of gardening in the afternoon—a way of rinsing my eye and feeling whole again. It is hard to say how tired I am of responding by letter, even to dear friends. The endless answering was always a problem, but now with diminishing energy— I have to remind myself that I *am* nearly seventy-five—it often seems beyond my strength and will.

I love writing to Juliette [Huxley], but she is really the only correspondent I look forward to answering. (p. 123)

Because I am well I no longer suffer from the acute loneliness I felt all spring and summer until now [August]. Loneliness because in spite of all the kindnesses and concern of so many friends there was no one who could fill the hole at the center of my being—only myself could fall it by becoming whole again. It was loneliness in essence for the *self*. Now that I can work, taking up the healthy rhythm of the days, I am not at all lonely.

. . . .

When I was ill I resented that I had some years ago called old age an "ascension" in an essay which appeared on the Op Ed page in the *Times*.

It did seem too ironic for words, but I believe there is some truth in it as I go back to it now. The ascension is possible when all that has to be given up can be *gladly* given up—because other things have become more important. I panted halfway up the stairs, but I also was able to sit and watch light change in the porch for an hour and be truly attentive to it, not plagued by what I "ought" to be doing.

But the body is part of our identity, and its afflictions and discontents, its donkey-like refusal to do what "ought" to be done, destroys self-respect. The wrinkles that write a lifetime into a face like a letter to the young are dismaying when one looks into a mirror. But this is the test, isn't it? How contemptuous I have been of women who try to look younger than they are! How beautiful an old face has been to me! So if I mind the wrinkles now it is because I have failed to ascend *inside* to what is happening *inside*—and that is a great adventure and challenge, perhaps the greatest in a lifetime—not sparing the rich or the famous, a part of accepting the human condition. At least, being well, I may be able to do better at it now than even a month ago. (pp. 124–125)

Yesterday there was a momentous event for me and that was to read Darlene Davis's M.A. thesis for Pennsylvania State at Harrisburg, "Johannes Vermeer and May Sarton: a Shared Aesthetic." I read it with amazement to find someone who has understood so well what I am after and has managed to relate it to the incomparable Vermeer in convincing ways. She used Vermeer's painting "A Woman Holding a Balance" as her chief anchor in the analysis and *A Reckoning*, my novel, as counterpart.

She defines the "shared aesthetic" as 1) light, so much the essence of Vermeer's magic and so often mentioned in my work; 2) the woman alone; 3) something that might be called the sacramentalization of ordinary life, the "ordinary" tasks of home-making. This work has given me great joy. Occasionally repetitious, she nevertheless uses a great deal of material including *Mrs. Stevens Hears the Mermaids Singing* and the poems with grace and wisdom. (pp. 163–164)

The last day of this bad old year full of illness, depression and death. I write that, it is the truth, yet it makes me laugh at the same time. For really, in spite of all my complaining, I am happy deep down inside me and that happiness turned into a short lyric two days ago.

But I am having to face at long last the unhealed wound of [Louise] Bogan's attitude toward my work. She did not, could not, perhaps, respect it as it deserves. But does it deserve to be?

What all this does is to exacerbate and bring to the surface all my doubts about the value in the long run of what I have achieved.

Bogan was an extremely good critic but could not bring herself to praise me in print—as a poet. So either she was right and I have given my life to a crazy delusion, or she was wrong. And if she was wrong and perhaps knew she was being "mean-spirited"—one of her favorite words—then jealousy is the only explanation. Both of these possible explanations cause extreme psychic disturbance in me. At night I pace around inside my head like a caged animal who can find no rest.

It would help if the correspondence between us could at last be published. Bogan's letters to me are at the Berg Collection in New York and mine to her at Amherst College's library—in all about two hundred. But Ruth Limmer's hostility and sneering attitude toward that relationship has, so far, stood in the way. At least it is now understood in academic circles that she has chosen to do so.

Lately I have felt covered with wounds like a tattoo—everywhere I look in the past there is pain. Why then am I on the whole a cheerful person and as someone writes me these days "a life-giver"? Why haven't I given up long ago? What has kept me going? Partly I have to admit the need for money. I am used to giving a good deal—in this last week for example, seven hundred dollars suddenly needed when Medicare gave out for an eighty-six-year-old friend who has had major surgery. Medicare paid for two weeks in a nursing home. I paid for the third.

In these last years I have felt rich, but when I was ill I realized that I have been rich because I was producing so much. What if illness or fatigue, the fatigue of old age takes over? I have no large amount of capital. A year in a nursing home would leave me dependent. So the necessity to earn has always been a spur.

But deeper than that is that I feel happy when I am working on a poem. "My cup runneth over with joy." Sometimes the poem has come as the direct result of a wound. Everything is part of the whole person, so tattoo, an external pattern imposed from outside, is not an accurate image. The wounds, I suppose, teach—force to resolve, to surmount, to transcend. I will not be put down permanently like a dying animal. I can recover and go on creating. (pp. 230–231)

I couldn't sleep last night and around midnight I went to the window in my bedroom and was dazzled by the moonlight on the snow and the extremely brilliant stars. I saw the Pleiades rather near the horizon under Orion—it was thrilling. Pierrot [the new kitten] often lies now on top of a suitcase which is held on the arms of a rather stiff armchair. From there he can look out and himself looks handsome, a white tiger. I wonder whether he sees the stars. He seems to be looking very intently *at something*.

Of course everything is brilliant in the snow dazzle since the storm. When I came home on Wednesday after Bedford, it was just after four and the sun was setting right in front of me as I swung onto the private road. It was a marvelous crimson globe going down and quite bearable to my eyes—an amazing sight through the dark pines and the snow-drifts.

Yesterday the cardinal was at the feeder again. (pp. 242–243)

. . . Much of the past is never resolved, for one thing, or one has resolved it by going on, by surviving, and in my case by writing poems. (p. 266)

So this is the anniversary [of the stroke] and I am well! It has been a long journey, but now I do not think about the past at all, only rejoice in the present—and dream of the future and a little dachshund puppy who will come here after my last poetry reading tour in California in April, and my seventy-fifth birthday on May third.

Then an open space opens before me—no more public appearances. There is much I still hope to do. And I rejoice in the life I have recaptured and in all that still lies ahead. (pp. 279–280)

Fiction

.... (ง͜ʖ͡ง)

AS WE ARE NOW (1973)

.... (ᵛ|ᵞ₁)

As you are now, so once was I;
Prepare for death and follow me.
   New England tombstone

I am not mad, only old. I make this statement to give me courage. To give you an idea what I mean by courage, suffice it to say that it has taken two weeks for me to obtain this notebook and a pen. I am in a concentration camp for the old, a place where people dump their parents or relatives exactly as though it were an ash can.

My brother, John, brought me here two weeks ago. Of course I knew from the beginning that living with him would never work. I had to close my own house after the heart attack (the stairs were too much for me). John is four years older than I am and married a much younger woman after Elizabeth, his first wife, died. Ginny never liked me. I make her feel inferior and I cannot help it. John is a reader and always has been. So am I. John is interested in politics. So am I. Ginny's only interests appear to be malicious gossip, bridge, and trying out new recipes. Unfortunately she is not a born cook. I find the above paragraph extremely boring and it has been a very great effort to set it down. No one wants to look hard at disagreeable things. I am not alone in that.

I am forcing myself to get everything clear in my mind by writing it down so I know where I am at. There is no reality now except what I can sustain inside me. My memory is failing. I have to hang on to every scrap of information I have to keep my sanity, and it is for that purpose

301

that I am keeping a journal. Then if I forget things later, I can always go back and read them here.

I call it *The Book of the Dead*. By the time I finish it I shall be dead. I want to be ready, to have gathered everything together and sorted it out, as if I were preparing for a great final journey. I intend to make myself whole here in this Hell. It is the thing that is set before me to do. So, in a way, this path inward and back into the past is like a map, the map of my world. If I can draw it accurately, I shall know where I am.

I do not blame John. That is the first thing. In his way he is fighting to keep whole, as I am, and Ginny was making life intolerable for both of us. Far better to dump me here than lose me in a quicksand of jealousy and hatred. He had to make a choice. The only thing I do not know is why he has not come to see me. Perhaps he is ill. Perhaps they have gone away. It does seem queer.

Also, although it is clear in my mind that I had to go somewhere, it is not clear why the place chosen should seem a place of punishment. But I must not dwell on this if possible. Sometimes old people imagine that everyone is against them. They have delusions of persecution. I must not fall into that trap.

It is better to smile at the image of that big white Cadillac turning off macadam onto a rough dirt road, the rain—of course it had to be raining, and not just a quiet rain, but a real downpour that would make almost anyone consider building an ark! I wondered whether Ginny had taken a wrong turning. When we stopped at a small red farmhouse that looked as though it had been gradually sinking into the mud for years, I thought it must be to ask directions. There was no sign, only two elms—the nursing home is called "Twin Elms." Five enormous geese stretched out their necks and hissed at us when we got out of the car. I noticed there was a barn over to the right. In the rain, the whole place seemed enclosed in darkness.

"Well," John said, "here we are, Caro." His voice had become unnaturally cheerful in the way voices do when addressing children or the feeble-minded.

There were two doors, but the front door opened into a sea of mud and was evidently not used. Ginny had parked close to the side door. We pushed our way in without ringing because of the downpour. Even in those few minutes I got soaking wet. There was no hall. We found ourselves in a large room with four or five beds in it. There was no light on. It took a moment before I realized that beside each bed an old man sat on a straight chair. One had his head in his hands. A younger man, whose legs were bandaged and who was half lying and half sitting in a sort of medical rocker, tried to speak but half choked. He was clearly out of his mind. However, he smiled, the only person in that room who did or who could.

Ginny called out loudly, "Here we are! Is there anyone home?"

Then an enormous woman filled the doorway, wiping her hands on her apron.

"Oh . . . well," she said, as if she had been taken by surprise. "My daughter is just making up Miss Spencer's room. But I guess you can go in now." She laughed. "We're up tight these days, no place to ask you to sit down."

I had had so many shocks by then that I felt quite numb and only wanted to be left alone as soon as possible. My heart started up and I was afraid I might faint. But it was a comfort to find that I had a room of my own, just big enough for a bed, an armchair, and a bureau. The bed was parallel to the window, and the window looked out, much to my astonishment, on a long field with tall trees at the end and, beyond them, gentle hills.

"Look at the view," Ginny said. "Isn't it marvelous?"

"What is that woman's name?" I asked in a whisper. I had the feeling already that even a whisper would be heard.

"Mrs. Hatfield—Harriet Hatfield. She is a trained nurse." (That is what Ginny said, but of course she must have known that Mrs. Hatfield's only experience had been as an aide in the State Hospital for two years.) "She and her daughter work very hard to keep things going here."

There was dust under the bureau and an old piece of Kleenex.

John disappeared for a time. They brought me a cup of tea and a cheap biscuit, which I didn't eat. They offered to help me unpack my two suitcases, but I managed to make it clear that I am not infirm. I set the photographs of my mother and father and one of me with John when I was fourteen and he was in college on the bureau, and three things I treasure: a Japanese bronze turtle, a small Swedish glass vase, and the *Oxford Book of English Verse.* I found my little pillow and lay down on the bed then. After a while I recited the Lord's Prayer three times. I do not believe this prayer is heard by the Person to whom it is addressed, but I find it comforting, like a rune, something to hold onto.

When John and Ginny left, he said, "We'll be seeing you."

After a while I slept. The rain drummed on the roof. I felt that for a time I must be absolutely passive, float from moment to moment and from hour to hour, shut out feeling and thought. They were both too dangerous. And I feared the weeping. Lately, since the hospital, I have cried a lot, and that may be one reason John felt I must go. Tears are an offense and make other people not so much suffer as feel attacked and irritable. When the inner world overflows in this way, it forces something entirely private out into the open where it does not belong, not at my age anyway. Only children are permitted tears, so in a way perhaps my being sent here is a punishment. Oh dear, I must not think about that now. Everything is dangerous that is not passive. I am learning to accept.

Harriet Hatfield woke me, not ungently, and pretty soon her daughter, Rose, came in with my supper on a tray. At least I do not have to eat with the others and watch them spill their soup. I can lie here and look out at the hills. Supper was cornflakes with milk and a banana that first evening. I enjoyed it far more than one of Ginny's "gourmet" concoctions. But then I could not sleep. I had to get accustomed to the noises, queer little creaks, the groans and snores in the big room where the men are. It seemed a terribly long night. When I went to the bathroom I bumped into a chair in the hall and bruised my leg. Perhaps John will bring me a flashlight when he comes. I will ask for note paper and stamps, a daily newspaper, and maybe a bottle of Scotch. It would be a help to have a small drink measured out each evening before supper.

That thought was a comfort when I wrote it several days ago. Now I know that good things like that are not going to happen. Old age, they say, is a gradual giving up. But it is strange when it all happens at once. That is a real test of character, a kind of solitary confinement. Whatever I have now is in my own mind.

Lately I have thought often of Doug, a former student of mine, who was put in solitary for two years by the Russians. When he came back he talked and talked about it and I listened. I thought I was helping him by listening. I never imagined that one day all he told me would be helping me. One thing he did was make a study of spiders, and later of mice. He remembered all the people he had known in school and tried to imagine exactly what had happened to them since, which amounted to making up novels in his head. He did mathematical problems. But he was under forty when this happened to him, and I, Caro Spencer, am over seventy—seventy-six. Time gets muddled up and what I lack, I fear, is the capacity to stick with a routine, to discipline myself—my mind goes wandering off. I see this all around me—when the TV is on, the old men stare at it in a daze. They do not pay attention for more than a few minutes, even to a ball game. I must try to pay attention to something for at least an hour every day. This last remark struck me as humorous and I laughed aloud after I had read it again. What difference does it make what I do or do not do? (No, that is the devil speaking. Do not listen to the devil.)

My first study became the two women who have me in their dominion. I observed them as if they were mice or spiders. It is better to think of them as beings remote from the human, as another species that flourishes on the despair and impotence of the weak. They are both grossly fat. When they make the beds and their enormous breasts jiggle, the old men leer and wink at each other. Harriet has a lover, an intense wizened little man ten years younger than she who smokes horrible cigars in the kitchen and rarely speaks. There are three children, Rose's, who come to play in the yard while she is here—she sleeps somewhere else. They chase the geese and climb trees and it is nice to have them around although they scream and fight a great deal—all girls. I would prefer boys.

Harriet is a dishonest woman so it is hard to pin her down. She puts on a terrific act when relatives come, coos over some old man whom she has treated roughly when changing his diapers a few moments before. She is full of false compassion at all times. "Imagine," I have heard her say, "we take them in, poor things." (We are talked about always as "them," as if we were abandoned animals thrown out of a car.) "Their families bring them here and sometimes never come back at all!" And the relatives look properly shocked and praise her for taking in these waifs and strays. But it is next to impossible for anyone "outside" to bear this atmosphere of decay for long, I have noticed. People come in, full of good cheer, bringing a carton of cigarettes or a magazine, but after about five minutes they begin to fade out, look hunted, have nothing to say after the first few exchanges about the weather and how their father or aunt is feeling. Paralysis sets in and suddenly they are compelled to flee.

I wonder whether a person who has complete power over others does not always become wicked. I try to separate what Harriet has become from what she may have been ten years ago. Her face is now that of a greedy and sullen pig—small blue eyes, a mean little mouth. It is true that both she and Rose are overworked. It seems as though they were always changing beds, washing someone, or bringing in trays. They too are no doubt affected by the atmosphere, tired most of the time, dealing with crotchety old people who are (let's face it) most of them not lovable. I gather the old men are chiefly on welfare.

It is terrible to have to admit that even here one does not change one's class. I am a snob. I went to college, taught school for forty years, come of gentle people. Most of the others here worked with their hands. Deprived of work, they have no resources at all. Two of the old men play cards for hours at a time. One reads the only newspaper very slowly for most of the morning. I have no peer, no one I can talk to. Harriet and Rose address me always as "Miss Spencer" with heavy irony. I am afraid to admit it even to myself but I feel sure that I was resented from the start as "superior."

The idea is that we are all one big family in a cozy old farmhouse, that this is to be truly a "home." Oh dear me! But we are free to wander about. Sometimes I am invited into the kitchen, the one really nice room in the house, with its good smells of cooking, its warmth and bright colors (red and white checked curtains, a new blue linoleum floor, and a big new stove and frigidaire). I sit for a half hour with the family and am given a cup of tea.

"How are you feeling this morning, dear?" Harriet may ask, but she never waits to hear my answer. With me she is subservient in a nasty way, never rude, but she has, of course, many ways to humiliate me. Thank Heavens I can wash myself and am not bedridden! My body is still my own, not to be degraded by those coarse, hard hands. For how long? At present I have a bath every day—rarely hot, but at least then I can lock the door and have total privacy for a quarter of an hour. The bath is my confessional. I can weep there and no one will see me.

Otherwise there is a house law that doors must not be closed. The two women are always in and out of every room, and one never knows when they are listening. Sometimes I go in and visit with the only other inmate who has a private room. Standish Flint is a retired farmer, American Gothic face, a noble man, but he is extremely deaf now and rarely gets out of bed. Since I have to shout to be heard, we converse more with signs and smiles, with ironic smiles, and sudden guffaws on his part. He whispers, "I never thought it would end like this," then looks hunted for fear "they" will be listening. I understand from Harriet that his wife is living but seriously ill, bedridden, being taken care of by a daughter. So that explains why no one comes to visit him—no one, anyway, in the two weeks I have been here.

Like me he cannot be beaten down yet. He is still his own man. So he is tortured in mean little ways—made to wait too long for the bedpan. Very often he refuses to eat what they bring him (he is on a dull diet of soft foods) and turns his head away. I sometimes think he is trying to starve himself to death. Every one of us still in his right mind must have fantasies of escape, and death is the only practical one. I have indulged in these fantasies myself—but I am still waiting for what will happen next. I want to see my brother. (He can't stay away forever.) There are things I have to do inside myself before I can die. And I have the belief that we make our deaths, that we ripen toward death, and only when the fruit is ripe may it drop. I still believe in life as a process and would not wish to end the process by an unnatural means. Old-fashioned of me, I suppose. Then I suspect that suicide is a kind of murder, an act of rage. I want to keep my soul from that sort of corroding impurity. My soul? What do I mean when I use that word?

Something deep down, true, detached from impurities, the instrument we have been given for making distinctions between right and wrong, true and false—the intrinsic *being* that is still alive even when memory goes. I treasure my soul as something given into my keeping, something that I must keep intact—more, keep in a state of growth and awareness whatever the odds. For whom? For what? That is the mystery. Only when we can conceive of it as belonging to some larger unity, some communion that includes stars and frogs and trees, does it seem valid to "treasure" it at all. I sometimes feel I am melting into the lovely landscape outside my window. Am floated. For an hour I do nothing else but rest in it. Afterwards I feel nourished. I am one with those gentle old hills.

Did they always hate me, my family I mean, because I was different, because I never married, because I didn't play bridge and went off to Europe alone every summer? A high-school teacher in a small town is (or was in the years when I taught math) not exactly suspect, but set apart. Only in the very last years when I was established as a dear old eccentric did I ever dare have a drink in public! And even among my colleagues, mostly good simple-minded fellows, I did not quite fit in. They had their own club and went off fishing together and on an occasional spree to New York, but of course they didn't want an old maid tagging along and their pleasures would hardly have been mine. I can go almost crazy with joy in a museum. I can get drunk on Vermeer or Brueghel, but the average nightclub is sheer misery to me because of the noise. My most intense pleasures were always reading, listening to records, and learning poetry by heart. That has come in handy here, as I sometimes spend two hours saying poems to myself.

"Talking to yourself again?" Harriet sneers when she comes in with my lunch. Why bother to answer? I am too old to try to make connections with boors and sadists.

I can still make connections with an animal and it must be said for this infernal place that it is in no way an "institution," and if it is dirty, at least there are a few animals around. There is a very old collie who wags her tail at the sound of a footstep and likes to be stroked around her ears. She licks my hand when I caress her. And, best of all, there is a cat called Pansy, a black cat with very soft fur, maybe a little coon in her. She has round golden eyes. I have been told categorically that she must not get up on the bed. But occasionally she manages to sneak in late at night and climb up, first curling into a tight ball then later, when I stroke her, uncurling to lie full length, upside down, sometimes with one paw over her nose. It is hard to express the joy it gives me to stroke this little creature and to feel the purrs begin in her throat. Those nights I sleep well, a lively sleep rather than a deathly sleep. It makes all the difference!

Everybody here is waiting . . . all the time. Standish has been demanding to see the doctor for days now, and I hear Harriet trying to get through. But I guess all the doctors around here are terribly busy, and it's a long way to come. Standish tells me he is in pain—kidneys, he says. He looks white and drawn.

Most of the old men are on tranquilizers, I have discovered—that explains why they are so dull and passive. Only the feeble-minded man, who is quite dear in his own strange way, is eager to talk and smiles when I go in there, but it is next to impossible to understand him. His speech is a sort of gurgle. I cannot imagine why his legs are bandaged all the time. He waits for his father to come; the old men wait for married daughters or sons. I wait for John.

I think it is almost three weeks since they left me here. I get frightened of losing all sense of time. I can't remember when it was I did come—some time in June, I guess. It has been too damp or too buggy for me to sit outdoors. But I could insist on going out at least for a short walk. Why don't I? I think it is because after a short time, even a very few days here, one begins to feel like an animal in a cage. Even if the door were to open, one would not dare move. It is the sense of being totally abandoned, so at first one goes way down deep into oneself and stays there just as a frightened animal does. I have an idea now that John was *told* to stay away. I have often thought about those visits to people in jail—a few minutes, a visit long looked forward to, but bringing with it chiefly wild nostalgia or despair. The difference is that it is hope that is hard to handle. Most prisoners foresee a time when they will get out. Here we know there is no way out, only down, little by little, till death do us join with whatever comes next, if only dust to dust. Hope is one thing of which we are deprived.

One of my problems is that John, after all, is eighty and has no very clear sense of time passing. He may honestly believe that he has left me here only a few days. Or Ginny may have forced him to go on a trip to her people in Ohio, or somewhere. I have thought of writing but I wonder whether the letter would be mailed, and I cringe at the thought that it might be read and thrown away. Also, if it did get there, Ginny might do the same.

Lately I have come to see that John and I never really understood each other. We took each other for granted, I suppose. But I cannot remember any real talk we ever had—about ourselves, I mean. We talked for hours about books and about the state of the world. We had fierce arguments that we enjoyed, but our parents were troubled by our ferocity. Their philosophy was peace at any price, and if possible under a Republican administration! The fight went out of John when he married Ginny. Thank God I never got married, never gave my body and soul into the keeping of anyone. Unregenerate I surely am, but I'm myself alone. There is some dignity in that. And I guess that is why I have not written—"dumb from human dignity" as Yeats said, but that was about passionate love.

The other day I was lying on my bed having a rather good think about Alex, the Englishman I loved, off and on, for twenty years, married of course, so I saw him only in the summer for brief weekends, and only twice for journeys we made together, once to Greece and once to Italy. Harriet interrupted here, and with her sharp needle thrust into this reverie.

"What are you dreaming about, Miss Spencer?"

"My lover," I said.

I saw her gesture as Rose came in, pointing to her head, saying without words "crazy as a loon, of course. This poor old thing never had a lover—senile." It was written on her face as clear as clear.

Am I senile, I wonder? The trouble is that old age is not interesting until one gets there, a foreign country with an unknown language to the young, and even to the middle-aged. I wish now that I had found out more about it. Loss of memory—but some things remain so vivid! In some ways I am not myself, that is true. In the first days I tried setting up mathematical problems, but I couldn't seem to concentrate. It is not so much that, though, as that I am not interested in the abstract cogitation any longer. I am interested in me. I am a long way still from the fulfillment, the total self-understanding that I long for now. I remain a mystery to myself. I want to get right down to the core, make a final perfect equation before I am through, balance it all up into a tidy *whole*. If I could think of this place not as the House of the Dead but as the House of Gathering—the house where I have to come to terms with everything, sort it all out, accept it all, I think that might be salvation, a rock on which to stand at least. It is all quicksand and threat still. I cannot get used to being here. It feels so makeshift. No paintings on the wall. Dust under the bureau. I never thought I should be asked to sleep in muslin sheets, or have to swallow daily doses of sheer vulgarity and meanness of spirit. If this is Purgatory it is hard to imagine Paradise as in any way attainable, or only in the imagination as a self-created place.

I am amazed at how much time I can spend apparently doing nothing, when in fact I am extremely busy with this kind of dreaming-awake that sustains me.

I have never liked women very much, too intense. I have been passionately attracted to one or two in my life, but that is different from liking. I like men much better. No woman would bear what Standish does in the way he does—so tart and bitter, so authentic. He is too angry most of the time to be sorry for himself. Anger keeps him alive. It is truly hard that we cannot *talk*. If only he were not so deaf. He looks at me with very bright clear eyes when he is awake and (how absurd this is!) I find that I try to look as well as I can for him. My hair needs washing and a rinse. They promise, but of course these things never do get done. But Standish notices a bright scarf or a piece of jewelry and gives me a wink of approval. I would write him messages, but apparently they have lost his glasses—he says he can't read any-more. But sometimes he talks about his life, how hard it has been, how hard he worked, how finally he realized he would have to give up the farm as he couldn't take care of the herd of cows himself and could not afford help. He had saved ten thousand dollars but it all got eaten up when his wife became ill, or almost all—he *says* he pays for himself here. I do hope it is true. Probably it is or he would not be allowed a room of his own.

What keeps him alive is a deep, buried fire of anger that never goes out, apparently. Out of rage he refuses to eat anything for several days. I feel he is always planning a way to get around "them," a way to get back at "them" by sheer tenacity, by passive resistance. Among the sheeplike herd we two are a different breed, rebels. Standish manages usually to get rid of the tranquilizers, hides them, then gives them to me to throw down the john. "They won't get my head," he whispers to me. "They won't castrate me in that way. I'm still alive from here up," he whispers, his hand at his throat. He has good hands, worn, but thin and sensitive. Sometimes I wish I could take one in mine and hold it hard—"We shall overcome." I don't because he is a touchy old man, and probably his chief escape is sexual fantasy.

He talks about Harriet and Rose as if they were prostitutes, with considerable relish, and expatiates on their enormous bums and breasts. He has a repertoire of dirty jokes—childish jokes they are. I do not mind them and some are even quite funny. He gives a loud guffaw after telling me one, and then a quick look hoping he has shocked me. I suppose he imagines I am an old maid—I could tell him some things but they are not to be shouted. So I let him talk, and when he falls asleep I go back to my room. The conversational opportunities here are certainly at a minimum. But then we all talk to ourselves in a perpetual exercise of free association.

I never thought much of psychiatry, but occasionally I imagine when I am lying here on my bed that I am talking to a wise and omniscient listener, a Doctor of Souls to whom I can say things I might not dare say to myself alone. Next time Harriet asks whom I am talking to, I'll tell her, "My psychiatrist, so you'd better leave us alone." Then she'll be sure I'm crazy. And perhaps that is not a good idea. One could make oneself mad by pretending to be, I have sometimes thought. The borderline between reality and fantasy is so thin in this confined, dreadfully lonely place.

I have not been able to write for days. I feel very bewildered and undone by John's visit—at last—after *four* weeks! Of course Ginny stayed with us the whole time. It was a terrible failure on my part, because as soon as I saw them I began to cry so terribly that I couldn't speak. I begged them to take me away. That was my second mistake. John sweated it out, I suppose, and Ginny talked a blue streak. Luckily I had made a short list of absolute necessities and Ginny promised to see to them and to come back alone in a few days. The list was stamps, note paper, lavender cologne, to order me the daily Boston *Globe*, to see that mail is forwarded (there must have been *some* since I left their house, magazines if nothing else), a summer wrapper, a pair of comfortable shoes, a raincoat, and several books.

John did kiss me goodbye, but he couldn't offer any comfort. He gave me a ten-dollar bill to put in my purse. It was done rather awkwardly, and I did not thank him. They stayed about fifteen minutes. I witnessed in my own flesh that we become moral lepers here, untouchables, from whom relatives flee because they can't bear what they have done.

"It'll get better, Caro," Ginny kept saying in her bright sharp voice. "Change is always hard at your age." But I am *not* ninety, nor am I insane! They brought me a carton of cigarettes. The doctor warned me—they must know that—that smoking could be fatal after the heart attack. Well, perhaps, the kindest way of offering suicide! I shall ration myself, and see. More likely they simply forgot about the heart because they have shut me out of their minds.

Harriet kept lurking around the corner and just when I tried to tell them about how awful it is, she came in ostentatiously with a cup of tea for me, cooing, "Here, dear, this will make you feel better."

"Nothing will make me feel better," I answered. I had an impulse to knock it out of her hands, but restrained myself. Then she addressed herself to Ginny as if John and I did not exist.

"Miss Spencer has been very good," she said. "Of course she's a lady and we are a bit rough and ready for someone like her, but she never complains, do you, dear? They all go through a period of adjustment, you know, and visits are quite hard on them sometimes."

I was wracked with sobs from sheer rage and despair.

"Here's a Kleenex . . . blow your nose, dear, and you'll feel better."

I couldn't wait for John and Ginny to go. I felt as though I were breaking into pieces with shame and misery. Wanted only to be left alone, and now, damn fool, I am weeping again from writing this down.

How long a journey will it be and what must I do to myself to learn to control my feelings here? Let woe in and it's next to impossible to get it out again. The only person who helps me is Standish. He said, "Come in here, woman, and stop bawling. If I were you I'd say a dirty word. I'd say several. Didn't stay long, did they? Families are great until you really need them. I never asked a living soul for anything, and now look at me! Shit," he said, "shit on the lot of them!"

But I can't curse John. He couldn't even look at me, he was so miserable.

Later I took the tranquilizer Harriet gave me. But I must not do that again. It made me feel very logy and queer. All I have is my mind and I must keep it clear. Remember that, Caro. *Don't let them steal your mind.*

Today is a dismal day, pouring rain and wind. The trees bend and strain, and leaves and twigs are torn off, a chaotic world, even outdoors. I put on my pink blouse to cheer myself up, but it seems to me I look queer and gaunt since I came here—there is already a change in my face, so it startles me each morning. Can this worn-out, haunted old body be me? My eyes used to be so blue but they have faded. And my mouth, rather stern at best, looks thin-lipped; deep lines pull it downward. My neck anyway is pretty good for an old bird—none of those scrawny tendons showing. My pearl choker hides the wrinkles. But time at a mirror is worse than wasted time, Caro. It makes you feel depressed. Better turn the mirror to the wall.

Until lunch I am going to lie here and watch the rain and remember all the picnics Alex and I had together. We used to take sketchbooks and go off in his ramshackle little car, with a bottle of wine, cheese and bread, pâté when we were in France, a pear or an orange. We had our worst arguments sometimes about choosing THE Place. How ridiculous we were! But it had to be just right, with both shade and sun if possible—once high up on a hill in a beech wood, looking down over a field, brilliant shining gold with buttercups and marvelous swan-like clouds going over all that day. For a change it did not rain. What did we talk about all those hours? Alex worked at Barclay's Bank, some sort of junior officer—he never wanted to talk about *that*. But he read everything, a very wide-awake man with a bold, strong face, bright blue eyes and a wonderful chuckle when he was amused. And for some reason I amused him very much, the violence of my language, my American accent. We met in the National Gallery, classic encounter, in front of the Piero della Francesca Nativity. I always did feel that painting says something of great importance—stark, aloof, yet so moving because of the spaces. It struck me as a kind of spiritual equation and I pondered it that day, unaware until he spoke of the man standing beside me. "Rather a jolly thing, what?" I was so taken by surprise, to be addressed in that extremely quiet place, and to be addressed by an Englishman out of the blue, and what he said seemed so ridiculously inadequate that I laughed aloud.

"What's funny?" he asked, lifting an eyebrow.

"Such a jolly understatement!"

He gave me a keen look then, taking me in, American written all over me. "What do you see in it?"

From there we talked. He guessed I must be a poet, I guessed he must be a lawyer. We agreed that Piero would appeal to a math teacher. (Oh, I do wish I had a reproduction of the painting here!) Alex asked me very good questions. He really liked women. I decided long ago that American men really don't—and before I knew what was happening we were sitting at Rules eating salmon and drinking hock. It was not an instant love, but it was instant recognition, rather a different thing. We enjoyed each other. I felt cherished and admired in a way I never had been before. That first summer we were not lovers. I was frightened, and also dismayed when I learned that he was married. But we wrote long letters to each other the next winter and when we met the following summer we knew that we had become deeply attached. Forty-five years ago! A love affair was a momentous journey to undertake for a person of my sort. But it helped, of course, that I was far from home. No one at home need ever know. And Alex persuaded me, for my sins, that since his wife had a lover, there was no reason why he shouldn't engage himself in the same way. I got very fond of Sarah . . . life is so much stranger than anyone could believe! As I think back, it seems to me that we all behaved in a rather civilized way. There was no drama, no pulling and tearing. Alex did not want to divorce Sarah and I could see why. In many ways he was dependent on her. And she had an elusive charm, was extremely feminine, chic and capable. He liked comfort, order, and beauty, and all these she provided in an amusing little house in Chelsea with an infinitesimal garden at the back that she made into something as perfect as a scene inside an Easter egg.

Did I want to marry him or did I just screen that possibility out? At one time I hoped to have a child by him—quite mad, of course, and Alex would have been dismayed at the prospect. They had two little boys, away at school when I first met Sarah.

I believe that I wanted exactly what I had—that sense of adventure, those picnics, our zany travels together, the depth and range of our communion, yet without any of the usual responsibilities. I doubt whether I would have made Alex a good wife . . . the very thought of what would have been expected in the way of womanly grace and skill terrifies me even now. I was lucky. Only the goodbyes when I had to leave to go home each autumn were excruciating. I felt each time as though I were being asked to cut off an arm or a leg—an amputee. In those days we traveled by boat, of course, and the journey home was limbo. Often I stayed in bed for three days, tortured by missing him, and missing the part of myself that did not live at all in America. It was hard even to write for the first weeks, as words seemed an inadequate substitute for kisses, for all that touch made happen between us—and I am not one to write love letters. I find them embarrassing. Words, except in poems, were not meant to be used as counters in a sensual game. Alex wrote me poems but they were not very good—dear man.

By letter we exchanged our lives, what we were thinking and doing. As the months of separation wore on they became quite abstract, full of philosophical speculation. Amazing that it lasted nearly twenty years, and died, finally, chiefly because of the long separation through World War II. Alex was in some secret work and couldn't tell me, anymore, anything about his day-to-day life. I sent food packages to Sarah every week, and, strangely enough, she and I wrote more intimately at that time than he and I did—the tides changed, the emotional tides. I would like to write more about this but I am tired. The word "picnic" has taken me on a long journey into the heart land, and in some way has given me peace.

John's visit seems rather irrelevant now. I am over the shock. Perhaps it is better that they do not come again, or very rarely. It just seems so unbelievable that I, Caro Spencer, should find myself here *for good.*

Well, it turned out to be one of the worst days after that small interlude of peaceful memorializing. Our lunch was some sort of luncheon meat again, bread and butter, canned beans, and jello. I asked for mustard and was told there wasn't any, a patent lie. Standish threw his lunch in the waste basket. I felt he had been getting a slow burn these last days and was sure to break out sometime. I guess the lunch was the last straw (Jell-o and bread and butter are the only things on his diet). He shouted obscenities at Rose, who burst into tears. Then Harriet came and told him he was a dirty old man and would have to be forcibly fed. I could hear him yell, "You just try that and you'll be sorry!"

But he is so weak, poor tortured beast, that the anger left him white and exhausted. If only I had a bottle of Scotch: a little drink would have done him good.

The old men in the big room were unsettled by all the shouting, and even the always cheerful feeble-minded Jack had a fit of sobbing, a thing he rarely does. We are so like caged animals that moods spread. Today the mood was violently roused *against* our keepers. Apparently no one ate lunch in the end. I could hear Harriet and Rose muttering as they threw it all into the swill pail. They should really keep a pig.

Finally we all went to sleep, that drugged hopeless sleep that is the only escape at times. When I woke at five it was still raining and pitch dark indoors. I put on my light to read in the *Oxford Book* and Harriet came in in a fury and turned it off!

"We aren't millionaires," she raged. "No lights on in summer before six, do you get that, Miss Spencer?" (Heavy irony in her tone as she said "Miss.")

"What about a candle?" I asked. "Would that be allowed?"

"And burn the place down! Are you crazy?"

I held my peace. But one day I am going to break out and smash things. That is what I most fear—the anger that Standish also feels, as it burns its way, little by little, to where it cannot be controlled. I cannot afford the punishment. I am punished beyond what I can handle now. So, Caro, hold your peace, and endure, I tell myself. Or God tells me.

Today I saw the sun rise, peaceful burst of light across the misty field. It was a small red globe at first, then it got larger and the light touched everything in long gentle rays. I felt flooded with joy, as if some inner darkness had worked itself out like a poison at last. Perhaps it has been an inch-by-inch taking hold of myself, keeping anger at bay. I suppose at its most negative it is just "getting used" to the limits of my prison. For the first days, the first three weeks until John finally came, I was sick with fear and disgust. And, in a strange way, I still had *hope*. It was when hope left me after that visit that I began the road back, the road into the central self that no environment can change or poison. I am *myself* again. I know that I must expect no help from the outside. This is it. Here I stand.

And here I see what is to be seen. Today, now that the deluge is over, there are cows in the field, a great comfort. I often discussed with Alex in the old days why cows are so peace-inducing, the way they walk along, munching, in a slow-moving group, the swing of a tail now and then, the quiet pleasure of creatures leading their own tranquil lives, creatures eating. Soon the cows will lie down in the shade, dear things.

It has been altogether a memorable day as the days go here. At eleven I had not only a letter but the daily newspaper (so Ginny has at least attended to that for me) and it was a treat to read it slowly, every page. I suppose it is possessive to dislike reading a paper that has passed through several hands, that is slightly crumpled. I only wish there were someone I could discuss an article with now and then. I buzz with ideas, but they die away for lack of anything to hang them on, and because I find it hard to think in an abstract sense for very long at a time. It would be a good thing to regard my mind a little as though it were a body out of training, and to force myself each day to use it, to tone up the muscle, so to speak. Today I read at some length about two automobile accidents; one was the cause of death. Beside the copy about that, there was an interview with an officer back from five years in prison in North Vietnam. He said he had been appalled on his return to see how angry we Americans get at the smallest frustration. As he put it, a man gets into his car, and if it doesn't start on the first or second try, he becomes furiously angry. People held up in traffic for even a short while lose their tempers. Can it be true that everyone is so close to rage all the time that the equivalent of stubbing a toe leads to a tantrum? And how can we handle this state of disequilibrium? For that is what it is. Almost every day one reads about some crazy person who takes a shotgun and shoots several people simply to relieve intolerable pressure. But what has caused the pressure? And why must it be relieved only through murderous violence? Questions, questions I can surely never answer. . . .

I have saved writing about my letter till last, and now I am stupidly exhausted. It is a letter from one of my former students, married now and with children in high school and in college. Of course she has no idea what has happened to me. And she is far away in Indiana. Yet it felt like a breath of air sent to a person buried alive. For Susie I *exist*, and have existed all these years, maybe thirty-five years, for I was young when she first came to the school, a freckled child with red hair and immense curiosity, nervous, willful, battling her way through school, always in trouble. It was a happy chance for me that math was the one subject she could handle with grace and style—rare gift among girls at that time. So it turned out that I was able to help her with English, at which she was clumsy and inadequate. I'll always remember the day she chased me out to my car after school, breathless as always, and said, "Look, Miss Spencer! Is it a poem?"

I was so afraid of having to disappoint her. While she scanned my face, I read ten or twelve lines describing a seagull, a poem about freedom, I suppose it was meant to be.

"Yes," I said, "it's a poem."

"Oh Boy!" She shouted and jumped up and down with excitement. "Oh, thank you"—and she tore off without waiting for whatever else I might have found to say.

I was touched that she had asked me to read it rather than her English teacher, Miss Flood. Miss Flood was a stickler for grammar and punctuation, but she did not exactly inspire her students. And of course she resented me because I did.

I was a good teacher, as I look back on that self now. The point is that I loved math with a passion. I loved the order, the clarity of it, the absolute in it. And I think my students felt that, for me, something more than mere math was involved, an attitude toward life itself. I liked a straight answer to a straight question, in just the way that I felt the beauty of a perfect equation or, even more, a geometric figure.

"You're mad about math, aren't you?" Susie asked me once.

"Am I? Well, maybe. I suppose I see a certain order in the universe and math is one way of making it visible."

She was twelve or thirteen by then, but I always talked to her as if she were grown up. Her mind was worthy of that treatment. And she has not failed. Even when her children were small she got a job with a law firm as a secretary, then when they were in high school, she went to law school herself. Her husband is a Unitarian minister. She studied law with the idea of helping some of the indigent people he has in his ministry who keep getting rooked by loan companies or dealers who persuade them into things they can't afford. Apparently they live in a border district of their industrial town, the church still supported by "old families" who have moved elsewhere, the church building itself now in a part of the city that is at least half black. I'm proud of Susie.

How am I to answer? Shall I tell her my plight? How could she believe it? What can she do? I shall have to think about this—it will come up again. What is my stance as far as old friends go? Pride enters in. I want Susie to think of me as the vital influence I have been. Teachers should perhaps never let their students into their own problems. It is to lay an unfair burden, a little as if a psychiatrist allowed former patients into his private dilemmas. A teacher cannot become too human or too vulnerable or he ceases to be the rock every young person needs. But Susie is forty now—perhaps more. She is grown up. Am I not to honor that fact with the hard truth? How usable would that hard truth be for her? How devastating? And what is the truth? Perhaps there is none. People disintegrate and have to be "taken care of." Why haven't I had the guts to make an escape, she might well wonder. But it is impossible to describe how isolated we are here. The village is at least five miles away, and there is nothing there, no motel, nothing but a General Store which is the P.O. If I called a taxi—and I have thought of this—and simply left, where would I go? I cannot impose myself for life on some friend from the past. The fact is my friends are scattered and there is really no one in my own town, a hundred miles away, whom I could ask for help. I just about pay my own way here. Are there other better places? Horribly expensive and perhaps, *au fond*, no more agreeable. I am no longer the person Susie needed and perhaps still needs. I am an old woman, fighting for her sanity against the odds.

But before I rest, I am going to rough out a letter. Then I can change it if necessary when I copy it out and send it. It could be, at least, a test of whether anything at all can get through—whether a letter will be mailed or censored or thrown away. If I write I am sure she will answer, *if* she gets my letter.

Sometime in September

Dear Susie,

Your letter was a lifeline and I'm afraid I fasten onto it as the only helpful thing that has come to me for a month. I am now stowed away in an old people's home. My brother, who is eighty and remarried, has done this and cannot really help himself. After a serious heart attack some months ago, I had to give up the little house you remember and go to them. But it did not, and could not, work. So I am here, more or less denuded of everything that might make life livable. I am losing my memory, but otherwise intact. I believe that I have to take this as some final test of my courage and endurance. I want to meet death fully myself.

What is precious is your writing and remembering what I once was, and still am at times. I need your belief that I can make it to the end—not pity, *faith.* If I were tapping this out to you from a prison cell to a fellow prisoner it could not seem more strange or wonderful to communicate with a real human being. I am proud of you. Please believe in the foxiness of this very old party . . . I mean to outwit "them" in the only possible way, that is by not being brainwashed and by remaining,

Yours very truly,

Caroline Spencer

P.S. I still believe there is some order in the universe: only man seems to stray from it.

The day when I roughed out that letter that never got sent, and probably never will, was some time ago. . . . I do not know how many days have elapsed. I am back in my own room again, weak and grateful for small favors. What I had been most afraid would happen, happened . . . it was because of Standish in pain, his face to the wall . . . I heard him begging them to get the doctor. And when Harriet answered finally in that hard, bright, we-know-better voice, "You're not in pain. You're just stubborn, throw your medicine away, won't eat. If you're in pain, it's your own fault—" Well, I went berserk, I guess. All the frustration and anger and pity seized me like a fit. I screamed awful things at Harriet. I think I may have even tried to hit her, but she held me at arm's length. When she let go, I was blind with rage and tears and hurled a chair across the room and broke it. "You pigs! You horrible pigs!" I remember sobbing. Finally Harriet, Rose, and the woman's lover pinned me down and got me into a room without windows where I lay in the dark for several days and nights—I do not know how long— heavily sedated, I suppose. During that time Ginny came and left what I had asked for, but was not allowed to see me—for fear I would talk, I suppose. What a relief for her! That awful attack of anger tore me open to grief. Also I think the pills they give me are depressants. I wake up weeping about 3 A.M. and cannot stop. It is happening now, I cannot see to write and must lie down.

But I have to pull myself together. I can't let them win, not yet. So, Caro, you've got to build yourself back from scratch. I have to think ahead of things I can do. Tomorrow, perhaps I can copy the letter and get it off to Susie. Oh, dear, I am not strong enough to think of goodness and gentleness, of belief. They shatter me. I am not worthy, a leper—an old woman without control over herself. When I cried so much in the dark it was a small punished child crying, but that is what I have to battle against—the longing to be forgiven, to be accepted again. When they let me out and brought me back, even Harriet was horribly kind, kind as a master is to a slave who has been tortured and will now, presumably, behave herself. I am still in bed, not allowed to get up, but at least I can see the precious light, and the cows, and Pansy comes to purr on my bed. I did not appreciate how lucky I was to have these comforts before. Now I do. Ginny brought lavender water. I can put it behind my ears as my mother used to do when I was feverish. Ginny brought me a light pink summer bedjacket . . . that was so kind of her. Must I learn that even the wicked *mean* well, at least at times?

I have been a snob about these people, that is true. I have felt myself superior. It was one way of surviving. I have also allowed myself to hate. That is wrong. That is to be inferior as a human being. It takes so long to learn these things. It takes time and suffering, the worst kind of suffering, admitting that one has been wrong, admitting that one has failed, abysmally. All my life anger has been my undoing, and now I must pay for it. And I must begin the serious work of self-making that will conquer it forever.

What I long for with a deep ache inside me is sacred music. I long for the Fauré Requiem, for the Haydn "Mass in Time of War," for some pure celestial music that could lift me above myself, into that sphere where great art lives, beyond what man can be in himself, the intimation of the sacred—what cannot be dirtied or smudged by wickedness or by anger, which no threat can touch.

How can I help Standish now? He welcomed me back from the dark place with tears in his eyes and squeezed my hand—how frail his hand is now! I feared to break it with my clasp. But that amount of human trust did us both good. I am so grateful that, wrapped in dignity, and in pain as he is, he found it in him to do that. It was to thank me for fighting in his behalf, clumsy and bad though my fight turned out to be.

Did the doctor come while I was "away"? I hope so much that perhaps they did get him, but I do not dare ask. I would have to shout to ask Standish and I fear punishment. I do not dare ask Harriet or Rose as it will remind them of my tantrum. Would feeble-minded Jack remember? Would he hear a whisper? Do I dare risk it? The old men sit there like miserable caged owls, but they hear and notice everything.

Sometimes I dream that another woman might be sent. I have never wanted a woman around before, but I feel it would help a lot. The place has the reek of old men and old men's fantasies, sexual of course. I long for a woman with whom to share quite ordinary things, like how I can get my hair washed.

Since my outbreak I feel so unlovable, beyond the pale. And this is childhood again. How many times was I sent to bed without supper because I had a tantrum? And how is it that through all my life I never came to terms with this anger inside me? Yet, Caro, remember that anger is the wicked side of fire—you had fire and that fire made you a good teacher and a brave fighter sometimes. Fire can be purifying. It was purifying when the art teacher, a homosexual, was threatened with dismissal for moral turpitude, and I went to the head of the school first and then to the superintendent and managed to save Bob—he got his tenure. I withered those two affable and bewildered men and it was not by being gentle. So, Caro, try to think now and then that you are a human being, full of unregenerate anger and sometimes inhabited by sacred fire. "Child, you are not all bad!" Who said that?

Or am I thinking of Herbert . . . let me find it in the *Oxford Book* . . . Oh, what a comfort to find it again, *The Collar*:

> But as I rav'd and grew more fierce and wild
> At every word,
> Me thought I heard one crying, *Child!*
> And I reply'd, *My Lord.*

At least when I come to the very nub, to the place where there is nothing, not even belief in the self, I can still contemplate purity in Euclid, for instance, and in dear George Herbert. Now I can sleep. I have reached an island in the ocean of despair.

I think they want to persuade me that I'm not quite sane. Every now and then Harriet tells me I have done something (broken a glass, burnt a hole in my sheet) or said something ("I won't stay here another minute") that I cannot remember *at all*. There are also things I *have* done—or believe I have done—like copying out the letter to Susie, that I may not have done. Losing one's memory is terribly disorienting. The danger is to lose track altogether and begin to be whirled about on time like a leaf in the eddy of a brook—then you begin to wonder what is real and what is not, and where you are, and how long you have been there. And finally it is frightening because I can see that what happens next is a growing distrust of everyone and everything. How can I tell truth from falsehood if I can't remember anything?

Well, Caro, you do remember that you write things down in this notebook. Today, as a "temporary stay against confusion," I read it all. Here I have been for at least a month, maybe two—the leaves are beginning to turn. One swamp maple far down the field is scarlet already. Here I have been all that time and I see that this experience is real and that quite a lot has happened. And I am still able to experience it in all its agony and truth. That is something. The old men in the other room have given up or have become totally passive. They are covered over by time like weeds in water, swaying as the currents move, agitated by a change in the atmosphere, but so remote that it is as if they had ceased to live except deep down inside themselves—and what goes on there? A long daydream where food and sex loom large? In an abstract way, hardly real, or attached to reality—it is not a wife they remember but the titillation of watching Harriet's breasts waggle as she stoops, or Rose's immense bum. Ice cream brings a clatter of spoons and toothless smiles. They watch TV with the expressions of cattle, in a stupor, mesmerized but untouched. Is that the way it goes, the way it must go with me? As I re-read what I have written I see that I must make a constant effort to keep as alert as possible, not to let go even about small things—my appearance, for one.

I am keeping the tranquilizers concealed in the bottom of a box of Kleenex. I feel much more alert since I decided not to take them. And I still have that ten dollars John gave me. Someday I can pay someone to make a phone call *outside*, if someone ever comes whom I could ask. I could even get a taxi up here and escape! But if so, where to? No, Caro, there is no escape here. Don't begin to hope again. That is too dangerous.

I'll smoke a cigarette and take a rest from this writing. It is an effort to do it, yet it is also a satisfaction. Because it *is* written down and can be re-read, it is far more substantive than my idle thoughts, or even my most intense thoughts for that matter. It is *outside* me and because I can see it and read it *outside* my mind, I know that I exist and am still sane.

Today I shall ask whether I can go and sit outside. There are chairs out by the barn, fresh air, and the idiotic geese to watch dawdling about, and the leaves turning. Yesterday I was allowed to get up. I even had a cup of coffee in the kitchen. So maybe . . . if I am meek and cheerful about it. No tears, Caro, no abject pleas.

I did get out and it was wonderful. Just being outside this house was a breath of something like freedom. The sun was warm, so warm I took my sweater off. I took note paper with me and the daily paper and pretended I was an ordinary person on a vacation. I saw a cedar wax-wing, several robins, and heard a song sparrow. My hearing appears to be intact and my eyes (as long as I have on my glasses) do pretty well still. It was all such a change that I didn't read or write after all. I became entranced by the slight motion in the maple leaves as a light breeze touched them alive. I understood why Hopkins spent hours making drawings of small waterfalls and eddies in a brook. It is the same pleasure, the changes within a pattern as it is affected by a current or by motion in the air. Then when I looked down, the geese made me laugh with their ridiculous antics, their towering necks and hisses when a car drove up, their absurd waddly walk, so full of dignity. The jar leads them and his three wives follow with a young goose bringing up the rear.

"Do the geese have names?" I asked Harriet when I went back in at lunchtime.

"Only a goose would name a goose," she answered in her flat way.

"Well, someone named *me!*" It was an attempt at humor, but one might as well tell a joke to a pig.

She is tired and cross these days. There are rumors that she and the lover will go away for a month to Florida. The telephone is in the hall outside my room and I have heard her trying to get someone to take her place, not easy.

Will it be better or worse if they do go? Of course it depends on the substitute. Certainly it is a gamble as it is possible that we could do worse. On the other hand we might get a retired RN and then Standish would have the care he needs so badly. He has bed sores, I hear. He groans and curses a great deal now and sometimes does not appear to know who I am. He peers at me with a troubled look, trying to remember. I hold his hand, often ice cold, but he does not squeeze it hard as he did when I came out from the dark. He is past feeling that much any more. How long will he hold out? Will no one ever come to see him? I try not to think about him and that is cowardly.

How angry I was years ago when people refused to admit that the concentration camps existed! Then, when the evidence was there—those frightful photographs of piles of emaciated corpses, and the survivors nothing but bones and eyes—people said to me, "Why dwell on it?" I felt that if we turned away by an inch from experiencing the truth as far as it could be imagined, all these despairing people would have died for nothing, their agony itself denied them. The only thing we could do was to *know*. And after the first shock, and the horror that human beings had done this to other human beings, we had to face that, in some depth beyond the rational, we each have a murderer and a torturer in us, that we are members of each other. All my scientific ideas about progress went down the drain. It was a crisis of faith in man for any thinking person and, for some, a crisis of faith in God.

But almost all of us shut ourselves away from what is painful. Only our own pain brings us back into compassion. My father, a generous-hearted but rather limited man, imaginatively speaking, touched me when he had his first operation at over sixty. One day when I went in to see him, he was, much to my dismay, crying. I had never seen him weep. "What is it, father?" I asked, and could not have been more surprised by his answer. "The concentration camps," he said. "I have been lying here thinking about those wretched prisoners." Of course he was sublimating his own misery.

There is a connection between any place where human beings are helpless, through illness or old age, and a prison. It is not only the heroic helplessness of the inmates, but also what complete control does to the nurses, guards, or whatever. I wish I could have seen Harriet and Rose as they were before they opened this ash heap for the moribund. It may well be that they began not only with the idea that a nursing home is a sure-fire investment but with the thought that they would enjoy taking care of the old whom families abandon for one reason or another. Rose, so buried in her flesh, sometimes looks out with an innocent and childlike air, asks something like a human question. The other day she picked up my lapis lazuli pin (Alex found it for me at Cameo Corner in Bloomsbury) and turned it over in her hands with real appreciation of its beauty. (That intense blue, who has ever seen its like?). She said, "Someone who loved you must have given you this."

I was quite taken aback. "Yes—someone who loved me," I answered. Idiot to have started to weep.

"But Miss Spencer," she said gently, "that is not something to cry about. Let me fix your pillows and straighten things out here a little. The Reverend Thornhill is coming to pay us a visit."

A visitor? I felt wildly excited at the prospect but I was not about to play into *their* hands about this, so I pretended not to care one way or the other.

"And who is this gentleman?"

"Oh, he's the minister at the Methodist Church."

"No doubt it will be edifying."

(Oh dear, that was a mistake. The irony in my tone, unmistakable, and the use of a word beyond Rose's vocabulary, insulting to her. The moment of something like communication was shattered and she went about her business, banging the broom on the bureau, her heavy hands battering everything about.)

The news of an imminent visitor has thrown me off—I have lost the thread of what I meant to consider this morning. Oh yes, about what happens to people who have complete power over others. This would be a far kinder and better place altogether if anyone concerned with us took the trouble to look around, to *sense* things, to observe, and to keep an outsider's eye on our keepers. But initiative of this sort does not appear to exist—there is a fundamental shyness about interfering. After all, the daughters and sons of the poor old men here may think, it is none of our business, and Dad is losing his mind, so how can we believe what he says? They are told, no doubt, by social workers and perhaps even by doctors, scarce as they seem to be around here, that old people become "mental," a word that has always amused me, as it seems to suggest the opposite of what it means. They are told, I suppose, that old people are naturally depressed and that their depression is "built in," and that the way to handle it is with drugs, not with imagination or with kindness. And most of them are simple people, terrified of the very atmosphere of a hospital or a "home," ill at ease, not able to be themselves. Harriet's manner with them is conspiratorial. They talk in whispers to each other and in falsely jovial tones to the patients, and the son or daughter leaves feeling that he has done all he can by paying a visit. The rest is up to the "institution." They are not people who have ever had the courage to put up a fight. The police, their bosses if they are factory workers, the "company," the "government" are all terrifying powers they cannot control or even understand.

Harriet and Rose are really kind to only one person here, the feeble-minded Jack. He gets little treats. They make an effort to understand what he says and what he wants. More than once he has called them to help one of the old men. He is the pet, an easily distractable but sweet nature. Possibly it is his total helplessness that has endeared him, and the fact that he can do no harm, can never talk "against" them. He is visited by his very old father every week. (I presume he was brought here when his mother died.) They sit beside each other, almost silent after the father has said the same thing several times: "Well, my boy, you seem to be in good spirits." The father brings him hard candies to suck. The father is the only visitor I see who does not seem anxious to get away, who seems actually to enjoy seeing his boy. And he always thanks Harriet for taking such good care of "my boy," gives the rocker where Jack is permanently tied in a gentle rock or two, and tiptoes out to the taxi waiting for him in the yard.

I wonder whether homes like this are ever inspected? The deterioration in cleanliness is marked these days—I suffer from the smell of urine. Bedpans are not properly cleaned and are often left around not emptied for hours. Surely there are laws about homes like this? Is it so remote that the powers that be have never got around to inspecting? Or does Harriet (who worked in the State Hospital) have pull that makes her feel safe? Perhaps I can ask a question like this of Rev. what's-his-name if and when he comes—but I must be terribly careful. Impossible to have any privacy. All the doors are open, and Harriet and Rose *lurk* and make sudden appearances if they sense that any criticism is in the air. They will be particularly on the alert where I am concerned because I am articulate and still able to express my feelings. Now, Caro, you've got to *think* this out. Maybe the wise thing would be to try to impress this Rev. first as a human being, still *compos mentis*, only that. And then, when he comes back—but how long does that mean? In two months or more? He has never paid a call before. What I am afraid of, if he is at all sympathetic, is a torrential overflow of talk. I feel like a person on a desert island who sees a fellow human being swimming toward him out of the blue. Try not to hope, Caro. You know it is the most dangerous emotion now.

Well, Reverend Thornhill came. I had expected a sententious man in his sixties, I don't really know why—I suppose because the Methodist minister at home was like that! How wrong we are to permit ourselves any stereotype where human beings are concerned! Richard Thornhill turned out to be a youngish man, a little over forty maybe. I heard his voice in the next room, a nice warm voice, "Well, how are you people today? We're in great October weather—at least that is a tonic. The drive up the hill was so splendid!" I heard Harriet making the introductions and the quiet way he addressed each of the old men, some of whom mumbled and then were silent, lapsing into indifference almost at once. I had been so afraid he would insist on a hymn or at least read the hundred and first psalm, but he didn't. He was extremely polite to Harriet and Rose. "It must be very hard," I heard him say, "but you are doing something greatly needed." They were quick to explain that it was hard indeed, impossible to get help, but they did their best out of true Christian concern, etc. Standish, in one of his now rare rowdy moods (no doubt he was stirred up at the idea of a visitor from outside) suddenly shouted "Shit!"

There was a murmur—I couldn't catch the words. Rose ran in to tell Standish to be quiet and not to insult the minister. And Richard Thornhill, bless him, strode right past her and introduced himself.

"Mr. Flint, I'm glad to meet you. May I sit down for a moment?"

"Don't see why not. It's a free country, ain't it?"

"More than he deserve after that dirty word," Harriet sniffed, standing ostentatiously in the doorway. I could see her shadow on the wall, that mountain of flesh.

"Perhaps I could have a little talk with Mr. Flint," Richard Thornhill said gently but firmly.

"Of course. He's been poorly lately, has a lot of pain. And throws his medicine away. What can we do?" She shrugged and went away.

There was a silence. I could imagine that Standish was taking Thornhill's measure, could imagine very well the keen look he gave him. "Are you going to fool me? Are you honest? Who are you?" Then Mr. Thornhill murmured something, but of course Standish didn't get it.

"I'm deaf, God damn it! You'll have to talk louder. Can't hear a word!"

"I would like to help you if I can," poor Richard shouted.

"Help?" The answer shot back. "People in Hell get no help. They just get more Hell." Standish gave one of his bitter guffaws, a kind of curse on the universe. "Yes," he said, "try it you'll like it." (It was a commercial we had often heard on the TV and it always made Standish laugh. I would hear him saying sardonically to Rose when she brought his supper, "Try it, you'll like it.")

"I know it's not easy, Mr. Flint. It's hard going for you."

"Hard going all my life. That's no news. But just the same. I didn't think it would end like this." Again there was silence. I felt for Richard Thornhill and I admired him for being silent. Sometimes silence is the greatest sign of understanding and of respect. It is far more consoling than words of false comfort.

"Do you have no family?" he asked then, speaking loudly.

"Yes . . . no . . . what does it matter? You talk to Miss Spencer next door, the only person with her wits about her within a radius of ten miles, I guess. She has her hearing. You talk to *her*," Standish said, bearing down hard. "She'll tell you—"

"I will. God bless you."

But this, of course, was a red rag to a bull. "God bless *me?* You're joking! God doesn't have the address. God never got further than the general store in the village. God?" Suddenly he was in one of his rages. "Christ!" he shouted. "I'm an old man. I had a wife, I had children. My wife is dying miles away from me. I'm dying miles away from her. My children?" I could hear the sob wrenched out of him, then: "Talk to Miss Spencer, for Christ's sake."

So that was the introduction. I was lying on my bed in my pink blouse and blue tweed skirt. I had on my best shoes. Richard Thornhill sat down in the armchair beside me and murmured, "I upset him. I didn't mean to."

Harriet, of course, was there in the doorway. But while she said her piece I looked hard at this young man.

"Miss Spencer is our special, Mr. Thornhill. She is sometimes violent, but now she has learned her lesson, we think she is doing rather well. She's such a lady." (So I get back my ironies at their expense.)

I didn't care *what* Harriet said. I had heard it all a thousand times before. I cared about this young man. I liked his face, a little unformed around the mouth, good clear blue eyes, good forehead. He was no fool, and so far he had made no boners. His copybook, as far as I was concerned, was surprisingly clean for a man of the cloth (if that is locution). In fact, he appeared to be a fairly intact human being and I hadn't seen one for months.

"Yes . . . of course . . . I would like to have a little talk with Miss Spencer." The formula was repeated and forced a retreat, no doubt only a very short distance.

"Perhaps you would have the authority to close the door. As a usual thing it is not permitted." That was my first test of Thornhill and he responded at once by closing the door.

He himself appeared to be relieved no longer to have to try to straddle two opposed worlds. I saw he was troubled and decided to help him out.

"It must be very hard for you to come into a place like this, a place of despair. It is good of you to make the effort."

"Well, Miss Spencer," he said with a smile, "it's part of my job. I care about human beings or I wouldn't be a minister."

"The problem is that with the old, the senile, there is so very little to be done. I can see that the time you will have spent coming up here to this remote place might well, in your own mind, have been better spent helping some young boy on drugs or some desperate young mother who wants a divorce."

He gave me a rather piercing look.

"I have the care of souls," he said. "I don't believe the soul has an age in human terms."

"Really? That's very interesting. Very few people in this place have any soul. Or it's buried so deep that even you would have difficulty in making contact with it."

"Mr. Flint does," he said firmly. "What can be done for him?"

"Mr. Flint is committing suicide. That means refusing his medicine or managing to get rid of it (I sometimes help by throwing it down the john) and by starving himself. Would you deny him the privilege of dying as fast as he can?"

"You are asking me questions I cannot answer." I saw his face go pale. Poor dear, what has he known of despair?

"I'll try to ask one that can be answered. Has this place been inspected and if not, why not?"

"It's that bad." He was instantly alert. I have observed before that when moral dilemmas are involved, there is nothing more efficacious than something perfectly down to earth and practical. A bowl of soup or a letter to a representative in Congress can work wonders to relieve the conscience. "I have no point of comparison," I answered. "Perhaps this is better than it seems."

"You are not like the others here. What is your story?" he asked. I felt his strain, his fear of entering a private reserve. And I liked him for daring to ask the question.

"Nothing special." (Be careful, Caro.) "My brother, my only family, is eighty and remarried to a much younger woman. I had a heart attack six months ago—some time ago, my memory fails about such things. I had to give up living alone, and needed care. John tried to make a go of having me live with them. But his wife, Ginny, and I have nothing in common—it couldn't work. We were all three being torn to pieces. And this place was recommended by the hospital. So I am here."

I could sense that he was looking for a formula. What had I been "before"? "You were a professional woman, I presume?"

"A high-school teacher in our home town, a hundred miles from here or more. I taught math. That's all gone now, but I am sustained by poetry and the music I hear in my head."

"You compose?"

"No, but I remember Bach fugues (close to mathematical formulas) and can, so to speak, hear them in my head. Bach and Mozart."

"You have no record player here?"

"No. It is quite expensive—even a place like this is expensive. I can ask for nothing like that."

"No wonder you are sometimes violent!"

"Oh, not about that. I became violent because they wouldn't get a doctor for Standish when he was in great pain. But then I was put in a room without windows for an indefinite time—days anyway. Little by little, Mr. Thornhill, the spirit gets broken here. Maybe it has to get broken. There is no hope and the spirit lives on hope. I am now learning the ways of despair."

"How can I help you? I would like to."

I think that is what he said. I was agitated. I was trying not to weep. I focused on his kind, innocent face, so perturbed and helpless, poor young man. I think I answered, "The worse thing that happens to us here is that we cease to trust. We are lied to about a lot of things—when the doctor will come, what medicines we are taking. The only thing you could do for me would be, I guess, if I could trust you, and even more important, that you did not go away thinking, 'Well, the poor old creature is slightly touched of course, so can I believe her?' "

"You don't seem at all 'touched' to me, Miss Spencer, I assure you."

"I might be by the time you come back." That is the awful thing, that I cannot know how far I have slipped.

"I'll come back soon," he said and got up. "Could I bring some books?"

"That would be marvelous—a good rich juicy long novel, I would be grateful for *that!*"

He shook my hand warmly and we smiled at each other, an open human smile. It is a long time since I have received a present such as that from a stranger. In fact the whole conversation, short as it was, gave me a tremendous shot in the arm.

For three days after Richard Thornhill's visit I felt better than I have since I got here. I have sat outdoors every morning. Two days ago I woke and looked out and the whole field was silvered over, and that means the leaves are changing fast. It's a blazing world. Going out and sitting in the natural air is a relief from the stifling smells and atmosphere inside. For a little while I forget Standish's misery. For a little while I feel quite alive and myself. The jar comes and eats bread out of my hand. Pansy sometimes appears, a black panther in miniature, threading her way through the long grasses. The sunlight on my hand is a pleasure. I feel warmed somewhere down at that ice at the bone. I take deep breaths, and my heart, that testy animal, beats with a good steady beat.

Yesterday I went for a little walk, but I was scolded when I got back (I guess they feared I might have run away!) and told to tell someone if and when I did such a thing again. My walk was not a success, as I fell on a sharp stone and scraped my knee. This, too, was treated as a misdemeanor, just as it used to be when I was a child. Mother's attitude was that I had somehow been careless or hurt myself to get attention! Probably I think so much about childhood here, not because I am in my second childhood (What a myth that is—children have hope!) but because the humiliations are the same as the humiliations children suffer, like being treated as if they knew nothing or were incapable of adult emotions. I asked Harriet yesterday whether I had ever given her a letter to mail. (I am haunted by whether that letter to Susie ever got mailed.)

"You must be dreaming, dear. You never wrote a letter," she said with her sweet betrayer's smile.

And I am I not sure I ever did copy it out, you see. I have the letter as I wrote it and have re-read it several times, but I simply cannot remember copying it or sealing the envelope. I have discovered that one way to remember things is to associate them with an *action*. Years ago an actress told me that it was not hard to remember a part because each line was associated with motion or some physiological event—the body remembers *for* the mind.

I would like now to write a note to dear old Eva, who worked for me for years. I believe she might make the effort to come and see me. The trouble is that my town is fifty miles from where John lives and a hundred miles from here, so it would be an expedition. Her husband would have to drive her and he is terribly busy as he has two jobs, his own farming, and he works on the roads as well. I'm sitting outside now. It is easier to try to reach over the barriers and to wave my hand when I am not a prisoner in my room. So I'll do it now.

What is the date, I wonder? Sometime in September—fifteenth or sixteenth—that's close enough.

September 16th

Dear Eva,

I wish you could manage to pay me a visit here at Twin Elms home . . . I am not sure of the name of the village but you can get it from my brother, John, and directions as to how to get here. It would do me a world of good to see your face. It seems years, though I guess it is only six months since I left home. I am all right. Only it gets lonely.

Sincerely your friend,

Caroline Spencer.

Even if Harriet reads this, surely she will send it. It does not criticize or complain. And I think I have stamps that Ginny sent with some note paper back in my room.

Well, what an adventure! As I was sitting there in the late morning a small car drove up, and out got a pretty girl with a mane of soft reddish hair and very blue eyes, in jeans and some sort of blue sailor shirt, and in sandals. I wondered whose visitor she might be. I had never seen her before and for a moment I had the wild hope she might be a grandchild coming to see Standish. She looked so alive, getting out of the car with a bunch of garden flowers in her hands. She saw me just as the jar saw her and advanced, his neck thrust out, hissing at her.

"Is he dangerous?" she called out to me, half laughing.

He is rather formidable at a first encounter, and her laugh was a little shaky.

"Just showing off before his wives," I called back. "Pay no attention. He's more scared than you are."

(What astonished me was to hear my own voice, as it used to be, quite loud and cheerful for a change! I realized that we speak in whispers indoors. I have not *heard* myself for weeks.)

She ran over to where I was sitting then.

"I'm Lisa Thornhill. My father sent me over because he can't come till next week. You *are* Miss Spencer?" she asked, and when I nodded, "I felt sure it must be you. My mother sent these from our garden—the very end, but she hopes you'll enjoy them."

Impossible to tell the girl how deeply touched I was, not only by the kindness, but the flowers themselves, manna from Heaven.

I sent her in to put them in water, the sun out here would wilt them. When she came back, she went first to the car and picked up three books, two thick English novels (Heaven!) and an anthology of poems I had not seen before. Then she came and sat in the other wicker chair and for a half hour I was in the real human world again. How wonderful that I could see her outdoors, that I did not feel someone was listening. And how wonderful that I was poised, did not weep, and managed to be almost my old self with this charming girl. I did not talk about myself at all. I was eager to hear about her and the whole family.

She is in her last year at high school, the public school in the town, and will go off to Smith next year. What she likes best in school is biology and, next, photography. The family is one boy and one girl, like mine. But her brother is two years younger than she; entirely absorbed in baseball, she says. He also plays clarinet in the school orchestra. They have been here only two years. Before that her father had a parish in a small town in Connecticut . . . It is tiring to try to remember it all. That is what I shall do before I go to sleep, turn it all over in my mind, fresh food for thought for a change.

But what seems so extraordinary, even miraculous, is that at last I am being sent some help. The only thing I asked Lisa to do was to mail my letter to Eva. She waited while I went indoors for note paper and copied it out. Harriet, of course, followed me like a bloodhound into my room and asked me what I was doing.

"I'm writing a letter," I said. "Would you like to read it?"

That floored her for the moment. She sniffed and went away to badger poor Standish with more medicine he will try to dispose of, then came back to say, "Too bad to keep that nice girl waiting. . ."

But I have learned to keep silent when curses rise to my lips. I let that pass.

Anyway I got the letter safely into Lisa's hands, a small triumph, but there have been few such lately. It gave me an immense sense of accomplishment, of self-assertion against all the odds here. And Lisa offered to go and fetch Eva if she finds she can't get away otherwise.

"I love exploring the country," she said. "I just got my license, you see, and it's exciting to drive all by myself. It's mother's car, but she lets me have it." Then she looked at me candidly and asked, "Could I come and take you for a little drive one day?"

I had the queerest reaction to that. It frightened me, I don't know why. I hesitated and she sensed the hesitation.

"I have a bad heart," I said, but it was a lie. It wasn't my heart at all. I think I was afraid that such an expedition would rouse despair.

She was tactful about changing the subject.

"I'd like to come back and talk some more."

"Would you really?" It is beyond my ken to imagine that a charming young girl could *want* to see me, and I suppose there was a challenge in my tone.

"Yes," she said, blushing in a delightful way.

"All right. As long as we have a pact to tell each other the truth. Is that agreed?"

"I thought people always did."

That made me laugh—I'm afraid, a rather harsh laugh. "The truth does not exist in this place. It has become so rare that I can hardly remember what it is to believe what anyone says." But as I saw this hurt her, I added quickly, "I liked your father. It isn't easy to come here and not utter any platitudes or false comfort. I liked him because he was not out to *tell* me anything. He listened."

"And I've done nothing but talk about myself!"

"This time you talked and I wanted to hear. Come again, and I'll bend your ears back!"

"It's a deal," she said, and then it was time to go.

I am writing this in my room. I moved the flowers to the bed table so I could smell the two deep red roses and also the faint bitter smell of chrysanthemums. How starved I am! I realized in the presence of these flowers that every sense except my eyes is starved here—I do have the long field and the cows and hills to look at. But the smells are so awful that I sometimes hold my nose for a few seconds to be relieved of them. The food is not too bad, but everything is plastic, even the tray cloth (so it never needs to be sent to the laundry), the dishes, and even the glass! And I am very sick of mashed potatoes and colorless meat covered with thick brown gravy out of a can. I cannot even imagine what it would be like to feel a tender caress—my skin is parched like a desert for lack of touch. Of course Pansy, dear Puss, licks my hand and when I stroke her soft thick fur, it is an exquisite pleasure. What I am getting at is that in a place like this where we are deprived of so much already, the small things that delight the senses—food, a soft blanket, a percale sheet and pillow case, a bottle of lavender cologne, a linen handkerchief seem necessities if one is to survive. We are slowly being turned into passive, maltreated animals. I wonder whether memory itself might not be kept alive partly through the *senses*—a mad idea, no doubt. But I know that I felt *physically* refreshed by that lovely girl. And even animals respond to the environment. Pigs, I hear, are not naturally unclean, but so often kept in filthy pens that they *become* dirty and perhaps are more miserable than we know.

These days I take my book into Standish's room and sit with him. I am not sure whether he is unconscious a lot of the time or simply too depressed to communicate. He lies with his hands clasped over the coverlet, a way of keeping hold of *himself* I think. When he wakes or stirs he groans. Twice I have imagined that he was actually dying. Once I ran out to the kitchen and asked Harriet to come and see. She straightened his pillow, took his pulse, and then asked me into the kitchen for a "little talk." "It's a terminal case," she explained, "cancer, and there is nothing the doctor can do." That, she told me, is why she has not insisted that he come out. She was quite matter-of-fact about it all.

"But surely they could help him with drugs for the pain? Shouldn't he die in a hospital?"

The family have been notified that he can't last much longer and have promised to come next week.

It is such a lonely death. I feel someone must keep the vigil, one human being be at his side. So I am there. It is all I can do. I put lavender on a handkerchief and wipe his forehead now and then. I was horrified the other day to see his nails are *black*. But if I complain, they will simply beat me down. With his eyes closed, as they are almost all the time, he looks like a figure on a tomb. I pray that he may slip away each night, slip away . . . be allowed *out*.

When an infant is born, it would die if no one slapped its behind and elicited the wail that will help it to take the cruel cold air into its lungs. What rite of passage is there for the dying? I must ask Richard Thornhill about this. . .

Especially where there is no faith in God, what can one do except *be* there, to wipe the cold sweat from a brow or hold a hand (Standish's are ice cold) and try to warm it? I have been in a hospital only once, years ago, for an appendectomy. It was sudden and I had to be put in a room with two other women, one dying of cirrhosis of the liver. There was a curtain between us, but I could not but be present when a very young priest (he couldn't have been more than twenty) came to give her extreme unction. I was moved by his simplicity. When she tried to make a confession, he said, "All that doesn't matter now. God forgives you." How comforting to believe that! But what comfort is there for Standish? Or for me, for that matter? I long for his death for his sake, but when he goes I shall have lost my only friend here. I have needed the illusion that I could still be useful, be needed by someone. The bond between us was very fragile because of his deafness, yet it was *real*. I shall never forget his handclasp when I came out of the dark. We didn't need words. I did defend him in the only way I could. And he knew it.

It's very hard to write today, yet I must. This document is becoming in a very real sense my stay against confusion of mind. When I feel my mind slipping, I go back and rediscover what really happened. It must be true, I wrote it myself. If it were taken away from me I would be in serious trouble. This is my one worst fear. But so far, thank God, Harriet and Rose have not realized that it is dynamite and consider it the maunderings of a senile old woman, like a game of solitaire. I sleep with it under my pillow, and during the day they haven't time to try to read any of it.

Richard Thornhill acted quickly, bless him. But what has happened only shows that we *are* in Hell and anyone who tries to help may make matters worse. Two days after I wrote about Standish dying, state medical inspectors came. I presume they always come without warning and it had been a humdinger of a morning. One old man had a slight stroke; Jack, who is usually cheerful, had a fit of weeping; and Standish (perhaps fortunately) was lucid for the first time in days. The inspectors looked into everything, the unemptied bedpans in the hall, the dirty sheets on Standish's bed. ("We would have to change him every ten or twelve hours and we can't afford that," I heard Harriet say.) They tried to talk to me, but I was careful. After all, they will be gone and I shall be here forever. I was foxy as could be, praised Harriet and Rose, told how hard they worked, and whatever I communicated otherwise was done with a single wink at a crucial question that I answered loudly in the affirmative, "Oh yes, they are very kind here."

The result of this visitation was that Standish was put in an ambulance to be taken to the hospital. "Don't bother," he implored, "don't take me away!" At the stage he was at, any move was a threat, his only desire to be "let be," to die where he lay. He was not permitted that, and he died in the ambulance among total strangers.

I have to write this very factually, because it is so hard.

His family never came in time. His battle to die with dignity in his own way was lost. And I was not with him at the end. This, I feel sure, meant nothing to him, but to me it has been hard to bear.

Apparently the place is not going to be closed, the need is too great, and there is nowhere else available to send us. But I got it from the horse's mouth, Harriet, that they will no longer be allowed to take people as *physically* ill as Standish was.

"It's done us only good," she said to me with an air of triumph. "We won't have to take in the moribund any longer." Then she gave me a long hard look. "So whatever you tried to do, Miss Spencer, has worked only to *our* advantage. After this, mind your own business."

"But what have *I* done?" I asked miserably.

"Never mind. *We* know," she said. And I am I sure I shall be punished, but it remains to be seen just how.

Without the Thornhills—Oh, I do hope he comes to see me soon!— I would feel very much threatened. Reprisals are inevitable. At present I am ostentatiously ignored, not asked to the kitchen for coffee, treated like an imbecile.

"Poor Miss Spencer," I heard Harriet say to some visiting relative, "she means well, but she is quite cuckoo. We have to warn people against anything her deluded mind makes her invent against us."

To get away from this sordid business, let me think for a moment, now that I am outdoors and a little more free in my mind, about the *effect* of Standish's death on the other inmates. It took me completely by surprise. Of course they had little or no contact with him in the big room where the old men and Jack are. To them, he was hardly a *person*, as he was to me.

Well, when they heard he had died, there was quite a stir, not of compassion or grief, but of sheer exhilaration that *they*—Roger Thompson who has no teeth, Fred Smith who never speaks, Mr. Coughlin (he is always called Mr. I know not why) who is diabetic and comatose most of the time, and Sam Martin who reads the newspaper line by line—are alive and Standish is dead! The outer room has never been more lively. They got together and demanded ice cream. They had fits of laughter at obscene jokes Fred told. Since I came here they have seemed like the living dead. But apparently they are intoxicated by the thought that someone dies but *they* are still here, more or less alive (far less alive than Standish even when he was dying—his frail hands spoke so poignantly of a *soul!*). They have reached the stage almost of amoebas—open mouths and a digestive tract, what more? Yet life, even that primeval life they still hang onto, means this—triumph when someone else goes under! They have become incapable of pity.

They gave me salt instead of sugar for my coffee this morning. On purpose? I rather think so. I wept with aggravation, but I pretended it had not happened. I am too vulnerable these days—I have been tossed about on nights of very little sleep. (How wonderful then when the sky lightens over the distant trees at last, and the birds chirp and sing! Reprieve.) Worse than those nights are the ones when I *do* sleep and have nightmares. In the middle of one of those I got out of bed and fell, but at least nothing was broken. I badly bruised one thigh on a chair. It has a huge purple splotch on it and hurts quite a lot. At the time it was a relief to wake, even though I woke in pain on the floor, terribly frightened. I thought I was on a ship, running down horrible white corridors to try to get to air, but always I came to a locked door. I find it impossible to read. I just can't pay attention. Whatever it is going on inside me, like troubled ocean, gets in the way. Sometimes, lying here on my bed, I feel I am drowning.

"What's the matter with you?" Rose asked when she came in yesterday while I was having one of these spells. She felt my forehead. It was clammy with sweat and my hair soaked through. "Let me bring you a hot water bottle," she said quite kindly. And she actually did so. (I have an idea that Harriet, who certainly has it in for me since the inspectors came, was outside or had gone out.)

"There now," Rose said as she slipped the hot water bottle in under the covers, "that'll warm your feet, Miss Spencer. I expect you caught a chill out there yesterday in the yard."

"I haven't been in the yard for days."

She gave me a queer startled look. Perhaps I am now forgetting what happened yesterday or the day before, but I have no memory of going out. Everything here is materialistic and physical. It would never occur to Rose that I am in a spiritual crisis. It's my *mental* health that has been affected by Standish's death. I appear to be in a state of turmoil and even panic.

I wonder whether the Thornhill girl has come and had been told that I can't see anyone at present? Otherwise it seems strange that she has not come. I trusted her. It is strange that I am not weeping at all. Something is locked inside me, too deep to find the ease of tears. At times it feels like a whirlwind and I am drowning. I feel lost, abandoned, as if the whole of my life had been a long betrayal that led me to this.

Why am I being punished? It is a stark question. I ask it many times, but no one will ever answer. I feel that nothing I can do now will ever work. I am like a leper. What I touch is infected, so by trying to help him I deprived Standish of death on his terms, infected his death in some terrible way, so he died in an ambulance. What could be more forlorn? Carried away like a corpse in a hearse.

What is happening to me? When I reread what I have written here, it is clear that, far from making myself whole as I imagined might be done (that was the challenge before me) I am sinking into madness or despair, fragmented, disoriented even when I try to find comfort in the past. Is it possible that a mind can quite suddenly fall to pieces? A sort of explosion as when all the petals of a flower suddenly fall? But if so, would I be aware of it? Does madness know itself as mad?

I must somehow get under this panic to solid ground. Misery lives in me like a cancer. It is the misery of self-hatred and self-doubt. Why did I never marry? Selfishness? Some immaturity that was never ready for that lifetime commitment?

"Brightness falls from the air . . ."

What do I take with me into the darkness now? What am I? A bundle of fears and guilt, a spoiled child, whose every action reeks of self-involvement . . . Who can forgive me? Who will listen? To whom can I speak? Poor Richard Thornhill would be horrified by the depth of my depravity. He thinks of me, no doubt, as a poor dear old lady, white as the driven snow. But I am *black* inside, Mr. Thornhill, if you only knew! What is awful is to hate so much. There are times when I dream only of hitting Harriet hard across her mean, self-indulgent, lying mouth.

If keepers are corrupted by having absolute power, what about those they keep? We learn to ingratiate ourselves, to pretend we do not notice the slights and humiliations. Or we close ourselves off into that terrible place of anger, of rage and despair, where Standish died. Is that my way? Is that what is now happening to me?

"Forgive us our trespasses as we forgive those who trespass against us." That crucial sentence looms ahead of me now when I say the Lord's Prayer. I try to believe, in this turmoil, that my only salvation is to think a great deal about where I myself have failed and fail every day.

Trying to assert myself as a child, I took advantage of John, and at least once allowed him to be punished for something I had done. And in those last months, was I generous to Ginny? Did I make any real effort to adapt myself to her needs and to their life together? I did not. When John and I played Scrabble, as we did by the hour, she was pushed aside, and I pretended that I couldn't play bridge (it has always bored me) so that we would not have to get in a fourth for endless bridge games. I did it out of snobbism. I wanted her to feel that John and I share an intellectual world she cannot enter. Then there were the sharp political arguments, resuming the old wars when we were growing up. She was right when she begged me to lay off. "John gets tired," she said once. "He's not up to your fierce tone." Of course those arguments exhausted me also. At least once I had to lie down because my heart was beating that queer irregular beat. But I paid no attention, blind to her kindness where John is concerned, walled in by arrogance and contempt. The fact is that I have become dreadfully selfish—perhaps I always was. I feel I was fighting for my pride as a human being, that to survive their atmosphere I had to impose mine on them. So if I am punished, I deserve it.

Yet I can never become gentle here—gentle or loving. Standish was the only one I could practice gentleness on, or love. I hold myself together with anger, and perhaps also with a sense of being an outsider and wishing to remain so. What have I to do with such vulgarity, such crude horror? Must I take it in? Is that what is asked of me? . . . I am too tired to write any more today. Perhaps I can go to sleep now. The nights are so bad, but for some reason my nap in the afternoon is a different, gentler kind of sleep. It is so wonderful to slip slowly into unconsciousness after resting my eyes on the cows and the field, as if I could in some way lie down myself on the sweet grass and be a contented animal for a change—the sleep of exhaustion. Let the mind go, Caro—what use is it to you now? A machine that is running down and can only make an occasional sputter, never really get on the road. Or, as they say (it has always amused me as an expression) "cook with gas."

I didn't get a rest after all. Harriet, very *affairée*, came to tell me she could wash my hair. She is leaving in two days, it appears, off to Florida with her lover. A Mrs. Close, a farmer's wife, will come to help out. Harriet was rough with me, pushed my head down too hard into the basin and at one point I thought I would suffocate. The true nature of a person is communicated as much, perhaps even more, by touch than by the look in his eyes. That is something I have learned here. I am not sure whether Harriet is so rough because she feels hatred toward me, or whether it is her natural way of being. Her hands have no gentleness in them. She pulled my hair when she was rinsing it, so hard I cried out once.

"You're hurting!"

"Not grateful, are you? When I took my hour off to do this! She was suddenly furious and left me to dry it myself with a much too small towel. I finally went out and sat in the sun, shaking with emotion. I felt I had suffered an assault on my person. When I came in Jack made a supreme effort to tell me—I find him so hard to decipher as he gurgles rather than speaks—that my "friend," the Thornhill girl, had come again and been told to go away while Harriet was washing my hair. He shook his head several times as if to say, "not good, what they did."

So my worst fears are being realized. The door that had opened a crack is being slammed shut. Only there is a faint hope that Mrs. Close, Harriet's replacement, will fail to receive this ukase from on high. Rose,

with her mother here, would never have dared let Lisa in. Patience,
Caro!

Yet why indulge in hope? Quite possibly the time has passed for me
to be helped by anyone from "outside"—even dear Eva, should they
manage to get her here. I am beginning to feel beaten down in a new
way, as if resilience were slowly leaking away through these petty mis-
eries like salt in the coffee. What I am afraid of is that no one would
believe me if I tried to tell what is happening. It sounds crazy to accuse
someone of putting salt in one's coffee! They are building up an image
of me for the world at large that will brainwash anyone who tries to
come close. That explains my feelings of turmoil and panic—*that* explains
it and not my idea of past guilt that has to be expiated. I feel immense
relief to have the clue. Yes, I am afraid of a torture far worse than petty
harassments, the torture of not being *believed*. I am afraid of being driven
mad.

What if Lisa is persuaded that it *is* bad for me and depresses me to
have visitors at present? Then if she herself really wants to come—and
how do I know?—she will refrain out of kindness. Richard Thornhill
said he would believe me and that I could trust him . . . but for how
long? How easy it is to tell half-truths that distort the truth sometimes
more dreadfully even than lies. I do get stirred up by any visit. That is
true and the half-truth is to extrapolate this into a suggestion that therefore visits must cease, that they are bad for me. The only person who
can be called "well" in this establishment is he who is totally passive;
anyone who "resists" is mad and dangerous.

And so I am back again, battering my heart against the absence of
God, against the terrible need to be comforted by this imaginary Father
who knows the fall of a sparrow but who allowed Standish to die in
extreme indignity, alone. "For Thine is the power. . . ." God created
the cat who devours the sparrow. If He is the power, why do the wicked
flourish? Why are the old disposed of in places like this? "Who cares?"
is the ceaseless cry of those in Hell. It is absurd to believe for a moment
that it is in the divine purpose to prevent the old from ripening toward
death in a fruitful way. If we believe in God, then we have to believe
equally in a power sometimes stronger than His and in a kingdom other

than His, in evil more potent than we have faced before. Of course this is what came to us through the concentration camps. If God was not there, then who *was* there? *Christ Stopped at Eboli*, and the village described in the book of that title was depicted as a misery beyond good or evil. Standish's cry that day when Richard Thornhill was here (how long ago? It seems an eternity) that God never got further than the village store said the same thing, exactly. Are there those beyond the dominion of God, outside it? Am I among them now?

I will write a letter to Richard Thornhill and see if I can persuade Mrs. Close—close to God? Close to the devil?—to see that it gets mailed.

"And what's all that writing for?" Harriet asked when she came in with my supper, dead-tasting frozen haddock with congealed cream sauce over it and a boiled potato.

"A game of solitaire," I answered. "I'll need some new copybooks soon—decks of cards, you might call them."

She sniffed and went out. So, to my letter,

Late September

Dear Mr. Thornhill,

I need some copybooks for the journal I am keeping. It is a necessity or I would not ask. They have told your daughter I do better without visitors at present. That is a lie. It is true that I am very depressed. Depression is natural to anyone in my situation. I am being punished for telling you what I did and for the inspectors who came. All I ask now is to be believed.

Yours very sincerely.

But when I reread that letter, it sounded so desperate—even mad—that I shall wait some days before I send it, and probably decide then to hold it back. I am learning that any true cry from the heart of an old person creates too much havoc in a listener, is too disturbing, because nothing can really be done to help us on the downward path. So, mentioning the horror of growing old alone becomes an intolerable burden. There seem to be only a few responses possible. One is the dreadful false comfort of the cliché, "It can't be as bad as all that" or "Things will surely be better tomorrow, dear." (I suffer excruciatingly from endearments that are casual and perfunctory, because I am so starved for real feelings, for love itself, I suppose. My mother used to call me "Dear heart" and Alex called me "Lamb of God," I can't imagine why. I am and always was very unlike a lamb. My father called me "Kiddo," I suddenly remember—how old-fashioned that does sound!)

The most cruel response to a *cri de coeur* is not to believe it, or to pretend that it is a lie. That is Harriet's weapon, or one of them. "You just imagine you can't sleep, dear. I heard you snoring at four this morning." There is also the cajoling response, the one that treats the old person as an infant, the "Now, now, quiet down" sort of thing. "I'll bring you some tea."

One could only be answered differently by true caring, and that, I suspect, would show itself in silence, by the quality of listening or some shy gesture of love.

Old age is really a disguise that no one but the old themselves see through. I feel exactly as I always did, as young inside as when I was twenty-one, but the outward shell conceals the real me—sometimes even from itself—and betrays that person deep down inside, under wrinkles and liver spots and all the horrors of decay. I sometimes think that I feel things *more* intensely than I used to, not less. But I am so afraid of appearing ridiculous. People expect serenity of the old. That is the stereotype, the mask we are expected to put on. But how many old people *are* serene? I have known one or two. My granny was, but my grandfather, my father's father, became very violent and irascible. I was terrified of him and my father dreaded going to see him. He was forever going to court about some supposed slight or slander. He was a newspaper man, owner of a small-town newspaper for which he wrote most of the editorials, and by the time he died had squandered half his fortune, never very large, on perfectly absurd lawsuits.

My anger, because I am old, is considered a sign of madness or senility. Is this not cruel? Are we to be deprived even of righteous anger? Is even irritability to be treated as a "symptom"? There I go—and I myself have just accused Granddad of becoming violent when he was *old!* Was he not violent before? Of course I don't know, as I only knew him when he was past seventy, but I suspect that he always was, only it seemed outrageous in the old man as it had not seemed when he was young and "fiery."

How *expression* relieves the mind! I feel quite lively and myself again just because I have managed to write two pages of dissent about old age! Among all the other deprivations here we are deprived of *expression*. The old men slowly atrophy because no one asks them what they feel or why. Could they speak if someone did? And why haven't I tried? I look at them from very far away as if they were in the distance, across a wide river. We have nothing in common. Why pretend that we do?

I cannot quite believe in the miracle of Mrs. Close. The miracle has happened since Harriet took off two days ago, and I am stretched out on my bed like a swimmer who, near exhaustion, can lie on a beach and rest at last. The whole atmosphere has changed radically since this angelic person made her appearance in a clean white apron over a blue and white checked dress like some character in a Beatrix Potter book. My fingers tingle with pleasure at the very thought of describing her— her quick silent feet, her work-hardened hands that are so full of wisdom and gentleness when she does the slightest thing, and above all, her round, soft, pink face and her quiet gray eyes, observant, humorous, discreet. At first she simply set silently to *work*, cleaned the whole house as it has never before been cleaned, even washed the hall floor! There was a pink tray cloth on my tray this morning (where did she ever find it?) and a pink rose in a little glass.

"Anything more I can do for you, Miss Spencer?" she asked, and she did not hurry off without listening.

I would like to have kept her close to me all day, to smell her *clean* smell, as if some heavenly nurse had come to be with me. But of course she is fearfully busy. Rose follows her around making acid comments.

"You don't have to do that, Mrs. Close. They don't notice." She pays no attention and does what she wants to do. And I think Rose is daunted by the sheer speed and efficiency at work.

Later in the morning I heard laughter from the old men—amazing! And when she brought in my lunch, we had a little talk. She was pleased because I recognized the rose as a Queen Elizabeth. She had picked it early this morning in her garden, she told me.

"Sit down, Mrs. Close," I begged her, "just for a minute."

"Well," she hesitated. "I will if you want me to."

"You've done a marvelous job here this morning. We're spic and span."

We could hear Rose clattering dishes in the kitchen, and Mrs. Close whispered, "It's a disgrace, Miss Spencer . . . the dirt. . ."

"It's more than the dirt," I ventured.

"I know," and we exchanged a look, the look between two women who understand each other. The relief of that! Indescribable relief. I was too moved to speak, but she saw the tears in my eyes, took my hand in both of hers, and gave it a squeeze. It was not a sentimental gesture at all. It *affirmed* our humanity and regard for each other.

"You shouldn't be here," she said. "it's not the place for you or the likes of you."

"If someone comes and asks for me, you won't send them away, will you?" I whispered. There might not be another chance to get this across.

"Of course not. Are you expecting relatives?"

"A friend, Miss Thornhill."

Then Rose called out in her harsh voice, "Mrs. Close! Mrs. Close! The trays are waiting."

I must be very careful not to antagonize Rose—not to do anything that could poison this reprieve. Harriet will be away for two whole weeks, maybe more, who knows? Meanwhile I am alive in a way I have not been since I came. That is what a mere presence, if it is kind, can do. There is something to look forward to. I shall wake up thinking that Mrs. Close will be coming in to say good morning.

It is only a little frightening to be swept back into feeling so much. Don't make a fool of yourself, Caro! Old people, we are told, get infatuated easily. I understand it all so much better than I would have even five years ago. Whatever lives in us, the heart and its capacity for suffering and for joy never dies, and must have an object. The sin would be to stop loving. But I have only seen this dear woman for a day and already I feel less starved and ornery, less arid, less ready to break out in anger. A single rose, a tray cloth, the presence of goodheartedness, of imagination—now I am ready for Lisa. I know that I can still respond to life in a normal human way. I am not disintegrating into madness.

The rose has opened during the day. I have lain here for an hour really paying attention to it. And now I think I'll go and sit outdoors.

People have remissions from cancer when for a time they feel quite well. I am being given a remission from despair and decline. It may be my last chance to recover and sort out all that must be resolved, so I must use it well. Time had become slack, tedious. Now it races. But I am accomplishing quite a lot in my own nice quiet noisy way. Who used to say that? "Nice quiet noisy way" . . . My Aunt Isabel, of course! She was the black sheep of the family, not only went to college but got a Ph.D. in political science. At a time when ladies neither drank nor smoked she did both with zest, and I suppose she was the only person in the family with whom I could feel wholly at ease. She even made a trip to London to meet Alex and approved of our liaison. How strange that I have not thought of her since I came here. I suppose it was feeling myself again that has made it possible. The very thought of her energy and the great way she died, of a heart attack on the way to get an honorary degree from the University of Wisconsin, would have depressed me too much when I first landed here. I never quite met her standards of superior achievement, but at least she understood why a woman of some intellectual distinction might hesitate to marry. "Be yourself, Caro," she used to say. "No one can be that for you." She was a prima donna, of course, and of course the family resented her fame and her women friends, her getting away with murder and flourishing despite it all.

She was my mother's older sister; they could not have been more different. When she came to visit we had a family joke that Hurricane Isabel was about to strike. She arrived with huge amounts of luggage, two or three briefcases of papers and books, made demands no other woman would have been allowed to make, worked till the early morning hours after everyone else was asleep, got up at eleven and expected breakfast, demanded endless martinis before dinner, teased my father and treated my mother with what can only be called condescension. But when Hurricane Isabel left, the house seemed very empty and life rather dull, even to my parents. They resented her intensity, her drive, but without it, for a week or so, they saw the dingy aspects of their life rather too clearly. At least, if they did not, I *did*. I couldn't help comparing her life, so wide open, so luxuriant, with theirs, so closed in, prim and safe.

For years I was terribly jealous of John, in whom she took an interest. Children bored her and at fourteen and fifteen I was a rather boring child, no doubt. But John was interested in ideas, a worthy antagonist, and they went at it together. Often my parents went to bed in sheer desperation, while she and John went talking about "progressive education" or whatever was in the air, and I, solemn ghost at the feast, nearly went to sleep but refused to leave for fear of missing something.

Later on I suppose I was a little in love with her and her life, and later on she enjoyed what she called my toughmindedness, teased me about being a mathematician, took me one wonderful summer to Europe, a slow, rich progress to her favorite places—Chartres, of course, the Dordogne, St. Paul de Vence, Venice, and finally Sion, in Switzerland. What would she have been like if she had lived to be very old? When she began to lose her powers? Well, of course, faithful Daphne, the last one of her several "friends," would have looked out for her. She attracted people like a magnet, attracted by sheer vitality and zest for life. She was always surrounded by admiring students, male and female. And by women, jealous of each other. I do not believe, strangely enough, that she was a very passionate woman. She aroused passions rather than experiencing them, is my guess. Oh, what I wouldn't give to have her sail in here and demolish the place by the sheer force of her personality! She would have carried me off without a moment's hesitation!— Such fantasies, Caro. The truth is that the people who could save the old in places like this have died—that is why we are put here, because there *is* no one.

I had a note, at long last, from Ginny to apologize for the long lapse. John, it seems, has been quite ill with pleurisy and nearly died. So that explains that. She promises to come in before they go south later on. He cannot, say the doctors, stand the winter here. The winters! I think of it with dread. Snow piled against the windows, drafts, being marooned.

Well, I was sitting outdoors, reading, at peace with myself, when Richard Thornhill drove up late that afternoon. He brought four or five splendid copybooks and a powerful transistor radio on which he thinks I can get music at certain hours. It has an earphone thing so I can listen without disturbing anyone. He brought more flowers from his wife. But, far more precious, he sat down for an hour and we had a real talk. I am almost afraid of so many good things happening—what fury stands in the wings? It can't last. A gentle voice, gentle hands, the silent communion with Mrs. Close *and* a charming young man who treats me with respect and listens to what I say! Can all this be real?

Richard (we are on a first-name basis now, at least on my side; he cannot quite bring himself to call me Caro) asked why they had told Lisa I couldn't see her—was it my wish?

"No, that was Harriet's way of punishing me for having told you so much, for the inspectors coming."

"I can't believe it!" The words sprang out spontaneously. He had no idea how frightful they were to hear. I had a queer sensation of dizziness and covered my eyes with one hand. It all rushed in, the fear of madness, of not being believed. I didn't know what to say, how to tell him. But he must have guessed, for he added after a moment, "Of course I believe you, Miss Spencer, if you tell me so."

But his eyes were troubled when I met them.

"No one believes in wickedness until he meets it face to face. I never did before." I was trembling and could hardly light my cigarette. He took the lighter from my hand and did it for me.

"Please, Miss Spencer, don't be upset. I had no idea, of course, that my effort to help could go wrong."

"It didn't . . . only . . . you see they took Standish away and he died such a lonely death in the ambulance. I felt responsible. The inspectors won't allow really sick people here any more. And that's right. Only *they* hate me now."

It was an awful moment. I felt I was spoiling his visit for him and for me, too. Tears flew down my cheeks like rain. I couldn't help it. "Nothing can be changed here," I managed to say when I had pulled myself together. "It's a locked world."

"It doesn't have to be," he said firmly. "Next time Lisa comes she will force her way in. Of *that* I can assure you."

For me it had been a violent fall back into the grief I had kept at bay since Standish died. But with it came a flash of insight. I did not, of course, tell Richard what I saw in that flash. It was that things can be changed here, but only by violent action. If I lose my temper I will be put in the dark again. But if I burn the place down some day, I can open this locked world—at least to death by fire, better than death by bad smells and bedpans and lost minds in sordidly failing bodies. I was staggered by the flash of what I conceived. The tears stopped at once and I became crazily cheerful, talked a blue streak, told him about John, gave a quite humorous criticism of the long novel he had brought, as a strong but aberrant cartoon of life—what people want to believe, not what is true. And this led us back to old age and death. And finally to my King Charles' Head, wickedness, and what one does in its presence, how one handles it.

"People become wicked," I said in the flush of all this talk, "when they have absolute power. I think that's the answer. One reads about fathers who brutalize infants, for instance. "The battered child syndrome," I believe it is called. Have you run into it, Richard? It seems so horrible."

"Yes," he nodded. "It happens every day. A man or woman is frustrated for some reason, an unfair boss, or what have you—comes home to a crying baby and breaks its arm. I've seen it."

"What do you do about it? How can one help?"

"I don't know," he sighed. "I try never to blame, or at least try to withhold blame, try to understand what the frustrations back of cruelty are. It's never easy, Miss Spencer. Such people are eaten by guilt."

"My experience of wickedness is that it is Protean—you can't seize onto it. And you can't because the truly wicked perhaps live in Heaven, a Heaven of their own making. They do not admit even to themselves what they have done or are doing. Harriet Hatfield is a perfect example. Her image of herself, I feel sure, is that of a compassionately overworked human being who has taken over the responsibility of others toward their fathers, mothers, sisters, et cetera, for little pay. She feels superior to me, for instance, *because* I have been left in her care. In here own eyes she is perfectly good. *She* feels no guilt, I can assure you. It is the innocent, not the guilty, who live in Hell," I heard myself say. And I have been thinking about this ever since. (The wonderful thing about real conversation is that it stimulates one to new insights.) Richard fumbled when I pressed my point, "And if that is so, how can you believe in a just God?"

I liked him because he took his time. He narrowed his eyes and looked down at the hands clasping his crossed knee. He is rather an elegant creature and I enjoyed looking at him. He pleases me as a man and as a human being. Brilliance, intellectually speaking, is not required of the ministry, but integrity is. And it is becoming rare in any field. Richard has it, and I feel it in Lisa too.

"You are really probing my faith, Miss Spencer," he said with an odd shy smile.

"I suppose so. Well?"

"I don't know," and he suddenly laughed. "Perhaps part of me believes that we are every day making God possible as He made us possible—He fails us when we fail Him. Maybe," he said, "wickedness is what God cannot deal with Himself. We have to deal with it."

"Cancer, for instance," I murmured, "when normal cells go wild and overmultiply—you mean we can't blame God for that?"

"Maybe . . ."

It was time to change the subject and I did. But it has given me much to think about. In this little distance from Harriet and in the blessed presence of Mrs. Close, I must try to achieve detachment and to stop hating so much. Hate is corrosive. But how to deal with Harriet? That remains a mystery.

These are wonderful days. They begin with dear Anna Close and my breakfast tray—though actually they begin with sunrise. Sometimes the field is covered with frost and sparkles when the sun climbs over the trees. I lie in my bed as the grey dawn changes to blue and the round red sun climbs up. Frost has brought changes to the trees and now everything is red and gold at the end of the field. I do not really want to die at all these days. I am avid for life. Sometimes Anna can sit down for a minute after my breakfast when she has taken care of the old men and comes back to get my tray. She is not a talker. I feel perfectly at peace when she is there and we do not need words. She seems to understand me in a way I have needed for years. The room feels airy and clean when she has been there with her magic touch. No more dust under the bureau these days! But it is not that, it is being cared for as though I were worthy of care. It is being not humiliated but treasured.

"I wish I could take you home with me," she said the other day, "but my husband wouldn't hear of it, and there are no conveniences. Children pouring in and out."

"Don't let's think ahead," I said quickly. I wanted to ask her when Harriet is due back, but I was afraid to. The only way I can handle this inevitable disaster is not to think about it. "Let's count our blessings," I added. "You make me feel ten years younger, Anna."

That made her laugh her soft secret laugh. "I'm sure I can't think why. I'm no one for the likes of you, a plain farmer's wife who has never been outside the state, if you can believe it."

"It's not that," I said, brushing away what seems quite irrelevant. "You're an angel in disguise."

"Quite a disguise, I must say," and she laughed again and gave me an amused look out of her clear blue eyes.

I think she is a little afraid of my feeling for her. No doubt it seems absurd. And no doubt it is. But while she is here, surely I am permitted to bask in goodness—it will not last long in this place. She insists on taking my things home to wash so they won't be stuffed into the machine here. She brings them back beautifully ironed and wrapped in tissue paper. "I do like that blouse," she will say, giving the package a pat. "It has a label from Paris." I realize that a blouse from Paris dazzles her.

"Hermès," I murmur.

"I just can't understand their leaving you here," she says. For by now of course she knows all about Ginny and John. "It's all very well for those old men, this is the sort of place they lived in before. But *you* . . ."

"Nobody stays special when they're old, Anna. That's what we have to learn."

"I don't believe that." She is, for once, angry, and flushes. "I would like to wring that Ginny's neck."

But now I am defended I can be generous. "It's not her fault, you know. She's got her hands full. And I was beastly to her, so maybe I deserve what I got."

So we talk, but it is not the words that matter. When she goes she pats my hand and sometimes kisses me on the cheek, "You'd better get outside in the warm sun," she says, "and do your writing there."

My notebooks fascinate her. "What do you do it for?" she asked me once.

"Oh, to keep alive, I suppose—to tell myself I am still able to feel and think." But there is another reason. The notebooks are my touch-stone for sanity.

Anna's mother died last year. She was completely blotto for years, at the end didn't know who Anna was. When Anna tells me about her, I get terribly frightened. She turned against them all before the end and threw things. And Anna had a hard time keeping her at home for her husband had enough of it long before the end. He appears to be a rather hard man, hard but a man of integrity, nearly works himself to death with the cows. They still have a herd, and when Anna comes here at seven she has been up since five to give him his breakfast. He didn't want her to take the job, but finally agreed because they need a new frigidaire and her weeks here helping out will make the down payment. I sometimes ask myself what I do for her, she who does so much for me. I think perhaps it is a glimpse of a woman's life not entirely spent in physical struggle to keep going—pretty things, a blouse from Hermès. She does not want them for herself, but she gets a romantic delight out of what I am and plies me with questions about Europe. To her I suppose I am like some rare bird, a scarlet tanager who suddenly appears in the backyard. One day she asked me, "Why didn't you marry, lovely as you are?'

It was a hard question to answer. How could I tell her, perhaps that I am a failure, couldn't take what it would have cost to give up an authentic being, myself, to take in the stranger? That I failed because I was afraid of losing myself when in fact I might have grown through sharing an equality with another human being. And yet . . . do I really regret not marrying? No, to be quite honest, *no*. I must have been silent for some time, because she said, "I shouldn't have asked."

"I'm sorry, I was thinking," I answered.

"You don't have to tell me."

"I want to tell you the truth. That's the problem. What is the truth?"

But then she had to go, for Rose was calling her as usual. Rose deeply resents our intimacy. She senses, I suppose, that something is going on that cannot be controlled. But even Rose has become more human in Harriet's absence. She dislikes me because she senses a superiority I cannot hide however much I try to. But I do not believe she actually hates me as Harriet does. She is simply at a loss about how to behave toward me. She has been trained to treat the inmates as inferiors to be ordered about, controlled in every possible way. I escape the control simply by being myself. However meek I am, I am still myself. This, I presume, is what has to be destroyed.

I live in dread of Anna's leaving, but there is something I can keep. Quite often I can get real music on the transistor radio in the evenings. It makes what used to be long hours after Anna has gone home a time of marvels. I marvel that such beauty flows in through my ears, unheard by anyone else. What a miracle! Last night I heard the Faurè Requiem, sung by the boys' voices in King's Chapel, and the other night Mozart's clarinet quintet and a Beethoven quartet. I have never listened to music with such absolute attention in a long life of hearing a great deal of it. Here there is nothing to distract. I give myself wholly to listening as if an astonishing angel had come into the room. I force myself not to daydream, not to think about Anna, for instance. Giving the music my whole attention I sometimes actually see notes written on a page (a curious reversal of the usual thing of hearing what one sees). I get a distilled pleasure from it that resembles what mathematics did for me in the past—a total absorption in abstract beauty, I suppose it is. My feelings have nothing to do with this pleasure, at least when I am hearing music. The romantics, even Beethoven occasionally, have a less wholesome effect. There is the danger that the Vox Humana sound too loudly, and then some door into private never-solved conflict flies open and I am undone. I become a lover, not a listener. Who was it who said that Mozart *feels* like an angel? Perhaps Gide in the journals. That is not quite right, but my understanding of what Gide meant is clear nonetheless. Mozart always transcends the dung of human experience. It is all there but transcended, as, indeed, an angel might apprehend it. And does that mean detachment? Perhaps, but of a very special kind known only to the creators. I would like to write a poem for Anna. But in this strange time of my life, in this strange place, it appears that I must suffer feeling without expression—it is to be used, if at all, as a reason for not dying. And I am not a poet, God knows.

But I am about to die. Harriet comes back on Saturday, in three days, in three days, in seventy-two hours. When Anna told me this morning my breakfast tray had a deep red rose on it. I went absolutely blank and turned my head away. I was falling through space in a state of uncontrollable panic. I could feel the sweat on my upper lip.

"Are you all right, dear?"

I was unable to answer. I was afraid that a single word, even "yes," even "no," would open a floodgate, that I would cling to her like a baby and howl. Perhaps Anna sensed that the best thing was to leave me alone. I listened to her gentle cheerful voice talking to the old men, their murmurs and cackles like a crowd of starlings.

How can I handle Anna's leaving? It was always there, the darkness ahead, but until the time of Harriet's return had become definite, circumscribed, I could pretend that she might be killed in an automobile accident. I could indulge in fantasies. Two weeks is a very short reprieve for those in Hell. A two weeks holiday, one might say. I cannot imagine a way to get myself ready for what must come. I suppose it is a matter of closing the door. Battening myself down. My jaw aches from holding a grief back. And I cannot summon the courage to get up and dress. It is all very well to scold myself, "Don't be absurd, Caro," but reason tells me that it is a disaster, a real one. It cannot really be transcended.

When Anna came back at eleven with a glass of milk and a biscuit I asked whether she would come and see me "afterwards." Her words were reassuring but I saw the shadow of a doubt cross her candid eyes— would she be allowed to?

"Anyway I could write to you, couldn't I?"

"Yes, dear, of course."

"And you will answer?"

She looked daunted, for once at a loss. I could see that the idea of putting feeling into written words was disturbing. "I'm not very good at writing letters," she said with that secret smile that hovers about her lips as though she were about to say something that will never be said. "My son James laughed at me when he got back from Vietnam last year. Apparently all I ever said, was 'I miss you and come home soon.' I'll try, dear," she said quickly, "but you mustn't expect too much."

"But you will read my letters?"

"Of course." For a second our eyes met. Then she fumbled for words, "I think so much of you, Miss Spencer . . . you must know I do."

So I am busy making up letters. That is something to hold onto. How very strange that at seventy-six in a relationship with an inarticulate person who cannot put any of it into words, I myself am on the brink of understanding things about love I have never understood before. But then I remind myself that this is one of the proofs of true love: It always comes as revelation, and we approach it always with awe as if it had never taken place before on earth in any human heart, for the very essence of its power is that it makes all things new.

Have I ever before really understood the power and the healing grace of sensitive hands like Anna's? Have I even experienced *loving* as I do in one glance from her amazing clear eyes that take in at once what my needs are, whether it be food or a gentle caress, a pillowcase changed,

a glass of warm milk? No wonder so many old men fall in love with
their nurses! I used to think of them with contempt—old babies, old
self-indulgent babies. And now here I am in much the same plight! But
I cannot offer Anna marriage or take her into my life, or in any way
help her as she helps me. I cannot bind her to me.

Oh dear, that is what makes the separation so agonizing—our mode
of expression will be gone. She will forget me soon enough, no doubt.
She is still carried forward on the demands of day-to-day living. I am
frozen here in this "still pond, no more moving."

And I am crying again and cannot go on.

Yesterday I was unable to write, but I did get up, made myself dress
and go out, though the air was chilly. It was lucky I did because Lisa
came, and I can always talk more easily outside this jail. She came,
bless her heart, to say that she has arranged to bring Eva here next
week, and she must have seen what a tonic effect that news had, something to look forward to after the disaster tomorrow. I am quite proud
of myself because I did not break down. It is odd how *not* crying makes
my whole jaw ache. But I must try to appear at least to be normal. I
want this girl to believe in my sanity. It is quite necessary for my future
plan that she do so. I asked her quite casually whether she could bring
me a large can of lighter fluid when she comes next week—she brought
me a carton of cigarettes and a crossword puzzle book.

(I didn't tell her that ever since a very rough passage to Europe, years
ago, when I did crossword puzzles between bouts of seasickness, I can't
look at a crossword puzzle without my stomach heaving.)

It is a comfort to have a plan that would end the Hell here but the
strange thing is that the very existence of Anna (even though I shall see
her rarely if ever), the fact of pure human goodness having come into
the orbit, makes it harder to do anything drastic now. And perhaps it
was her presence, shaking out a mop as we talked, giving me a wave of
her hand in the doorway, that made it possible for me to get Lisa to
talk a little about her world, as shaken by love as mine is, avid for food
that will nourish that hunger—poetry, music. Her young man has gone
to Turkey this summer, the mecca for youth these days, a kind of new

world where they imagine they are Marco Polo all over again, bumming rides to cross mountains and deserts to Katmandu—I think she said Katmandu. She is afraid of losing him to the wandering girls, to the pick-ups, afraid of his losing his way. He had wanted to be a doctor, she said, but was wavering now before the arduous years of training.

"Peter is very young," she said, as women have said of their lovers from time immemorial. She seemed rather an old-fashioned girl this time, and I teased her and told her she had better go to Turkey herself.

"I'd be scared to death," she admitted, a quick wild blush rising to her ears. "I'm not adventurous."

"He'll be back with the winter birds," I told her. "You'll see."

With this visit I climbed out of that pit of panic and loneliness. It gave me back a sense of proportion. It's too easy in this place to go a little crazy as prisoners often do. The inner world blows up like a balloon. But now I can rest. I must prepare to say goodbye to Anna and do it with dignity. Compose the mind, Caro! Think of goodness. Think of courage. Think of all you know that a young girl cannot know, and be strong.

Words . . . words . . . words . . . I reread that last passage and it was dust and ashes.

Harriet has been back for two days. She is full of hearty cheer and hatred. I suppose she hated to come back as much as we dreaded her return. She is brown and has lost a little weight. The first morning she brought in my tray, the old plastic one, as before, she greeted me with "I hear you've been spoiled, Miss Spencer, but you must understand that I have no time for fol-de-rols."

"I understand," I said meekly. I am terribly afraid of her, irrationally afraid. I feel like an animal that growls at some perfect stranger as if meanness and cruelty had an actual smell. But I do not dare growl. The mean mistress has to be placated if possible.

"Did you have a good holiday?" I managed to ask.

"Good enough, but everything is so expensive, how can a person have any fun?"

I wanted to say, if you mean sex, that usually does not cost money, but I refrained. I suppose she pays for her lover, but perhaps it is mean-spirited of me to think so. At any rate she dominates Ned completely, and he looks exhausted. She is always cajoling him into doing some odd job. He comes home from the day's work—a mechanic, I think he said he was—looking as if all he wanted was a beer and some peace and quiet. Instead I hear her shouting at him, "You haven't been emptying bedpans all day! Take out the rubbish and stop babying yourself!" He never talks back. They have sex, as the saying goes, but it doesn't look as though they had much else. I breathe Anna in and out with each breath. Her name is my air. And today I reread all that I had written about her coming, the miracle that it was. But I am very sore inside as if I had been beaten. So sometimes "breathing Anna" is breathing pain.

My daily stint is to endure. It is different from conflict. Conflict may be fruitful, at least it contains in it the seeds of a future, of a resolution. I endure in a vacuum. What I endure will not end ever until my death. When I wake up I still imagine that I will see Anna, that her smile will soon come to me, and then I have to realize that the good dream is over and the nightmare is the reality. The early morning is the hardest time. I can hardly bear to see the sun rise, to see the golden leaves sifting down, down, and to know that I have to get through a whole long day. So I get up and dress. Today I cleaned my room myself, to no praise, I may say.

"What do you think you're doing with that dustpan?" Harriet asked irritably. "Isn't it clean enough for you here?"

"I just felt like doing it."

"Mind your own business, Miss Spencer. Please give me that dirt and I'll dispose of it."

Unfortunately it is too cold today to sit outside. Perhaps I can manage a little walk later on. But first I want to write a letter to Anna—I have waited two days to do it, two long days. I felt unable. And even now my hand shakes when I take the pen. It is as though I were somehow contaminated already, not the person she knew. Hatred seeps in, the fear of madness. Anna, help me.

I will try a letter out and see what happens. But words are no help.

She is not a word-person. She is back in her own life now. What did I mean to her? She is "outside," safe. I am inside, in danger of despair and madness, in danger of appearing ridiculous—even to myself.

Yet I must believe. I must try to keep intact what is gentle and loving—as long as that is possible. So I lie here on my bed and look out at the sky, pure and brilliant, the wholesome world outdoors, where there are seasons, the leaves change and fall. . . . The chipmunks are busy these days. I love to watch their swift runs, tail in air—they are harvesting. And I must harvest, too, stow somewhere in the depths of my heart all I have been given to sustain me, all I can keep of Anna. And give her all I can summon today to tell her what she has given me. . . .

End of September

Dearest Anna,

You have been gone now for two days. And I have wanted to write you. I hope that you miss me sometimes, although I am sure your own life has filled in whatever emptiness you may have experienced at first. It is different for me, of course. I do not lead a normal life any longer and so, perhaps, am not quite normal myself. You may think I am a loon when you read this, yet I must try to trust you. You are the only person whom I can trust now. Lisa came and told me she would bring me down to see you next week if that is all right with you? You must imagine how much I need your answer. I feel so hopeless.

I want to tell you that you have brought me back from Hell to Heaven, from nothing but hatred and despair to love. You must understand that this is a miracle. I shall never forget your face, your gentle hands . . . I want to tell you what touch can do to bring life back to the dead. The first time you clasped my hand I became a little child. I felt safe for the first time since I came to his dreadful place. Every morning I woke before sunrise and knew you were coming soon, I was filled with joy like a child. When you were busy working I heard your voice. The rose you had put on my tray was beside me. Of such small things is Heaven made when one loves again. But all the time I knew it was only for a little while. Perhaps that is why my feelings were so intense. It all had to be experienced immediately for it could not last. I wonder whether you ever felt like this—that we had very little time.

You gave me so much and I could give you so little, that is what bothers me. But once you said you liked my blouse from Hermès. I want to give it to you and when Lisa brings me I'll have it with me. We won't be able to talk at all, I fear.

I bought the blouse to please Alex, the man I loved. So it comes from my old love to you, my miracle of new love, with all my heart.

This letter says too much and too little. But I have found it very hard to write. What we had was a *silent* communion. Words are leaden by comparison. God bless you and keep you, and do not forget that I love you.

Caro

I have read and reread this letter, so inadequate. But I doubt whether I can do better. I have to hold so much back. I will copy it out this afternoon. Now I must go for a walk, get *out*. Perhaps I can manage to walk this ache out, get myself really physically tired.

Did I go for a walk? I don't even remember. I must have, yes of course I did, for that was how Harriet got hold of the letter. I had left the copybook open on my bed. Since then—how many days?—I am being tortured. Harriet read what I had written. She has made everything dirty and destroyed it.

"I didn't know you were a dirty old woman," she said when she brought my lunch in that day—when was it?— "At least the old men think about women. They are not filthy like you."

"It's not filthy to love Anna," I said. "She's a beautiful person."

"And she kisses you, no doubt, and she clasps your hand."

The sneers fell like stones, well aimed. Every one found its mark. "This is no place for queers," she said. "We'll have you in the State Hospital if you ever dare send such a filthy letter."

I was silent—silent with dismay.

"At least I've saved Anna from your dirt," Harriet said smugly. "She *is* a good wife and mother and grandmother. She doesn't need your smears, Miss Spencer."

How much was I supposed to take in silence? I got up and walked out of the house. I felt I would walk till I dropped dead. But they soon caught up with me in the truck, she and her lover.

"Oh no, you don't run away," Harriet said as they came to a halt and the man jumped out. "I undertook to take care of you and I will."

Every word of this is grooved so deeply into my mind that I write it down now, days later. I was put in the dark when they got me back, and I suppose Lisa, if she came, was sent away. Now they think I am tamed out of any reaction. I am back in my bed. I am given light again. I am very meek and mild, of course.

Today I was handed a postcard from Ginny and John, from Florida. It said, "A bit hot here, but John is getting along nicely. We both send our love."

Love? I have come to loathe the word. I hope never to utter or to hear it again as long as I live.

Harriet holds over me the threat of commitment to the State Hospital, but I doubt if she would have the legal right. I suffered real panic about this and have lain low. But sometimes I long to be put out of my misery. At least there they have drugs. I would be put to sleep, I suppose, kept in a state of lethargy. Wouldn't that be better than my present anxiety—am I a dirty old woman?—guilt, and despair. I have spoken, I feel, lightly of despair before this episode. Now I know more about it. Now I begin to understand Standish. There is a point of no return, a point when the only question is whether to choose to starve to death or to use a more violent means.

The Lord's Prayer has ceased to be of any comfort. I cannot forgive my enemies. I have been murdered. Murdered in the most cruel of ways possible. How can I ever forgive Harriet? Why should I? If Richard comes I shall refuse to see him. I cannot offer him my humiliation or even talk about it. I have become a leper to myself. I cannot contaminate lovely innocent Lisa. I am beyond the pale. Very well—I have my own ideas of what those beyond the pale do—the blacks, for instance. They finally come to see that violence is the only answer to oppression. They make bombs. What was good in them becomes evil. They want only to destroy. I understand them now very well. I have been punished enough. Once I believed in mercy and had a supreme example of it in one who shall be nameless now. But mercy fails against wickedness. God, if you exist, take me away. Blind me, destroy my every sense, make me numb. Drive me mad. It is all I can pray for now.

Days have gone by. It must be October, mid-October I think, because the leaves are flying fast. The great maples are skeletons against the sky. The beeches are still a marvelous greenish-yellow, a Chinese yellow, I have always thought. Pansy, now the nights are cold, sometimes comes to sleep with me, and slips out (clever cat) before anyone has stirred. The only time I weep is when she is there, purring beside me. I, who longed for touch, can hardly bear the sweetness of that little rough tongue licking my hand.

There is nothing to say any longer. And I am writing only because Lisa is to bring Eva today. Harriet doesn't want them to see me as I was—dirty hair I hardly bothered to comb, an old woman, a grotesque miserable animal. She washed my hair and it is drying now. This time she was gentle, thank God. I suppose she can be because I am just a passive bundle. She brought me a clean and, for once, properly ironed nightgown. I do not dress very often any more. I feel safer in bed. I suspect they are putting sedatives in my coffee, for I feel very sleepy after breakfast. I am too tired now to go on writing—anyway why go on? I once believed I could keep myself alive here, partly by recording the experience. But I had not reckoned with . . . but I simply must not think about that. The only thing a tortured being asks is not to be tortured any more. I wonder whether X—I shall never speak her name again—has tried to reach me. But who knows? I may have made the whole thing up. Mad people do have dreams, I suppose. Anyway, it was all such a long time ago, if it ever happened. How am I to hide my misery from Lisa, from Eva? How not to hurt them and hurt myself by spreading this leprosy? I do not address myself any more as Caro. Caro is dead. I cannot say "Pull yourself together, Caro" for that person has ceased to exist. Someone else, mentally ill, tortured, hopeless, has taken over my body and my mind. I am in the power of evil.

I wish they were not coming. I do not know how to summon anyone to meet them. There is no one here.

Harriet of course came in with them . . . I heard her whispering in the hall, "Miss Spencer has failed rapidly in the last weeks . . . be prepared for a change . . ." (This to Lisa, I presume.)

Lisa ran in and, much to my surprise, kissed me. "I am so glad to see you, and I've brought you Eva." Poor dear Eva was clearly in a state of shock, and I don't wonder. At first she was so overcome with shyness and not knowing what to say to the wreck before her, that she hardly looked at me. She sat in the chair by the bed, her hands clasped, and a look of fierce determination on her face to see the ordeal through. Lisa tactfully withdrew and closed the door behind her.

What did I say? Some casual remark about its being good of her to come, and good of Lisa to bring her.

"Oh, my dear Miss Spencer, you've been crying," she wailed. "It's a terrible place!" I had tried to imagine what it would be like to see her again, but it had never occurred to me that she would break down herself. She fumbled in her bag and drew out a box of candied ginger. The dear old thing had remembered that I love it.

"Let's have a piece right away. It'll cheer us up," I said.

But all I felt was an immense weariness before the effort of making contact across such an abyss of time and pain. We talked for about a half hour and by the end she was able to tell me a little about herself, the arthritis in her hands (they are quite warped and gnarled) and news of various acquaintances . . . but it is all so far away, I could only pretend interest. Harriet came in twice, officiously, to bring cups of coffee and coffee cake.

"She seems kind," Eva murmured, but with a look of bewilderment in her eyes. I suppose she sensed things she could not really get hold of. And there is no point in my even trying to tell anyone about torture. Too easy for that to be laid aside as senility, the paranoia one hears about. I don't know what I said in answer. The visit was simply a disaster. It is far too great an effort to try to pin down all the reasons. When Lisa came in, poor Eva was crying uncontrollably, and hardly able to say goodbye.

Dear Lisa looked upset, too—I suppose I have changed since we had that good talk in the garden. She kissed me goodbye and whispered in my ear that she would send her father to see me.

I did not cry even after they had gone. I have become numb where human beings are concerned. I cannot afford to feel anything at all. I am walled in. I do not want to see anyone and shall have Richard turned away if he does come. The time for hope is past. Shall I ever have the strength for action? I have hidden the lighter fluid in the top drawer of the bureau under my scarves. Must find some way of getting two or three more cans.

When everything else has died, does violence still remain? I am kept alive only for one purpose, to end things here while I am still sane enough to do it. But I must, to succeed, be clever, appear to be passive and weak. Appear to be tamed, even grateful for small mercies. (The ginger, after so much flat-tasting food, is delicious.)

Now Eva has come and gone, I remember very distinctly my little house, the porch hidden by vines, so it was very cool and green, the front parlor where I kept a wood fire burning all through the winter, and my books . . . oh, my books! The trouble is that the relationship Eva and I had was clear and simple, but it had to do with keeping the house shining clean. I guess there was just no substance we could fall back on here, no thread to pick up. At this season I was apt to be

outdoors planting bulbs when she came. Then at noon we had a sand-
wich and tea together. And what on earth did we talk about? I cannot
remember—the gossip of the town, I suppose, the cost of living. There
is nothing left of all that. It's all gone.

Just now I looked out and it was snowing, the sky closed down, hard,
relentless. I used to love the snow. Here it feels ominous. Even the
weather slowly turns into the enemy—except, if we got snowed in, that
would be the time for a cleansing holocaust!

I am full of panic these days. I wake sometimes with the hair clinging
to my scalp, the sweat of panic. What am I so afraid of? I am afraid of
Richard because he is so good he might manage to puncture my resolve
to put a violent end to this place. I do not want to see anyone at all.
Yet at the same time I wonder whether, if he does come, I should not
give him the three copybooks I have filled, a kind of testament, should
I be committed to the State Hospital, or in case I manage to carry out
my plan. Perhaps if this story of despair could be published it would
help those who deal with people like me, the sick in health or mind, or
the just plain old and abandoned. I could not bear to have him read the
last pages since X left but I believe he can be trusted not to, until I die.
What will it matter then that I became infatuated with a woman and
longed for her touch?

As I reread those words they make my spirit shrivel into itself. Have
I allowed something real, something pure, to be corrupted? Am I so
unsure of myself that I have come to believe what "they" say about me?

No, it is more that there is some truth in what they think, yet, if
people know nothing about love they will always make it into a sexual
matter. The limit of what I longed for with X was simply to lie down
somewhere beside her and to hold her hand—Why that? Because words
were not a possible means of deep exchange between us, because I
longed so to rest in her, to believe too that she might rest in me.

Now in late October I am able to listen to music again, but not in
the way I did before. It is a drug. I do not listen, just go long wandering
journeys and fantasies—music is a door into escape now. I go over and
over every word Anna ever said to me. She said I was beautiful. And

that she had never known anyone like me. She used to look at me with such a tender, amused look sometimes—is that what women have most deeply to give to each other? Tenderness? Oh, I should never have started on this taboo subject.

The trouble is I have little else to feed on. Lately it has been hard to concentrate. I read the paper and that's about all. Everything I do is done to kill time. When I try to read a book, my mind wanders—I find I have read the same paragraph a dozen times.

The atmosphere has changed since Harriet came back, changed for the worse. I mean *their* atmosphere. Rose is in the doghouse, perhaps because she permitted Anna to raise the standards. The old men are restless and peevish. Several have refused to eat. Rain for several days. The mud around the house is a morass. Only the geese are cheerful and I hear they are afraid of foxes and huddle in the doorway at night, poor creatures. Harriet talks about getting rid of them. I am not asked into the kitchen for a cup of tea or coffee anymore—not, perhaps, since the inspectors came. I am not trusted. That is the frightful joke on me. I, who can trust no one and who have been betrayed, am the one who is *not trusted*. Everything here is twisted around into reverse. I long only to manage to burn the place down. But I am losing my grip, even the grip on anger. Wouldn't it be wonderful if the house were struck by lightening? An act of God!

Richard Thornhill has been here. He brought me five novels and stayed quite a while. I learned by his visit that I have changed for the worse. I simply did not have the gumption to receive him as he deserves. I didn't want to talk at all. I must have seemed churlish.

I could not bring myself to give him the copybooks. I feel they should be in a safe place, my last will and testament. But if I let them go, and can no longer reread to assure myself that I exist and have not dreamed all that has happened here, I shall have lost my last hold on reality. Today I could not remember Standish Flint's name!

The trouble was I could not tell Richard about Anna. He asked me how things were going, but did not inquire directly about her. I wanted so much to ask him to remind Lisa that she had—how long ago?—said she would take me there for a visit. I am afraid of everything now. It would be an immense piece of courage to go and see Anna in her own home, for the very idea fills me with a tumult of emotion. So I am glad, in a way, that I was silent on this matter, as on so many others.

I cannot read the novels.

All I want is to sleep and to be left alone.

It must be mid-November. The leaves are all gone. Harriet found Pansy on my bed and now locks her out every night. The walls close in on every side. I do not remember things very clearly . . . is my brother John still alive? Where has Anna gone?

Soon it will be Thanksgiving. I used to help my mother stuff the turkey and make cranberry sauce her special way, so each cranberry shone like a jewel in a coat of sugar. The aunts came, though rarely Aunt Isabel. My father carved very skillfully and made little jokes, his jokes as much a part of the ritual as creamed onions and squash and mince pies. John and I thought dinner would never end—we had to stay till the nuts were cracked and a glass of port had been consumed by the adults. I can remember very well how hard the back of my chair felt and how we raced out into the chill fresh air, got on our bikes, and once rode way out into the country and got lost. Is John still alive, I wonder? Who but me remembers? It's all melting away . . . like snow . . . a whole lifetime . . . nothing.

The fact is that I am dying for lack of love. Exactly as though the oxygen in my lungs were being slowly diminished.

Mr. Coughlin, the diabetic, died yesterday. His nephew and niece came, of course. They, who had not bothered to see him more than once a month, if that, while he was alive, hurried over at once to arrange for the funeral. This time I notice that the vivid reaction among the old men when Standish died is not there. They seem hardly to have noticed when the body was removed. Strangely enough, Rose mourned him. She was weeping when she brought in my lunch.

"He is better off, Rose," I said gently. "He's hardly known where or who he was for months."

"It's just . . . just . . ." but she couldn't express what she felt and ended by saying quite angrily, "I hate this place!"

"You're not alone in that," I murmured. Probably she didn't hear me, and that is just as well. But I am interested in the violence of her feeling. I suppose she is caught just as we are. Being with the moribund day after day can't be easy on the psyche, and her way has been to be on the defensive against compassion. Compassion would cost too much, I suppose.

When I reread this journal or whatever it is, I am amazed at the vitality I had when I came here—about six months ago. My mind was alive. Now it is only alive in spots and moments, maybe a half hour a day when something like Rose's unexpected tears wakes it. I no longer function as a human being. Even weeks ago I had ideas of taking action—violent action—of burning the place down. I still have the lighter fluid. It is like the little baskets of food or ornaments that were laid in the Egyptian tombs beside the mummy of a king or queen—a talisman.

The day after Thanksgiving—no Saturday, I think.

Yesterday the walls of Jericho came down to Lisa's trumpet! She appeared out of the blue, looking full of surprises, bringing me an Advent wreath, so pretty, with candles on it. (My idea is to hide the candles for other purposes. They will be part of my arsenal of matches, lighter fluid and other combustibles.) But she came also to help me dress and to take me down to see Anna. It all happened so quickly I had no time to think or to say no. I put on my pink sweater and tweed skirt and my liberty scarf, and remembered to take the Hermes blouse, still wrapped in tissue paper after she had washed and ironed it for me when she was here.

Luckily Lisa talked a blue streak the whole way. She is finding the freshman year very exciting, especially a course in cultural anthropology. That and Russian are her great enthusiasms. She poured it all out, and I listened gratefully. It's been months since I've left the home—everything we saw was vividly exciting—a black dog barking as we went by, the lovely withered beech leaves, pale brown against all the blacks and grays, a flock of jays, a woodpecker, and once a startlingly blue pond, reflecting the cloudless sky.

Anna's farm is about five miles away, along a winding road that follows a brook. I felt I was inside a painting, a Brueghel perhaps. Children in bright red caps and stockings. A man with a gun, out for deer. Why am I writing all this down? I suppose to keep from remembering what it was like to see Anna again.

The farm was just as I had imagined it, classic even to geraniums in the windows, a huge red barn, and a big vegetable garden in the field to one side, nothing but pumpkins and withered stalks now. Anna came out before Lisa had even come to a halt. Anna herself. I have dreamed this woman so deeply, then buried the dream so deeply, I felt nothing at all. I felt encased in armor. It was something to go through as well as possible, like death.

"Dear Miss Spencer," she said, taking my hand warmly in hers, and thanked Lisa for bringing me. "Come in." We sat down a little self-consciously in the front parlor, only Lisa at ease.

"I've been waiting for a letter . . ." Anna said with her sweet, slightly teasing smile. "How come I never got one?" Of course she didn't know the horrible truth.

"I wrote, but I guess it never got to the post office."

"Oh, my," Anna said miserably. "Do you think she'd do that?"

"It doesn't matter."

"I've thought about you every day, wondered. I called once and they said you were sick. But, you know, they don't welcome a call. I should have tried again. We've been that busy, first getting the hay in, then the vegetables. I've put up hundreds of jars, it feels like . . ."

Anna, usually so silent, was voluble. It came from shyness. I sat there, numb and dumb, wishing Lisa would have the sense to leave us alone. Then hordes of grandchildren came in to be introduced, and the husband, a tall dark man with a scowl who made his escape as fast as he decently could. But—saving grace!—he asked Lisa if she'd like to see the cows, and they all trooped out to the barn.

Then Anna and I sat, in the parlor, on stiff chairs, not daring to look at each other, while the immense silence flowed in, not the silence of companionship and understanding that we had known in the days at the farm, but the silence of psychic discomfort. A wall of silence between us. I could not speak, lit a cigarette, and Anna went out to fetch an ashtray. When she came back, I gave her the blouse.

"Oh, but you shouldn't Miss Spencer—it's so becoming!

"I want you to have it," I said firmly.

"Well," she had grown quite pink, "I'll think of you when I wear it. It's very kind of you."

For the first time she really looked at me. And I looked back.

"You don't look well, Miss Spencer. You look dragged out."

"I'm on the downgrade, Anna. Might as well face it."

"I wish I could take care of you!" For the first time she sounded like herself and I had to laugh, for the sheer relief of it.

"We haven't got much time." Suddenly anxious lest someone spoil this moment, I rushed in to try to say something. "I'm so glad I knew you for a little while. I wish I could tell you what it meant, what I tried to say in the letter . . ." Then I almost broke down and told her how they had killed my love, and I wish I had. But sitting there in the parlor it all seemed a little strange, too strange to utter. Perhaps I kept my self-respect and her respect by not saying it.

I didn't see anything all the way back, I was just hoping I could get back to my bed and turn my face to the wall and not weep in front of Lisa. Neither of us said very much. As soon as she left I ferreted out the tranquilizers—I suppose that is what they are—that they used to give me, and swallowed three. I slept the whole afternoon. I'm dead now, or might as well be. Something has gone, some spring, some fresh response to life I used to have. Is this old age? Not caring? I would not have believed that until now. I would have said that was a myth created by the young so as not to worry about the old. "They don't really care any more."

The tide goes out, little by little; the tide goes out and whatever is left of us lies like a beached ship, rotting on the shore among all the other detritus—empty crab shells, clam shells, dried seaweed, the indestructible plastic cup, a few old rags, pieces of driftwood. The tide of love goes out. Anna is now one with Alex and all the others, hardly distinguishable. I can say of them all, "I loved you once, long ago." and what is left of you? A lapis lazuli pin, a faded rose petal, once pink, slipped into the pages of this copybook.

But, ironically enough, I, Caro, am still here. I still have to manage to die, and whatever powers I have must be concentrated on doing it soon. I want my death to be something more like me than slow disintegration. "Do not go gentle into that good night" . . . the words, so hackneyed by now, come back to me like a command from somewhere way down inside, where there is still fire, if only the fire of anger and disgust.

I feel quite sure that Harriet puts tranquilizers in my coffee and that it is Sanka. Today I threw it down the john and asked for a second cup, "real coffee"—I went out into the kitchen and they couldn't very well hide anything there. I sat at the table, but they were at their antics again, and told me I had heard from John last week. I have no memory of this.

"Oh yes, Miss Spencer, I brought you a card from Florida."

(Of course they are spies as well. If there was such a card Harriet must have read it and thrown it away.)

They are very clever about confusing me and it's quite evident that they do it on purpose.

"Is it December?" I asked. Outside it is a grim, cold day with a high wind rattling the dead leaves.

"No, dear, it's November 28th. Thanksgiving was last week."

But how am I to believe the slightest thing? Even to the date? They are driving me slowly to the wall, driving me into senility, and for them that means complete passivity. When I am a vegetable they will be glad.

"Miss Spencer is more cheerful these days," Harriet said to Rose in that way she has as if I were not in the room. "She doesn't cry anymore, do you, dear?"

"I expect not."

"Do you remember how you used to cry?"

"No," I lied, and saw them exchange a look—mad as a hatter!

Later when I lay down and began to write, I realized for the flash of a second what this atmosphere does. They never tell me the truth, and I pretend to believe their lies. Then I lie to them and little by little every shred of truth, of reality, is destroyed. I have stopped crying because I am dead inside.

Anyway, I won about the candles. Harriet came and took the wreath away, to hang in the front window, she told me.

"Didn't Miss Thornhill bring candles?"

"Maybe she forgot" I prevaricated.

"Hmmm," Harriet sniffed and went away.

I have hidden the candles under my underwear in a draw but I've got to think of a better place. Under the mattress they might break. Maybe in my empty suitcase? No one would think of looking there. I am not about to go on a journey.

The best news is that Ned brings the trash cans in every night because a raccoon has been knocking them over and makes a fearful mess outside. Harriet is trying to cajole him into building a shed that could be padlocked. But so far he has shown no interest at all in performing this task.

"Why bother?" I heard him say. "It's no trouble to bring the cans in."

If I can set the trash cans on fire all will be well. Ned and Harriet sleep in a bedroom off the kitchen so they would hear any loud noise, but my guess is they sleep soundly, and the door is locked. Tonight I'll practice going out there, so I know just what I might run into. If they wake, I can pretend that I feel dizzy and sick and was looking for some Alka Seltzer.

I have to be sure that Panzy is not indoors. Thank goodness the old dog was put to sleep some time ago. He would have barked. I could put some lighter fluid on the curtains—a quick blaze.

I must also find out whether there is a fire extinguisher and see if I can manage to put it out of commission. I really feel awake and able to cope for the first time in weeks. The adrenal gland seems to be working again. And that cup of real coffee excited me.

I wonder what it's like to die in a fire? I guess you suffocate. It can't take very long.

But now I must be very careful. It has to be done in a blizzard when the fire engines either can't get up here or are slowed down. And how can I keep myself alert that long? December, January . . . the big snows don't come till January. And what if I lose my nerve? Right now I do not feel ready. Something is still to happen—I don't know what—before I can feel ready.

The only person I mind about is Jack . . . is there some way to get him out? Warn him? No, that would be too risky. The old men are better off dead. I have no compunction whatever about giving them a quick blazing end. It's more than they deserve, poor creatures.

My Aunt Isabel would fully approve of this criminal act. I can hear her saying. "Only cows go meekly to the slaughter. You're a brave women, Caro. And you're not crazy enough to let them have it their way, to carry you out addled totally gone to seed . . . no, Caro, you'll go out in a blaze!"

At present all this is still a fantasy, something to keep me going from day to day. And I repeat with ironic satisfaction Eliot's lines,

> We only live, only suspire
> Consumed by either fire or fire.

There is only one fire in me now, a fire of disgust and hatred, and there is plenty of fuel to keep it going till January in this place.

It is strange that now I have made my decision I can prepare for death in a wholly new way. I feel free, beyond attachment, beyond the human world at last. I rejoice as if I were newborn, seeing with wide-open eyes, as only the old can (for the newborn infant cannot see) the marvels of the world. These late November skies are extraordinary . . . great open washed-in color, a transparent greenish-blue, a wonderful elevating pink. The trees are so beautiful without their leaves. I lie on my bed and sometimes just look for hours in a daze of quiet pleasure.

I listen to music again. Last night the Mozart Adagio and Fugue for Strings in C Minor. It is years since I listened to it with Alex at a concert in London. Now I listened to it quite differently . . . the memory of passion added nothing. The music alone was with me. I felt exalted and purified.

I have believed since I came here that I was here to prepare for death, but I did not yet know how to do it. At first I felt I must cling to myself, keep my mind alive somehow—That was the the task set before me, a losing battle, for the best I could hope for was to stand still in the same place. Progress in an intellectual sense was clearly out of the question. It ended in greater and greater frustration and anger.

I see, now that death is not a vague prospect but something I hold in my hand, that the very opposite is required from what I thought at first. I am asked to listen to music, look at the bare trees divested of all but their fine structure, drink in the sunset like wine, read poetry again. I have laid novels aside. (The human world in the sense of relationship is not mine to worry about or to partake of any longer. It is not my concern.) I am gathering together all that matters most, tasting it for the last time. As I do this, everything mundane falls away. Why, it seems quite stupid that I have minded drinking coffee from a plastic cup! How foolish can one be?

Harriet and Rose come and go through the room like ghosts. They have no power to irritate or confuse. So for the first time I am able to be kind to *them*. That is because they have lost their power to hurt.

And how has this immense change taken place? It came from seeing Anna again and letting that whole burden of love and shame fall away, all tension of that sort gone from me . . . and it then came from making the decision to end this whole business in a cleansing burst of flame. I am knotted up to a single purpose now. What a relief! I am stripped down to nothing, needing no protection anymore. All needs have been fulfilled. Is this madness, God?

I believe it is close to it. But perhaps at the furthest reach and in the presence of death there is no distinction to be made. Absolute nakedness may be madness. It doesn't matter. It is what is *required*.

And when we have achieved it, then perhaps we are able to give the ultimate things. At some earlier stage it might have been love. Now it must be an end to misery and corruption for the body, a clean quick end. We give when we have nothing. Then there is no wall between us and the living or the dead. We are all one.

I look at the old men with a new tenderness, the curious way they revolve around Jack, the only youngish person in the house. There he sits rocking all day, always cheerful except very rarely when he gets angry . . . as who doesn't? The other night a fox must have been in the vicinity for the geese were restless, squawked in fear and huddled against the door. At about ten there was a real commotion and Jack called out in his strange strangled voice. I got out of bed to see what the matter was, opened the door, and whatever it was got frightened off. By then Harriet had arrived in her wrapper, bare feet, furious at being awakened.

"Jack was worried about the geese," I explained. "He thinks there may be a fox out there."

"And what if there is?" she screamed. "Can't I get a night's sleep for once? Who cares about the geese? Good riddance, I'd say."

At this rough speech, Jack suddenly howled and sobbed like a child. "P-p-poor geese," he stammered, "Jack doesn't w-w-ant them to die!"

"Now, Jack," she said more gently, "they'll be all right. I'll send Ned out with his rifle. Go to bed, Miss Spencer, you'll catch cold. All we need is an epidemic of colds around here."

I fled, fearing worse. But none of us slept the rest of the night. Mr. Thompson had a nightmare and gave a muffled scream. Fred Smith, who so rarely speaks, went off on a jag of some kind, some childhood memory about a goose. "He was a holy terror," he kept saying, "goosed the schoolteacher one day." Then he giggled and nearly choked to death. "Chased old Mr. Brown half a mile down the road," and he gave a whoop. Jack repeated the phrase and laughed and laughed. That room of old men had become a nursery in the middle of the night. I was dying to get up and make them cups of cocoa, but I didn't dare.

And now I have just heard that Harriet plans to have the geese killed and put in the freezer. It will be a relief as I have been anxious about them. They should not have been left with no shelter these cold nights. I myself feel the draft from the window, a thin stream of icy air. It gives me neuralgia. Tried to stuff Kleenex along the sills, but Harriet tore it all out.

"I'm cold in the night," I explained.

"Nonsense, you have two blankets. Pull one up over your head."

And still I wait for whatever it is that has to happen. Some outrage or cataclysm, some galvanizing event that will give me the courage to act.

It's December, they tell me. I have stopped reading the newspaper. Marooned. The trouble is that now I have come right up to the inexorable FACT: I have to admit that I do not want to die. Soon it will snow. Soon I will have to be ready. But I am not. I feel terribly restless and have taken to pacing about, a thing that irritates Harriet and Rose— I always seem to be in their way when they pass with a bedpan or broom. But how does one fill time waiting . . . waiting.

I have to admit that in some ways I am treated with kindness these days. Harriet washed my hair yesterday, maybe to try to tire me out! Tomorrow Richard Thornhill is to pay a visit. I really have no wish to see him . . . I have to conceal so much. Can't tell him my plans, of course. Might pretend mad . . . and should I give him the early copybooks? I cannot bear to part with them. Yet how to save them when the time comes? I am all at sixes and sevens, pacing around in limbo.

"We have to get you out of here," was what Richard came to say. Why was my reaction so violent? Even a month ago such words would have been a reprieve, but I burst into tears and begged him not to do anything, not to take me away. "I have to die here," I said. "It's too late . . . too late!"

He took my hand and held it then and calmed me down.

"No one is going to force you, dear Miss Spencer."

"Having one of her spells, is she?" Harriet came in with warm milk. I held the cup in my two hands like a baby.

Then Richard closed the door.

I lay on my bed as heavy as a corpse. A very strange sensation. I had my eyes closed. I didn't care whether he stayed or not. But he did stay, silent there beside me for a while. Then he talked about other things— how much Lisa is looking forward to seeing me when she comes home in two weeks for a weekend. Her young man has decided to go back to college and become a doctor after all. While Richard talked I managed very slowly to come back to the surface. At last I could open my eyes.

He reached over again and took my hand. His felt so warm and comforting. I looked deeply into his eyes for a second.

"I am stripped down to nothing," I said. "So somehow I can see you very clearly, and everything else. I want you to know that whatever happens you did all that you could. You have been a good friend."

"We are all wound round in mystery," was his answer.

It was as though we were the last people left alive on earth. I do not really know what happened, why it was like that. I felt I was speaking to someone very far away, yet someone who would hear a whisper, and perhaps I did whisper,

"Can you forgive me now?"

The strange thing, the marvel was that he did not say what at any other time he might have said, something about my not needing to be forgiven. He understood that I was in extremity and he did not question it.

"I believe we are forgiven at the instant of asking forgiveness, for asking forgiveness is an act of faith. It places the soul in eternity."

"But I am thinking of terrible things, Richard. Do you believe in damnation?"

"I don't know. Do you?"

"Yes. But I think I am going to risk it . . . when the snow falls."

Then there was a long silence.

The man was clearly suffering with me and for me. His silence was so intense I felt almost as though he was a laser beam, probing, probing, trying to reach to the very marrow of my thought. I saw the sweat on his forehead. It was all very strange.

Then something snapped. Like people who have been dreaming, we woke.

Richard coughed. We were back in the normal world. I noticed a spider web in the corner of the room, and the way a band of sunlight lay across the floor. I looked around me.

"You are a great person, Miss Spencer."

"I wish you could bring yourself to call me Caro."

"I think of you as Miss Spencer. It is a sign of respect. I don't come across so very many great human beings."

I had to smile at that. It seemed so nonsensical.

"No, I mean it. Don't smile. I have seen in you what courage can be when there is no hope. I have seen the power of a human being to withstand the very worst and not be corrupted, and not change."

"I have changed."

"Not in any way that affects the essence. You are beautiful."

He must have gone then, or someone knocked on the door. I can't quite remember now. I remember that I felt terribly tired and perhaps I slept.

"Well, thank goodness, you've come to!" I heard Harriet's voice, "you've been lying there like a corpse. Your pulse was so low I could hardly catch it. What *have* you been doing?"

I was given a drink, a thimbleful of brandy.

I felt shivery and queer and decided to have a hot bath before supper and get into bed. When I was in the bathroom running the water, I realized that in my confused state I had forgotten my soap and face cloth. I was barefooted and must have made no sound at all, for when I came to my room Harriet was sitting on the bed reading the last copybook. I had left it open there with the pen inside it. She looked extremely startled to see me, and for just a second we stared at each other. Then I felt such a flood of fierce strength rise in me that I must have lunged at her like a wild animal, torn the copybook out of her hands and in doing so knocked her off balance so she fell to the floor.

"Rose! Help!" She screamed, but she was not hurt, only panting with anger and the effort of lifting her two hundred pounds up. I met Rose in the corridor as I ran to the bathroom, still clutching the copybook, and locked myself in.

Harriet stood outside shouting at me, "I know your evil thoughts, cursing us! Attacking me! That's assault and it's a federal offense in case you're interested!"

"Come on, Harriet," I heard Ned say. "She's crazy, poor thing . . . leave her be!"

"She'll go without supper, that's for sure."

I could have laughed at the impotence of this punishment. What do I care about supper?

I have been here now for a long time. Maybe hours. Everything is as I dreamed it would be. It is snowing hard. I can peer out of the bath-room window at whiteness, a fur of whiteness against the panes. All I have to do now is wait for them to go to bed. I wish I had my watch on, but I took it off when I undressed. But I can tell by the sounds, and eventually by the silence. And meanwhile I am going to lie down on the bathmat with my back against the door and have a little nap. I feel at peace. Death by fire will come as an angel, or it will come as a devil, depending on our deserts.

Only one thing, THE important thing I must manage to do is place all the copybooks in the frigidaire. To you who may one day read this, I give them as a testament. Please try to understand.

·· *Afterword* ··

This manuscript was found after the fire that destroyed the Twin Elms Nursing Home. In a letter found inside the cover, Miss Caroline Spencer requested the Reverend Thornhill to have it published if pos-sible. This had been done with the permission of her brother, John Spencer.

FROM *A RECKONING*

·· (ゾY)

·· *Chapter One* ··

Walking down Marlboro Street in Boston, Laura Spelman saw the low brick houses, the strong blue sky, the delicate shape of the leafless trees, even the dirty lumps of snow along the curb as so piercing in their beauty that she felt a little drunk. She now knew that she was panting not because she was overweight, but because her lungs had been attacked. "I shan't need to diet, after all." The two blocks she had to walk from Jim Goodwin's office seemed long. She stopped twice to catch her breath before she reached her little car. Safely inside, she sat there for a few moments sorting out the jumble of feelings her interview with Dr. Goodwin had set whirling. The overwhelming one was a strange excitement, as though she were more than usually alive, awake, and in command: I am to have my own death. I can play it my own way. He said two years, but they always give you an outside figure, and my guess is at most a year. A year, one more spring, one more. . . . I've got to do it well. I've got to *think*.

She needed to get home as fast as possible. She started off, swinging out into the street so quickly a passing taxi nearly hit her. "In your own way, Laura, you idiot!" she said aloud. "Sudden death on Marlboro Street would never do!"

A half hour later she was standing at her own front door in Lincoln, fumbling for the key, and greeted by excited barks from inside. For the first time since Dr. Goodwin's verdict she froze, immobilized by a sharp pain in her chest, but the barking was hysterical now and she finally found the keyhole, opened the door, and knelt down to hug Grindle, the old sheltie, and to accept his moist tongue licking her face, licking the tears away as he had done when Charles died.

"Oh Grindle, what are we going to do? What are we going to do?" Leaving Grindle and Sasha, the cat, was going to be the worst.

"Grindle," she said severely, "I've got to get over this right now. Stop licking, and I'll stop crying."

Sensing the change of tone, Grindle went and curled up in his bed, the pricked ears following her movements as she stumbled to her feet.

She went to the kitchen, poured herself a glass of claret, and took it into the library where she put a Mozart flute concerto on the player. She lay down on the sofa with her hands behind her head and reasoned it out. Grindle would go to Brooks and Ann, her son and daughter-in-law. Their children loved him. Sasha, shy and intense—what about her?

There were going to be some things so awful she must begin now to learn how to set them aside. One part of her being was going to have to live only in the present, as she did when Sasha jumped up and began to knead her chest. Laura pushed her off to one side where loud purrs vibrated all along her thigh. She felt herself sinking down, down into the music, the flute calling like a celestial bird with a thousand songs instead of only one in its silver throat. While she listened, she absorbed the brilliance of the light, light reflected from snow outside so that the room itself was bathed in a cool fire. Grindle gave a long sigh as he fell asleep in his corner, and Laura felt joy rising, filling her to the brim, yet not overflowing. What had become almost uncontrollable grief at the door seemed now a blessed state. It was not a state she could easily define in words. But it felt like some extraordinary dance, the dance of life itself, of atoms and molecules, that had never been as beautiful or as poignant as at this instant, a dance that must be danced more carefully and with greater fervor to the very end.

Poor Mamma, she thought, sitting up. She has been deprived of this. She is stumbling to her death, only half conscious, if conscious at all, of what is going on. Her attachments now are only to those who serve her, Mary whom she hates and Annabelle whom she loves—ambivalent to the end.

Laura pulled herself back from those thoughts of her mother, so terribly grand—and so terrible, thoughts that always had mixed her up, made her feel uncentered, at a loss. Lay them aside now, Laura, you'll never solve that mystery before you die.

I shall have to tell Jo—and Daphne, of course. But Jo, the eldest of the three sisters, was the stumbling block: powerful, blunt Jo, wrapped up in her job; she had late in her life taken over the presidency of a small women's college. She repeated these facts about Jo, turning them over in her mind. No, she wouldn't tell Jo for a while. Besides, was there a real connection?

Here the record stopped. Without music, the house, the room where she sat became suddenly empty. I'm not scared exactly, but if there is no real connection with my sister, who is there? What is there? Only now did the full impact of Dr. Goodwin's verdict reach Laura, and she began to shake. Her hands were ice-cold. Fear had replaced the strange elation she had felt at first, and she rose and paced up and down, then leaned her forehead against the icy window for a moment. I'm not ready, she thought, I can't do it alone. But I want to do it alone, something deep down answered. And even deeper down she knew that she would have to do it alone. Dying—no one talked about it. We are not prepared. We come to it in absolute ignorance. But even as the tears splashed down on her hands, or perhaps because their flow had dissolved the awful tension of fear, Laura felt relief. After all, she told herself, we meet every great experience in ignorance . . . being born, falling in love, bearing a first child. . . . always there is terror first.

In the few seconds of silence it had become clear that she was going to have to reckon with almost everything in a new way. "It is then to be a reckoning." And Laura realized that at this moment she felt closer to Mozart and Chekhov than she did to her own sister. "I shall not pretend that this is not so. There isn't time. The time I have left is for the real connections.

The real connections? The question aroused such strange answers, all beating their wings in her mind, that she lay back again and waited for all this to quiet down or sort itself out.

Tell the children? No, not yet. Ben, so far away in California, struggling with his painting; Brooks still taking his father's death hard, that sudden death only three years ago; Daisy in New York with her lover, working long hours. But Laura knew she would have to tell Brooks and Ann pretty soon—they lived only a mile away. The children—the last thing she wanted or needed was to think about them, though she was leaving them in the lurch, of course. But I just can't cope with all that today, she thought. Family. I'm not asked to cope with it today.

Disposing of the house, things, money, lawyers—oh, dear, she had thought only of dying with grace, of making a good death, but not of all the affairs involved, the decisions! Tomorrow—not today.

Today, "the real connections."